THE CI THEORY

Rise of the doomsday sun

T. L. BEVERAGE

ISBN: 0615719562

ISBN 13: 9780615719566

Library of Congress Control Number: TXu001708767 / 2010-07-19

Science Fiction

Hemet, CA

CONTENTS

ACKNOWLEDGMENTS

To John, Mom, Dad, and Stephenie: Thank you for listening to me boast and complain about this book as if it were a favorite, yet unruly child. Over the years, you have listened to me bemoan the challenges of writing a novel. At times, you read my rough drafts that now make me wince a bit…okay a lot.

To my friends, coworkers, and the rest of my family who read this story: You have all unwittingly served as inspirations for the characters. If you read carefully enough, you may find yourself in the pages somewhere.

I would also like to express appreciation to my content editor, Mike Foley of *Writer's Review,* and the *Amazon* project team. All of your feedback helped polish this book into a better work.

To my niece, nephews, step-grandkids, and all other kids: I hope that we adults make this world a better place for you. It is our duty to strive for no less. Earth does not belong to one generation over another. We are passing tenants who should take what we need while making sure there's enough for those who come after us.

Finally, I'd like to acknowledge my beautiful animals—you'll always have a place in my heart for your selfless loyalty and for teaching me to be a better person.

All that is necessary for the triumph of evil is that good men do nothing

– Edmund Burke

PART I

THE STATUS QUO

SAT 12/31/2129
TIMES SQUARE
NEW YORK CITY, NY

Daniel covered his ears as several firecrackers popped behind him. Fighting his irritation, he squeezed forward in the packed intersection. He jumped back when a stream of white sparks shot up from the street and barely missed his face. Three NYPD cops pushed past him on their way toward the offenders. He couldn't believe he'd let JoMarie dupe him into coming here on New Year's Eve.

Realizing there was no quick escape, Daniel stared at the sky and searched for a hint of calmness. The millions of people in the intersection and their crude pyrotechnics faded to the backdrop of his awareness. A cool breeze brushed over his face. The sky seemed to be looming above New York like a tidal wave cresting over unsuspecting beachgoers. He sensed the upcoming meteor storm was deliberate, targeted.

He furrowed his brow. Logic told him that this was a ridiculous notion. Such claims were propaganda used by the end-timers who were scattered throughout the Square, ranting at anyone who dared to be halfway civil to them. This storm was an act of nature, oblivious to the lives it would soon injure and kill. Just like the African Plague that took out two hundred million people last year. Then Daniel's raw superstition butted heads with his scientific edict.

There's something more going on.

The crowd started clapping and shouting when the clock progressed to 23:40. Daniel shoved his way to JoMarie, who was standing nearby with her husband and kids. He realized how lucky he was to have a boss who'd adopted him as part of her family. She and Ed probably cared for him more than his own parents did.

Daniel smiled a little. Even though JoMarie sometimes nagged him and treated him with tough love, her intentions were in the right place. She was always trying to pull him out of his shell or talk him out of his dark moods.

In his peripheral vision, he tried to ignore the sky, which looked like it was getting heavier by the second as if ready to split open. He turned to the sidewalks where the police had set up shelters from the meteors. Most everyone still insisted on staying in the intersection. Had to watch that ball drop.

"Well," Daniel said in JoMarie's ear, "not to put a damper on this festive night, but we have another meteor storm pulling the curtain down over the stage. Nobody in this mob seems to give a shit."

JoMarie's eyes shifted toward him. "Many of them are drinking and dare I say celebrating. And you know how often the projections are wrong."

"They can have their fun. I should've stayed in my room. Not in the mood to be here."

"All you would've done was brood about the presentation."

Daniel's stomach tightened when he thought of Wednesday's meeting at the UN and the five-year mission they'd be speaking about. "The only reason I'm here is because you prodded me."

"Join the club," JoMarie said. "I'm here because Ed and the kids prodded me."

JoMarie began clapping with Ed, Seth, and Kara. Daniel could see why nobody had mistaken them for his parents and siblings as of yet. First, they were too upbeat. On top of that, his beige winter skin clashed against their warm African pigment and he was nearly a head taller than all of them. He was grateful that DNA wasn't the only thing that bonded people.

"Be glad you get to spend time with your family before the mission starts," Daniel said.

"That's why I've decided to enjoy tonight," JoMarie responded, "meteor storm or not, presentations or not. Happy New Year."

Pulling his Epad from his pocket, Daniel aimed the camera lens at JoMarie and Ed. "Or if nothing else, Happy New next Year. We have fourteen minutes until 2130 lowers into the Square, so give me a smile."

JoMarie forced a huge grin and grabbed her husband's arm. "Okay Ed. Let's make happy faces for Daniel."

Ed bulged out his eyes and hiked his brows up toward his hairline. "Is this good enough?"

The Epad flashed and Daniel looked at the picture. "Okay, smart asses. Be that way."

"We're just being like you," JoMarie said.

JoMarie and Ed's exaggerated grins glowed on the Epad's screen. Daniel turned the image toward them. "I'm posting this on the EPA community net site."

"Please do," JoMarie said as she swatted her hand at the Epad. "Maybe a few bureaucrats there will crack a smile." She and Ed resumed their clapping and started singing with the music.

Daniel shook his head and chuckled. Suddenly, the blaring cross-winds of different bands brought on some sort of déjà vu. He rubbed his face and tried to stop thinking. Even this holiday celebration couldn't stop him from slipping back into his December funk and thoughts of Hannah.

His daughter had lived four years, four months, six hours, and thirty-two minutes. She would've turned thirteen on December 5 but instead left the planet on April 5, 2121. He blinked wetness from his eyes as her memory shoved through the colorful night. So many years had passed since she'd died, but the pain hung over him like a knife, plunging in his chest at unexpected moments.

Looking back up, he again sensed that the sky was bearing down over the city. A billboard-sized holovision hanging from the side of a building caught his eye. The *Galax.net News* was reporting about the storm. Daniel read the words scrolling across the bottom of the screen. The meteors were expected to hit New York City within ten to twenty minutes. No one else seemed to notice or care.

The overlapping of loud music was becoming insufferable. JoMarie and her family appeared deaf to the chaos as they clapped and sang, creating a separate, terrible song in itself. He squinted and stared at the ground to deflect the noise. Thoughts of Christmas Eve 2116 flowed through Daniel, seemingly carried by the breeze that was shuffling his hair in different directions.

At nineteen days old, Hannah lay in a crib at Boise Children's Hospital, diagnosed with organ damage and a leukemia that was supposed to be curable. Blood was trickling from her nose and her body was dotted with small bruises. She looked like someone had beaten her. And someone had—the human race.

Prenatal exposure to agricultural toxins, that's what he and Cherril had been told. The lab where he'd worked to make pesticides safe had been built on a three-kilometer slab of poison. They had lived a few kilometers away. In that housing tract, Cherril was exposed to pesticides while pregnant.

The music and shouting came back as Daniel's thoughts redirected to the New Year's ball suspended over the crowd. He gazed at the few stars willing to reveal themselves through the solid sky. He hoped they'd share a smidgen of their wisdom with him. They'd seen pyramids built, cars and computers invented, and witnessed the savagery of wars and genocides.

No response.

Daniel assumed the stars' stony silence meant he was going to have to figure out life's lessons on his own. Cherril hadn't had the stomach to help him with such challenges. Years later, he'd figured out that during their marriage he'd behaved as if he was flying solo. And soon enough he was.

He stuffed his hands in his pants pockets thinking back to February 2119 when he, Cherril, and Hannah headed for North Carolina. He'd been hired by the EPA and would be mentored by JoMarie Sanford, one of the United States' top waste management experts. Hannah was going to be treated at a renowned hospital in Raleigh.

The thrill of his daughter's upcoming state-of-the-art treatments and the new job was short-lived. That May, Cherril filed for divorce and then moved to her own house with Hannah. After their daughter died, she headed back to Seattle to live near her parents, unable to tolerate him or the malfunctioning kinfolk that came as his dowry.

As the stars continued to ignore Daniel's pleas, he stared down at his shoes. Every December around Hannah's birthday, memories of her flooded back as if they had happened yesterday. As if life was still trying to teach him something or punish him. He wasn't sure which. He wiped his wet eyes with his jacket sleeve.

Daniel watched JoMarie and her family sing. It was no small wonder he'd failed at the family thing. That's why he didn't spend New Year's Eve with his parents, why he missed the Christmas dinner again. Dad's declining health had muted his violent temper and he probably didn't have much time left. However, Daniel's recollections lingered in his mind like a slight headache that exploded like a bullet in the brain whenever there was a homecoming.

He looked around him. People were starting to aim binoculars and telescopes upward. *Finally, they notice something.*

JoMarie wrapped her arms around Seth and Kara. Daniel remembered when both kids stood just past his waist. Now young adults, Kara had JoMarie's wide-set black eyes and slim figure, but passed on her mom's cropped afro by sporting a long, straight style. Seth looked like Ed with green eyes and a husky build. They even shared facial expressions. Daniel wondered why so many sons were doomed to resemble their fathers—just as he did. Why couldn't genetics be a little more flexible?

"Slip on your head covers," JoMarie said to her kids. "Your dad's wearing his."

Kara held her shield under her arm and shook her head at JoMarie. Seth stared straight ahead. JoMarie looked pissed. "He doesn't care if he looks embarrassing," she said pointing to her temple. "He values this thing in here called a brain."

Daniel laughed. Kara's pouty resistance wasn't going to work. JoMarie didn't care if someone was ten feet tall. If they were younger than her, she mothered them.

"Put them on now!" JoMarie commanded.

Seth and Kara looked at each other and begrudgingly slipped their caps on.

He heard the voice redirecting its aim.

"Daniel?" JoMarie said.

"I didn't bring one." Daniel raised his closed shield. "This should be enough."

Walking in front of him, JoMarie motioned to the shield. "That thing can shift sideways and expose you."

"Maybe I wanna get hit."

JoMarie shoved a cap in his hand. "That's too bad because I brought an extra. You're not skipping out on Wednesday."

Stuffing the reinforced cap under his arm, Daniel patted JoMarie's shoulder. "You're not letting me escape that UN meeting for anything, are you?"

"That is part of my sinister plan."

Trying not to watch the news, Daniel considered how being clueless wasn't so bad. Besides, the Square may not be hit and they would have done all this worrying over nothing. Half the time, *Galax.net* was wrong about the exact location of the meteor storms. If this time it happened to be right, the rooftop lasers would disintegrate the bigger rocks, like they did to the surface-to-air missiles occasionally shot their way.

Daniel frowned as JoMarie gave him her special glare, the one she made before she started to really nag. Ed smiled at him and turned away.

"Okay, mister," she said. "You're sniping about everyone else not facing reality about the meteors, yet most of the crowd now has their head covers on except for you and a few others with death wishes."

Groaning, he shoved the brown cap on his head.

"That's better," JoMarie said. "Now keep it on until the last rock hits the ground. And get that shield ready to open."

"Yes, ma'am," Daniel grumbled.

JoMarie seemed to sense his despair. "I know December's a tough time for you. Remember how important the mission is. We're gonna make a big difference."

"Okay," he said. "I'll try."

"Not just try. Do."

Meteorites tails began to glow in the distance. Some people took refuge under the shelters. Daniel watched more shields pop up in the crowd. JoMarie and her family held the shields over their heads like umbrellas. She narrowed her eyes at him and he complied.

As Daniel stared through his shield's clear cover, he watched the burning rocks fall down from the sky. Lasers shot from rooftops like glowing spears and blew them apart. More people started backing onto the sidewalks. Others gasped as if they were at a fireworks show. A nearby group of teenagers tossed their shields in the air then started clapping and howling. Police officers, wearing protective gear, headed toward the kids who saw them coming and pushed through the crowd, running away and laughing.

Daniel felt his heart start to palpitate. He'd never been in the middle of such a storm, through he'd read enough about them. The lasers' defenses intensified, lighting up the Square as if it were noon.

Rocks too small to be zapped by the lasers, but heavy enough to dent a person's skull started pouring over the crowd. Daniel dropped and stared down. Popping sounds like gunfire filled the air as the meteors hit the streets and buildings. He cringed as he heard wailing. He lifted his gaze and saw unprotected people running to the shelters. Not all of them made it. Collective screams merged into a ghostly chorus. Those too proud or too stupid to listen to common sense paid the price—just like he almost did.

Warm dust from the blown up meteors drifted onto the street. Daniel's throat closed and he started to gag. A wave of nausea hit him. He remembered Hannah's remains being divided between him and Cherril; the stream of grayish powder pouring first in one urn and then in another.

A meteor slammed his arm and knocked him forward. The offending rock that bounced off his elbow onto the ground was smaller than a walnut. Daniel squeezed his eyes shut trying to forget about the urn. He listened for the thuds to slow to a stop.

* * *

A loud voice from the HV announced that no more meteors were expected to fall. Daniel stood up and closed his shield. He pulled off the cap and stuffed it in his coat pocket. Smoke was rising from the street. His jacket had a black scorch mark from where he'd been hit, but the sting was fading. While most of the crowd was upright, the blood pooling around his shoes proved that others weren't so lucky, or perhaps not so smart.

JoMarie checked with Seth and Kara to make sure they were okay. Ed was shaking his head. "Can't wait to get back to North Carolina."

She nodded. "As much as I want to see you guys, I'd like you home too."

Daniel watched EMTs running toward injured people. While he agreed with other scientists that gravity was pulling meteors to Earth, his take was that the rocks were aiming at people. Not any particular person, just any person. He laughed. The other scientists' take was that Daniel was a little—maybe more than a little—crazy.

"The mission's got to succeed," Daniel said to JoMarie. "I'd like to get married and be a father again. Almost nine years have passed since Hannah died, but this time of the year, I don't feel much better than I did on day one."

"Mental garbage doesn't dispose of itself," JoMarie said. "It piles up in your brain, turning your head into a dirty attic filled with anger and pain. You need help cleaning your attic."

"I try to make Hannah's memory a motivation to succeed."

"That's what she'd want." JoMarie smiled. "As for me, I'd like to live past sixty-two. I also have an interest in my children and my two-year-old grandchild."

JoMarie gave him a solemn stare. "My octogenarian mother has dreams too. We all do."

"Didn't mean to come off as a narcissist," Daniel said.

"More like self-preservation. The mission's success has to rise above our own wants. The reward will be worth the sacrifice."

JoMarie pinched her lips tight as if she knew Daniel wasn't buying her sales pitch. "Academically, we've been told this a thousand times. But we gotta believe it in our bellies."

Daniel began to thank her for working him a few steps out of his funk but paused. NYPD Slojets hovered over the crowd, sweeping their spotlights as they searched for injured people. FDNY trucks headed toward fires triggered by the meteorites. Smoke billowed above the Square, making the sky even more one-dimensional.

Embracing Ed, then hugging Seth and Kara, JoMarie looked at Daniel. "We should've stayed in our rooms tonight."

"I don't think so," Daniel said. "The only people who got hurt were those who chose not to protect themselves."

"Daniel's right," Ed added. "And we're all fine."

JoMarie left her cap on while Ed and the kids pulled theirs off. They started walking down Seventh Avenue back to the Westin Hotel.

Daniel trotted after JoMarie and her family. He remembered the four years he'd been given to worry about Hannah's safety, and the whole time that was all he'd done.

"Those rocks fall everywhere," Daniel said, trying to bring his thoughts to a different place. "Tonight, Times Square was hit. North Carolina or Moscow could be smacked tomorrow, in two months or in six months."

An explosion blew streams of fire from one building and ignited another.

Ed grabbed JoMarie's hand. "The Carolinas are startin' to look pretty good."

Daniel pulled his Epad out of his pants pocket. "Okay, Pokey, give me the latest."

He read the news scrolling down the computer's small screen. "According to *Galax.net*, the financial district was hit the hardest, but not many people were there. Twelve deaths so far."

"All we can do is focus on the mission," JoMarie said, looking at the Epad.

Kicking a smoking rock, Daniel scowled. "Between tonight's storm and last month's terror attacks in Russia, the end-timers must be in ecstasy. And maybe we finally *have* screwed up the planet to the point of no return."

He stopped. Before Hannah died, she'd made him promise to never give up. While he was accustomed to working in laboratories or out in the field, his mission role would be using artificial intelligence to analyze data. That would take some getting used to. But he knew the less that people were involved in the mix, the less unclean motives there would be to sully up the science. Using AI programs as a primary research tool was a little out of his comfort zone but for his daughter's memory he'd do anything.

"Okay we're not at the point of no return yet."

JoMarie nodded. "That's better."

"The public's been dragging its heels for too long," Daniel said. "Like a couple hundred years."

"And you'll say that at Wednesday's meeting?"

"I'm not sure I can make it." Daniel started coughing. "My throat's starting to get sore. How many days do I have to get sick?"

JoMarie shook her finger at him. "Don't you dare."

Daniel thought of how much he wanted to go to Unity Space Station, start the mission, and escape the chaos. "Forget the public dog and pony show. I want to solve the problem."

JoMarie stopped at the corner of Seventh and Forty-Second Streets and motioned toward camera crews piling over the meteorites. "*Galax.net's* media stumps distract from the mission's goals. Maybe after our meeting, the protests will ease up."

Daniel followed JoMarie and her family as they walked toward their hotel. EMTs rushed to a man and woman lying against a curb. The woman's face was soaked with blood. She stared ahead, her eyes blinking with fright and disbelief. The man, whose face had been smashed by a rock, was clearly expired.

Turning back to Times Square, Daniel became still. *Galax.net*'s spotlights were blinding. Hissing Slojets, bloody bodies, and dense, smoky air yanked his sense of balance into a dizzying flow of sensory overload.

A woman and man draped in blue satin cloaks stood in the Square. They held flashing signs that read, "THE END IS NEAR! For Salvation Go To: *TheEndisNearExceptforUs@Galax.net.*"

The New Year's ball that everyone had waited for had dropped as scheduled. Few had noticed. Daniel watched the numbers 2130 blink inside the glass sphere like a lone, optimistic eye.

SUN 01/01/2130
WESTIN HOTEL
NEW YORK CITY, NY

Daniel stretched across the bed in his hotel room. A pillow cradled his head like a soft, maternal arm. So far, the meteorites had killed twenty-one people and injured over a hundred. One large rock missed by the lasers had crashed through the glass walls of the Westin's penthouse nightclub, killing two people.

He looked at Pokey. The dalmatian cartoon had displayed on the Epad that he'd magnetized to his forearm. Another New Year's morning spent alone with his animated friend. Daniel set his Epad upright on the end table so it faced him. It was hard to believe that in spring 2116, he was twenty-seven years old and had it all—a PhD, his first research job, and he was married with a child on the way. Now with nearly fourteen more years under his belt, he had far less of everything, including time.

"See you in the morning, Pokey," Daniel said.

"Goodnight, Daniel," his Epad answered. "Your pulse is ninety-four. Blood pressure is 120/70. Blood alcohol percent is 0.04."

"I had two beers with dinner. That sounds too high. So does my pulse."

"I can test your breath instead of your perspiration. Your fast heartbeat tells me that you're bothered. Probably your December funk bleeding into January again."

Daniel sunk his head deeper in the pillow. "Yeah."

"Stop blaming yourself for things that weren't your fault," Pokey said. "I am programmed to be honest but not punitive. If the divorce and your daughter dying were because of you, I'd say so without feeling bad. After all I'm not a touchy feely type."

"With my dad's genetics, I probably would've ended up abusive anyway. Maybe fate's put me in an isolated state for a reason."

Pokey projected the Unity Station roster on the screen. "Now you're feeling sorry for yourself. I suggest you see one of the three counselors who'll be on the space station."

Daniel dimmed the lamp. "Have you been talking to JoMarie?"

"No but I've been listening to her," Pokey replied.

"I'll probably talk to someone. Goodnight."

"About time," the dalmatian said. "You're exhausting to listen to sometimes. I'm also tired of Casey's voice messages."

"He wants to come to New York. I've told him no fifty times."

Pokey laughed. "He should've been born a mule instead of a golden retriever."

"Maybe," Daniel said. "But he's not getting his way."

"He'll keep bugging me until you give in."

Daniel didn't want to deal with a mouthy dog that had human intelligence. "I'll call him pretty soon."

"Please do. Pokey Griffin, Electronic Personal Assistant and Database, is entering hibernation mode."

Daniel rolled on his back. Casey didn't want to come to this mess of a city for any good reason. The dog wanted to go because he couldn't. He looked at his blood-soaked shoes from Times Square. Lying on the floor near the window, they were a sober reminder of life's frailty. The cap he'd forgotten to give back to JoMarie lay next to them. He shook his head.

Humans thought they were an exception to the fate that had befallen so many other major species before them. Forget the dinosaurs and all the other life that had come and gone. *Hah!*

Like every other January 1, people believed passing the torch from one year to the next would bring new prosperity...as if one moment could hold precedence over another. Humans had an impulse to control the planet and each other, even trying to hold captive the intangible notion of time, of one instant melting into another.

Brightening the lamp and sitting up, Daniel grabbed a bottle of water from the end table and took a few swallows. Looking at the label with his name and job title, he felt guilty that federal employees had priority for receiving clean water.

Slojet lights shone between the partially open drapes, reminding Daniel of the security around the UN Multiplex back on July 22, 2119—a date that could've changed the world forever. A coalition had been formed to address Earth's collapsing ecosystem, repair human infrastructure, and build a space station for top world leaders. The coalition was named HEPCOM, an acronym for the Human and Environmental Preservation Committee.

Grimacing in disgust as he remembered the hoopla, Daniel took another swig of water. The leftist protestors had been stomping the streets, angry about the money to be spent on the space station. The right-wingers stomped about the money to be spent on the environment.

That night had been balmy and the crickets loud. Cherril had dropped off Hannah, who had just finished her cell purification treatment. Sitting next to him on the couch, she was upbeat and playful. They watched the news and played computer games together. Daniel had held hope that HEPCOM would make the world a better place for his then two-year-old daughter.

Daniel finished off his water and laughed aloud at his naiveté. He'd joined the HEPCOM citizens' group and attended virtual meetings for years. Phase I was the name of the ecosystem and infrastructure part of the program. Phase II was to follow—the space station for world leaders to maintain order. Named the United Nations Earthstar Compound, the station would hold seven hundred and fifty people.

The compound would float four to five hundred kilometers above ground, away from pestilence and supposedly any terrorist threat. Earthstar would be the ultimate kings' castle. The primary residents would be world leaders served by underprivileged citizens who could bring up to two kids thirteen or older. All would be service workers. The rest of the world was stuck at ground level.

Forcing himself off the bed and walking to the hotel window, Daniel watched EMTs and police trek the streets. Cleanup crews cleared the debris from Times Square.

He wondered if his efforts in HEPCOM had made any difference. On the weekends that Hannah was with Cherril, he'd attended meetings, leaving optimistic and, he realized later, stupid. HEPCOM was eventually pressured to focus on the Earthstar compound that became Phase I, demoting the ecosystem and infrastructure work to Phase II. By June 2128, Phase II was named the Global Restoration Mission. HEPCOM became an oversight agency that was more symbolic than meaningful. *Kind of like the UN.*

Pokey released a startling bark. "Why haven't you changed for bedtime?"

Staring down at the streets, Daniel shrugged. "Can't stop thinking."

"What's new?" Pokey groaned. "Dwelling on things you can't change only makes things worse."

"Can't help it," Daniel said.

"Why didn't you go to your parents' holiday dinners this year?"

"Didn't want to depress myself."

"Your dad's condition has improved," Pokey said. "I've been reading your mom and sister's social network pages."

"Good for him," Daniel responded, not quite believing that he was defending himself to his Epad again. "I'm dreading Wednesday. I hate talking in front of groups, being in groups, looking at groups." He tightened his arms around this chest. "There will be protests, of course."

"Be prepared for rude people. If you get out of sorts, pretend your audience is naked, sitting on a toilet, or both. That goes for the protestors, too."

"I'll settle for meditation and deep breathing."

The cartoon snickered. "The toilet option really brings things home."

Daniel figured the imagery would make him laugh or get sick to his stomach. "Thanks but no thanks."

"Look at the politicians out there," said Pokey. "They yap in front of crowds all the time."

"They don't mean what they say. I care about the things I'll be talking about. Besides, sometimes I think better under stress."

"Think all you want," Pokey said. "I'm going back in hibernation."

Daniel couldn't fight off his second wind. "Goodnight."

"You mean good morning," Pokey snapped back. The dalmatian cartoon took a deep breath and started snoring.

Daniel fixated on the geometric glass skyscrapers and small brick structures throughout the city. Sweepers wiped debris off the streets and into large, robotic scoopers. He likened the buildings to chess pieces, the city blocks serving as the game board. The knights were the smaller glass buildings that represented bigger, private businesses. Rooks were represented by the run down brick stores that were the small businesses. Pawns were the little human figures scattered over the board who never really owned anything. All bowed to the shimmering glass castles towering over New York City—the kings and queens of the financial district.

Grabbing his binoculars, Daniel took a closer look at his city chessboard. Impulse led him to the corridors of metro life where pawns trudged through an existence that held little chance for promotion. Graffiti and strewn trash embodied the dejected human spirits that lived there. A streetlight shone on rodents sipping from a puddle of dirty water that had settled in a cleft in a broken sidewalk.

Much of the old financial district, once called Wall Street for reasons Daniel couldn't remember, was gated off. Bombed by terrorists fifty years ago, the remaining buildings were eroding toward ground level. Some investment group had bought the land cheap and did nothing with it. The glass and concrete remnants were a sad reminder of a United States that once had competition rather than a few monopolies.

He zeroed in on spotlights aimed at an old structure on the poor side of the tracks. The building appeared freshly textured and painted. A crane was lifting something onto the building's wall. *What's being done at this time on New Year's morning?*

Closing in on the object of his curiosity, Daniel set his binoculars on the windowsill and shook his head. This wasn't a heartfelt gesture by the Public Works Department to dignify pawn turf. The wall had been repaired to hang a larger-than-life billboard featuring the face of US President and People's Party leader, Victor Clemens.

Lights cast over the painting. President Clemens' cropped, grayish brown hair and sculptured face matched well with his powerful, yet soft hazel eyes. His paternal expression reeked of compassionate intellect, yet somewhere beneath the topcoat of shaven skin and probably the scent of the most expensive aftershave, Daniel sensed a dark underbelly.

Clemens' eyes seemed to harden as if telling Daniel to keep his mouth shut and better yet, his mind. The Statue of Liberty still strut her stuff on Staten Island, but she was one of few who did or could. Something had gone terribly wrong.

TUES 01/03/2130
FLC FAMILY TRUST PENTHOUSE
MANHATTAN ISLAND, NY

Ribbons of fire swayed in Shaune's thoughts like the neck-high legs of his favorite lap dancer at the Kat Shak. He leaned against the barber chair in his master bathroom. After showing up late as usual, Clarissa brushed through his damp hair with the comforting warmth of a blow dryer.

Today's exercise would be another step toward victory. On the first day of spring 2131, the Utopian Society Alliance would announce that a global takeover was forthcoming and act accordingly. No longer would Alliance members have to use the conventional election system to gain power through the People's Party. And the name was genius. USA members could code talk in front of others and be mistaken for patriots.

A gust of warm air grazed Shaune's face. Wasteful elections would no longer be necessary. A one-world government was so close to being real.

Shaune glanced at his pewter George Washington statue sitting on a shelf and couldn't help but feel elated. Earth would finally have a governing system that worked. Democracies based on the selfish and stupid wants of the masses were doomed. The most intelligent world leaders would work together and actually solve problems.

Glancing out of his penthouse window, Shaune saw city workers picking meteors off the street. The public's distraction with the end of the world nonsense was an unforeseen gift. Visualizing the different colors of flames produced from various weapons and bombs, Shaune realized that he was flushed and starting to sweat.

"Why's it so damn hot in here, Clarissa?"

Clarissa yawned and ambled in her droopy green sweat suit to the thermostat. She walked back to Shaune, her brown eyes barely open. Her maroon hair was pinned into a bushy wad on top of her head. Being a young, partying bimbo, Shaune figured she was probably hung over again. He hoped his hair would end up looking better than hers did.

"The heater's been set at twenty-nine Celsius since midnight," Clarissa said. "I lowered the setting to nineteen."

"Who the hell set it at twenty-nine?"

She changed the dryer's setting to air temperature and continued working on his hair. "Maybe Bernard did."

"True," Shaune said. "The old fart probably can't tell the difference between a one and two anymore or maybe his circulation's shutting down and he's cold all the time."

Clarissa turned off the dryer and then combed through Shaune's hair, shaping it into small spikes with a light gel.

Shaune stood and stretched. "Good enough. That's all for now. Now go home and sleep."

"Am I that obvious?" she said, grabbing her purse.

"Utterly so." He swatted his hand toward her, dusting the air of the once useful but now intruding cobweb.

After Clarissa left his master suite, Shaune stood in front of the sliding glass walls and admired his reflection. He gazed over Manhattan and the Atlantic Ocean. Morning clouds enclosed the city like a fitted bed sheet. The weather was just what he needed.

"Bernard, I'm ready."

Within a few seconds, Shaune heard feet shuffling down the hall. The suite's sensor recognized the sound and the two entry doors slid open.

Bernard gave him a condescending squint. "So this is the day."

"Yes. Do you remember what'll happen if you tell?"

The butler's oblong face overlapped in dull, pasty folds as he frowned. "I'll be soaked in battery acid and thrown in an alligator pit after I'm shot in what's left of my kneecaps."

Shaune shot him a single nod like an approving schoolteacher. "Correct, through the gators weren't my idea."

"Thank you for not being part of the gator conspiracy," Bernard mumbled.

"This morning your bank account was increased by the agreed-upon amount."

"With my newfound wealth, I can replace my bad kneecaps, which feel like they've already been shot."

Shaune looked out the windows again. "Good idea. This morning I found out that we can't fly to the airport. Before I could ask why, I was hung up on. Those triple-decker downtown streets really suck."

"They do," Bernard said. "But flying could draw attention."

Shaune slipped back in his dressing room and grabbed the Washington statue. George's pewter gray eyes were heavy-lidded and foolish. His clenched teeth were so stern, as if staunch in his belief that any population could manage, of all things, itself. Autocracies would be the governing bookends in human history. This new order would be different, not founded on bloodlines, money, or ethnicity but something much more legitimate: superior intelligence.

* * *

Even with the truck windows closed, Shaune felt bombarded by the honking buses and semis groaning below on street level one. Bernard slammed on the truck's brakes after a taxi cut him off. Shaune lurched forward in the backseat. "Let's get on level three, away from these idiots."

"As you wish," Bernard said as he cut off a van and slid onto the level three onramp. A middle finger shot out at them from the van's driver window.

Shaune lowered his window and returned the favor. "Level two's the shits."

"I couldn't agree more."

Looking down at the freeways below, Shaune watched taxi drivers, mass transporters, and road raging suits pump in and out of the concrete aorta. An airbus filled with people flew over the street layers toward the financial district.

Looking up at the undercarriage of a police car soaring above them, Shaune pushed his chin into a frustrated pout. The tires lowered from the car and landed on a level three on-ramp.

"You know what's bullshit?" Shaune said.

Bernard looked at him in the review mirror. "What now?"

"Only military and law enforcement can drive skybrids."

"Most of the general public can barely manage cars on roads. Adding altitude would bring pandemonium."

Shaune grabbed his Epad and winked at his Washington statue lying on the seat. "I'll get one soon. I'm by no means the general public."

He accessed the target building's electronic security portal on his Epad. Pressing his thumb on the screen's reader, his DNA and thumbprint were confirmed. GlobeTek's logo flashed on the screen. His hackers had done their job well. He navigated to the building's surveillance system and accessed the internal cameras. Inserting an earpiece into the Epad, he could now hear and see the office workers on the thirty-second floor.

A chubby woman with puffy brown hair was slumped in an office chair as she browed a shopping website on *Galax.net*. Decorative characters reading "Tuesday, January 3, 2130," were displayed on her daily organizer. Shaune doubted she would live to see the page changed to Wednesday, because she was being studied by the person was who was going to kill her and her coworkers in less than one hour. The gold nameplate propped on her desk read, "Lucinda Bertinelli, Administrative Analyst."

Shaune grinned and increased the audio. What kind of job was an administrative analyst*? Expendable—like the person.*

He watched as Lucinda scooted her rolling chair to the other side of her L-shaped work module. She shoved some boxes across the floor and groaned. "How in the hell can anyone get this done in a fifty-hour workweek? Two years and I'm hitting retirement road."

Shaune noticed the other employees staring blankly at their computer screens like they'd heard this many times before.

Sliding on a thin vinyl coat, Lucinda stomped over to a young blonde co-worker. "Hey Rosanna? Wanna take a break? I won't survive 'til noon without a nicotine fix."

Rosanna looked up "I'd like to, Luce, but I'm swamped."

Lucinda sidled over to a stout, middle-aged Hispanic man. His name and title, Joseph Martinez, Financial Analyst, were engraved on his desk nameplate. Shaune figured he must be called something else. Few people named Joseph went by that. Usually they were Joey or Joe.

"Joe," Lucinda said, "hoist up that seat warmer of yours and walk with me." Her lips bent into a terse frown. "Please? Nobody else will."

Just as Shaune figured. The guy was Joe. He found himself pulled into the conversation of these two sacrifices. Bernard's glossy head faded in the background.

Joe pulled a wallet from his pants pocket and counted his currency. "Hey Luce, did you really get your ex-husband's Y-chromosome in the divorce settlement?"

Shaune didn't laugh easy, but that was good. Some of his friends' ex-wives had attempted such extractions. No women were trustworthy except, of course, his sister and dear mummy.

"No," Lucinda said. "He didn't have one to give. Can I assume by your newfound attitude that you've passed your job probation?"

Joe stood and stretched. "Yes, I have, and despite your irrefutable charm, m' lady, you appear to have no other takers. So I will visit the vending machine and stroll with you."

Shaune's Epad shifted on his forearm as the truck jolted and squealed again. "What the hell are you doing now?"

"Sorry," Bernard said. "One of the disadvantages of using level three is exiting. What are you doing back there? Sounds like you're spying."

"I'm observing GlobeTek's employees."

"You're watching your sacrifices before the attack. Why?"

"A way of paying homage to their useless lives," Shaune answered. "When do we hit Interstate 80?"

Bernard pointed to what was now a very obvious sign. "We already have. We'll be at the hangar in thirty minutes."

Shaune smiled. "Time is 10:40. Good." He searched for his robotic pigeon perched on a tree branch in the park next to what would be Ground Zero. He logged out of GlobeTek's security network and accessed the pigeon, where he watched his sacrifices with amusement.

Lucinda and Joe walked toward the food courts. Joe stuffed a candy bar and soda in his coat pocket.

"I'm hungry," Lucinda said. "Maybe we could take a quick lunch and go home early. After all, life could end any day. Mine almost did this morning when I tripped over a meteor in my driveway."

"Let's combine our break and lunch," Joe said. "We just have to get back by noon and if the world ends before then, we won't even have to do that."

Shaune felt more energized and smiled. *No, you won't even have to do that.*

Lucinda nodded and pinched her lips around an electric cigarette.

"You know those things will kill you," Joe said. "Have you tried Savvy Cigs?"

Sucking the air into her cigarette, Lucinda blew white vapors from her nostrils. "Savvy Cigs taste how dog crap smells. Besides, my smokes won't kill me any faster than that set of triplets hanging around your waist. You know—sudden cardiac arrest, instant flatline."

Sliding the candy bar out of his pocket, Joe waved the silver wrapper in the air. "Maybe, but I'll go quick."

"Quicker than you know," Shaune said to himself, submerged in his dual role as predator and empathizer. He closed the pigeon's eyes.

TUES 01/03/2130
CENTRAL PARK
NEW YORK CITY, NY

Daniel flipped the hood of his sweatshirt away from his head. The water in Jacqueline Kennedy Reservoir swayed in a light morning wind that was cool but not cold enough for an east coast winter. Green artificial turf sprawled across the park like soft carpet, making him want to fall into the landscaping and sleep until after tomorrow's presentation. He saw remnants of the New Year's Eve meteors scattered across the grass and sidewalks. The probability of pending disaster was real.

For most of the world, the monster isn't scary enough—yet.

Shifting on the fiberglass bench to relieve his aching tailbone, Daniel expanded his tablet screen from twenty centimeters to forty. A few people jogged past him as they laughed and talked. Their minds were seemingly at ease; something he was desperate for. The presentation was tomorrow and the sore throat he was hoping for was cruelly distant. As he reviewed his and JoMarie's key points for the presentation, he wondered if they were trying to dump too much science into a Q & A event.

Daniel turned away from the tablet. Working in a park was unnatural. JoMarie had already stopped reviewing her notes and was leaning against a tree. She was talking on her Epad, probably to Ed, who didn't want her on the mission. Daniel could imagine the conversation. Ed was telling her that after thirty-two years at the EPA she could receive eighty percent of her retirement. She could spend more time with him and the family. Dillon was only two and needed his grandma. But Daniel knew JoMarie would have none of that and deep down so did Ed.

He rubbed his finger on the tablet. Hannah's baby picture displayed. Daniel's stomach ached with guilt as he touched her cheek. Feeling a hint of warmth stirring in the breeze, he looked up. There was enough sunlight pushing through to illuminate the thick clouds. He felt his heart slow and stomach relax. The vastness of space calmed him down, shrinking his problems to a manageable level when compared to infinity.

Daniel changed the screen back to his presentation notes. He forced a hard stare at the words, trying to concentrate on the key points—world falling apart, meteor storms, children in the hot continents dying from a plague, and his unofficial point, the something else going on that he couldn't quite figure out.

JoMarie walked over to him and clicked the phone off on her Epad. "I just talked to Ed. I already miss my grandbaby and kids."

Daniel looked up at her. "I know."

After working with JoMarie for thirteen years, Daniel knew her empathetic nature the end-result of her piercing intellect and authentic spirituality. She'd supported him after his divorce and Hannah's death more than his parents ever had. When it came to the mission, she knew how close Earth was to some type of disastrous shift. And she wasn't going to allow her children, grandchild, and other people's children to suffer.

"Family's a big deal," Daniel said. "Be glad yours is somewhat functional."

"Somewhat is the key word," JoMarie said. "After the mission I have to retire. Ed's driving me crazy and deep down, I know he's right."

"The mission's five years, not five months," Daniel said. "That's a huge commitment. He knows you have to do this, right?"

"I'm not so sure."

Daniel stood and rubbed his lower back. He knew that if he and JoMarie were on the mission for personal gain, it would be easy to walk away. She could be a dean at a college. He could be a professor.

The denial of Earth's weakened state was the poison and the only antidote was action. The scientific knowledge they'd ingested over the years was inescapable, fully incorporating its brutal reality throughout their bodies and minds.

JoMarie stared at her Epad. "I have to ride this to the end." Turning to Daniel, she added, "And so do you. Ready to walk around the reservoir?"

"I guess so," Daniel said. "I've been slouching around since we got to New York. Haven't memorized the support for our key points and somehow I'm sweating."

"My Epad says the temperature's nine Celsius," JoMarie said as she gazed at the reservoir. "That's higher than normal for this time of year, but hot? Not even close. You're getting the jitters about tomorrow."

"Or maybe I'm getting the flu," said Daniel.

JoMarie headed toward the water. "Sounds like your December funk hasn't been told that the month switched over."

Daniel followed, thinking more than he cared to. "Not the first time that's happened. I was looking at Hannah's picture. Whenever I see her, there's a new sparkle in her eyes, a dimple in her cheek or curl in her hair I never noticed before." He shrunk his tablet to eight centimeters and shoved it in his coat pocket.

"Hannah was a smart little girl given her short time on Earth," JoMarie said. "Remember when she took my lunch order for Mexican food from Olivia's? She scolded me about how unhealthy my meal was!"

Daniel watched the small waves in the water ripple like sand in the desert. "Then she sent you those healthy taco recipes from *Galax.net*. I swear on my life I won't let her down."

JoMarie read mail on her Epad as she walked. "You never will. After Ed and I finished our little discussion, Dillon and I talked. Tomorrow you and I will be the voices for Dillon and Hannah."

"Somebody needs to be," Daniel said. "I'm tired of the shit talk about how people say they love the children but don't pony up."

"So you'll help sell the mission tomorrow by memorizing the support to our key points?"

"I can't think straight enough," he answered. "The support will have to drop out of my mouth on an as-needed basis." Daniel pulled his vibrating Epad from his pants pocket.

Not again. Casey's grumpy face was staring at him from the screen.

JoMarie picked up her pace on the sidewalk bordering the reservoir. "We need to head back to the hotel and get more work done. I'm thinking about home too much."

Daniel trekked after her as the Epad switched to ringing mode. The golden retriever had phoned him three times yesterday and each call had ended in an argument.

"Can you take Casey home to your cabin? He's calling me again and I don't want to answer."

JoMarie kept walking. "He'll know you're letting his calls go to voicemail. That'll make things worse."

Daniel groaned and answered the call. "For the tenth time you can't come to New York."

Curling his lips up in a big smile, Casey lifted a paw and waved at Daniel. "Look forward to seeing you tomorrow."

"Casey," Daniel said, "Nielsen doesn't want you going to public events yet. If you want people to see you talk, make a video and stick it on *Galax.net*."

"Everyone will think the footage is faked."

Biting his lip, Daniel tried to stay calm. "Dr. Nielsen is in charge of the mission. He won't let you go. Plus, you're not prepared."

Casey laughed. "I don't have to be prepared. I'm a talking dog."

Daniel could see the other enhanced animals snickering in the background at their persistent alpha male. But Daniel was a bigger alpha. "Nielsen won't let you leave Unity Station. This is also a safety matter. You could be kidnapped."

"You're just jealous that I might get more attention than you."

"You know better than that."

"So delude yourself," Casey said. "I'm not being held prisoner on this space station."

"Why do you want to go?" Daniel said feeling more exasperated with each word he uttered. "There will be hundreds, maybe thousands of people at Public Hall. Remember your college graduation? You got stage fright in front of a hundred people at DHS."

"I had a cold that day."

Daniel swung the Epad toward the sky and shook his head. Dealing with Casey was like arguing with a spoiled ten-year-old boy. Hannah was more mature when she was two. He zoomed into a close up of Casey's face. "Crowds give you panic attacks. You wouldn't like New York."

"Yes, sirree, I will," Casey said as he sat in a lotus position and took three deep breaths. "I can control my breathing now."

"Casey I have to go. I'll call you tomorrow after the presentation."

"You won't have to. I'll see you there." The dog stuck his tongue out at Daniel and the screen went dark.

"Did he hang up on you?" JoMarie said.

"Again." Daniel put his Epad back in his pocket. "Part of me feels bad but he'd get in the way. There's no chance he'd be let off Unity Station anyhow."

"And he'd be a huge distraction. He's getting too big for those furry britches of his."

"Getting?" Daniel watched a man and woman walking a Saint Bernard in the distance. "Whose idea was it to give dogs the ability to talk anyway? Especially that one."

"Sure wasn't me," JoMarie said. "Casey got his rebellious attitude from being in that rogue lab before he was rescued."

"He was probably already that way," Daniel commented. "His original owner was a prominent civil rights attorney in LA."

"I never heard that story but now that you mention it...."

As they reached the end of the reservoir, Daniel watched Slojets soar under the clouds. He hoped Casey didn't call back until after the presentation. He had to prepare better and didn't feel like arguing.

A Skyguard scaling over the park caught his eye. He thought of President Clemens' face on the billboard and the fishbowl called Earth. Almost nothing was private anymore, yet Daniel suspected that most evil truths on this blue orb remained hidden in plain sight.

TUES 01/03/2130
FLC FAMILY TRUST AIRPORT
MORRISON, NY

Bernard stopped the truck at the airport's security checkpoint. Shaune lowered his window and submitted his DNA and thumbprint to the guard. The two iron gates opened. A surge of warm boldness filled his body as if he'd just downed a shot of tequila. They drove past several guards and to the hangar's rear entrance. Shaune couldn't believe how much his family owned. Having access to a private airport kept him from having to be crammed in the public terminals with the commoners.

He and Bernard got out of the car and walked into the terminal and down the hall toward a remodeled and furnished apartment. A security guard opened the front door then motioned toward the bathroom. "The chemical armor stall is in a separate section of the shower. The dispenser's set up. All you have to do is push the 'On' button."

"Will do," Shaune said as he set his Epad and Washington statue on the bathroom countertop. He stripped in front of the bathroom door after the guard walked off.

Bernard stared at him.

Shaune rubbed his stomach, the muscles feeling like coils of damp clay. "What are you staring at? You're improperly equipped and even if you weren't, you're too old."

Bernard winked. "Same to you."

"You're such an asshole."

"Same to you," Bernard said. "I was remembering you as a nine-year-old kid. What a little monster you were. Not much has changed."

Shaune laughed and walked through the shower and in the stall. He slid an oxygen mask over his face and then put on goggles and a hair cap. He pushed the 'On' button and vaporous liquid sprayed from all directions, coating his body. After a few minutes the mister stopped. Warm air blew on him and he walked in the living room, dry.

Bernard had placed the combat gear across the couch. "After putting on your monkey suit you should be almost indestructible."

"I hope so." Shaune rubbed his arm and felt the pliable film encapsulating him. Strutting to the vanity's mirror, he admired himself from different angles. The cut physique he'd earned on his own. The head of thick, reddish brown hair he inherited from his mummy.

"The new stuff lasts pretty long, I'm told," Bernard said.

"It's supposed to. I'll be resistant to bullets for at least a week or until I apply the deactivating solvent. The body armor suit is probably enough, but I didn't want to take unnecessary risk when the fix was so easy."

Shaune forced his legs and body into the tight undergarment. He pulled the straps over his shoulders and grabbed the mesh pants and shirt that would serve as body armor with g-force control. "I hope these things compress right. I don't tolerate pressure well past Mach One."

"If not, you'll pass out," Bernard said. "You're not flying the plane so that wouldn't be the worst thing."

Anxious about the loss of control that goes with fainting, Shaune frowned. "I don't like being unconscious."

"Better than what your sacrifices will go through when they're burned alive. You'll be as good as new by tomorrow after a good night's sleep."

"Let's hope."

Bernard squinted as if in deep thought. "I am concerned about one thing. What if someone shoots you in the face?"

Shaune rolled his eyes. Sometimes Bernard was so dense. "The helmet and visor are ammo proof. Plus, I have these." He lifted a small box from the counter. The package read, "US Navy SEALs Eye

Enhancers." He leaned toward the mirror, pried his right eyelid up, and pressed a lens on his eye.

"They're stocked with nano-computers that adjust to night or day lighting. Very expensive and hard to get."

Shaune inserted a lens on his left eye. "There's a screen on the lens that displays maps and other images, if needed. More important, they have an anti-projectile feature that'll divert a small, fast-moving object coming toward my head."

"And remember," Bernard said, "you can always get another cornea."

Shaune magnetized his Epad on his forearm and stepped into the fireproof jumpsuit. "In the blink of an eye."

Sitting on the couch, Shaune yanked on boots and grabbed the gloves. He shoved the Washington statue in the leg's large side pocket. The new world order was embracing him like a hug. "See you tonight at the pier."

* * *

Holding his helmet, Shaune walked inside the main hangar. Armed guards stood against a wall and stared straight ahead. Three Slojets shimmered in technological glory. The crafts' triangular black wings were topped with red sirens.

A man wearing the same gear as Shaune stood by one of the jets. His gloved hands were propped on the fuselage. The guy waved him over, his stony scowl showing through his face shield.

"I'm Paul O'Brien. Finally, we meet in person. You gave me a lot of work to do but I think everything's covered."

"Everything's as it's supposed to be?" Shaune said.

Paul glared at him. "The work was done according to your specifications. Whether that's how it's supposed to be is your problem." He motioned to the plane's undercarriage. "The laser power is as requested: military grade with the capacity to bend a building in half."

“Sounds great,” Shaune said, trying not to lose his temper. “Someone checked to make sure these look exactly like the NYPD units?”

“Whatever you specified,” Paul said his tone a little snarky. “As I’ve told you in previous conversations, the USAF’s X-1000s are similar to the New York units. We had to make minor body changes to duplicate the PD 850s. We used original paint, NYPD logos, and authentic ID numbers. The hackers will monitor and adjust the IT system to get us past the Skyguards.”

Shaune nodded. *He’s as much of a jerk-off in person as he was in his emails and phone conversations.*

“Nobody will know until after it matters,” Paul added.

The other four advocates walked into the hangar and stood around the Slojets. Shaune lifted up his sleeve. His Epad read 11:20. *Gotta hurry.* He pulled his gloves from his back pocket and slid them on. Taking a deep breath, he snapped on his helmet. Paul handed him a small flat air tank that he set over his back. The suit was already tight and he hoped it wouldn’t have to compress much more when adjusting to supersonic speeds.

* * *

The three jets crawled outside of the hangar and rose into the sky. Shaune and Paul ascended over the clouds, which hid them from the city like dense foliage. The others followed. A NYPD Slojet passed. No response. Skyguard satellites watched them like curious but unalarmed children.

Shaune reviewed the surveillance screens. “The NYPD and Skyguards aren’t responding.”

“As planned,” Paul said.

“We got thirty-five seconds left,” Shaune breathed. They cut through the cloud layer toward the financial district below. “We’ve broken past the security shield. I can’t believe this is real.”

Paul stared ahead. “Don’t forget that it is.”

Shaune took mental aim at the target and checked his suit's diagnostics. "There it is. GlobeTek Finance." The emerald skyscraper grew closer.

The Slojets lowered to the building's face. Paul programmed the laser strength on the control panel. The other jets levitated on each side of Shaune and Paul and then took aim. Taxis and buses inched down the streets below. Suddenly, streams of glowing ammo seared across the huge glass windows. GlobeTek began hemorrhaging fire like a slashed throat. Glass screeched as it crumbled and landed on the sidewalks and streets, asphyxiating the city's everyday white noise.

Slipping a uniflyer over his back, Shaune squeezed out of the jet's hatch and glided through the large cavity blown into the building. One advocate from each of the other jets followed. His lenses displayed animated replications, showing him where objects were located in the gray smoke.

He quickly realized that no visual aids were needed to see the people collapsing into walls and choking on burning plastic and metals. Flames were breaking out and spreading. Desks, chairs, and storage cabinets slid into an expanding sinkhole. The building's floor began wavering and sagged like a shallow bowl.

The faint smell of burning flesh penetrated Shaune's mask, or maybe he was imagining things. He couldn't be getting outside air. A large number of people were wearing uniflyers and escaping through the building's massive gashes. "Shit! I didn't know so many people had those," he said aloud.

Paul radioed Shaune. Their one minute was up. Shaune shouted in his headset to the advocates, "Time to go!" He swam through the smoke and floated outside, followed by the others.

Shaune and the advocates climbed back into the Slojets. Paul struck the GlobeTek Finance logo anchored on the building's roof. It exploded into flames. Parachutes billowed to the ground. Men and women squirmed from under the chutes and ran. People poured from the still upright bottom floor while others jumped from the floors above. Shaune turned his head, searching. He looked toward the park. Lucinda and Joe were cowering behind a van in the food court.

Shaune felt relief and then dread. He'd never again observe his victims before a kill; see their faces and hear their voices. He realized he'd formed an unhealthy sentiment that could affect his ability to follow through.

"Blast the target one more time," he said. "This is the first workday after a three-day weekend."

Paul pinched his mouth back in one corner. "That will cause too much damage to the buildings next door. Our casualty profile was specific."

"I didn't become a part of this to go easy," Shaune replied.

Streams of lasers blew into the glass and exploded. Fire whipped throughout the building. The floors started slowly collapsing like falling dominoes. The blazing, gold skeleton of GlobeTek Finance bowed into a twisted metal sculpture. Shaune opened the plane's hatch. He tossed his Washington statue onto the chaos to give investigators something to analyze. Seeing the porkers showing upon the observation screen, he slid off his uniflyer.

Paul aimed the Slojet at a sixty-degree angle and shot into the sky. A sonic boom jolted Shaune's insides. Two more booms shook from the advocates' jets. Shaune's hands and feet were numb, squeezed to the bone by his suit's g-force protection. The porkers were fast, but they couldn't reach Mach 8.

Paul examined the NYPD crafts in the screen. "Their engines can't be 850s. They're moving too fast. Could they have upgraded and you didn't know?"

"You think I'm a chump?" Shaune said. "Our connections said they had standard 850s. Never seen anything else on patrol."

"Sounds like your connections missed something."

Shaune didn't want to admit that he was afraid.

* * *

Growling under his breath, Paul rammed the jet upward. "We're two thousand kilometers over the Atlantic and the PD is still on us. I'm activating the holographic cloak, but if we still get caught I'm selling your ass out."

Shaune clenched his fists, ready to tell Paul to go fuck himself. He hesitated. Maybe that wasn't such a good idea. He'd never be a Utopian Society Alliance leader if he was ejected from the plane with a nano-grenade hidden somewhere on his person. And he figured Paul was perfectly capable of such treason.

Within a few seconds, their jet's exterior was adjusting its colors to the surroundings. Paul motioned to one of the screens that displayed the advocates. "The NYPD deactivated the cloaks of the other units. In a few minutes they'll be close enough to disable the crafts."

Shaune stared at the panel, observing the police closing in on his comrades. "Once the PD disables the crafts, the advocates will be captured. They'll be interrogated until they shit their pants."

Paul nodded.

Shaune felt lightheaded as he closed his eyes. "They'll talk before our connections at Oval can intervene."

Looking down at the jet's control panel, Paul frowned. "Oval won't reach them in time."

"They're one of us," Shaune said.

"They knew the risks, but you have to make the decision."

"Activate the self-destruct feature," Shaune whispered.

Paul pressed his right index finger onto the reader. The command registered, reading, "Implode selected crafts." Submit right thumb to verify print and DNA. "

Paul pressed his right thumb onto the glass.

"Command verified—destruction complete," the screen read. The observation screens showed two fireballs exploding across the sky. Gray, billowing smoke followed. The NYPD blips slowed, treaded air for a second, and started heading toward Shaune and Paul.

"Paul, are we gonna risk capture or are you going to fly this thing right?" Shaune yelled.

Paul shot the jet straight up even further. "The PD must have engines and other technology you didn't know about. I should toss your spoiled, rich carcass in the shark-ridden waters! I'd bet those hungry fish can eat through body armor." Then, smiling, he added, "Probably for the best that the others didn't make it. Dead lips speak softly."

Paul brushed his fingers over the steering controls and corkscrewed the jet down. Shaune's suit wasn't acclimating to the g-force fluctuations like he'd hoped. Despite his preparations for this ride, he didn't know if the Atlantic Ocean was below him or above him. He was just wildly spinning in a blue tunnel.

The jet lunged forward.

Shaune gasped, "What the shit!"

"We gotta dump the bird," Paul said. "I contacted our subs. They're almost under us. I was gonna dock the jet in mine but that'll take too long. We got twenty seconds."

Shaune's eardrums popped. A sting shot through his head and a wave of nausea followed. Why hadn't he remembered to take a damn motion sickness pill?

"I think we sacrificed a couple thousand," Shaune said. "Too many escaped with the uniflyers and chutes. I failed to maximize the kills." He slammed the jet's side window with his forearm. "We should've gassed them! Less drama, more trauma."

Paul grabbed Shaune's wrist. "Would you knock that off? We're not supposed to make these too big. Besides, we could've gotten two thousand sacrifices a lot easier and cheaper than this."

Folding his arms with tight conviction, Shaune shook his head. "Success doesn't come cheap. Penetration through the Skyguards will create fear in Mr. and Ms. Public that will transcend any measurable damage."

He tapped on his helmet. "The imprisonment we seek isn't of the body. I'm after primordial manipulation—fear of death, gradual thought conversion. That's power. That's the future of the Utopian Society Alliance, which will soon be transforming this disaster of a planet into paradise."

Through his face shield, Paul's tanned, middle-aged crow's feet stood firm around his gray eyes. "You can explain that."

The display reported that the plane was hovering a thousand meters over the ocean. Shaune's Epad vibrated under his flight suit, indicating his waiting sub was ready for him.

The jet's hatch popped open. He slipped his uniflyer on and drifted toward the water. In the distance, Paul was closing in on his own sub. Skyguards and the NYPD flew in the distant sky. The police would be here in a few minutes, but he'd be out of reach by then. The jet sliced the ocean's surface and submerged in premature death. Bubbles rose from the water, assuring Shaune that the craft had imploded.

Shaune raised his fist in victory. This exercise was a steppingstone to a cause so great that humanity would someday thank him; maybe even sell pewter statues of him in the White House. He closed in on the assigned coordinates where he'd be picked up. He zeroed in on his sub. Act One complete. Acts Two and Three to come, then the take-over. And finally—peace on Earth.

WED 01/04/2130, 08:55
UN MULTIPLEX
NEW YORK CITY, NY

Daniel sat at the table on the Public Hall coliseum stage. *Find hope somewhere.*

Find it in the smoke puffing from GlobeTek's aftermath. Find it in the meteorites. Find it in the children of the hot continents, like those he'd seen during his Peace Corps trips in college. He remembered what a bad hand those kids had been tossed. Yet they played and laughed in their meager and often vile surroundings. His job was to find a future for them in the AI programs.

He stared at the two computer screens on the panelist table. The presentation outline and key points he and JoMarie put together displayed on screen two. Looking behind him, he saw the giant holovision hanging over the stage. The HV would display whatever was on screen one, which right now, was blank. Turning back, he glanced at his Epad. Pokey was looking at him from the table with a sad dog look that seemed too real for a cartoon.

Daniel had called Casey last night and was sent directly to voicemail. He shouldn't have snapped at the dog yesterday. Casey's emotional maturity was still developing since he'd only had human intelligence for ten years.

He looked around the coliseum that was far too full. There had to be at least two thousand people, waiting for what he had deduced was a mission infomercial. They had to sell Phase II of the mission by convincing the public that investing in the environment was worth the time and money. Phase I would happen regardless and he expected arguments on that too. He sighed and shook his head when he realized that the UN had provided headsets so attendees' voices could be amplified. *More people to yell at me.*

Daniel was breathing fast and he struggled to calm down. At the same time, he didn't want to fade off after sleeping only two hours. He had three espresso shots and a bottle of antacids on the table for easy access. He turned to JoMarie. Her face was tense as she reviewed her Epad.

The town hall meeting would be starting in five minutes. Daniel thought of the shouting protesters outside the Multiplex who believed the mission was nothing more than elitist preservation. Laughing a little, he couldn't help but love the bomb-sniffing dogs waiting outside the entrance for suckers like him. *Talk about gratuitous.* They shoved their noses against the most discrete body parts long after knowing there were no explosives or weapons to be found.

Daniel cringed when he saw Vladimir Chistyakov walk onto the stage to introduce the presentation. The audience applauded as the UN leader and Russian president stood behind the podium next to Daniel and JoMarie's table. The eighty-six-year-old guy looked like a bent tree that had weathered too many Siberian winters.

"Good morning, Public Hall guests," Chistyakov said. "The United Nations and New York City are honored to welcome today's panelists, Professors JoMarie Sanford and Daniel Griffin. Before this mission, they oversaw industrial waste management at the National Exposure Research Lab in North Carolina for the EPA."

Daniel faced the audience that was blending and shifting in a dizzying pattern. Huge and distorted images of his and JoMarie's faces popped up on screen one and above the stage. He downed one of the espressos and swallowed an antacid pill.

Chistyakov thankfully changed the display to other scientists and turned to the HV. "Our panelists will be working on the Global Restoration Mission to help repair the world's ailing ecosystem. Maybe the meteorite mystery that has taunted us for almost forty years will be solved too. The mission's goals and our speakers' bios are in your programs."

He smiled at Daniel and JoMarie. "Thank you for coming here." Chistyakov walked off the stage and sat in the front row.

The spotlight shifted to Daniel.

"Keep your chin up," JoMarie said. "We're gonna do great."

Daniel walked to the side of the table and adjusted his headset. The audience gave him low-grade applause. Someone out there with a reasonable head had to be listening. He aimed his mouse pointer at the scientists on the screen.

"Six hundred researchers will be working full-time on the mission," he said. "One hundred of them will live on Unity Space Station, including JoMarie and me. We're two of five project specialists who'll use artificial intelligence and creative problem solving as part of our scientific analysis. Today we are here to answer questions and provide information about the mission. Please send your *Galax.net* user name to the UN mission website, *USRG.net* for random selection."

He turned back to JoMarie, who was operating the computer. She looked up at the audience and read, "Sebastian Mac."

Daniel scanned the audience. A man who appeared to be in his mid-thirties rose from the second row at the far left of the coliseum. His long copper-colored ponytail dripped with arrogance. The guy adjusted his headset and braced his hands on the waist of his denim trench coat. He leered at Daniel.

"I'm Sebastian MacDonald, reporter for *Galax.net EU Media*. Mr. Griffin, I have a question about the Earthstar compound that I'm dying to ask. Who will get to live there? You and your elitist buddies?"

Just as Daniel's luck would have it, the first question was coming from a smart ass.

"As one of twenty senior researchers," Daniel answered, "I was given the opportunity to live in Earthstar. I donated my two slots to a Kenyan woman and her daughter."

"How convenient," MacDonald snapped back. "Even if the planet's soaked in poison and piss, you can escape."

Daniel tightened his jaw. "I could've sworn I just said I donated my slots. I'll be living on Earth after the mission."

"Sure you will. Until the air seizes your lungs and a glass of tap water makes you shit for two days."

Feeling heat rise to his face, Daniel fought what he knew was his dad's temperament. "The ecosystem's a mess and hundreds of millions of people have died from the African Plague. And as a reporter, you must know that the meteor storms are scaring everyone. You're against us trying to find out why these things are happening?"

MacDonald coughed out a mocking snort. "You're not going to find out why. Earthstar and your sorry ass are all you sell-out scientists care about."

President Chistyakov stood from his seat. He turned to the reporter and spoke into his headset. "Mr. MacDonald, our guests do not decide who lives on Earthstar. Take your yellow journalism elsewhere. Be serious or be out."

"I am serious," MacDonald said. "And why is public money being wasted on a space station for research? You spent a fortune so this outer space lab could have artificial gravity. How many kids could've been fed with that money?"

"UN leaders, including me," Chistyakov responded, "believe that having scientists willing to live away from their families and focus on their jobs was best for the mission, like soldiers in battle."

"What a bunch of bullshit."

Chistyakov raised his voice. "Sir, we're at war with our own imminent destruction. The artificial gravity was provided by NASA at a reduced cost. It makes the five-year stay more tolerable." He pointed at MacDonald. "Now sit down!"

MacDonald pouted and dropped in his chair. Several people around him cheered.

Daniel glared at the sulking reporter. JoMarie should've opened this. Her three decades of wading in political sand traps at the EPA had seasoned her nerves.

He heard JoMarie announce the next selection. "US Senator Wharton," she said.

A conservative US senator stood from a front row seat near the stage. Daniel balked a little, but the man was better than the People's Party members wearing those ridiculous matching yellow and lime geometric ties.

"I'm US Senator Terrell Wharton from Montana," the man said. "Are we going to find out what's causing the meteor storms? They're terrorist attacks in and of themselves…and they seem to be aiming at things!"

"Just people," Daniel responded as he glanced back at JoMarie.

JoMarie glared at Daniel from the table as if wanting to elbow him. "I think we may need more evidence to conclude that."

"He's got a point." The senator paused then added, "Washington DC seems to be a favorite striking area."

The audience laughed and started clapping. Some stood and turned up the microphones on their headsets as they cheered. Daniel couldn't help but join them.

After a minute of enthusiastic applause, the senator waved his hand at the audience to calm down. "I know that's funny, but we really need to see results."

"I feel your pain, Senator," JoMarie said as she stood and walked in front of the table. "We're not selling a chick magnet car with low monthly payments. The mission's offering a boat-sized wagon for twice the cost of a Benz. Daniel and I aim to convince you that the wagon's the better deal."

"Why can't anyone figure out what's causing the storms?" Senator Wharton shot back.

JoMarie folded her arms and looked at the senator, her face tense. "The storms seem to be caused by a gravitational phenomenon that's attracting the meteors to Earth. We're not sure if this relates to the ecosystem's breakdown or not."

Yes, this relates to the ecosystem's breakdown, Daniel thought as he stared down at the stage. *But there's something more.*

Senator Wharton squinted at them in what appeared to be a high level of skepticism. "Wasn't the UN green tax supposed to pay for the meteor research?"

Wincing a little, JoMarie answered, "That money was diverted to clean up bacteria-laden water."

"I thought the UN water safety tax was used for that."

Daniel walked to the table and downed espresso number two. He knew that even with antacid pills, the caustic drink might agitate his ulcer, but he didn't care.

JoMarie displayed her email address on the HV. "I don't know what the taxes were supposed to cover, but I'll mail you a summary of what research I have."

"Thank you, ma'am," Senator Wharton said as he sat down.

* * *

Two hours had passed and Daniel was mentally exhausted. Not so much from the scientific concepts they were trying to explain, but from the banter. JoMarie was back at the computer and he was tired of standing. At least lunch was in the near future. He swiped his remote computer mouse at screen one that displayed Earth's newest Central American plains on the HV.

"In 2050 this was a rainforest," he said. "Due to overpopulation and slapstick regulations, it has become flattened by farming and manufacturing." Startled, he turned to a shrieking shout in the audience.

"Why are we wasting our time hiring people from the EPA?" MacDonald shouted. "They've been given four bloody decades to find out what's causing the meteor storms, which by the way are getting worse!"

Four UN security guards surrounded MacDonald. They grabbed him under his arms, lifted him out of his chair, and escorted him up the now-moving escalator. They unceremoniously shoved him out of the coliseum. His supporters followed; shouting and raising their fists like a herd of gorillas. The doors closed behind the red ponytail and his posse. Restraining gloat, Daniel bared his teeth a little.

"To address Mr. MacDonald's question," JoMarie said, "the situation we're dealing with is unknown. Frankly, we've had other crises to deal with."

Daniel changed the HV display to Tokyo Nuclear Power Plant. "For the past two centuries, Earth's been on a bad diet, losing five kilograms and gaining ten, over and over."

He used his pointer to form a cluster of animated oranges hanging over the power plant's cooling towers and waste storage units. "With solar and other energies stagnant for the last half century, nuclear power has become the largest part of the world's energy mix."

He thrust his pointer like a pool cue, stabbing the oranges. They fell and splattered into pulp on the structures.

"One drawback to the everlasting nuclear reserve is the discarded orange peel. Like a broken record from the twenty-first century, I must again say that we must resolve contamination issues and stop terrorists from accessing spent fuel."

A man with a shaved head and brown goatee stood from the third row. This guy wasn't waiting for his and JoMarie's primitive selection process. His tie and matching clip told Daniel that he was a high-ranking People's Party member and more likely than not, another complainer.

"Hatton Robertson, Senior VP for International Refuse Eliminators. Sticking IRE storage units in your presentation is cliché even for you NERL scientists. You're nothing more than taxpayer funded boogeymen."

"I didn't mention names," said Daniel as he clenched his fists to divert his contempt. "But since you did, let me finish. Moscow and Barcelona were hit in 2123 with nukes made from spent fuel that was traced to stolen waste from IRE warehouses. Two million people perished in the bombings and another three million from the radioactive aftermath."

The audience started booing at Hattan Robertson.

"The traitors who stole that waste were executed," Robertson said. "That was a fluke."

Daniel shook his head. "Not good enough. Without proper management there's always more accidents to come."

Hattan Robertson stabbed his finger at Daniel then at the audience. "How about this? Nuclear waste is less toxic than the excess world population. Any scientist will tell you that."

Turning to JoMarie, Daniel paused. She mouthed to him, "You can do this."

Walking behind the table and sitting down, Daniel was ready to confront someone more offensive to him than the most fire-breathing conservative or pointlessly defiant liberal—a member of the People's Party of America. He thought of why he was on the mission and about

Hannah, his beautiful daughter, dead because of people like Hattan Robertson. Daniel's hands trembled as he tried to think away his grief.

Pokey flashed a message on the Epad screen. *He's naked on the toilet!!* A computer-animation of a bare Robertson on a commode displayed.

Daniel looked away from the Epad. "Thanks, Pokey," he said under his breath.

He looked back at the audience, trying to forget the image. "Proper waste management is a necessity and an overpopulated world, while a huge problem, is not an excuse to ignore corporate responsibility."

Glancing at the discussion points on screen two, Daniel realized the presentation was taking on a life of its own. This tidy outline that JoMarie had insisted on was hurdling off a cliff.

"Mount Yucca One and Two are far beyond capacity," he continued. "Spent fuel and transuranic waste does not belong, and should not be put, in the ground. I also have an issue with this garbage being dumped on the moon. Print that in your PR pamphlets."

A round of applause came from the back of the coliseum. Daniel's stomach felt relief that someone seemed to be on his side. He turned to JoMarie and she smiled, reassuring him that he was doing fine.

"Mr. Griffin," the IRE executive replied, unmoved, "Phase I, the construction of the Earthstar compound, is your first priority. That's the reason I pay the ridiculous green tax that Senator Wharton mentioned. Your environmental ambitions are Phase II. Since you have a PhD, I assume you're familiar with how numbers work? Phase I is before Phase II." The guy sat down and started laughing with a man sitting next to him.

Keeping his expression blank, Daniel was still. *Push away Dad's DNA*.

JoMarie walked in front of the table and stood next to him.

"In Africa and some higher industrialized countries," she said, "water infrastructure is either collapsing or is non-existent. We have to be careful about disposing waste in the underground facilities."

Using her mouse, JoMarie faded the splattered oranges and the Tokyo plant display. The room dimmed and a spotlight shone on her. "The world cannot be managed without everyone's help. The conditions we've discussed are ominous, but one of the biggest threats to our survival is human overpopulation."

Daniel felt relief but didn't know why. Maybe sharing this information would affect people in the audience who could make change happen. Pacing back and forth across the stage, JoMarie seemed hesitant. Daniel understood why. What she was about to say was going to stir controversy. She walked to the edge of the stage.

"Some of you may have heard that in 2135, a new UN global population reduction plan will begin. This is true. All babies born in a medical facility will be sterilized at birth. When a person turns twenty-five years of age, he or she must pass a psychological test to reproduce. A person will then be sterilized after having two biological children."

Murmuring in the audience told Daniel that there was a mixed reaction. He couldn't argue with the naysayers. Being a part of Hannah's life and death made him realize how much love he could have for another person. He wanted to have that again but under the new rules would probably fail the psych test. Of course, his parents would've failed too, making the point moot.

JoMarie nodded sadly at the grumbling in the audience. "The impact will be measurable in thirty to fifty years. Stabilization should start occurring around 2180 to 2190."

Daniel knew that media spin and human rights challenges would follow. He pondered the irony of a dead species eradicated by unleashed freedoms. The audience fell silent as if they were becoming resigned, knowing that options were shrinking and would soon disappear.

As JoMarie finished, Chistyakov walked back to the podium. "We're almost at noon," he said. "The presentation will resume at 13:30. Thank you."

* * *

Lines of people rode the moving escalators up and out of Public Hall and headed toward the food courts. Daniel followed JoMarie toward the middle exit with the last of the crowd. "Those damn meteorites seem to be aiming for humans. Has an animal ever been killed by one?"

“How would I know?” JoMarie smirked at him. “They can’t report if they’ve been hit.” She smiled. “At least most of them can’t.”

Daniel stopped outside the coliseum’s exit. “You know what I mean. Not a single documented case! On top of that, *Galax.net* has compiled patterns of the meteor storms and has found a relationship to terrorist attacks. People are starting to panic. New York City was hit on New Year’s Eve and GlobeTek was attacked yesterday.”

“But other places were hit, too,” JoMarie said, “and were not being attacked. There could be a connection or all of this could be a coincidence.”

Daniel checked the news on his Epad. The protests were getting worse outside the Multiplex. Footage from *Galax.net* showed the protesters around the UN buildings. Most of them appeared to be college age. They charged down the street chanting, “USRG saves itself!”

Retreating to the food courts with JoMarie, Daniel pressed on his stomach. He always knew that the mission’s progress would be snared in conflicts of politics, protests, and funding sources. But he was beginning to understand that this aloof understanding bore little resemblance to marching into the conflicts and beyond them.

WED 01/04/2130, 08:52 PST
SOUTHERN CALIFORNIA ELECTRICAL DIST. INC.
SAN CLEMENTE, CA

Sanya Vasquez's eyes opened and she blinked several times. The room looked monochrome and generic. She wasn't sure where she was. Who was that horrible man she saw in the fire? Her heart started pounding hard. As the color started to return to her surroundings, she stared at the screen saver spiraling on her computer monitor. Rubbing her eyes, she looked at an HV on the wall with the caption, "*SCED Employee New Year's Resolutions*" followed by contact information for support groups.

Crap, Sanya thought. She couldn't believe what had just happened. She'd faded off at work a few times before. Today was the first time she'd ever fallen completely asleep and was dreaming.

She pulled a compact out of her purse and looked in the mirror. Her hazel eyes had lost the spark they had in her mid-twenties. Now they were framed by loosening skin that didn't attract men like they once did. Of course, if she could get more than four hours of sleep a night maybe her eyes wouldn't look half shut all the time.

Sanya patted her tired eyelids with powder. She pinched a violet eye pencil in her fingers and drew a line right below her lower lashes. Gotta bring out the green flecks in that hazel. Stuffing her makeup back in her purse, she ran a brush through her hair, grateful that she had pigmentation pills that made her wavy, grayish hair brown. Of course the highlights were added manually. No pill for that yet. She felt a pang of loneliness. She was only forty-five, not eighty-five. Ever since she pushed Aaron away, no one else had crossed her path. Thank God for her daughters.

Suddenly, the face she saw glaring through the smoky flames in her dream came back to her. A man inside a burning building was wearing a uniflyer and gliding carelessly through a collapsing building as people burned to death. The man was thinking of something called the…cat shack? Ugh. She knew what that was. Too much like her ex-husband.

She also knew this tied to something much worse. Sanya sensed her dream was related to the New York terrorist attack. She laid her head on her desk. Nobody would believe her and she didn't have a clear enough vision of the man to identify him. Pushing herself out of her chair, she walked toward the break room to fetch an energy drink. Her head throbbed a little with each step.

This was no haphazard, fictional movie playing out in an imaginary world. Death and destruction were again infiltrating her sleep. This man and his evil deeds were a reality that belonged to someone else and had duplicated in her head. And once again she had no choice but to make it hers.

WED 01/04/2130, 13:30
UN MULTIPLEX
NEW YORK CITY, NY

Daniel settled in his chair at the panelist table scanning *Galax.net* stories with his Epad. He couldn't really tell how their Phase II sell was going. The preliminary blogs were showing a mixed reaction but then the complainers always voiced their opinions more loudly than the silent majority. The audience had returned and seemed more voluminous and loud. He laughed as he finished off his last espresso. Maybe there weren't more people. Perhaps they were full of food and took up more space. The protestors had been removed from outside the Multiplex and taken to jail after the police blasted them with tranquilizing gas.

He nodded to JoMarie. "You first."

JoMarie narrowed her eyes at Daniel and stood in front of the table. "The desperation and pain in our world is apparent," she said as the audience quieted down.

She turned to the American flag draped on the stage next to the podium. "Death rates are rampant in the poor continents. This is often blamed on doctors relocating to Los Angeles Valley or to other exclusive communities, but most have not."

Displaying the underground city on the large screen, she continued. "The city can hold only two thousand people, so there's a limit to how many doctors can live there. The real problem is the scarcity of doctors and abundance of patients."

A voice shouted from the audience, "Death to LA Valley! Death to the bastards that escape to the trillion-dollar amusement park!"

From the front row, Chistyakov scribbled notes on his Epad, ignoring the latest rant. Daniel figured he was avoiding confrontation that could trigger more civil unrest.

"I don't agree with LA Valley's costs either," JoMarie said. "But that's not why there's a doctor shortage. Part of the problem is that government and private doctors have changed their focus to intelligence enhancement research. Their logic is that the benefit to humanity would be enormous in so many ways. However, the research isn't progressing as fast as hoped."

Daniel cringed as Hatton Robertson rose for an encore. He was glad JoMarie would get to deal with him.

"Why not focus on enhancements, Dr. Sanford?" Robertson belted out. "Bankrupting the financial markets to provide healthcare and food will only maintain a surplus population, which you agreed earlier was our worst problem." He shifted his tie clip, as if wanting to draw attention to his affiliation. "Thank you."

JoMarie forced her scowl into a flat expression as scattered boos came from the audience. "We don't consider anyone a surplus human being."

She sat back at the panelist table and directed screen one and the HV to a group of shouting women in the audience. With their blackened and leathery skin, Daniel assumed they were from the hot regions of Africa. They stood up and shook their fists at Hattan Robertson.

One of the women gripped a tablet displayed with her child's picture. "Our children are dying! How can you value wealth over the lives of innocent babies?"

Squirming in his chair while he watched the IRE executive ignore the despondent woman, Daniel paid penance for his espressos. He thought about how he was disturbed yet intrigued by enhancements. He wasn't surprised that a People's Party member would support Hitler's dream come true. He also knew that nothing would stop the operations whether they were for good or evil. There'd always be people like Hattan Robertson and right now they ruled America and perhaps more.

The audience started booing Robertson more as the women sat down and consoled each other. He and his security guard stood and stomped up the escalator and out of the coliseum.

JoMarie clapped lightly after Robertson made his exit. Daniel walked in front of the table and acknowledged US Senator Margaret Powell, who was motioning to him from the front row seat next to Chistyakov.

"To what extent is the enhancement surgery occurring and how effective is it?" she asked. "The ban apparently isn't working."

"Despite the high failure rate on animals," JoMarie said, "private researchers receive huge contributions to enhance animals and possibly even humans. We don't have much information because everything's underground. Based on data in computers seized in raids, we're estimating a ten percent success rate."

"More policing is needed," Daniel said.

"You say that Daniel," Chistyakov interjected, "but you're one of the scientists who recommended that four enhanced animals live on Unity Station to work on the mission. With only a few years of analytical capability, I doubt they'll offer unique input."

"The animals care more than most people do," Daniel replied. "The world means a lot to them because their instincts are more aligned to the earth."

Chistyakov folded his arms and shot a sarcastic look at Daniel. "I've seen footage of the others in Sweden and I'm skeptical. Though I haven't yet met the four on the mission, I doubt they're much better."

"The Stockholm Six have been enhanced three years," Daniel said. "The Unity animals have been enhanced ten years. They're team players, especially the dogs. According to USRG neurologist Sharon Caldwell, their analytical skills are highly developed. All four are college graduates."

"That's not saying much." Chistyakov grinned. "Dr. Caldwell is their rescuer. Of course, she's going to say how wonderful they are. If the animals' only specialty is they have intelligence similar to humans, heaven knows we have plenty of those."

"Their potential remains to be seen," Daniel said as he looked at JoMarie. "Can I show the audience so they know what we're talking about?"

"Yeah," JoMarie sighed. "Show us something that will make us feel good."

Daniel changed the screen from LA Valley to footage in a hospital room. Two cats and a dog were lying in clear capsules. Liquids pumped through tubes that had been placed in the animals' shaved skulls. The display then zeroed in on Casey, who was in the room lying on a couch with his head on a pillow. His eyes half-closed, he stared at the HV and yawned. He pulled a remote control from under his pillow and changed the channel from *Galax.net News* to *Cartoon.net*.

Seeing Casey made Daniel feel like a piece of guilty shit. He'd called the dog twice during lunch and was again sent straight to voicemail. He liked working with Casey and the other animals when training for the mission and had gotten attached to them. While they weren't Hannah, they often reminded him of how she may have been if she'd gotten to live longer—innocent, curious, and looking up to him like a parent.

"The golden retriever watching HV is Casey," Daniel told the audience. "He slept in my room on Unity Station during our training. Sometimes he'd turn off the gravity feature during the night and I'd wake up floating near the ceiling."

A few mild chuckles came from the audience. Daniel smiled through his regret. "These creatures of science can now be seen on *Galax.net*. The footage on the screen is from late 2119. The gray cat in the closest capsule is Cindera. The orange tabby in the middle is Kosmo, and the yellow dog in the third capsule against the wall is Rushton, another golden retriever."

A voice shot out from the audience. "How do you know they're smart?"

"They tell us," Daniel said, gleeful about his comeback to such a stupid question. "Along with the neuro enhancements, their vocal cords are modified so that they speak in human-sounding tones. The flexibility in their leg joints have been expanded so they can sit and use their front paws similar to how humans use their hands and feet. That was done to help them acclimate to the office and other work environments."

Chistyakov's melon-sized fist slapped the arm of his chair. "Americans are still in denial. Your national infrastructure is a mess. Your social services are inadequate just like the rest of us. Your government spends way too much money to research this science. Creating talking pets in laboratories is a waste of resources."

JoMarie walked from the table and stood next to Daniel. "This research is for human neurological health."

"I haven't seen anything useful in that regard," Chistyakov said.

Daniel wrung his hands as he paced the stage and turned to Chistyakov. "You remember 2125 when Casey's astute senses linked evidence to terrorists who'd planned to attack Buckingham Palace with a dirty bomb?"

"I know," Chistyakov said dryly. "Casey helped save the Queen. I assume you're aware of the latest media blitz on the money spent to enhance these animals?"

Daniel's forehead pinched into a deep frown. "Ten trillion dollars over five years."

"Don't you find that preposterous?"

JoMarie walked forward on the stage. "The animals have been working hard to prepare for the mission. They want to contribute their fair share. Sharon tells us that in five years we can start using the technology on humans."

"Except the side effects make people crazier than they already are," Chistyakov said.

Daniel hoped to get the Russian president to see the practical side of enhancements so they could move on. "Mr. Chistyakov, nuclear and conventional terrorist attacks have killed two hundred million people since 2100. The United States is doing everything possible to prevent megakills on their soil."

"Russia knows of megakills," Chistyakov said his voice trailing. "One million deaths by terror. Who'd have thought there'd be a name for such a thing? While the GlobeTek Finance attack was terrible, you Americans should feel lucky that you've only had kilokills so far."

"We need to use whatever resources we have," Senator Margaret Powell interjected. "If enhanced animals can help find the answer to this scourge, why not use them?"

Chistyakov turned to Margaret. "But enhanced animals could end up in the wrong hands and be used to conspire against us."

"That'll happen whether we use them or not," said Margaret.

A woman in the audience raised her hand and stood. Daniel could tell by her oversized tablet and sneer that resembled Sebastian MacDonald's that she was a reporter.

"Gina Romero, New York Times," she sniffed. "Mr. Griffin, information about the enhancement process is such a big secret. Can you tell me why this procedure is so expensive?"

Daniel knew this would happen. He'd get questions that had nothing to do with the mission, at least not directly. Reporters too often assumed a panelist table exuded a power that gave omnipotence to anyone sitting behind it. "I don't know the medical specifics," he said. "I can tell you that a tiny computer is implanted in the skull. The computer releases nanobots that carry stem cells inside the brain and converts them into neural tissue."

He walked to the computer and changed the display on screen one. The next images would be graphic, controversial, and of course…his fault. Photographs of bloody brains rotated on the HV. He displayed the implant in the brain's base and then zoomed in the bots.

"The lab-created stem cells require less organic support," Daniel began. "They have to be made smaller than regular brain cells to avoid pressure on the skull. In theory, when the procedure is used on humans, the skull won't have to be expanded to make room for a larger brain."

The woman seemed to be entering something in her tablet. "This seems very invasive and risky," she said loudly into her headset.

Daniel nodded. "That's why human testing hasn't started yet, as far as we know. And the bots don't stay in the brain permanently. The subjects are placed in a medically induced coma. The bots take about a week to convert the inert cells into brain cells then return to the implant, which is removed."

"Those images are repulsive," the woman commented, "and the risk for abuse seems tremendous. Haven't we messed with nature enough?"

"Like the nuclear bomb," Daniel said, "the technology was already in place. Rogue facilities have to be rooted out. The hazards are obvious."

"As a species we're still in our adolescent phase," JoMarie said, pacing the stage. "We're intelligent enough to get in trouble, but not always wise enough to get out."

“I assume these animals are aware of their mortality,” the reporter responded. “Are they afraid to die?”

Facing a diva reporter was more than Daniel could bear, but he knew this stuff was coming. He thought of his and JoMarie’s talking points still displayed on screen two. *So much for those.*

“They were afraid to die before the surgeries,” he said. “Luckily, the manufactured stem cells slow the cellular life and death cycle, tripling the animals’ life spans to forty-five years. The effect on the human lifespan is unknown.”

Daniel restored the images of the cats and dogs and added, “The bad news is that with all science, side effects must be addressed.”

“You still haven’t explained why the costs are so high.” She glared at Daniel as if he was pulling food out of children’s mouths to finance enhancements. He fought the urge to snap at her. “The operation gives animals with small heads human intelligence. I presume that’s difficult and thus, expensive.”

“Why couldn’t you use animals with bigger heads?”

Her tone scraped Daniel’s patience like a razor across a scab, but what else could he expect from a member of the press? “I’m not the person who picks the animals. So far, animals with bigger heads and brains adopt psychopathic characteristics. This is because the cell growth is harder to control and can cause massive tumors. That’s why enhancements haven’t been approved for humans.”

“Sounds like a Frankenstein experiment,” the reporter said as she sat down. Her pout told Daniel that enhancements were all his fault and tomorrow an editorial column in the New York Times would say so.

WED 01/04/2130, 15:00
UN MULTIPLEX
NEW YORK CITY, NY

Standing under the HV, Daniel rubbed his forehead. Time for the final topic, the one he was dreading the most—child mortality. JoMarie had offered to introduce the subject, but he had to do this for Hannah. He started by displaying footage on the HV.

In imagery so textured and vibrant that it seemed to be taking place in Public Hall, the HV and screen one projected people in an African village walking in a long, single file line. Women, young and old, wore brightly colored dresses and skirts as if going to a festival. But when the camera zoomed closer, it showed that their eyes were swollen and teary. Their mouths wailed out mournful chants. Their children were dead and dying from African Plague.

Daniel looked at the women that pushed Hattan Robertson into making his welcomed exodus. He couldn't see their eyes but he knew they were red like his.

In the background, dead babies, kids, and teenagers were piled under trees like mounds of hay. Groups of men in hazmats tossed the bodies into the beds of trucks parked nearby. Seeing corpses in 3D gave Daniel a sick chill in his stomach. In the background, smoke seeped from several chimneys in a stone building that was probably the crematorium. The Public Hall audience appeared hypnotized, hopefully by the bleak faces of death as they finally realized what was at stake.

"The bodies will be cremated en mass," Daniel said. "In the past five years, we've lost over six hundred million children and one hundred million adults to the Plague. It is spreading to China, Europe, and the US."

He paced across the edge of the stage making eye contact with his listeners. "Soon, these bodies won't be of kids in a faraway land. They will be your children." Daniel's voice tapered to a whisper. "And already mine."

Losing his composure just in time for JoMarie to start speaking, he sat back at the table. He sighed with relief as she stood with her tablet.

Daniel remembered that on Hannah's final morning on Earth, she managed to push out a few raspy words. She told Daniel how she loved him and Mommy and wished them a good life. He wiped his eyes as blood filled his face.

Suddenly, the HV shut off. He looked to the screen one—same thing. He looked at the screen's backside and checked the computer. Daniel furrowed his brow. Everything looked okay, so now what? JoMarie made small talk with the audience while he waved over a stage technician. The guy slipped on a uniflyer and shot up to the HV's back panel while Daniel bent down and continued to check the connections to the computer.

Daniel heard what sounded like a barking dog blaring from the HV's speakers. When he looked at the HV, he recoiled not wanting to believe what he was seeing. A giant image of Casey's face was staring out to the audience. Daniel bowled over. *No.*

"Sorry to interrupt the presentation," Casey said. "But I'd like to share some tidbits I learned in college."

The technician lowered to the stage and looked at Daniel. He smiled and shrugged then walked away.

The guilt Daniel had felt earlier transformed into anger. Staring at the screen and HV, he wondered how Casey had pulled this off. And the technicians at the Multiplex had to be in on this too. Where was that dog at?

Casey sprayed his mouth with breath spray and cleared his throat. "We the people and enhanced animals of the United States, in order to form a more perfect union, establish justice, insure domestic tranquility, provide for the common defense, promote the general welfare, and secure the blessings of liberty to ourselves and our posterity, do ordain and establish this Constitution for the United States of America."

Trumpets blared from the speakers. Daniel turned to light coming from one of the Public Hall entrances as the doors slid open. The escalator below it started moving down. Six Unity guards marched inside the door and stopped. A spotlight hit the guards as Casey walked between them wearing a black tuxedo jacket with rhinestone trim. With the spotlight following him and his guards, the dog jumped on the escalator and headed down toward the stage.

Daniel put his hands on his face and shook his head. Looking back up, he saw people starting to applaud. Casey stood up on two legs and waved like a beauty pageant contestant. When he got to the front row he hopped off the escalator and onto the stage. He growled as he passed by Daniel and then trotted to JoMarie.

"Casey!" Daniel said, waving him over. "JoMarie and I were in the middle of a very serious part of our presentation. How did you finagle your way here? Nielsen's gonna have a fit!"

Casey stomped back to the table. He yanked a document from inside his jacket and shoved it in Daniel's hand. Daniel read a signed release allowing a neurologically enhanced canine, Casey Caldwell, to leave Unity Station and travel to New York for the UN Public Hall town meeting. Nielsen's signature was below the text. Daniel set the paper on the table. Anything to pander a buck.

Sticking his nose in the air, Casey ran back to JoMarie. He motioned to her headset and she warily handed it to him. Slipping the piece over his face, he walked to the front of the stage. His guards stood on each side of him with arms folded.

Daniel found the scene pompous and embarrassing for the mission. From his seat, Chistyakov glared at him and JoMarie as if they'd staged this. Any headway they'd made with the public was wiped out by this nonsense. All anyone would remember was the dog in a Las Vegas tuxedo jacket.

Looking back to the stage, Daniel noticed that Casey's legs were wobbling.

The dog started to talk but his voice began tapering off. "Article one, section one: All legislative powers herein granted shall be vested in a congressss...."

Fighting to keep his balance, Casey tried to mouth out more words but no sound came out. Daniel narrowed his eyes. *Stage fright.* He had warned the dog over and over not to come here and he showed up anyway.

Casey's neck lurched back and forth like he was going to get sick. Taking a deep breath, the dog struggled to speak again. Instead, he expelled a guttural belch magnified by the headset and fell sideways on the floor. People started looking at each other and murmuring. A few boos started coming from the audience. *Thanks, Nielsen.*

While JoMarie ran to Casey, Daniel stayed put in his chair. "The only thing wrong with that dog is that he's overflowing with melodrama," he said.

Casey slowly got back on his feet. He pointed his front paw at Daniel. "You're a butthole! If you hadn't yelled at me yesterday, I wouldn't have gotten stage fright!"

The audience started applauding as they heard Casey speak again. The dog bowed and grinned. Daniel closed his eyes as country music started playing. That was a deliberate jab. Casey knew that Daniel hated country music.

Standing on his back legs, Casey shifted his hips back and forth in some type of awkward dance. Some of the audience started pointing above the stage. Daniel looked behind him at the HV. Cindera, Rushton, and Kosmo were waving their front paws at the camera from Unity Station. Donovan Lu's smiling face popped in front of the animals and then disappeared. Nielsen even had the mission's IT director in on this.

Daniel didn't know whether to laugh or cry. Nielsen had allowed a showboat dog and his entourage to make their live debut at the worst possible time. Grabbing his Epad, he brought up Hannah's picture, the one he took of her two weeks before she died. Her thinning long brown hair covered part of her face but her striking green eyes still had so much life ready to live. *I'm so sorry.*

He hoped she wouldn't be mad at him and JoMarie for this complete breakdown. In her four years, four months, six hours, and thirty-two minutes of life on Earth, she'd had a sense of humor. Maybe she'd think the dancing dog was funny and her dad was a stick in the mud.

Chistyakov stormed onto the stage, shaking his head at Daniel. The music stopped. The UN leader glared at Casey and then pointed at a side door that led to the dressing rooms. Casey froze for a second, snarled at Daniel then trotted through the door with his guards.

As he walked to the podium, Chistyakov raised his hand for the audience to quiet down. Staring angrily at Daniel and JoMarie, he said, "I don't know what that little sideshow was about but we have children dying every day and there's no sign that it's stopping soon. Humanity is at a crossroad. Let's take the right path for a change."

Daniel followed JoMarie as she walked to Chistyakov. The three of them stood together trying to recapture the mindset of the mission.

Chistyakov turned to JoMarie and Daniel. "Past generations assumed someone would compose a magnum opus that would lick the wounds that humanity has cast upon itself."

His voice softened as if realizing that Daniel and JoMarie would never concoct something so ridiculous. "You and the other scientists are now our opus makers. We're your students. Please continue with your presentation."

The audience started applauding. Daniel managed a smile and waved. *Good save, Chistyakov.* Still, he couldn't wait to get backstage to call Nielsen.

JoMarie sat at the table and restored the image from Africa on the HV. Daniel stood next to her and acknowledged a stout security guard by the fifth row raising his hand.

Something in the guy's palm flashed red like a pupil possessed. He wasn't asking a question. Or was he? Maybe he was holding a hand-held HV or one of the new Epads. Blood rushed through Daniel's face. A surreal daze softened what would have been an incontinent panic if his adrenalin had run its course.

Time warped, no longer linear but passing diagonally, like a mud-slide easing down a hill—slow in its gait but certain to reach its destiny. His tongue writhed, pushing bitter salvia into his mouth. *A bomb?*

A bomb.

"The Roman Empire of the United States will fall!" The guard shook his fist. "You spend poor people's money building a space station! How dare you mock their suffering with dancing animals?" As another security guard ran toward the man, he swung his hand in the air hurling the bomb toward the stage.

The object closed in, the demonic eye glided toward Daniel. If the techno-beast had a mouth it would surely be smirking with blood-stained teeth. People screamed and charged toward the escalators. Streams of light from Bulletasers knocked the object off course and a loud boom shattered the walls. Flames exploded in front of the stage as Daniel dove under the panelist table. Water from the fire sprinklers rained over the audience. Casey was backstage, but where was JoMarie?

Daniel realized the left arm of his jacket was on fire and melting onto his skin. Heat carved through his muscle, settling in his bones. Trying to scream, he could only hear himself wheezing in agony. He rolled out from under the table and let the sprinklers pour water over his body.

WED 01/04/2130, 15:45
UN MULTIPLEX
NEW YORK CITY, NY

Daniel opened his eyes and realized he was backstage. His shallow breaths barely passed through his clenched teeth as pain seared his body. His face and clothes were saturated from the fire sprinklers but the water provided no relief from the consuming burn. JoMarie was kneeling over him, her clothes damp. Casey lay at his side with a guilty and noticeably dry frown. The Unity guards stood around them. Daniel's left arm was covered with a steamy, melted jacket sleeve. He turned to Chistyakov who was leaning against a wall, wiping his face with a towel. Several Russian Secret Service officers guarding him were also wiping their faces.

"Help is on the way," JoMarie said as she pressed Daniel's Epad in his right hand. "This was on the floor of the stage. One of Chistyakov's guards grabbed it."

"Thanks," said Daniel as he looked at Pokey, who was displaying an image of the bomber sitting on a toilet. He winced and stuffed the Epad in his pocket.

"I didn't mean for anyone to get hurt!" Casey said, sitting up. "I'm sorry." His cheeks and mouth sagged in a big pout. "I was acting like a butthole."

Daniel managed a smile despite a tortuous pain shifting up his shoulder and over his chest. He extended his right hand and croaked out a hoarse, "Gimmie a high five."

Casey swatted his paw on Daniel's palm. "Done!"

Daniel turned to the paramedics running toward him. Hissing Slojets circled the building. A rogue bomb stank of collusion. Technology could detect explosives and weapons stashed in the most discrete body parts. For all the motion-sensing devices and bomb-sniffing dogs in the world, not much could be done about an inside job.

He shouted in pain as he was lifted onto an ambulance bed. Daniel turned away when an EMT aimed a needle at his arm that looked like an ancient spear. "I don't take medicine unless I have to. I can handle this misery."

The EMT slid the needle under Daniel's shirt and into his shoulder. "Trust me buddy, you don't want to feel what we're gonna do." Instantly, the left side of Daniel's upper torso fell numb.

Pouring solution on Daniel's coat sleeve, two EMTs slowly cut and peeled the material from his skin. Then they coiled Dermawraps around his purple and black arm. After Daniel's arm was wrapped up to the shoulder, the guy who gave him the injection radioed a Slojet that was apparently on its way to take him to the hospital.

Chistyakov walked over to Daniel, his face pink and rumpled. "You don't look it, but you're pretty heavy when you're unconscious. JoMarie and I dragged you back here to safety. Just tell me you didn't plan that brouhaha with the dog."

Daniel closed his eyes. "I told Casey not to come here. Nielsen overrode me."

Chistyakov's old, almond-shaped eyes showed a smidgen of compassion. "Gallant, but very distracting. I'll have to call him and try to understand his logic."

"I knew Casey showing up would cause commotion."

"And that he did," Chistyakov said. He shrugged and glanced at the golden retriever. "But maybe a good kind. Without him, the meeting would have really been a downer."

JoMarie patted Daniel's good arm. "Most of the audience loved Casey and they liked us too. Public opinion is positive on the *Galax.net* social sites. They were very impressed with his language skills."

"That's a start," Daniel said as he struggled to breathe from his numb chest. "What about the Plague and foreboding resistance to bacteria and viruses? And we need to find out about the meteors."

"You need to wait until your arm's taken care of," JoMarie said.

Chistyakov reviewed his Epad. "My staff is telling me that the bomb was knocked off course by another guard's weapon. The guy that threw the bomb worked at the UN six months. So now, we have terrorists integrating our workforce. The navigation was programmed to redirect to the stage if diverted. Instead, it blew." He looked up with a pained expression. "There are at least twenty dead bodies out there."

His chest unbearably weak, Daniel struggled not to sob. He stared at JoMarie. "Why does this happen? Maybe our species needs to die off!"

JoMarie shook her head. "No. The people with common sense need to take a stand."

The group fell silent for a moment. Daniel noticed the EMTs grimacing at Casey's tuxedo jacket. He couldn't help but laugh aloud despite not being able to feel himself breathe.

"What's so funny?" Casey said.

"That thing you're wearing," Daniel answered.

Casey straightened his bowtie. "I'll have you know this is from the Elvis Collection. He wore this design in the early 1960's when he was still a little classy."

Shifting his body weight away from his injured arm, Daniel groaned. "That jacket is not classy."

"Well it was expensive," Casey said as he sat up and brushed his paw across the rhinestones. "Had to be custom made. Cost me two week's pay."

JoMarie hugged Casey. "Elvis, wherever he is, probably finds you delightful in his tuxedo."

Daniel was glad that the mood was shifting to a better place, even if gaudy stage costumes were part of the mix. Feeling like a frightened child, he looked at JoMarie. "Tell me it's going to be okay."

She nodded. "It's going to be okay. The mission will win and we shall overcome."

The EMTs raised the bed from the floor and started rolling Daniel down a corridor. One of them looked at Casey and started laughing. He turned to Daniel. "Sorry. Not making fun of you but that dog is too much. The jet's ready to take you to New York Medical. We gotta bring you to the shuttleport on the top of the building."

Daniel wriggled off the bed and onto the floor. "Let me walk so I can teach that murderer a lesson. I won't be stopped."

"You're better off lying down," one EMT said. "Most of your trunk muscles are as dead as dirt right now."

Daniel grabbed the EMT's arm and tried to take a few steps. He wondered why he was limping like he had been shot in the leg when it was only his arm that was injured. *Must be the same illogical reason I squinted to quiet the music at the Square.*

After a few steps, Daniel's legs folded under him and he dropped onto the carpet. The images of fires, piles of children's bodies, and a dog wearing a tuxedo jacket faded into the air like a saxophone's closing wail.

WED 01/04/2130
FLC FAMILY TRUST BEACH HOUSE
BRIDGEPORT, NY

Slapping a tranquilizer patch on his arm, Shaune walked across his lawn toward the condominium. Even though he'd eaten a heavy dinner, the food was burned away by excitement from yesterday's attack. The night sky was darkened by residual smoke from GlobeTek. He thought about after he'd boarded the submarine. He'd received a brief text message telling him that the exercise's results were being reviewed. Shit, he'd gotten past the Skyguards and the kills were just over two thousand, right in the projected range.

What more do those assholes want?

He turned to Bernard, who was trying to maneuver the limo inside the condo's garage. The car's parking feature seemed to be playing games—driving sideways and then backward toward the street. The limo finally rolled forward, parked crooked in the garage, and shut off its engine.

Bernard walked toward his compact sedan and waved. Shaune waved back. Must be depressing to be seventy-three and driving for people in their thirties. Bernard was seven million dollars richer for keeping his mouth shut. And for all his years of loyalty, he was under consideration for Utopian Society Alliance membership. Maybe he was doing all right.

Shaune's Epad rang and the face he was expecting appeared on the screen. He jogged to the front porch, pressed his thumb on the ID pad, and flung open the door. Bolting inside, he slammed the door shut. He dropped on the couch and set his Epad upright on the coffee table. Answering the call in speaker mode, he smiled at the face. "Yesterday was a smashing success."

"You destroyed three X1000s," the face snarled back. "Your extra lasers killed a hundred and fifty kids in a daycare center at the bank next door."

"And your point?"

"Your little fieldtrip in the building gave the PD an extra minute to find you, resulting in the deaths of four advocates. And you could've been killed yourself had that building collapsed while you were inside!"

Shaune could never do anything right. He felt like slamming the Epad on the floor and could only scream out the curse words in his head.

"Any coward can use a remote explosive or suicide bomb," Shaune answered. "But I attacked, danced inside the belly of the beast, and got out alive—that's courage."

The head stared back. "It could also be stupidity and arrogance."

"What I did was nothing new. Through the People's Party, the Alliance has kept the public on edge with kilokills. You know how quickly they forget with *Galax.net* switching headlines every five minutes."

"Sounds like you're making excuses," the head replied.

Shaune's hands trembled in fury. What a bastard. "You're forgetting the strategy. The Party gets credit for preventing the worst assaults in the United States. The Utopian Society Alliance keeps its access to power and US government resources. Because they're doing the megakills overseas, they have to do something here or other nations will get suspicious."

"I know," the head answered. "But this exercise didn't scare as much as it pissed people off because you killed kids."

"It's nothing compared to the African Plague," Shaune said, "and that's nature, not terrorism. By killing thousands in the United States and millions abroad, the People's Party will stay in control. This will position us for takeover."

Rubbing the vacant scalp on top of his head, the man's brow furrowed with questionable conviction. "Listen to me."

Shaune leaned over and shook kindling chips from a bag into his fireplace. He ignited the gas, anticipating a fire like the ones he set as a kid. White flames rose from the pipe and gradually stretched above the wood like the ethereal fingers of a grim reaper musician. He was impressed with the fire's almost instinctive drive to overtake.

The face suddenly gasped. "What the shit is going on with the news?"

"What's wrong now?"

"Turn on channel 405, dammit!"

Shaune sat back on the couch. The Epad showed his boss's face engorging with furious blood. This sudden bloating brought to the forefront a rotten purple yolk of a soul inside a head that was more fitting for a jack-o-lantern. Turning on the HV, Shaune navigated to channel 405. The porkers were in a lab standing around his Washington statue.

"So I left the PD a souvenir; nothing useful, just bullshit. I'm mocking the concept of democracy." He grabbed a bottled martini from his bar, popped the cap, and took a deep swig.

"We can't take any chances!" the head exclaimed. "Listen to me. You can get drunk later."

Shaune set the drink on a coaster and said, "What are you so worked up about?"

"You don't leave information for the police that could lead anywhere. How could you be so arrogant?"

Shaune sipped on his fiery drink and blew out a stem of warm air. "I'm not arrogant just self-assured. Like you taught me, Dad."

SAT 01/07/2130
JFK AIRPORT
QUEENS, NY

The Unity shuttle doors slammed shut. Caution lights flashed in preparation for takeoff. Flight attendants walked the aisles and checked passengers' restraining belts. Daniel sat down and buckled himself in. "Thanks for letting me have the aisle seat," he said to JoMarie.

JoMarie looked up from her novel. "I'm gonna read and it's only for a couple hours but you're welcome."

"Right now any closed area feels suffocating." Daniel squirmed in his seat trying to get comfortable. Even the padding seemed to squeeze him like a vice grip.

"I'm glad the Public Hall bomber was killed," he said, "but he ended up taking twenty-five people with him." Daniel propped his bandaged arm on the seat's armrest. "Probably someone that asshole EU reporter knew."

JoMarie nodded solemnly, "He's been cleared. While evil will never be completely stopped, enough's not being done to minimize it."

The shuttle slowly lifted off the runway. Daniel waved at the window with his still-functioning right hand. "To that I say good riddance, Planet Earth. Hello Unity Station."

He rubbed his fingers over the transplanted tissue healing on his forearm. The muscle cell implants and skin wraps were worth the three-day hospital stay, but the first project specialist meeting was supposed to be yesterday and because of him, it was postponed to Tuesday. He'd already screwed things up and he hadn't even started working yet. The others were waiting for him and JoMarie to arrive. Casey had left for Unity Station yesterday and was no doubt telling everyone who'd listen about his adventure.

The shuttle's nose turned toward the sky and shot up above New York. The evening surface lights receded into yellow dots. Daniel's grim prognosis of humanity's fate deepened. The sky diamonds would jewel the universe millions of years from now. The fate of the lights below ended with a question mark at best. It didn't help that *Galax.net*'s stories were focusing on the bombing and Casey's dog show.

Daniel felt something hit his hair. He cranked his head around. A toddler was strapped to the seat behind him, holding a bag of cookies. Forcing a smile at the dark-haired boy and the person whom he assumed was the child's mother; he slid wet crumbs out of his hair and into his hand.

The woman blushed and gave Daniel a Warmwype. Turning to her son she snapped at him. "Brandon, don't spit out your treats! Do want me to take them away?"

The boy shook his head from side to side.

"I'm sorry," she said. "I think he's nervous."

Daniel forced a smile. "No problem."

Patting his hair with the wipe, he turned to JoMarie and whispered, "I can't believe this was the only flight available today."

JoMarie kept reading. "Why don't you get a snack?"

"That'll make my heartburn worse," Daniel said as he picked up a *Celestial Mall* magazine and flipped through the pages. "Why does that child's mother sit there with that impish grin on her face?"

"She's in tantrum prevention mode," JoMarie answered.

Daniel felt the back of his seat being kicked. He forced himself not to turn around and explode at the kid's mother. He rubbed the back of his neck.

"Wait a minute," JoMarie said, grinning at him. "I thought your dream was to have a family again."

"I wouldn't have a bratty kid like that. Hannah never threw food at people."

JoMarie stifled a laugh. "You've never had a boy and I have. You know the researchers' spouses and a few kids are visiting one last time before the mission officially starts Monday."

"I'd rather fly in the lunar disposal shuttles with spent fuel. This damn flight's overbooked."

JoMarie turned back to her novel. "Is that sour attitude following you into open space?"

"I just want to relax for more than five minutes," he said as he pulled a beanie from his carryon and slid it over his head. "I feel like I'm in a psych ward with these kids screaming. Can't these parents control their offspring?"

He turned to the sound of a man clearing his throat. Jake Brighton was standing over him.

Jake squeezed past Daniel and JoMarie, and then wedged in his window seat. "You look like you belong in a psych ward wearing that cap inside this stuffy spaceship."

"Where were you at take off?" Daniel asked desperately trying to ignore the thumping on his seat.

"I was calming down a passenger who was having a panic attack."

"Well, it's a good thing you warmed up your skills because you're gonna be busy. I'm one of the more functional researchers your counseling team will be dealing with when the mission gets crazy."

"Don't flatter yourself." Jake pulled a small comb from his pocket and ran it through his cropped red beard. "Although I have to admit, you'll probably be easier than Matt Bertrand."

"You think Matt will be a problem?"

"No." Jake grinned. "Matt is a problem but only for me so far. He's not crazy, just dysfunctional."

JoMarie looked up from her book. "The kid's been traumatized. He was only eight when a drunk driver killed his mother."

"Matt's twenty-two," Jake said. "I've seen six-year-olds with more tact. He was overindulged by a guilty father and in need of a big brother figure." He pointed his finger at Daniel. "Watch out. He started wearing fatigue pants like yours near the end of training."

Daniel clenched his jaw. "I'm not ready to be anyone's example."

Shrugging, Jake replied, "Think of this boat ride as a practice exercise, a prelude to the stress you'll be subjected to on the mission."

“Oh, Jake.” JoMarie reclined her chair and strapped a small pillow to her seat’s headrest. “Don’t get him riled up.”

“He’s not giving me an attitude that I don’t already have,” Daniel said. “I get my ass reamed inside out by the security scanners and those dogs, and still an explosive slips in and murders innocent people.”

“I did hear the body scanners were rather curious, as were the pooches,” Jake said. “The problem is we’ll never be one hundred percent safe. That’s been the human condition since we starting tossing pointed sticks at each other.”

“Speaking of curious, I’m curious.” Daniel leaned toward Jake. “What do you think of the project specialists? Besides JoMarie and I, of course.”

“They’re fine, just fine. Even Matt’s psyche’s within one and a half deviations of the bell curve’s average.”

Daniel pinched his mouth closed. Psychiatrists always managed to find a technical term for someone who was plain crazy or a hateful bully like his dad. “Don’t stonewall me.”

Jake rubbed lotion on his hands. “Let’s say that for those of you who dance on the fringes of neurosis, we counselors will do everything we can to ensure that calmness prevails. It’s for our own good to treat you effectively.” Leaning back toward Daniel, he added, “To be frank, the enhanced animals are probably the most stable.”

“I’d agree with that,” Daniel mused. “What do you think of Robert Landry being one of the project specialists? He’s conservative, you know.”

“So’s JoMarie, and you like her.”

“She’s a conservationist conservative. That’s different. She believes in conserving, not hoarding.”

“Based on my talks with him, the senator’s prudent but open to reason.”

Dreading the idea of having to deal with people of any type, especially conservatives like his father, Daniel cringed. “But some of his ideology conflicts with the mission’s objectives. He’ll question everything we do.”

“That’s his job,” JoMarie said. “He was sent to provide balance.”

“The guy’s on the mission for political reasons,” Daniel shot back. “Three months before the start date he’s added as a fifth project specialist. We were in training for eighteen months. I bet he wants to run for president."

"His polygraphs and neuron readings indicate otherwise," Jake said. "He believes people should stop blaming others for their problems. That's what I try to get them to do—after they've made peace with their inner child, that is." Jake motioned to a stern-faced guard. "I'd be more worried about the goons in the ruling party."

"I am, but the conservatives' stubbornness led to their rise in power," said Daniel.

"And the liberals weren't obstinate?"

"I suppose," Daniel said. "You're well-versed in human behavior. How did people who were labeled right-wing and left-wing mesh into the People's Party?"

"Passion," Jake said, "like some marriages. They had big dreams to change the world. Most of us sit around and do our own thing. They're macro-focused, we're micro-focused."

"Something is disquieting about that union," Daniel said. "Extreme views coming around full circle to converge."

"I have my concerns."

"Do you think Senator Landry will stall the mission's progress?"

"Stop grilling Jake," JoMarie said as she read her book. "He can't do anything about the People's Party or the senator. Besides, Bob didn't have to train as long as we did because he's a layperson mediator."

"Oh, so now Senator Landry is Bob, an average dude wearing his folksy cowboy hat."

JoMarie set her book down and turned to Daniel. "Senator Landry served his country fighting in Central America and was a POW. When he came home, he discovered that his wife had run off with another man and left their daughter and son with his parents. Over the years, I've learned to keep my ears, eyes, and mind open before judging."

"He may not understand what we're dealing with," Daniel said. "The mission's success may take years, and in some cases decades, to be measurable."

"We have to start somewhere," JoMarie answered.

Daniel pressed on his burning diaphragm. People expected him and the rest of the USRG to save the world. They were the opus makers.

Whatever. *Hannah's memory is why I'm spending five claustrophobic years on a space station.*

"I don't know if all the researchers are on the same page. I'm not even sure about Sharon."

"Sharon's trustworthy," Jake said. "However, she feels guilty for her family's wealth and exploits, which makes her hypersensitive at times. Her heart is filled with compassion—a true physician." He stared at Daniel. "Unfortunately, like some people in this aircraft, she stereotypes people."

Daniel looked back at Jake. "Stereotyping is efficient."

"And often wrong," Jake replied as he slid off his shoes and shoved them under his seat. "Pardon me, but she's bloody rich, single, and a cute strawberry blonde. You're athletic, unmarried and forty-one. What's stopping you?"

"I have an ex-wife that dampened my enthusiasm for emotional commitments."

"Join the club. That doesn't mean you give up."

Microgravity began to set in and Daniel tightened his seatbelt. "Sharon reminds me of my younger sister—attracted to derelicts and drunks. Her family is even more ominous than the men she attracts."

JoMarie looked at her Epad and then at Daniel. "I'm assigning you your first mission project. Turn on the *Galax.net News* to someone you don't like. That should be easy. Listen to what they have to say and practice negotiating. You have two days to polish your diplomacy."

Daniel's body tensed even as the gravity faded to near zero. "Now you're starting to sound like Jake. I got tired of holding back when I was a kid, living in a home where you hoped your famous army general father would slug you in places covered by clothes. What do you tell people? Oh! I fell down the stairs. Oh! I slipped on a banana peel! I couldn't stand up for myself then because my dad was five times my size. I can now."

An image of his dad's size fourteen boots formed in his mind. He remembered how that polished black shoe kicked things across the floor, sometimes, on bad nights, kicking him across the floor.

JoMarie's voice was soothing but not convincing. "Take a pain patch and get some rest. And try to have mercy on your dad. He has a bipolar disorder."

“Which he could have treated and still can,” Daniel said. He noticed that the pounding on his seat had stopped and looked behind him. The child was asleep in his mother’s arms. Suddenly, he felt more relaxed.

Jake tapped Daniel’s arm and looked him quizzically. “How long has it been since you lived at home?”

Realizing Jake had been listening to his and JoMarie’s exchange, Daniel was embarrassed. “Twenty years, but he passed his shitty genes to my sister and me.”

Looking at him with a “you’ve got to be kidding me” face, Jake shook his head.

Remembering one of his dad’s late night rants, Daniel rubbed his temples. “What if stress from the mission triggers an onset of his illness in me?”

Jake’s ruddy brows pressed into one. “The likelihood of ending up bipolar at your age is minimal. Besides, the treatments are no big deal. A nurse inserts a neuropatch in your neck and replaces it once a year.”

“I don’t want to be dependent on patches, shots, or pills for my sanity. Half the world lives off them.”

“Your dad could’ve been treated for his illness,” Jake said, “but his pride destroyed your family. When you were a kid, did you get the shot that prevents bipolar onsets?”

“Hell no.”

Releasing a frustrated sigh, Jake stared ahead. “We’ll never know why your parents made that choice. Make an appointment with me and take your pain patches like JoMarie said.”

Daniel remembered when Hannah was in the hospital and diagnosed with leukemia. He’d made the mistake of calling his parents, who flew in from Virginia. Dad showed up drunk and belligerent. He ranted at the doctors until Mom dragged him to a taxi and sent him back to the hotel.

“I’ll set up an appointment but I don’t like taking meds. I can psych myself out of pain and illness.”

Jake shook his head. “Tsk, tsk. Many a dead and crazy person has skipped down that path.”

“I’ll think about it,” Daniel said. His arm started sizzling like meat on a grill as if to prove a point. The Public Hall fire had returned to finish the job. JoMarie had dozed off. He grabbed a pain patch and feverishly tore open the wrapper. Pressing the fleshy rectangle over the skin wraps, he breathed relief as a stream of numbness melted into his muscle. Staring at the shuttle's ceiling, he felt his December funk bleeding into January 2130. Jake and JoMarie meant well. They just didn't understand.

* * *

Raising his fist in victory as the shuttle closed in on Unity Station, Daniel watched as satellites and other space stations floated in the distance. Speeding through the thermosphere toward the exosphere and finally outer space, he was almost home. Passing the UN Peacebuilder station, the shuttle chased down Unity. The pilots exchanged commands with the spacecraft controllers at Unity's docking station.

The toddler behind him started squealing. Unable to bear the sound, Daniel pulled a station tourist pamphlet from the pouch in the seat in front of him. Opening the small booklet, he turned his seat around to face the boy to show him diagrams of Unity. The kid looked at him blankly and then stared at the images.

"Who are you going to visit Brandon?" Daniel said.

The kid turned away and whined louder.

"His dad," the mother answered.

Daniel reviewed the booklet. The diagrams detailed Unity's basic configuration. Each level was made of six rectangular train car structures attached with horizontal tubes that formed a hexagon. Four hexagons hovered a bit over each other, connected by vertical tubes, making the structure look like a building. Skewered in the middle was a rectangular module. This was attached to the hexagons with more tubes. To Daniel the station looked like a toy; quite fake if he didn't know better.

"Who are you visiting, Brandon?" Daniel asked again.

The kid pushed his bottom lip out and uttered, "Da-da."

"Brandon's too young to come up here," his mother said, "but since I'm a USRG researcher working in California and my husband's on Unity we get to visit. I'm Heidi. My husband's Doug Klaussen."

"I know him," Daniel said. "He works in IT with Donovan Lu."

Heidi grabbed a magazine. "Thanks for putting up with Brandon."

"I can't blame him for not liking the ride. I'll try to keep him busy while we dock." Daniel turned the page of the booklet and pointed to the bottom hexagon.

"Okay, Brandon, we are going to dock the ship here," Daniel said. "Our food and supplies are also in this hexagon." He pointed to the center rectangle. "We do our work in the first four levels of the rectangle. Your daddy works there with Donovan Lu."

The kid's eyes widened. "Don Poo."

"Brandon." Heidi turned from her magazine. "That's Lu."

"Poo."

"Don Lu, honey."

"Don Poo."

"I think he's made up his mind," Daniel said with a smile.

Heidi began stuffing Brandon's toys in a backpack. "Thanks for keeping him from fussing but he probably doesn't understand much of what you're saying."

"You know, I started this ride in a bad mood. I'm okay now." Daniel shook the boy's small hand. "Thanks Brandon." He heard himself hum a little and he turned his seat back. The shuttle was now hovering over the platform that protruded from Unity Station's bottom level.

The shuttle closed its wings around the fuselage. The front end slid into a cavity. He looked at the HV showing the docking process. The shuttle's back half was being sealed by panels that slid out from Unity's outer wall then closed around the tail section. As the shuttle coasted deeper in the front cavity and into the interior port, the panels flattened back against the wall. The front cavity opened, allowing the shuttle to stop and lower the landing gear on the port's floor.

Feeling a little flushed, Daniel closed his eyes as the shuttle door opened. Messages flashed over each passenger's seat, instructing them to release their restraining belts and begin to exit. Jake scooted past Daniel and JoMarie to the aisle. JoMarie sat with Daniel as passengers pushed forward to exit the shuttle.

Daniel promised himself to always remember why he was on this mission—to stop the destruction that killed his daughter. Instead of starting her teens and thinking of what high school to attend, Hannah was almost nine years dead. He lowered his head and rubbed his eyes with the now dirty wipe Brandon's mother had given him.

He'd always planned on working for the private sector and maybe someday he would again. But after Hannah's death, he realized the importance of a system that monitored people willing to risk poisoning themselves and others in exchange for cash flow. After almost eleven years, he had no regrets.

Shoving the cookie-coated wipe in his pocket and standing up to exit, Daniel felt sad. People didn't seem to understand that his daughter was more than a child that could be replaced with another. She was a person named Hannah Leanne Griffin, born December 5, 2116. The RIP date, April 5, 2121, etched on the small urn in his condo bedroom, would always be a reminder of why he was on the mission. And because of an immune system that often forbade his daughter from contacting even the most docile of germs, she rarely got the chance to spit cookie chunks onto a stranger's hair. He smiled as he followed JoMarie down the aisle and out of the shuttle. Not that she ever would have.

TUES 01/10/2130
UNITY SPACE STATION
ALTITUDE 415 KM AT 27,250 KM/H

Daniel wondered if time passed at an accelerated rate when circling Earth at supersonic speeds. Three days had gone by so fast since arriving at Unity Station and the first day of work had arrived. He was glad he'd be able to squeeze in a short spacewalk beforehand to get the creative juices flowing. As he walked in the prep area, he suddenly started floating above the lockers.

Dammit! He'd forgotten that the artificial gravity was shut off in this area. He didn't think to bring the magnetic-soled shoes that would hold his feet against the carpet. He swiped at a bench and missed. Pushing his palms against the ceiling tiles, he flipped himself around and faced the floor. Outer space was beckoning him through a small, square window. The absence of traffic, trees, sunsets, and now gravity reminded him of how far from home he really was.

Maneuvering in a state of float was art submitting to science. Daniel swung himself down. He lowered his body to the padded bench and tightened a strap around his waist. Opening his assigned locker, he studied the space suit and black neoprene undergarment hanging inside. He took off his clothes and stuffed them in a second locker then pulled on the stretchy garment.

Daniel was intrigued by how the exterior suit's numerous components served as a life support system. The headpiece was unfashionably big and the transparent bubble made the wearer look like a giant, humanoid insect; much scarier than the helpless creature inside. The hands and feet were attached like the kiddie pajamas that he and his younger sister wore in more innocent years.

He looked up. A tall, husky man with salt-and-pepper braided ponytails and a goatee stood over him. His lined brown skin and chiseled features told Daniel he'd had a lot of experience doing something—hopefully overseeing spacewalks.

"Nice to meet you, Daniel," the man said. "I'm Cal Medina. I'll be in charge of your spacewalk."

Daniel nodded and shook Cal's hand. "Thanks for responding to my emails and setting me up for this."

Cal winced at him. "How's your arm doing? Casey's been telling everyone you got burned pretty bad."

"That dog should work for the *Galax.net News,*" Daniel said. "The Dermawraps and muscle implants seem to be growing into my tissue well. Will my injuries be a problem with the walk?"

"You'll be fine." Cal started examining Daniel's space suit. "That attack was really chicken shit."

Daniel nodded, his heart pounding light and fast. His stomach twisted as the reality of going on a spacewalk hit him. An anxiety attack was struggling to be let out of its cage.

"So how long have you worked for NASA?"

Plugging a small computer into the suit, Cal observed the readings. Daniel could see he was running a diagnostics test. "Twenty-five years."

"Oh," Daniel squeaked.

Cal smirked as if sensing Daniel's uncertainty. "I graduated from MIT with high honors. I have a doctorate in astronautics and grew up on the Seminole Indian reservation. In high school, I repaired slot machines at my tribe's resort. Do I meet your qualifications?"

Daniel shrugged and then started laughing. "I don't know if fixing slots helps, but the rest seems good. I guess I'm asking if you've ever lost anyone on a spacewalk."

With a furrowed brow, Cal stared at the ceiling as if in deep thought. "Only the ones I didn't like," he said as he pushed a few more buttons on the computer and looked at Daniel.

"That was a joke. NASA and I are completely committed to your safety."

"Hey, humor's good."

"We have you down for a one-hour hike," Cal said. "That means you'll travel with the space station around two-thirds of Earth's diameter. You'll be on the hot side for part of the time and the cold side for the other. The temperature will vary between negative and positive one hundred and fifty degrees Celsius, but you won't know the difference."

"Good thing," Daniel commented.

"If you didn't have a suit it would be a bad thing," Cal said, "but only for a very short time."

Daniel stared out a window to look at the stars. "I'd like to hike longer but an hour is all I can get away with. My first project specialist meeting's in an hour and a half. I'm hoping this walk will open my consciousness to expand my problem-solving skills."

"You did mention in your email you're one of the brainstormers. I'm glad spacewalking may be used for that. About time."

"I'll do whatever I can to live up to the public's and the mission's expectations."

Cal motioned to the giant insect headpiece. "And if you don't, hang free on a spacewalk. Renew your thoughts. Other people's demands will be secondary. That's a promise."

"You've been on lots of these?"

"You betcha, Danny," Cal said. "I've hiked over five hundred times and never get tired of it. It's kinda like skydiving without the fall."

Looking up, Daniel saw two assistants walk into the locker room. They unstrapped Daniel and guided his floating body into the bulky suit. In a few minutes, the sack of manmade materials would unite him with infinity and shield him from a brisk and certain death.

Minutes passed as seals were checked, zippers were zipped, and finally the headpiece was set in place. After several tugs, Daniel forced his heels in the back of knee-high boots, which were then bound with straps. Cal performed a final diagnostics test. Holding onto the locker to keep from floating up, Daniel commented, "Pretty comfortable for a one hundred kilogram suit."

"That's one of the reasons we have zero gravity in here," Cal said, studying the computer's readings. "You wouldn't want to walk around in that suit otherwise."

"What if I have questions when I'm out there?"

"Your vitals and spacesuit will be constantly monitored," Cal answered. "We can read your Epad and the suit's monitoring equipment. If ether one acts up, we'll come get you. If you feel nauseous or want to come back in for any reason, let us know. We can always hear you. If you don't want to hear us, then push the black button on your sleeve."

"Thanks," Daniel said, feeling a bit silly, but safer that Pokey was magnetized to his forearm. "Any suggestions?"

Nodding, Cal pointed to a red button next to the black one. "To see things a little differently, press this one. Your head covering will change its optical capacity to infrared viewing. Push again to return to normal. The view's exhilarating."

"I remember reading about the infrared experience," Daniel said.

Cal winked at Daniel. "Better than drugs."

He led Daniel down a hall into the transition room. "Stand here for five minutes before we open the hatch. We'll be monitoring your suit's operating system. If you're warm and can breathe comfortably, wave both arms and say 'Ready.' We'll be coming to get you if we see or hear anything else."

"I can't wait," Daniel said as he stepped in the room and took several deep breaths. They attached a cable to his suit and then walked inside a control room.

Daniel couldn't help but stare out the large windows. He remembered reading about how space hiking was like nutrients for the soul, an experience best shared verbally and through body language. In pre-cyber societies, elders passed wisdom to new generations through storytelling. He sometimes yearned for a world before computers, holovision, and other contraptions that often alienated more than they integrated.

Suddenly Cal's voice blared into Daniel's headset. "You okay?"

Startled, Daniel took a deep breath and waved his arms at Cal. "I'm okay and ready!"

The hatch slid open. Stars lit the stage of perpetuity. Turning to Cal and the assistants one last time, Daniel stepped through the exit.

He pushed the black button so that their exchanges of technical chatter were silent to him. The door slid shut except for a small hole that allowed the cable attached to his suit to reel out like a fire hose.

He grabbed his chest as his heart skipped. Daniel felt like he'd been pushed out of a womb and into another world. Millions of stars and planets glittered like tiny but powerfully lit diamonds strewn over black velvet. They seemed to watch him with curiosity and amusement. His tourist status was immediately apparent. He was trekking in an alien region not designed to accommodate the fragile bodies of curious mammals. Yet somewhere in this vast depth, he felt warmth. He laughed. Maybe he was on the part of Earth facing the sun.

Unity glided next to Daniel like a techno butterfly as if having not a care in the world. She meshed well with her environment as a beautiful work of space architecture designed for traveling these parts of the woods. She didn't seem to be a tourist like him as she soared effortlessly around the planet whose inhabitants had constructed her. Traveling at twenty-seven thousand kilometers per hour, Unity circled the oceans and continents every ninety minutes. As a creation of human ingenuity, he was proud of her. *Maybe kids like Hannah have a chance after all.*

The stars appeared to blink in consensus. Daniel heard himself shout, "Awesome! Nothing like big picture awesomeness. Makes worries like report due dates, demanding UN leaders, and penny-pinching governments fade into the universe's filing cabinet of Obsolete Matters."

Starting to feel like a welcome visitor, he submerged his thoughts in the heavens' offerings. Swimming, dancing, and wrapping his arms around a mottled distant moon, Daniel addressed the celestial audience. Feeling completely solitary yet forever linked to the universe, the presence he felt seemed friendly. He began to chat with his audience.

"I'll sing something," he said waving at the stars. "What do you guys wanna hear? My mom used to sing me a song when I was a kid. I sure miss seeing her, but with Mom comes dear ole Dad."

He hummed a series of tunes, hoping his memory would be triggered. Then the words came to him and he started to sing. "Would… you…? Would you like to swing on a star? Carry moonbeams home in a jar?"

In what Daniel knew had to be tone-deaf harmonies, he crooned to his coliseum. He didn't care. He was at home with friends. After finishing his song, he pushed the red button. His clear helmet suddenly changed to an infrared lens. Reds, pinks, whites, and stellar colors vibrated.

Earth slipped into Daniel's peripheral vision. He wasn't sure if studying the planet during the walk would be depressing or inspiring. Bowing to his impulses, he looked again to see not a Pacific, Atlantic, or the other oceans, but one cloud-swirled body of water interspersed with land. Geographical divides and nations were evaporated by distance and the magnitude of infinity. He pushed the red button off.

Through the clear headpiece, the planet looked like a sapphire and amber jewel softened by a protective mist. Humans had complicated life with their over-categorization of everything; shoving all thoughts inside assigned boxes of names, compartments, diagrams, and flowcharts. That was okay, but they had failed to look at things from afar. He thought of JoMarie's assignment on the shuttle. *Find someone whose opinion I disagree with and learn to schmooze better. Screw that.*

Daniel hesitated, realizing that on Sunday morning Robert Landry was one of the first people to offer his condolences for the Public Hall bombing. The senator seemed like a decent guy but Daniel had never joined any political party because he didn't believe in them. Divisive and outdated, they attracted carnival barkers over problem solvers. And with the People's Party, he suspected far worse.

He had to admit he'd been spoiled since arriving at Unity. He was injured but compared to the other Public Hall survivors he was doing okay. Matt and Sharon had cleaned his room and helped with laundry. JoMarie was cutting his food into bite-sized pieces. The animals were staying in his cramped living area and Casey had insisted on sleeping in the bed with Daniel, reminding him that he was a bomb-sniffing dog who'd saved the Queen.

After Casey had squeezed next to Daniel on the small mattress with him last night, he turned off the artificial gravity with the remote. Daniel had woken up with a sore neck and floating in the middle of the room facing the dog's hairy behind.

He laughed at the visual and turned to Unity. Recalling his space station anatomy lessons from USRG training, he was disappointed when he found out that the ship's sprawling solar panels were subsidized with nuclear power. Later, he saw the station's energy requirements as inevitable with present technology.

Daniel had always been skeptical of how progress of alternative energy stalled in the mid twenty-first century. The whole thing made no sense. Maybe the USRG would reveal the bottleneck, the conspiracy, whatever the case. Coal was clean, but not much was left. Nukes were cheap and easy, and deemed the necessity of the moment, but their reign should've ended. Why was the world a half century behind where it should have been in energy technology?

Rolling in a somersault, Daniel considered the possibility of energy systems designed to accommodate a region. Start with fundamentals and then customize to the furthest extent possible. Some areas could go one hundred percent natural while others probably never could. The AI programs would help eliminate the human bias. If mission scientists could actually be allowed to implement what they wanted, maybe something big could happen.

His forehead pressed into a frown. For Hannah and the other children who died, the answer had to include safety. The journey had to be realistic yet aim for the stars. The future generations of kids deserved a fighting chance. He stared up at his audience's blinking nods of approval and danced some more.

* * *

The sound of loud hacking startled Daniel.

"Dude," Cal said. "Time's up. You've been out an hour and twelve bonus minutes."

"I feel like I've been out here five minutes. It's been over an hour?" Daniel replied.

"Afraid so, Danny."

The hatch opened and Daniel was reeled inside the transition room. He sulked a little as the hatch shut behind him. The assistants walked in and disconnected the cable. Then they escorted him to the locker room and dismantled his suit. Strapping himself to the bench, Daniel removed the black interior suit and redressed. Cal tested his vitals, though Pokey had already registered that he was fine.

Cal stared at him. "Enjoy yourself?"

"More than words can describe."

"I understand completely," Cal said, rubbing his goatee. "You know, when I went out there the first time, I got weird…one might say spacey."

His face drew close to Daniel's ear. "I even sang that "Moonbeams in a Jar" song written God knows when. I don't know why, but it seems like everyone sings that song on their virgin walk."

Daniel suddenly felt less special. "Oh."

Cal looked at his assistants then burst out laughing. "Just screwin' with you! We never heard anyone sing that before. We were listening to you the whole time. Remember?"

Daniel bit his lip. Cheap voyeurism. That's why these jokers eavesdropped.

"Come again and bring your friends," Cal said, patting his back. "By the way, your comment about the obsolete filing cabinet was great. Before you go, take your pick from the snack basket in the waiting room."

Struggling not to be pissed off, Daniel snatched a donut from the basket. He walked out of the NASA module. Weight landed on his shoulders as his feet bore down into artificial gravity and the mission.

TUES 01/10/2130
UNITY SPACE STATION
ALTITUDE 410 KM AT 27,400 KM/H

Standing outside of the Thinkers Room, Daniel brushed his thumb over the DNA reader. He took a deep breath, trying to be optimistic about using AI programs as the first level of ecosystem analysis.The double doors slid open and the room's pine walls eased his return to civilized life. The clock on the wall read 08:12 UTC. Twelve minutes late. The other project specialists were sitting around the table and looked up as he walked in.

A fake log glowed in the potbelly stove. Daniel welcomed the earthy decorum intended to encourage analysis and debate. If he'd walked inside a cabin in the Blue Ridge Mountains, he wouldn't have known the difference. Except when he looked out the window saw satellites float by and lasers zap meteorites that loomed too close.

JoMarie was sitting at the head of the table. Daniel plopped in his chair to her right and across from Robert, who was wearing his trademark cowboy hat. Casey was asleep on the floor with Rushton and Kosmo. Cindera was sitting in her high chair at the table and also appeared to have nodded off. Despite their tendency to sleep and criticize, Daniel looked forward to the animals working on the mission.

On a large HV built into the wall, footage of a stern Dr. Nielsen was on display. The mission leader was describing the format that the project specialists would use for progress reports. Daniel snorted in disgust. The guy had some nerve making a film about protocol after allowing Casey to make his live debut at Public Hall.

An icy breeze blew from JoMarie as she paused Nielsen's spiel on the HV. "Daniel, did you get a phone message and email from Carla Macias? She called me and said you never replied to either one."

"Nielsen's assistant? Yeah, I'm sorry. I'm also sorry that I'm late."

"I don't care that you're a little late." JoMarie glared at him. "And?"

Having no idea what he'd done wrong, Daniel groaned. "Last week we lost two thousand people at GlobeTek and three X-1000s were stolen from Socorro Air Base. Did anyone find out who destroyed GlobeTek? No. Did anyone find out who gassed the fifty base employees to death and stole the jets? No. I'm sick of hearing about evil shit that goes unpunished. What happened to the assholes that masterminded the Public Hall attack?"

"I know this is overwhelming," JoMarie said, "but at least read your emails, not just the subject line. Carla told me that Dr. Nielsen's brother-in-law was a GlobeTek vice president who died in the attack. She was taking contributions for the children of the victims."

Daniel twirled an electronic pen between his fingers like a baton, struggling to preserve the mood that had added an extra skip to his walk a few minutes earlier. "You know I'm devastated about GlobeTek but I hate the way Nielsen treats us like naughty kids, so I avoid any message from his office. I didn't know he lost a family member."

"Daniel."

He wrote in the air with his pen. "He composes a courteous memo in his UK dialect with the stake he drives though your heart." Daniel made a stabbing motion to his chest trying to humor his peers, who always laughed at his Dr. Nielsen jokes.

JoMarie pointed at the frozen image of Nielsen on the video. "GlobeTek."

"I'm sorry," Daniel said. "I'll call him at lunch and I'll get out my wallet for Carla."

"Great, but please call them both on our mid-morning break. We need our sensitive, caring Daniel to return to us."

"This is your sensitive Daniel," he said. "I took a spacewalk this morning. I sent all of you an email about it last night."

"How'd it go?" Robert asked.

Daniel guarded his words, not wanting to step into political sand traps early in the mission. "I got a few ideas for regional power systems, like using several sources that work together."

Robert nodded. "One size fits all normally isn't comfortable for anyone."

A loud sneeze interrupted them. Matt sniffed and then slid a handout across the table to Daniel.

"Go to the bathroom and get a tissue for that germ blaster," Daniel said. "Haven't you noticed we're in an enclosed space station?"

Matt sniffled again and wiped his nose with a napkin. "My blaster is the least of your problems. Take a look at this booklet. Since I'm in charge of energy projects, Nielsen emailed this to me yesterday and I had to read it."

Daniel read the cover: *Chronology of Power System Development for the Global Restoration Mission.* "Is there something in here I'm supposed to care about?"

"Check out page eleven," Matt said. "I can forward you the E-copy."

"Don't bother." Daniel turned to the page and scanned the first paragraph. He closed the book not believing what he read, though he should have known better. "We're supposed to perfect Earthstar's energy structure before starting on terrestrial systems?"

"Not only the energy structure." Matt stared at Daniel. "Just like with your emails, you didn't read the whole text. Earthstar's construction and the subsequent move in of world leaders must be completed before Phase II can officially begin."

Thumbing through the booklet's pages, Daniel read the entire section. July fourth was the planned move in day. "Six months of bullshit. I'm calling Chistyakov."

"The UN had no say," JoMarie said. "I found this out late last night. The People's Party threatened to pull US funding if Earthstar wasn't completed first. The compound has been under partial construction on the ground for years. We'll be working on Phase II at partial speed by August and full speed by November."

Matt grabbed the book from Daniel. "For six months after the compound move-in, we'll probably have bugs to work out."

JoMarie waved at the group and restarted Nielsen's video. As the mission leader continued to give painstaking detail on how to format their proposals, Daniel felt his heart weigh heavy with sadness over Hannah and his hopes for the mission. He remembered Hatton Robertson from the Public Hall presentation. The bastard was right. Phase I and Phase II—in that order.

TUES 01/10/2130
FLC FAMILY TRUST LAKE HOUSE
BRIDGEPORT, NY

The tapping on his bedroom door was a tortuous sound, like a chainsaw cutting through metal.

"Shaune?"

Hearing his dad's voice, Shaune pulled the blankets over his head. *Ah! It is a chainsaw.*

He threw off his blankets and sat up, seeing his dad's face poking in his bedroom. To Shaune, Poppy's head seemed to be getting bigger, yet his body was the same size. If a pumpkin were capable of envy, it would surely be pining after this mug.

"Shaune," Poppy said, "Clark Bowers is here with me. I want you to meet him. He's a biochemist at the CDC."

"Are you kidding?" Shaune grumbled, still shaking off a dead and comfortable sleep. "I thought you two were coming here this afternoon. It's only 06:00."

"Clark and I have work in DC this morning. Sorry to interrupt your busy schedule, but you can sleep until noon after we leave. We'll be waiting in the living room."

Shaune moaned and put on a pair of sweatpants and a t-shirt. He shuffled in the living room and there was his bigheaded dad and Clark Bowers. The guy looked more like Clark Kent but with red hair. "And he's supposed to do what?"

Poppy looked agitated. “Get you started on Act Two. You’ll be the last leader brought in before the takeover.”

Falling onto the couch across from his dad and Clark, Shaune rubbed his eyes. “That one’s not scheduled until November.”

“And it will take some time to prepare,” Poppy said. “The consequences of error in Act Two are far worse than those of GlobeTek. Do you have any idea how much Clark and his advocates will have to do in order to set this up?”

“No,” Shaune said flatly. “I’m not sure I give a shit this early in the morning.”

Clark walked to Shaune and extended his hand. “This will be one of the best attacks yet. Not in body counts but in terms of public fear. Act Two will be unprecedented in this country’s history.”

Shaune shook the guy’s hand. He already liked Clark’s style. “So you think the exercise will be that good?”

“That good and better,” Clark said pulling a tablet from a folder. “The information I have access to will work with whatever approach you want to take. We’re talking really advanced science. You’re gonna love it.”

“Love is a strong word,” Shaune said. “The only things I love are sex and power and those are Siamese twins.” He begrudgingly turned to his dad. “And of course my adoring family.”

“This is pretty sexy stuff,” Clark said as he displayed the names of different biological weapons on Shaune’s HV. “All of these agents can be used in your next assignment. Do your research and let me know which ones you want. I’ve sent a link to your Epad.”

“When do I have to make a decision?” Shaune said.

“By the end of June,” Clark said. “This is fair notice. You’ll have to be educated on bios so you can make the right choice.”

“And,” Poppy interjected, “it will give the Alliance time to evaluate your plan.”

Shaune yawned and reclined against the arm of the couch. “So you don’t trust me?”

Poppy’s face seemed to bloat like it always did when he got mad. “We can’t trust anyone completely. The USA needs a leader that has the ability to soundly reason in critical matters. They don’t mind if you’re nuts the rest of the time. Most of us are according to the US Psychiatric Association.”

“The inferiors will never understand us,” Shaune said.

“You’re not that smart yet,” Poppy said. “Your surgery’s scheduled for July third, after your preliminary plan for Act Two is submitted.”

“I’m plenty smart enough now,” Shaune said as he tried to focus his tired eyes. “If I can plan this without the enhancement, imagine what I can do afterward.”

“We’ll see.” Poppy stood and headed toward the door. “You can’t screw up like you did with GlobeTek. There are consequences for repeated mistakes.”

Shaune glared at his dad. “There won’t be a ‘repeated mistake,’ as you call it.”

Clark followed Poppy to the door. “Nice meeting you Shaune. I’ll be in touch in the next month or so and we can get started.”

“Yeah,” Shaune said.

Poppy gave Shaune a snide look. “Make sure you start on your USA lessons. You need to get those done before your surgery.”

“Fine.”

The door shut and Shaune shuffled back toward his bedroom. Biological weapons were particularly fascinating to him. Forget bombs and fires. The power of the unseen was the ultimate tool of fear. He dropped on his bed, excited about the prospects of Act Two.

TUES 01/10/2130
UNITY SPACE STATION
ALTITUDE 410 KM AT 27,400 KM/H

While the others had left the Thinkers Room to take their breaks, Daniel stayed in his chair and sipped on a bottle of iced coffee. He grabbed a chocolate muffin from a snack box on the table, knowing that these carbohydrate fixes were interfering with his fitness protocol. But the aroma of cocoa and sugar was hard to fight off. Taking a big bite, he savored the sweet taste. Would alien beings someday land on Earth and declare these chocolaty cakes a prime example of human gluttony? Nah…they probably eat them too.

Having called Dr. Nielsen and giving his condolences, Daniel felt relief. Since the mission leader was grieving his loss, he didn't bother bringing up Casey's Public Hall fiasco. He'd also felt better after sending Carla a donation for the children of the GlobeTek victims

His other call, the one to Chistyakov, pissed him off. He wasn't mad at the guy but at the situation they faced. How had the People's Party become so powerful that they could dictate the mission's direction? He turned to the sound of rustling in the kitchen.

JoMarie was holding a bag of carrot chips. "Did you call Nielsen?"

"Yeah," Daniel said. "The conversation made us both feel better. Then I called Carla and donated." He hesitated. "The other call reactivated my ulcer."

Her eyes bulged a little. "Who'd you call?"

"Chistyakov."

She walked to the table and sat next to him. "If you make him mad, you could be gone, off the mission. You're a brilliant scientist and I want you to replace me someday but you must restrain your emotions."

"Hear me out," Daniel said, a bit slighted. "Chistyakov and I discussed the chronology of Phase I and Phase II. I voiced my concerns and he understood. He didn't seem mad at all."

Grabbing Daniel's muffin from him, JoMarie took several bites.

"So if he wasn't angry, what's the problem?"

Staring at his bottle of iced coffee as he swished the tepid liquid back and forth, Daniel was engrossed by the swirls of cream dancing against the plastic.

"I wasn't stupid enough to be a jerk. When I sounded off a bit, I figured the worst he might do is dole out a Siberian tongue-lashing. Instead he told me that the People's Party was funding much of the mission, so we had to comply. He agreed with me."

"He is the Russian president. He's not going to like the United States running too much of the show, regardless," JoMarie answered.

"But the People's Party's controlling everything," Daniel said. "I can't place what is wrong, but something is. They make my skin crawl."

JoMarie sighed. "No mystery there. That's because a lot of them are creeps, as many politicians tend to be. But he who holds the purse strings holds the power."

"I can't help but feel there's something more going on."

"You've been saying that since I met you," she said handing the small remaining piece of the snack back to him.

"I'm sorry." Daniel ate the last piece of his muffin. "I'm not trying to be a crazy conspirator."

"I know." JoMarie smiled. "You're just a natural."

Laughing, he grabbed another muffin and checked his Epad. Pokey frowned and gave him *Galax.net*'s top stories. A group of Europeans had been arrested for the Public Hall attack. He looked at their young faces, desperate and self-defeating. Generation after generation of humanity did the same ignorant things—the same old violence, same old game. When would they figure it out? Would they figure it out?

* * *

Daniel heard the doors slide open. Matt, Robert, and Sharon walked in and headed for their chairs. Casey woke up, stretched, and then slipped on the thin, neoprene USRG t-shirt he'd been sleeping on. He went in the kitchenette and came back with a bottle of water. Trotting to Daniel, the dog hopped in the chair next to him. Kosmo and Rushton were still asleep and part of Daniel wanted to join them.

Robert shook his finger at JoMarie and sat down. "The USRG's role in Earthstar's completion is a concern. What if this bleeds into two or three years?"

Feeling a flash of hope that Robert could be an ally in some areas, Daniel nodded and answered, "Good question from Bob. What about that JoMarie?"

Raising his paw, Casey answered. "I'll take that one. When money and power are involved, human resourcefulness blossoms. I oughta know."

"Their selfish desire to move in will help us," JoMarie said.

Robert pointed at Casey. "That dog knows his stuff about the People's Party."

Casey grabbed an apple tart from the snack box. "This dog knows his stuff about all you humans."

Sharon sat on the other side of Casey and Matt returned to his chair. Daniel was hoping for a little productivity but figured the first day of work would probably be mostly orientation and bullshitting. JoMarie took the computer out of hibernation and displayed a map of Earthstar's residential sections on the HV.

"Structural components with plumbing and wiring are complete," she said. "They are ready for transport to space. We'll use the AI programs to address bugs that come up when NASA and the other space agencies start piecing things together."

Daniel seethed, drumming his fingers on the table. “Several nations have full functioning space stations. So many people are suffering from the deteriorating ecosystem. That has to be contributing to the African Plague’s rapid spread. Why are mission scientists testing the energy systems when other researchers can?”

Matt handed Daniel the booklet. “If you go to page fifty, there’s an FAQ section by USRG scientists. Read questions one and seven.”

Daniel flipped the booklet to page fifty and read the first question.

> Question 1: Why is completion of the UN Earthstar Compound a top priority? Why can’t Phase II occur concurrently with Phase I while world leaders live in the existing space stations until Earthstar is complete?
>
> *Answer: The accommodations and defense systems are inadequate in existing facilities. World leadership must be stable should a crisis or crises occur. Earthstar will be equipped with the world’s most advanced weapons and disaster management plans. The station’s military capacity will be capable of halting any major conflicts.*

Shaking his head in disgust, Daniel read the other question.

> Question 7: Why are USRG scientists addressing the UN Earthstar energy systems when other researchers are available?
>
> *Answer: Unity researchers have been honorably selected to work on Earthstar’s energy systems for the same reason they are participating in the mission: their high level of specialized expertise combined with practical big picture problem solving.*

“That’s a crock of shit,” Daniel said. “What’s the latest count on world leaders who’ll be moving to Earthstar?”

“Look at the next page,” Matt said. “That’s another FAQ. Three hundred of Earthstar’s seven hundred and fifty residents will be one hundred and fifty world leaders with one guest each. One hundred and sixty will be military and other personnel. We’ll take up forty if all twenty

USRG leaders bring one person. The two hundred and fifty others will be impoverished parents and kids that will serve everyone else."

Daniel handed the booklet back to Matt. "How generous."

"The children will receive the best education," Matt said as he set the booklet down. "What are you sniping about? We've been offered residency."

Casey rolled his eyes at Matt. "All for the children."

Groaning as he squirmed inside the shrinking walls between science and politics, Daniel stared straight ahead. The two were different species and should never cross-pollinate, as far as he was concerned.

"Don't tell me that the EU reporter who stomped my ass at the forum was right. I defended our position of being on the mission for the good of humanity."

Coughing onto his sleeve, Matt managed a muffled response. "Speak for yourself," he said before motioning to Casey. "And I saw that smart ass look, canine."

Daniel took a deep breath to stay calm. He thought of Jake and JoMarie's conflicting takes about Matt: *I've seen six-year-olds with more tact; the kid's been traumatized. He lost his mother.* "Both of you need to stop," he said.

Matt leered at Casey. "I'll mind my business when that dog does. Besides, I'm sure we can work on the ecosystem as long as there isn't compound work, right JoMarie?"

"That's my plan," she said laughing. "Don't worry about Casey's behavior. Focus on monitoring yourself."

Nodding as if in agreement, Matt downloaded database images from his Epad to the computer. He projected them on the HV.

Daniel's muscles tensed as he watched a desert windstorm. Waves of blowing sand rained last rites over human and animal corpses. A dead bird's wing reached out of the rippling sand, its dark feathers twitching in the air as if demanding justice.

"My daughter died because nobody gave a damn about safety when times got tough," Daniel said as he folded his arms and leaned back. He fought back tears. "Her tiny body was exposed to garbage that no human or animal should have to endure. I'll do everything in my power to make sure other kids don't die like she did. Fuck Phase I."

"Ouch," Casey said.

"Yeah. Ouch is what you feel when your kid dies."

"I'm sorry," Casey said taking a drink of his water. "I wasn't making light of that."

"I know."

"I don't agree with the priority change," Matt said, "but I'm stuck in the system like you are."

"No system's going to paralyze me. It's already killed my kid."

Matt motioned to the HV. "I wish the mass deaths weren't inevitable but I don't see another way."

"There has to be," Robert said.

Sharon jotted notes on her tablet. "Our mission is tough but I don't think a large reduction in the population is necessary."

"Don't kill the messenger," Matt said motioning to the storm on the HV. "This is Nicaragua. I'm sure JoMarie and Robert are old enough to remember when this place was green. Once half the world population expires, which shouldn't take more than a century or two we'll be at a balanced population of eight billion or so. Death is the unfortunate solution to maintaining quality life on an overburdened planet."

Daniel felt like going home to North Carolina to sit with his daughter's remains. He felt at peace there. Matt's ideology seemed only a peg or two above Hatton Robertson's.

Sharon ran her fingers through her straight hair. "When I took the Hippocratic Oath, I took it for all people and earth creatures, not just world leaders."

Matt shot out a sarcastic sniff. "Your mythological angels aren't gonna descend from the clouds and invalidate Charlie D's universe."

Sharon narrowed her eyes at Matt. "Charlie D?"

"Charles Darwin. Who else?"

Daniel grinned as JoMarie rose from her chair. Casey's eyes got big as if he knew what was coming. Now it was Matt's turn to get that special look she gave. Apparently he'd forgotten that she got quite put off by young scientists who scoffed religion and faith.

JoMarie's gold cross draped around her neck. "I know you're cynical about spiritual realms and the like, but many scientists reconcile science with faith. Others don't. Being a humanist is your right, but don't mock those who do otherwise."

"I believe in God," Casey said.

"Of course you do," Matt answered. "By human standards, you're a ten-year-old boy. I used to believe in one too, until my mother was smashed to bits by a drunk driver."

JoMarie's face softened. "God didn't kill your mother and I hope you can realize that someday."

Cindera woke up and jumped from her chair to the table. She sat front of Matt and cocked her head sideways. Daniel had a feeling this debate wasn't over. Maybe Matt had justification for his beliefs, but now he'd likely offended the cat.

Matt scratched Cindera's gray shoulders and bobbed tail. "C'mon, JoMarie. She understands what I'm talking about. I'm sure she's killed mice, bugs, perhaps a spider or two, but does she care? Nah. She works for Charlie."

Cindera growled and ran across the table, jumping on JoMarie's lap. Turning to Matt, she stuck her tongue out. Daniel laughed. Matt had met his match: a fifteen pound cat with an IQ that rivaled his.

JoMarie rotated her index finger around Cindera's ears. "Maybe Charlie can thin herds without conscience, but we're going to work overtime for Phase II. Our goal is to save everyone and everything."

"Overtime?" Matt said, his mouth gaped open.

Casey's face scrunched into the scary clown look he made when he laughed. "That's right. Overtime for Matt. No time for the one girl in ten years who wants to date him."

"Can someone remove these pseudo-scientists from the debate?" Matt said. "When the scenario of saving everyone is run through the AI programs, an error message spits out. Ask Donovan Lu in IT."

Looking at Matt, Daniel almost felt sorry for him. That spiel wasn't going to sell. It wouldn't even make it off the shelf for a quick peek. He watched Robert take notes on a tablet probably wishing he were back in the more amicable halls of Congress. There had to be easier ways to run for president.

"No, I won't ask Donovan," JoMarie said. "I'm his superior and I'm telling you what our goal is."

Matt pointed to the desert scene on the HV. "Think of Planet Earth as the *Titanic*. There's only enough lifeboats for some of the passengers. This isn't our fault. We didn't build the ship!" He screamed out a string of sneezes.

“As the doctor in this room,” Sharon said, “I’m asking you to cover your mouth and disinfect your hands every five minutes.” She walked into the kitchenette then came back, tossing him a small tube of gel and a tissue pack.

He wiped his hands and face with the medicine. “I need to take a nap. None of the crap I’ve taken for this cold has helped.”

Cindera smiled, her fangs overlapping her lower jaw as she spoke to Matt. “Maybe you have that new strain of the African Plague. The treatment’s hard to come by. Only the VIPs get it.” She imitated Matt’s expression by pushing her lower lip into a pout. “You’re probably not important enough.”

Matt shook his tissue at Cindera and Casey. “I’d say I am.”

Casey winked at Daniel and Cindera. “Oh my little Matty, the world is filled with young know-it-all scientists, just like you.” He lifted his paw to his ears. “Hark? Could those innocent sniffles be the sounds of preliminary herd thinning?”

“Could be,” Daniel said trying not to laugh. “You know how cheap Nielsen is. Treating your illness might break his budget.”

Pulling a pill bottle from his coat pocket, Matt shoved two pills in his mouth and swallowed. “That dog needs to shut up and know his place. Where’s Jake?”

JoMarie’s glared at him from across the table. “Jake had to make an emergency trip back to Florida. His mother’s had a heart attack. You can talk to one of the other counselors.”

“He’s the only one who understands me,” Matt said. Turning to Daniel, he winced. “I’m showing the symptoms of African Plague?”

From his peripheral vision, Daniel motioned to Cindera as he saw Robert look up from his tablet and shake his head. “Ask her. She’s been helping Sharon in her Plague research.”

Matt looked at Cindera and shrugged. “Well?”

Cindera nibbled at her front paws and smiled at Sharon. She looked at Casey who shrugged.

“I’m not sure,” said the cat. “I’ll have to observe you a little longer.”

* * *

The mental hydration needed to water the seeds of invention had gone AWOL. Daniel felt like he was being yanked into the eye of a whirlpool; lots of movement going nowhere but down. Sharon's eyes were tired, bloodshot. Robert and his cowboy hat had gone limp. Casey had left for lunch with Kosmo and Rushton fifteen minutes earlier. Cindera was sitting on the table staring at Matt. All were signs that lunch was forthcoming.

"JoMarie, can we take a lunch and eat real food?" Daniel said. "These muffins are doing us more harm than good."

Glancing at Cindera, JoMarie smiled. "Well…should we let them go?"

Cindera aimed her paw at Matt. "Everyone but him. Food will give him more energy to be creepy."

JoMarie whispered in Cindera's ear loud enough for everyone to hear, "I say let's give him a break."

The cat flung her paws over her head. "Okay. You know human nature almost as well as I do."

"See you all back at two o'clock," JoMarie said. "Clear your heads. Maybe even get a good laugh or two."

TUES 01/10/2130
UNITY SPACE STATION
ALTITUDE 408 KM AT 27,490 KM/H

Swiveling in his chair, Daniel could smell meat and potatoes in his head. Even the freeze-dried variety seemed mouthwatering. The others were eating at the snack bar except him, JoMarie, and Cindera. The cat was sleeping on Matt's chair and JoMarie was picking up lunch. He checked his Epad for mail.

Pokey yawned. "Have you signed up for your counseling appointment?"

"You know the answer," Daniel said.

"Just testing your honesty."

Daniel had considered changing his eHelper to a more adult character like most people his age, but he figured that Pokey was a constant in his life. And he wasn't overloaded with those. *Fifty emails*! He skimmed through the subject lines.

"I'll talk to Jake when things are more settled." He pressed his Epad on his forearm.

JoMarie walked in the room and handed Daniel his boxed lunch.

"As a reminder, don't get too huffy with Robert," she said. "He could recommend replacing us if he decides we're not making progress. As head of the Senate Intelligence Committee, he's got clout, like it or not." She shook her finger at him like the crotchety database librarian from high school and added, "Try to be nice."

"I have been nice," Daniel said pulling a sandwich from the box. "This mission's becoming a political nightmare. I can't make Chistyakov mad, can't make Robert mad. I'm basically okay with the guy but his insistence on wearing a cowboy hat in space tells me he's not overly scientific."

"We have much bigger concerns than Robert's hat," JoMarie said.

Not able to shake off his uneasiness Daniel clenched his fists. "I gotta gut feeling about the People's Party."

"Anything's possible, but we can't input gut feeling into the computer."

"I think we should with that group." Daniel bit into what should have been labeled a cardboard sandwich. The Thinkers Room's doors opened and a twang pierced his ear.

"Donuts! Get yer donuts!"

Robert walked in and set a pink box on the table. Sharon and Matt followed him like clone-bots for sale on *Galax.net*. Casey, Rushton, and Kosmo trotted in and gathered around the box. Daniel grabbed the empty muffin box and tossed it in the recycler. *Pastries make strange bedfellows,* he thought.

Matt walked to his chair. He waved his donut at Cindera, who was in the midst of a muscle-twitching dream. "Outta my chair before I boot you on a spacewalk au natural."

Blinking her eyes, the cat snarled at Matt and jumped under the table.

"Was that necessary?" Daniel said.

"Yes." Matt sat down holding his powdered donut and laughed. "She needs to know who's in charge. I'd like to thank her for warming the chair, however. The heating element in the cushion will take effect much quicker."

Daniel turned to the man in the cowboy hat. "Robert, I question the People's Party's support of the mission. I think Clemens is too much of a jerk to care about the ecosystem."

"Good analogy," Robert said. "Remember when Clemens pushed those waste regs though Congress? The EPA was giddy. Then, when no one else could compete, IRE took over and did a lousy job. And you know who owns it." He motioned under the table. "Ask the cat. She knows."

Daniel bent his head down and looked at Cindera.

The cat glanced up at him. “Key members of the People’s Party.”

“That was our naïve mistake,” Daniel said, “and we’re still paying. We have to make an impact with Phase II. I’ve had an idea for some time about building temporary camps for people. They’d live there while the worst areas are cleaned. I’ll talk to Donovan and Info Systems. Maybe he can write an AI program for that. Can I show you all real quick?”

Matt, Sharon, and Robert nodded. JoMarie waved him to the front of the room. “Give us what you got.”

Daniel walked to the computer screen on the table feeling the extra skip he had after the spacewalk. He used his ePen to scrawl diagrams that displayed on the wall HV.

“*Galax.net*’s media spin about space stations being built for millions of people creates more crap to respond to. Reality needs to be better publicized.”

“Good luck with that,” Robert said.

Giving Daniel a frown sooner than he expected, JoMarie motioned to the HV. “Can the camps avoid damaging Earth’s fragile wildlife areas?”

“The lodgings could be aerodynamic,” Daniel answered. “We can use canvas walls embedded with solar cells for energy. Supplies would be transported in and disposed items removed or recycled. We might need a compact nuclear reactor. Fauna would be watered as needed. Native habitat would be preserved to the greatest extent possible.” He smiled. “We’ll have the AI program weed out the problems.”

“Camps won’t come cheap,” she said.

“This will only be for mothers, their young children, and the elderly. The rest can help clean.”

Robert set his wallet on the table. “Money—we need to figure out who must be evacuated, how many camps can be built, and how often people can be rotated. Then we gotta create a budget.”

“The costs will be prohibitive,” Matt said as he waved the energy book in the air. “Aren’t any of you paying attention? Phase I is before Phase II.”

“Call this Phase III,” Daniel said. “The US probably won’t fund this, but the other nations might.”

Matt sneezed. He motioned to Kosmo and the dogs that had fallen asleep under the table with Cindera. Throwing two more pills in his mouth, he choked them down without any liquid and sneezed again. "If you want to see where the money for your camps are, look at the animals. Instead of spending trillions of dollars to make them smart, we could've helped people. All this group does is sleep, eat, and complain. In economic terms they're free riders, welfare recipients."

Daniel swallowed acid reflux. Taking a drink of water, he shoved the rest of the stale sandwich in his mouth. Maybe the supplements they were taking to live in a space were making them moody.

Sharon's hand slammed on the tabletop. "Canines and felines are nocturnal, not lazy! The intelligent enhancements are only five years away from treating human illnesses."

Daniel looked at JoMarie, who smiled. They both saw the same thing. Casey was padding to the potbelly stove. He lay down in front of it, spread out flat like a bear rug, and started snoring. Robert followed their gaze and buried his hands in his face Daniel didn't want to disagree with Sharon, but maybe the animals were a little more laid back than the human scientists.

Sharon walked back in the kitchenette and came back holding a surgical mask. She shoved it in Matt's hand. "These animals were destined to die in shelters or labs. They were castaways. Now, they're more honorable than a lot of people. Put this on just in case the animals are right about you."

"I'm not wearing that damn thing," Matt said. "We can all die together."

"All right you two, nobody here has the African Plague," JoMarie responded. "Matt, stop complaining and start suggesting."

Daniel realized that some of the project specialists needed to work on their diplomacy skills, namely Matt. "We're not all going to die, at least not yet. I'd like everyone to think about the camp idea tonight and give me any suggestions you have."

JoMarie studied his diagrams. "The concept's promising. Matt and Robert's concerns about costs are also true, but I'd like to think outside the box today." She whipped the *Chronology of Power System*

Development for the Global Restoration Mission from Matt's hand. "Here, my friends, is the box."

* * *

Daniel stared at Earth through the porthole in his cramped bedroom. The oneness he'd felt from the spacewalk had faded. Humanity's self-inflicted geographic divides had returned along with the five oceans.

He walked to his bed. Casey was upside down in the zero-gravity capsule and had left the artificial gravity on in the room. That was okay with Daniel. Despite JoMarie's claim about how well she slept in zero gravity, he preferred being stabilized on a mattress. He lay on the bed and pulled a sheet over him. Closing his eyes, he took a deep breath. Finally, he could resume his walk through the stars.

TUES 02/14/2130
FLC FAMILY TRUST RANCH
SOCORRO, NM

Shaune stared at the computer screen. *Screw Valentine's Day.*

All three women he'd pursued on the Sassy Sexy Singles network had given him thumbs downs. The symbols seemed to be the size of real hands. Somewhere in the images, there were concealed fingernails—pointy and condescending. He checked his Epad. No emails. Same as a thumbs down. The computer screen in the family library was far too big, magnifying the burn of an electronic snub.

Shaune closed the *Galax.net* page and opened files on the USA network.

He selected Lesson Two from the study file. There were five required tests to complete the USA curriculum. He always knew that despite his naturally high intelligence, homework and studying weren't his better talents. The file opened and the lesson's theme flashed at him.

TOGETHER, THE UTOPIAN SOCIETY ALLIANCE, WILL ACHIEVE WORLD PEACE THROUGH RULE BY QUALIFIED INDIVIDUALS WHO ARE LEGITIMATELY SUPERIOR TO THOSE RULED.

While Shaune read the introduction to Lesson Two, he heard the malfunctioning library door groan open and then screech shut. He turned and saw Bernard tottering toward him holding two bottles of water. What a perfect match for the sickly door.

Handing Shaune a bottle, Bernard looked at the screen. "You're just starting your homework? It's almost 14:00. Isn't Lesson Two due on Friday?"

Shaune opened the bottle and took a drink. "What day is it? Not Friday. Not even Thursday. Plus, it's the day of romance."

Bernard sat on a chair by the computer and folded his arms. "Your homework's more important."

"Is there anything wrong with wanting to get laid on Valentine's Day?"

Touching the computer screen with his wrinkled hand, Bernard moved Lesson Two to the next page.

"No, but the group you're trying to join is preparing to institute a totalitarian one world government. You have to be prepared. Besides, if getting laid is your idea of romance, your odds of such a conquest plunge considerably."

Shaune sipped on the water and gazed out the library's expansive window to the city of Socorro. The place was known for its artsy culture and space alien encounters. "There has to be a downtrodden female sculptor down there who'd accept the seduction of a guy whose family has a trillion dollar-plus fortune."

"What's wrong with the Kat Shak?" Bernard said.

Setting the water on the desk, Shaune scowled. "The closest one's in Albuquerque. I don't feel like driving that far."

"I'll drive you as long as I get to go, too."

"Don't feel like being in a car for over an hour."

Bernard advanced the lesson to the learning objectives page. "You shouldn't even be in this city. You're way too close to the crime scene."

"Using nerve gas on those guards to steal the Slojets was Paul's gig. There's nothing pointing my direction."

"You've got those stupid Washington statues in the closet. Do you know how angry this city is about the killings? Socorro Air Base is their jewel."

Shaune was furious that he was forbidden from leaving the statues at any future attacks. "Those idiots are descendants of other idiots who thought space aliens landed on Earth in the 1960s. You know that's why the base was built—to find and capture little green men?" He laughed. "Never found 'em."

"The idiots, as you call them, are in charge for now," Bernard said.

"Not for long. The human race was never supposed to be governed democratically. It's about time the world is ruled by people with more than half a brain." Shaune turned and fixated on Lesson Two's learning objectives.

- *The future leader is to understand the necessity of creating a superior race not based on color, creed, physical form, or wealth, but on something much more legitimate: intellect.*
- *The future leader must understand why human beings in their current state of evolution are too ignorant and emotional to rule themselves.*
- *The future leader must understand why superior intellect is necessary to properly rule over the inferiors.*
- *The future leader must learn how to manage the psychological and physical changes that enhancement surgery brings.*

Shaune read the last objective. He wasn't thrilled with the idea of anyone messing with his brain. It was fine as it was.

"Shaune," Bernard said, "you can't be careless with the stuff you leave behind at the attacks."

"I'm not concerned."

"The logistics must be perfect. If outsiders find out, the plan could be stopped."

Shaune stared out the window, wondering where his artist friend was. She had to be in the art district, waiting. "You sound like my dad."

"Shaune, do your homework."

"Now you sound like my mom," Shaune said as he changed to the next page in the lesson and winced. The dead rats were quite a sight; subjects of the newest nerve gas. Piled on each other like a mountain of yams, the rats were a metaphor for what was to come.

"I'm not sure if I should use a biological agent for Act Two."

Bernard gave him a pained look. "Are you sure you want to be a USA leader? I'm gonna be a member and I don't have to kill anything."

"Geez, now you sound like my sister," Shaune said changing the screen to one from his GlobeTek scrapbook.

"She doesn't fit in with the rest of you," Bernard replied.

"She gets too attached to the inferiors," Shaune said, and paused. That was something he didn't want to do, even if the inferior was a beautiful, sexy woman. "As a leader, I must be able to put the cause first. Maybe someday I'll be the Supreme Leader."

Bernard took a drink of his water. "If the promise of creating ageless bodies comes within my lifetime maybe I'll have a chance."

"Your psychological age would still be that of an old fart," Shaune said.

"Age is a state of mind."

"Even in a modified body," Shaune countered, "you can still get killed."

"Not if you're a smart old fart," Bernard said.

Shaune reopened the Sassy Sexy Singles site. Women with painted smiles and airbrushed bodies mocked him. He wanted someone nice that he could trust. Of course, she still had to be hot. "I'm sick of trolling these sites."

"Good," Bernard said. "They're filled with gold diggers." He toggled back to the rat picture.

"Yeah, I want someone that actually likes me for a change."

With a deep frown, Bernard shrugged. "You'd have to reconsider your decision to seek USA leadership. A nice woman probably wouldn't want to date a terrorist who's killed two thousand people with more to come."

Irritated at Bernard for interfering with his fantasy life, Shaune minimized the rats. "I want world peace. The only way that can happen is for the inferiors to be ruled by the superiors."

Bernard touched the screen and displayed the rats again. "If you want to have your cake and eat it too, that's fine with me. I'm just not sure how obtainable that is."

"I can make my reality. My nice girl won't know," Shaune said as he minimized the rats and returned to his scrapbook of the GlobeTek aftermath. "This attack was too confined. It didn't incite as much fear as it did rage. The next one has to be more frightening, more fluid. It has to have a life of its own."

"Ruling an angry public is not what you want."

Shaune entered a restricted DHS site. "What would the world be without hacking?"

"Pretty boring," Bernard said.

"And hopeless." Shaune found the DHS assassination site. He pressed his right thumb on the ID pad on the computer screen. He watched the computer read his DNA and transmit the results to the DHS computer on the receiving end. He would learn the methods of top-secret kills by the United States government. The introduction page opened and Shaune scanned the contents. "I need something that kills a large number people, not something like an exploding crow-bot that takes out a handful."

"Your dad and Clark detailed the biological possibility," Bernard said.

Shaune navigated to the bioweapon pages. "I hate following his orders."

"He didn't get to where he is by being stupid."

"Oh, I think he's pretty stupid," Shaune responded as he studied DHS targets from varying nations, each of them dead, some with blue, bulging faces and others who had more peacefully passed. A picture toward the end grabbed his attention. "I got my brains from my mummy. My dad's an intellectual simpleton even with the surgery."

Bernard shrugged as if exasperated.

Shaune zoomed in on a pile of human bodies inside a tent.

Shaking his head, Bernard sneered. "That's ugly."

"I feel worse for the rats," Shaune said as he studied the image. The bodies appeared to be adult males. Their skin was covered in horrific sores with some of the limbs and faces missing flesh.

"These guys killed US soldiers in Burma," Bernard said. "I don't feel bad that they ended up like that. But on civilians?"

Shaune read the caption: *Streptococcus Exotoxin Version 4 (SEV4); other terms include necrotizing fasciitis and flesh-eating bacteria.* "Very visual and fluid and scary as shit. According to the info here only those directly exposed are affected."

Navigating through the SEV4 website, Shaune grinned. "Like they say at the Kat Shak, this is purrrrfect!"

Bernard nodded at the image. "Your imaginary nice girl sculptor probably wouldn't think so."

"Can you stop talking about that?" Shaune said as he turned back to the screen. "This is exactly what I need. Now I gotta find a vehicle of dispersion, among other things."

Studying the close ups of the deteriorated flesh, Bernard pushed out his bottom lip. "You have a point. The burned bodies from GlobeTek were dramatic but this is more as you said—fluid."

Shaune knew he needed to get this planned. The order was to hit Los Angeles during Thanksgiving week and shoot for twenty thousand deaths. The exact time and place were exciting possibilities to be worked through. Fear, not rage. He closed the website and shut down the computer.

Bernard grabbed a printout of the Lesson Two objectives. "You haven't finished your homework."

"Between you and me, I don't need to learn that shit."

"You still have to answer the questions and submit them."

"Tomorrow," Shaune said. "Today's Valentine's Day and I believe there is a festival in the art district today. Can you get the limo ready?"

"I'll have a couple of the guys wash and vacuum the car," Bernard said as he walked out the library.

Shaune could see Socorro Base in the distance. The gas attack had been the only way to get the X-1000's and move toward a world government that would achieve the unthinkable—peace on Earth. He was ready to patronize the art festival and find himself an artist. Maybe Valentine's Day wouldn't be so screwed after all.

PART II

THE RESPONSE EXPANDS

TUES 05/16/2130
UNITY SPACE STATION
ALTITUDE 460 KM AT 27,900 KM/H

Daniel leaned away from the Thinkers Room conference table. He couldn't believe over four months of the mission had already passed. *Must be that supersonic time warp in motion again.* Days passed like hours as he and the other project specialists studied AI program output and tested any questionable results with lab work. Perhaps his sense of urgency was creating the warp in his mind. He didn't know.

But alas, this hard work was not directed at improving the ecosystem but for Earthstar—testing energy, oxygen, and climate control systems and other things he didn't care much about when it related to space stations. After several sessions with Jake, inner peace was a more frequent visitor in his life. He knew he needed more counseling but there was too much work to do. The sooner Earthstar was ready, the sooner Phase II could get moving. Turning his Epad toward him, Daniel browsed through his camp proposal. Switching to the *Galax.net News*, he scanned the day's headlines, his thoughts drifting back to the urgency of Phase II.

The months had dissipated into the stars he'd hiked with back in January. But the stars had no worries. For them, the months wasted building a massive international space castle were inconsequential grains of sand passing into infinity. But for humanity the particles were finite, sliding down an hourglass, the capacity of which was nearly spent. Daniel's arm was long healed from the Public Hall bombing, but his heart remained fractured. His precious Hannah was a water drop in an ocean of death and agony. How her small body must have ached.

Unable to hold the thought, Daniel watched the HV. The final phase of Earthstar's construction was broadcasting. Construction shuttles floated in space, their robotic arms gripping sections of exterior modules and setting them into the compound's framework. Laborers in spacesuits floated around the structures like white ants manually inspecting the robots' work.

Displayed in the HV's upper left corner was a small screen showing a construction shuttle's interior. People rushed back and forth between control panels. Suddenly, in the larger screen, one of the workers floating in a spacesuit seemed to be seizing. Other workers surrounded him, attached equipment to the suit, and tried to drag him inside. After a few minutes of frantic effort, the body in the suit went limp. Daniel felt sick.

Too many laborers were dying from malfunctioning lower-cost spacesuits. Everyone knew that after twelve continuous hours of use, these suits could sputter to a stop unpredictably. He was taken aback on how his comrades were so preoccupied with their *Galax.net* shopping, snacking, and watching sitcoms on their Epads and various computers. *And this is supposed to be the Thinkers Room.*

"What's the matter with you guys?" Daniel blurted out. "Are we living in 1850? How many workers have died or suffered brain damage from spacesuit malfunctions? And we've heard nothing from the UN about my transition camp proposal."

Matt looked up from his laptop. "Like I've said before, Phase I is before Phase II. You keep trying to change Charlie's system."

Daniel noticed Robert fixated on the HV, his eyes glazed as if wishing a magic genie would materialize from his cowboy hat. Sharon rummaged through a bag filled with the newest dietary supplements for living in space. The animals were taking their afternoon naps except for Casey, who was lying on the floor playing games on his computer tablet. The dog understood exploitation when he saw it, probably more than Daniel did.

Coughing, Daniel raised his hands in the air. "Hello! Is anyone home?"

"I forwarded you an email last week," JoMarie shot back. "For the hundredth time, if you'd read your mail, you'd know what's going on."

"What did the email say?" Daniel asked.

JoMarie walked to him and braced her hands on her hips. "I'm sorry, Daniel. I saw that laborer die. The whole thing is sickening but we have to get through this to start on Phase II."

Shaking his head, Daniel grumbled. "If it ever happens."

"It will," JoMarie said, "and Chistyakov liked the camp idea. He and HEPCOM are reviewing your research. And yes, I've voiced my concerns to Nielsen over the treatment of the Earthstar laborers. You were copied that email this morning." She sat down at her place at the table, pulled a nutrition bar from her pocket, and watched HV.

"I'm sorry," Daniel said. "I'll eat my foot."

"Just don't choke on your toenails. We have to work this weekend."

Daniel turned to Matt, whose face was buried in a large tattered black book, *As Timeless as Infinity—The Complete Twilight Zone Scripts of Rod Serling.* "How can you be so apathetic? Doesn't this labor exploitation disturb you?"

"Retro sci-fi is more worthy of my attention."

"You need to focus on reality."

Matt shoved the book in Daniel's hand. "There's a goldmine on human nature in this relic. The pages are filled with Twilight Zone television scripts. You remember when video mediums were only two-dimensional?"

Opening the fragile cover, Daniel thumbed through the pages. He reviewed some of the scripts' title pages—"THE TIME ELEMENT": Airdate: 11/24/1958, "WHERE IS EVERYBODY?": Airdate: 10/02/1959.

Daniel noticed that Matt's tablet was on a website detailing the symptoms of African Plague. He grinned at the irony of the book's last script title, "THE DUMMY." He was amazed at the vast ravine that often divorced IQ and common sense.

"I remember the TV series from a media history class," Daniel said as he gripped the book. "The stories focused on the weakness of the human character. Have you ever bothered to pay attention to them apart from entertainment?"

"To the extent my psyche is capable, I suppose," Matt answered. "Your concerns about the Earthstar workers are well intended but misdirected. They're getting paid overtime at one hundred fifty percent of their standard rate and they sign a waiver. They know the risks."

"That doesn't make it right."

Matt leaned down and whispered toward Casey, "Still, that's more than I can say for us on salary."

Casey pinched an ear back and burped.

Matt grunted at Daniel. "That canine's a slob."

"You always give the animals a hard time," Daniel said. "That's why they respond in kind."

JoMarie waved at Daniel. "I gotta question for you. Due to the relaxing of labor laws for Phase I, two crews currently work in twelve-hour shifts. I think they should have three crews working eight hour shifts. You know, like the good old days. What do you think?"

Daniel watched a group of laborers surrounding an Earthstar module that was dangling from the main structure. "That's fine with me. I'm not confident that will happen."

"Twelve hours isn't a big deal," Matt commented. "We work days that long and worse. Nobody gives a shit about us."

"We're not floating in half-baked spacesuits," Daniel said, feeling like a beaten down parent worn out by a child's banter. *The kid's been traumatized. He lost his mother.* "You're a physicist," he continued. "You know those suits are more likely to have problems after they're active more than twelve hours. Almost all deaths have come in the eleventh or later hour that the suit was in use."

"Well, I guess that's a problem," Matt muttered.

JoMarie sat next to Matt. "Speaking of problems, what's your update on Earthstar's power systems?"

Matt turned from his tablet and snatched the Twilight Zone book back from Daniel. "The solar tube bugs are worked out," he said to JoMarie. "Remember, two weeks ago, our AI program rejected the Earthstar tube configuration as only functional and not optimal? Siemens redesigned the tubes according to the program's recommendations then shipped the tubes to Houston yesterday. Texas Nuclear informed us that the tubes and the nuclear reactor hybrid system will be ready for installation in a few weeks."

Scanning through a copy of the Phase I timeline, JoMarie nodded. "Sharon, update us on the supplements."

Sharon handed JoMarie a report. "On our last voyage to Mars, we learned a lot about living out of Earth's atmosphere. Even though we've addressed the physical effects, the psychological impact is still an issue. The latest supplements help the brain adapt faster to a closed and foreign ecosystem, namely the space station."

Feeling weak and lightheaded, Daniel's internal clock was weary of the days passing in a series of never ending midnights. "All we hear and talk about is the relocation, supplements for Earthstar residents and Phase I. This huge investment saves only a few. In the big picture, it's inconsequential. Virtually everyone else has to live on Earth."

"They're world leaders," Matt said. "That's always made a difference in how people are treated. Your children of the hot continents will get their chance. And remember Earthstar is for us too."

"I've already passed."

"We'll see," said Matt.

As he studied his Epad, Daniel's jaw stiffened. "I wonder if Phase II will happen at all. Regardless of what Chistyakov tells JoMarie or Nielsen, when I bring up the subject, he just mumbles about HEPCOM meetings."

Daniel imagined the gleaming compound in outer space, pristine and glorious. The flying penthouses attached to a central hub would be hundreds of kilometers above Earth. The residents wouldn't have to see a planet littered with piles of dead children. Kids like his daughter would be invisible. He felt a surge of anger, realizing that the separation of space didn't matter anyway. To these people, the flies, the crematories, and the agonies of Earth had been irrelevant all along.

"Okay," JoMarie called out as she walked back to her chair, "obsessing about things you can't control must occur during your free time." She yawned as she tapped on the computer, changing the HV display to a group of rectangular glass buildings. "This is an industrial park ten miles west of Detroit."

"This place used to be a real armpit," Matt said. "Cold as hell and tons of crime."

Trying to ignore Matt and at the same time having empathy for him, Daniel turned to JoMarie. "This is where Earthstar's components were manufactured?"

"The parts were manufactured in China and shipped to Detroit," JoMarie answered. "This building is where they are assembled into modules that will be shipped to the Earthstar construction site."

"This project's created a lot of jobs," Robert said. "The positive economic effect of Phase I can't be ignored."

Daniel held up his Epad. "Look at our world, or what's left of it. I'm sick of economic stimulation being an excuse to exploit people. *Galax.net's* reporting that deaths tolls this year from the African Plague are expected to rise again. Then there's the damn meteor storms. Am I the only one who sees this as being some type of endgame?"

"Giving people food to eat and homes to live in is important, too," Robert said. "These jobs are saving lives. We all see the same calamity you do, Daniel. That's why we're here."

Daniel clenched his fists. Robert and Matt's vanilla words and their underlying assumptions about life's basics were different than his. There was an oblivion in their perspectives that he found appalling. JoMarie's comments on the shuttle ride came back to him again. *He served his country...POW...wife ran off with another man.*

Daniel relaxed his hands. He knew that he couldn't change them but hoped he could negotiate their policy positions.

"Maybe we all need a few sessions with Jake," he said.

JoMarie gave him that pointed glance she'd been giving him for years. "Now that Daniel is finished venting, let's watch the final Earthstar components being constructed by workers in the United States."

"This is happening live?" Robert said.

"Sure is," JoMarie said as she sipped her iced coffee.

Station construction workers rode forklifts down white, stark aisles. Towering space station components dwarfed the people walking underneath. Music blared over the gentle hum of heavy equipment. Tunes of romantic struggles and job-shoving anthologies played in different workstations.

JoMarie turned up the volume. "The disadvantaged citizens are being chosen for Earthstar residence as we speak. Results are expected this afternoon."

Robert looked at his Epad and motioned to the HV's second screen that showed the surviving worker bees floating around Earthstar. With a pained squint, he said, "At least they have jobs, can pay their bills, and can save some money. Their kids are fed and clothed, and their families are provided for. Life isn't bad for them, really." He sighed and his shoulders slumped.

Daniel remembered the ousted EU reporter with the arrogant pony-tail from Public Hall. "Yeah, until the outside air seizes their lungs and a glass of tap water makes them shit for two days."

WED 05/17/2130
SOUTHERN CALIFORNIA ELECTRICAL DIST. INC. SAN CLEMENTE, CA

Sanya's watch read 14:10 as she walked in the administration building lobby. Passing through the metal detectors, she walked faster. Damn! No more weekday lunches with friends. Picking up her pace even more as she approached the IT department elevator, Sanya hoped no one would notice that she was late. An alarm suddenly screeched behind her and she spun around. Julio Ramos, one of the plant's security guards, waved her down.

Keeping her stride, she looked at her watch—14:12. "I was already cleared in the parking lot," she said.

Julio trotted over to her. "Sorry about the trouble but we have an extra security layer today. IRE's prepping for the spent waste transport to Mount Yucca. Anyone who accesses the elevators or stairs must pass a second scan."

"Oh yeah, that's tonight."

Julio walked to a computer on the counter. "Won't take but a minute."

Sanya followed him and pressed her thumb on the computer's DNA reader. The screen displayed her company vitals—SCED: Sanya Vasquez, Computer Programming Manager, Security Level Eight.

A picture of a much younger Sanya popped up under her name. She felt her face drop into a pout. She'd forgotten how young she'd been when she started at the company.

Julio nodded and motioned to the elevators. "You and your DNA are good to go back to work."

"Thanks," she said dryly.

Sanya headed toward the elevator. Suddenly, two loud booms shook the building and she felt her legs buckle. Her black pumps slipped from under her and she slammed on the floor. Looking up, she saw meteorites pounding on the building's security glass. Chandeliers swung over her like gold spiders on strands of webbing. She reassured herself that the admin building's walls could resist the impact of commercial jets, so a few meteorites weren't a big deal. She sat up as the banging of the rocks on the glass slowed to a stop.

Julio ran up and pulled Sanya to her feet. "You okay?"

She wiped dust from her beige pantsuit. "What were those explosions?"

"Probably the new lasers," Julio said. "They blow the big meteorites into smaller bits better than the old ones did. Frankly, this whole meteor thing is spooky."

"Very spooky," Sanya said. "And my head's starting to hurt from the jolt of falling."

"Let me walk you to the company doctor. I have to complete an accident report for this, anyway."

"I don't have the time," Sanya said as she turned and walked toward the elevator. "If I got checked out every time my body hurt, I'd never get anything done."

"Okay," Julio said. "HR will contact you either today or tomorrow."

Shooting a wave at Julio, Sanya stepped in the elevator and brushed her finger across the sixth floor button that led to the IT department. She paused and then pushed floor twenty. A mild throb had started above her eye and she leaned against the wall. She hoped this wasn't the onset of a migraine.

A light jumped up the series of numbered elevator buttons and then stopped. The doors opened. Sanya felt her hip burn when she tried to move her legs. She limped into the security department corridor, held onto a post for a few seconds, and then walked slowly to Aaron's office door.

After a few seconds, a smiling hologram popped up. "Hello, I'm Aaron Willis, Director of Security. Good afternoon, Sanya!"

The metal door slid open. Sanya hobbled toward Aaron, who was sitting in his chair with his back facing her. He turned from the surveillance screens on the wall behind his desk and smiled. He pointed at a chair next to him.

"Hey, Sanya! Sit down and relax. I promise that there's no whoopee cushion waiting to surprise you." He bent his head sideways. "Maybe I need to add one to put a smile on your face."

Once a fiancé and now "just a friend," Sanya fought her irritation. She lowered onto the padded chair and winced as pain stabbed through her hips.

"We've been hit by meteors. How can you think of whoopee cushions?"

"I was trying to lighten the air no pun intended," Aaron said. "After getting that afternoon wake-up jolt from Mother Nature, I thought some humor might be in order."

"Not funny."

Aaron walked behind Sanya and started rubbing her shoulders. "I gotta be calm to get my job done," he said. "Humor helps me stay focused."

Sanya closed her eyes. Normally, she resisted Aaron's shoulder rubs. However, the throb in her head was picking up speed, her hip ached, and she didn't know what was next.

"Do you know what's up with the meteors? When they hit the glass I was taken off guard and fell on my butt in the lobby."

"The warnings don't get out if we don't know exactly where the rocks are gonna fall. Sometimes they seem to have a mind of their own."

Sanya opened her eyes halfway. Her shoulders dropped as her muscles started to relax. "Was anyone hurt?"

Aaron dug his fingers deeper in Sanya's muscles. "Two guys outside the storage units prepping for the waste run got hit. Both are headed to the hospital in critical condition. One may not make it."

"That's awful," she said. "What's this building designed to withstand?"

"A commercial jet impact, a nine point earthquake, and any meteor storm, but preferably not at the same time. This admin building is stable because it's shaped like a giant boob."

Shaking her head, Sanya frowned. *Why did I come up here?* "I think in architecture it's called a dome."

"After we built the guard station on the roof, the issue was settled," Aaron answered. "It's a boob."

Moisture seemed to be shifting from Sanya's dry mouth to her clammy palms. Her heart was pounding fast. "The mammary physics theory is reassuring, I guess."

"Comforting people is my job, too," Aaron said as he turned to one of his screens that showed the IRE storage units. "Even though IRE's down two workers and one truck, they'll get the spent fuel to Yucca's temporary storage."

"Haven't both Yucca facilities been at capacity for years?"

"Yeah, since they started storing all types of industrial waste." Aaron patted her back then he sat in front of the screens. "They're supposed to transport the spent fuel to the lunar station in a few days. That'll make more space."

"We shouldn't need so much storage for waste," Sanya said as she watched the IRE employees on one of the screens.

"We're still not relying enough on clean sources," Aaron replied. "That said, I've seen gals in Admin fit more thigh in less pant than I believed possible. Maybe some of them should go visit the Yuccas and show 'em a thing or two."

Though Aaron was intermittently offensive with his jokes, Sanya couldn't argue with the truth.

"That's not a bad idea. I hope the meteors are done today," she said as she stood and rubbed her hip. "Thanks for talking."

Aaron put his arm around her waist. "Are you gonna see the doctor about your fall?"

"I will if I don't feel better soon, but I've got painkillers at home. If you ever figure out what's causing this madness, let me know."

Giving her a big hug, Aaron smiled. "You'll be the first."

Sanya pulled away and headed out of the office. She walked down the hall toward the elevator. She used her Epad to send her boss a message about her fall and to tell him that she was going home early. Sometimes she wished she hadn't broke things off with Aaron, but she knew what happened whenever she got too happy. The clacking sound from Sanya's pumps pushed against her left eye. She started to feel dizzy. Her upcoming migraine was taking its miserable course and the preventive meds still didn't work.

She stepped in the elevator and pressed the lobby button. Sanya stared at the light moving down the buttons. She saw herself in the all too reflective chrome and winced. Pale suits made her look squatty, even though she was average height. She managed to keep her pants at a size eight, which was not bad for a middle-aged office worker with two kids. Besides, Aaron always thought she looked good. She closed her eyes, soothed by subtle movement of the elevator.

The elevator bell rang, jolting Sanya back into reality. The doors opened and she stepped guardedly across the lobby. She waved at Julio as she headed outside.

Last night she'd slept terribly. She hoped that she didn't dream about the GlobeTek attack again. At least once a week since January, fiery images would flutter in and out of her sleep like a shadow passing by a wall. She could see just enough to know something or someone was lurking near. When a good night's sleep did find her, it offered relief. But too often, sleep was the most vengeful of all enemies, failing to douse the bonfires of worry and instead igniting them into flames from *Dante's Inferno.*

THURS 05/18/2130
SANYA VASQUEZ'S RESIDENCE
MISSION VIEJO, CA

Sanya's eyelids were heavy, but stuck half open like jammed window shades. She set her Epad on the end table, noting that the clock read 01:06. Sinking into her pillow, she smelled the pumpkin spice fragrance circulating from her night-light.

Her lunch was lost to the toilet hours ago and the thought of trying to sneak a small dinner in her empty stomach passed with each painful hiccup. Worry settled over her like a heavy fog. At least Jessie was home. Even at fourteen, her daughter provided a sense of safety. *I wish Marika hadn't stayed at her friend's dorm.*

Suddenly a sharp pain stabbed through her hip. She sat up and rubbed the saucer-shaped bruise on her leg. A cruel pulse inside her eye accelerated into a sucker punch. She grabbed her medicine off the end table and squeezed two minty green drops onto her tongue. Her alertness dissolved in a gleaming pool of shapes and colors.

* * *

All was black, and then came the moon. The spotted mass orbited Earth like a nervous spectator. Sanya realized that she was floating over SCED near the IRE warehouses that were built underground with the reactors. Her nightgown billowed in the cool breeze like a large kite, keeping her airborne. One of the warehouse's ground-level roofs was sliding back, exposing the interior. Semi-trailer trucks were backing down in the driveway that led inside the structure. Armed guards and a motorcade waited above.

Sanya watched steam puff into the sky from the nearby cooling towers. Inside the warehouse, robotic arms grabbed the encased spent fuel rods from their storage ports, packed and bound them on large pallets, and then raised them onto the trucks. Once the trucks were loaded and had driven up to ground level, the warehouse roof slid closed. The motorcade surrounded the semis as they pulled onto the Interstate 5 South Freeway.

Maneuvering forward by swimming midair, Sanya glided after the motorcade.

Why aren't they going to Nevada?

Passing through a void, she now hovered over the trucks as they backed up to a pier where a large transport carrier waited. Ocean waves collapsed on the coast. A Mexican flag draped from a large pole. She knew that they were in Baja. She glided on the deck. People walked past her and through her and continued on their way. Cranes pulled the waste containers from the trucks and slid them into the cargo section of the huge ship. Commands were being swapped between crewmembers.

A man shouted, *"Tirar la basura en el mar!"* Sanya wished she didn't understand the words: Throw the garbage into the sea.

Sanya spun through a dark tunnel and dropped into the ocean. The sea was cool against her skin, the dimness refreshingly dark like a peaceful tomb. Through a deep, olive green haze, she saw pallets drop past her toward the ocean floor like rocks tossed in a pond.

Inhaling as deep as she could, Sanya released salty water from her lungs. Metallic blue and green dolphins swam around her. A shark as big as a car swam nearby. Looking blandly at her, it proceeded on. She realized she'd lived near the beach most of her life and was oblivious to the ocean world, trading her curiosity for work and other daily grinds.

A group of whales with transparent fins swam past her a few seconds later. She struggled to remember what they were called. Little, black serpent fishes swayed in groups, their sharpened teeth revealing their carnivorous nature. Eels stopped and surrounded her but they became bored after a few minutes and swam away, their tails whipping onward.

A razor-sharp edge of a rock sliced Sanya's foot and a cloud of dark blood swirled from her toe. She grabbed her bleeding foot. More water gushed into her chest and she casually exhaled. In front of the rocks lay a metal drum. In the distance, she saw drums piled beyond her field of vision. Turning from her wounded foot, she scissor-kicked toward the casks wedged in the sand. Floating over what looked like piles of landfill, she recognized the labeled containers—Class B waste from SCED. Stacks of pallets grabbed her attention. She gasped and more water spilled inside her chest. *Spent fuel. This can't be.*

Some type of fury must have heated the water she was breathing. Sanya's chest felt hot. Rocks and plants began trembling under her. The ocean floor was draining into a large cavity. Suddenly, orange liquid exploded from the opening, blowing her and the casks toward the water's surface.

* * *

Sanya heard herself shouting. She sat up and kicked the blankets to the foot of her bed, gasping as her sore hip jerked sideways. The smiling star night-light glowed yellow by her bathroom door; the pumpkin spice aroma still filled the room. Residual orange outlines of casks faded into the ceiling. She rubbed her toes. No wound, no blood. Crickets chirped outside her window. Those damn migraine drugs.

She kept inhaling, relieved her lungs were filling with air. The throbbing in her head had almost stopped but she didn't want to take more medicine. If only the preventive shots helped her. But they were useless because her headaches weren't typical migraines. They were predictors of upcoming nightmares. The fall probably didn't make a difference, this headache would've happened either way. Her loyal shepherd, Buster jumped from the floor and sprawled across the bed. She scratched his back.

Was she was tumbling into the depths of madness only to be pulled back right before she fell to her demise?

Her brain shivered like cold, damp skin. Sanya returned to a private, icy planet, where twenty years ago a dream leapt past the threshold of her mind and into reality.

It seemed like yesterday when the thunder cracked its knuckles and bitter cold rain poured over a death dark night. Her younger brother Javier was nineteen years old, driving from their parents' cabin in Lake Arrowhead. Before that night, Sanya's memories of her family on the mountain had always been something she'd cherished. But that night, the hill was a predator and Javier the victim.

Wind sprayed rain in saturating collisions. Javier had caught his girlfriend cheating on him. He put the top down on his car and shut off the obstacle avoidance function. A beer bottle was shoved in his drink holder and an empty twelve-pack carton lay on the back seat floor.

He soared down the mountain highway, vulnerable and dejected, daring life to take another shot at him. His vision blurred by grief and alcohol, he didn't see the giant pine that seemed to leap from nowhere until it was too late. Tires screeched like a frightened animal and Javier's car spun and folded around the unyielding tree. Airbags collapsed into flat balloons and the steering wheel plowed against Javier's chest. Pain seared through his rupturing organs. Blood spilled out of his nose and over the blue jacket Sanya had given him for his eighteenth birthday.

A few minutes later, US Forest Service rescuers darted around him. Javier's eyes were blinking and scared. He was sorry for what he'd done. To him, the rescuers looked human at first but soon deepened into vague shadows. They slowed to a crawl and then faded to whiteness as Javier's body became numb and limp.

Rescuers pried his body from the narrow strip of space between the steering wheel and driver's seat. They slid Javier in the back of an ambulance and attached electrodes and other life support to his head and caved-in chest. They released warm blood into his veins and his body arched up several times from the electric currents but was otherwise still. Javier's eyes closed and his life shut down. The rescuers shook their heads solemnly and pulled a sheet over him.

Sanya had woke up screaming that night. Her dorm roommate was shaking her and shouting, "Wake up! Please wake up!" She had opened her eyes and heard her Epad beeping. Dad's tear-stained face was in the screen. Sanya had already known why.

She turned to Buster who now slept next to her in comfort. She looked at her nightlight glowing from the wall and wiped a tear from her eye. For all the injustices animals were subjected to in this life, the beasts were often the lucky ones.

THURS 05/18/2130
UNITY SPACE STATION
ALTITUDE 425 KM AT 28.025 KM/H

Daniel stared at outer space through the glass walls in Unity's viewing room. He was pining for another spacewalk, but Cal and his group had been diverted to research involving the malfunctions in the spacesuits worn by the Earthstar construction workers. The blackness of infinity lit by countless stars was inviting. He wished he could submerge himself again.

A faint reflection of his frowning face stared back from the glass. Is that what he looked like to everyone else, a grouchy man approaching middle age? Would cynicism congest his attitude throughout the mission like a stubborn tickle in the throat?

Damn, he thought. *Here I thought I was the most positive force in my family.*

While he was far from perfect, he'd assumed Jake's sessions were helping. That was, until Casey said he overheard USRG researchers saying that Project Specialist Daniel Griffin was a downer. He brought up Hannah's picture on his Epad. *How many of those assholes have lost a child?*

Dreading the update at 09:00 with Chistyakov, the US President, and other political leaders, he walked past Casey, who was snoring on a chaise lounge. He quickly checked his email and pressed his Epad back on his forearm. Sitting on a stool in front of a telescope, Daniel stared through the scope's lens. The caressing glow of stars softened the sting of peer rejection.

A succession of taps suddenly jabbed his shoulder. Daniel turned and saw JoMarie walking away from him toward the lounges. She was wearing dress shoes and a smart maroon pantsuit under her lab coat as if ready for an important business meeting.

Her posture told him that she was depressed. Feeling a little underdressed in a lab coat covering canvas pants and an oxford shirt, he combed his hair back. His disposition swung with political pendulums and holiday funks, but JoMarie's moods were often the result of more practical things like fights with her husband, kids, or worst of all, her mother.

Looking back in the scope, Daniel studied a distant nebula. "What's up?"

"I need to reconnect with my spirituality."

Dreading one of JoMarie's religious discussions, Daniel turned from the scope anyway. "Care to talk?"

She sat sideways on a lounge chair. "Part of me wants to vent but the larger part begs to forget. Mama's fighting with the kids and Ed again." She closed her eyes. "You had breakfast?"

"No." Daniel said, rubbing his fingers in circles over his abdomen. He knew his food choices had to be made warily. "Got the ole stomach burn."

"You need to see a doctor."

Daniel fidgeted with the telescope's star tracker. "Just stress from everyone hating our guts. The public thinks the USRG is a whore for politicians. The politicians think we're incompetent and are threatening more oversight."

Feeling his eyes well with tears as he thought of Hannah, he looked up at JoMarie. "I can hope fixing the polluted ecosystem will slow the African Plague. I could make a better paycheck in a lot easier ways."

JoMarie leaned back. "Nobody hates us, Daniel. The USRG's doing a fine job. The loud mouths always get the press."

"I don't want to greet the residents when they arrive at Earthstar. What a dismal way to celebrate Independence Day."

"We're also greeting two hundred and eighty people who are disadvantaged," she said. "The added thirty are from fifteen of the mission leaders waiving their residency."

"Matt too?"

"He's one of five who hasn't responded," JoMarie said. "I'm cautiously optimistic."

"I knew almost from the start that I had no interest in living there," Daniel said. "I hope Matt's wrong about Earthstar being the final refuge. Earth could be for all practical purposes, a coffin."

"That's not a vote of confidence for Phase II."

Daniel folded his arms. "Haven't heard anything lately about the camps."

"We will," JoMarie said as she stood up. "I'll feel better if I eat breakfast. You want me to pick something up for you?"

"You could fetch me some french toast, eggs, and bottled coffee."

"No problem."

Adjusting the telescope, Daniel tried not to let the challenges get him down. "I wonder if we have a fair chance with the protests and politics."

JoMarie walked to the viewing room's glass. "We'll save as much life as possible. Everything works together—inanimate, animate, doesn't matter. It's nothing short of a miracle."

"But there is a scientific explanation," Daniel said.

JoMarie glared at him and then turned back to the glass. "Not for all of it." Checking her Epad, she walked back to her chaise and sat down.

Daniel remembered JoMarie's stories about Ed's NASA trips into deep space. During those voyages, Ed and his fellow astronauts said that they felt the presence of something living, self-aware, and frighteningly smart. And they sensed that "something" was watching them. Daniel was intrigued and even dared to have hope because that meant he might see Hannah again. But he was leery of the dogma that seemed to spawn when too many people gathered in one place for any reason. Especially that reason.

Releasing a big yawn, Casey jumped off his chaise and trotted to JoMarie.

She scratched his head. "Ready for breakfast?"

"You need to ask him?" Daniel interjected.

Casey narrowed his eyes. "Aren't you supposed to be busy with your telescope?"

Daniel smirked as the dog rubbed his muzzle against JoMarie's hand. Canines had been good beggars before they could talk, but now they'd reached new heights.

JoMarie patted Casey's back. "You're such a sweetie. Why can't people be more like you?"

"Thanks, JoMarie," Casey said. "I wish they were, too. I also wish you could hire us animals a nanny that could groom us and rub our shoulders."

"I can't even get a masseuse for us humans!"

Casey sat on the floor. "What are we, second class?" He unzipped a canvas pouch that was strapped around his harness. Pulling out an anti-bacterial wipe, he cleaned his face.

JoMarie scratched under Casey's chin. "I'm sorry. My ancestors feel your pain. I should've known better than to speak like that."

"He's trying to schmooze for extra food," Daniel said. The defense attorney who had that dog as a puppy taught him well.

"What did I say about the telescope?" Casey said as he picked at a curly tuft in his fur and pouted. "I'm not a dog or a human, anyhow. I'm a guinea pig."

"You're a member of the Unity family," JoMarie said. "Be glad the Feds raided the lab you were trapped in."

Casey grinned. "Too bad five percent of the people cause ninety-five percent of the problems. The rate for dogs is much better. We live in packs. We don't abide by the 'me first' blahooey like you humans."

JoMarie braced her hands on her hips. "That means the other ninety-five percent are sitting around on their duffs. I'm getting breakfast for Daniel and me. What do you want to eat?"

Daniel shook his head at Casey who was staring at the ceiling as if faking deep thought.

"Three pounds of chicken from white meat cells," the dog said. "Make it the fresh stuff, not the freeze-dried gristle."

"Three pounds!" Daniel said. "Do you think that's enough? Why not ten pounds?"

"Maybe if it were lunchtime," Casey answered.

JoMarie laughed. "You do like the good life. I'll ask the cook what he has."

Staring back out at the universe, Daniel swore he recognized some of the stars from his spacewalk. They were, after all, the same ones. And he hoped, for Hannah's sake, that they were watching him back.

* * *

The Milky Way was the perfect refuge. Daniel found the Sagittarius constellations and studied the Lagoon Nebula. Turning to Casey, who was talking on his Epad, his thoughts shifted to rouge enhancement labs. He always suspected the research had been expanded from animals to humans, despite the international ban. Urban and tabloid legends traveled through media channels claiming that mentally ill and brain damaged people were being transformed into homicidal zombies.

Daniel heard clanking noises. He looked up and saw JoMarie gripping a large breakfast tray as she walked back in the viewing room. Cindera, Rushton, and Kosmo were trailing after her. He walked over to her and grabbed the tray, setting it on the coffee table in front of the lounges. Lifting the clear lid off his breakfast, he embraced the fragrance of toasted sugar and bread. Rushton snatched a chunk of Casey's chicken and ducked under JoMarie's lounge.

"That was rude," Casey said.

"Excuse me. Thanks for sharing your chicken," Rushton replied while chewing with his mouth open.

"You steal food and you lie," Casey said as he grabbed his plate with his two front paws and sat back on his lounge.

"That was too much for you, anyway," Daniel said. He took his food and coffee, and carried it to a table next to a long-range microscope. He piled his eggs on the toast, sat on a stool, and faced JoMarie.

"Too many people see the world through one pair of glasses and reject alternative views. I realized this on my spacewalk."

JoMarie passed out pieces of meat to the cats. "True."

Rotating the scope's base, Daniel examined the mechanics. This scope could view molecules millions of miles away. Only five of its kind existed and he'd always wanted to check one out. Aiming the instrument at Chicago, Leningrad, and then Tokyo, he examined oxygen, carbon, and ozone molecules. There were the same dirty layers of industrial crap hovering over all of the cities; not a very exciting scope. No wonder there were only five of them.

Daniel gulped down his toast and coffee. His stomach seemed to be cooperating so far. Maybe this was a sign that the mission update was going to be successful. "On my spacewalk back in January, I looked through the infrared lens and got a new take on human eyesight."

"You wore a new pair of glasses," JoMarie said.

Daniel started touring the solar system with the scope. Stars blended into hazy clouds of carbon and helium. He froze for a second and stared through the scope again. His peripheral vision had caught something that looked like light spearing through Earth's solar system. Redirecting his lens, he followed the bolt. It was a single beam coming from the Pacific Ocean.

He had the scope calculate the object's diameter and recorded the result in his Epad: .01 of a micrometer. He followed the beam from the ocean and discovered it extended into space beyond the scope's capacity.

"JoMarie," Daniel said. "Take a look in this eyepiece and tell me what you see."

She walked to the scope and pressed her eye against the viewer. "Looks like a beam coming out of the ocean to the sky."

Daniel nodded. "To be exact, the bolt is coming from the Pacific Ocean between South America and Asia."

"The beam is so narrow yet extends into the solar system…so odd," JoMarie said. She motioned to Daniel's Epad. "Save the images and email them to NASA. Maybe it's one of their experiments." She walked back to her lounge and sat down.

Daniel transferred several images to his Epad and emailed them to NASA researchers in Florida. He felt chills running through his arms. The meteor storms were coming from outer space. The beam was shooting *out* into the solar system. Was there some type of communication between the two? Had someone or something found Earth? Could one of the world governments be attacking other countries with the meteor storms? *I always thought those damn things were targeting something.*

Daniel took a deep breath. He wasn't going to burden JoMarie with his concerns just yet. He'd done enough of that and she had too much to think about. Walking to the breakfast tray, he set down his empty plate and bottle. He sat on the lounge next to JoMarie and the animals and reviewed the mission updates on his Epad.

JoMarie set her plate on the tray. "The meeting starts in an hour. You ready?"

Cindera and Kosmo jumped on Daniel's lap and he petted them. "We may be defending ourselves like at Public Hall, bitch and moan."

Walking back to the windows, JoMarie bit her lip. "I came here before the meeting to reconnect with God and the universe. I'm not looking forward to this morning's drivel either."

"I envy your ability to connect to spiritual things," Daniel said. "Maybe the staff researchers are right about me being a jerk."

"Who said that?"

"Casey overheard people saying I was a downer."

She turned to Casey, who had fallen asleep. "He shouldn't be gossiping. Try to meditate and be more spiritual. Maybe that will help the good side of you shine more. There's plenty there."

Daniel squinted, pained by the suggestion. JoMarie was so damn hopeful with her belief in spiritual realms. He'd grown up in a world where intangibles were for weaklings and only measurable concepts were acceptable. As much as he hated how he was parented, he couldn't shake off the side effects.

"Spirits might have a problem breaking the hide of my psyche." He thought for a few seconds and decided to clarify. "At least the good ones."

"I know you better than that," JoMarie said. "Now I do admit that some of the politicians we're gonna see in an hour could be dining with the bad ones."

"Especially President Clemens," Daniel noted. He thought about his dad, who'd have a fit anytime a person questioned the perfection of the United States. Daniel understood his dad's military background would bring him to a patriotic place, but that shouldn't include oblivion. "The only way one can improve is to accept there's improvement to be made."

“We can all be better people,” JoMarie responded, “and that includes the United States of course. I understand what you’ve been saying about the People’s Party. We just can’t prove anything.”

“Not yet,” Daniel said opening his Epad to the January 2105 issue of *Galaxy Today* magazine. On the cover was a picture of a young Senator Clemens. He remembered his mom being excited about the third party. They were going to get results and they did. Twenty years after they took control of the government, poverty was widespread, but mediocre social services were abundant. And those few who had a lot had trillions.

JoMarie walked back and glanced at Daniel’s Epad. “Whatever the People’s Party is, the old government dismissed the early victories. That was their big mistake.”

Daniel started to read the article filled with promises. The People’s Party had offered the public a crystal goblet filled with shit and nobody sniffed. They’d gotten rid of most of the terrorist attacks on the mainland and there was less crime, but something was still wrong. “Why can’t people be moderate?”

Sitting back on her lounge, she answered, “Because everyone thinks they’re moderate.”

“There’s nothing about this country’s rulers that are moderate,” Daniel said starting to scare himself a little. “Power mongers convince the voters of their superiority. That’s how they keep winning.”

JoMarie nodded. “That’s how they keep winning.”

“My dad thinks he’s superior,” Daniel said feeling inadequate and angry. Sadness came over him as he had to keep facing a truth he wished was different. “Yet he’s crazy.”

“He’s mentally ill,” JoMarie said, “caught in a tail-chasing cycle of being too sick to know he needs medicine. Most crazy people think they’re superior.”

Daniel’s stomach twisted as it always did when he thought about his dad for more than ten seconds. Because of the effect he allowed his father to have on him, he’d moved to where the big job was. His daughter was exposed to pesticides before she was born. Cherril divorced him and a couple years later, Hannah was dead.

“That December funk I get around Hannah’s birthday always drifts into the next year.”

“Once a parent, always a parent,” JoMarie whispered.

Daniel knew that more than he cared to. He smiled a little as he watched Casey snore on a lounge with a blissful look on his face. Kosmo lay on Daniel’s lap and licked his paws. Cindera was asleep next to him, or at least appeared to be. Rushton was licking food off the breakfast plates. They were now his kids too.

Cindera’s eyes popped open and she shot him a piercing gaze. “Don’t be afraid to consider what seems impossible. Hannah deserves no less.”

Casey opened one eye and winked at him. Daniel realized that they were never completely asleep.

He balked a little as he came to a sudden realization. Ultraviolet light—he was pretty sure that’s what that bolt was made of. But then other scientists must’ve seen it through these scopes, so why hadn’t anyone said anything? What was it? If he had to search through trillions of obscure molecules to find the answer, he would.

THURS 05/18/2130
UNITY SPACE STATION
ALTITUDE 435 KM AT 27,500 KM/H

Any hint of enthusiasm that Daniel had embraced at breakfast evaporated as the Thinkers Room HV displayed live images of the UN shuttle docking. His stomach took a turn for the worse, making him regret his big breakfast. He switched the channel to an old 2050s comedy. He'd heard a lot about the fifties from his grandparents. It seemed like a good time to live. As he watched the show, he kept wondering about the bolt of light and what NASA would have to say about the images he'd sent them.

Sharon was in the kitchen refilling the first aid kit with Warmwypes and antiseptics that had been emptied by Matt and his frequent colds. The guests had exited their shuttle and were heading straight to the Thinkers Room. Daniel was ready to go back to the 2050s, live in a small town, and grow corn for fuel. Almost anything was better than this. He noticed Matt walk in wearing a wrinkled shirt and pants under his lab coat. *At least I'm not the only slob in the room.*

Matt sat down and entered the guest's names into the electric name-plates to be set around the table. "Has anyone seen the prodigies?"

Robert, wearing a suit, stood in the room's entrance then walked in and hung his hat in a cabinet. "You mean the animals?"

"Who else?" Matt said.

"Lucky for them, not here," Robert said as he started setting extra chairs around the table.

JoMarie grabbed chairs to help Robert, and then turned to Matt. "Do you want me to go get them?"

"No," Matt answered. "Just curious where they're loafing."

She laughed as she grabbed more chairs. "Loafing is such a harsh word. They ate breakfast with Daniel and me. Let's say they're in the viewing room recuperating."

"Loafing sounds about right," Matt said.

Sharon's voice quivered as she starting talking. "Listen, you…."

Daniel ceased to distinguish further words. He stared at the walls. Their wood grain flowed like melted fingerprints. Perhaps the room would ooze some type of sap to cleanse itself of the banter.

The doors slid open. A finely suited President Clemens and his Secret Service agents scoped the room and found the most superior chair at the head of the table where JoMarie normally sat. Repulsed by the US president's power play, Daniel moved to a chair set at the middle of the table. Chistyakov walked in, surrounded by guards and wearing his suit. With a pained look on his face, the UN leader sat in the seat to Clemens' left. Robert sat on the other side of the US president across from Chistyakov. Casey's tuxedo would fit in well with all the silly pretentiousness.

Clemens' powdered demeanor was more transparent in person than on the glossy New York billboard Daniel saw back on New Year's. His assistant pranced to the president's chair and posed behind him like a net site pin-up girl. One of the DHS agents snatched the nameplates from Matt and began setting them on the table. Matt scowled at the guy and sat on Daniel's right side.

Wearing traditional formal clothes, the president of China, Ming Cheng, and Saudi Princess Nabeeha were projected as holograms from the UN Peacebuilder Space Station. Their images appeared on the far side of the table. Dr. Nielsen sat to Daniel's left, no doubt as a subtle warning to give a good update. Sharon, having no great love for Clemens, sat next to the holograms. Daniel wished he were with the animals, snoring in the viewing room.

JoMarie sat next to Chistyakov and asked, "What's wrong?"

The UN leader motioned to Clemens. "You tell 'em."

“Before we get started on the mission update,” Clemens said, “I need to inform you all that a terrorist attack occurred a few hours ago in the United States. San Clemente Electrical Distribution Plant and IRE were hit in California.”

“What happened?” Nielsen said.

Clemens shifted his jaw and was quiet. To Daniel, this seemed to be a pause to sift out the harder truths. “We delayed the story until a few minutes ago. Nobody knew what to report.”

He looked at the HV. “Someone turn off this ridiculous show and give us the news.”

Daniel bit his lip and changed the HV to *Galax.net*. A news release was scrolling down the right half of the screen while footage of something being pulled from the ocean was displayed on the left. Reading the text, Daniel shook his head disgusted.

> *Today at 04:02 Pacific Time in California, San Clemente Electrical Distribution Plant known as SCED and International Refuse Eliminators known as IRE, were victims of a terrorist attack. One IRE security employee was killed and another critically injured.*
>
> *Forty storage drums filled with nuclear waste were propelled from what was determined to be an illegal dump in the Pacific Ocean west of Baja Mexico, striking both SCED and IRE buildings.*
>
> *The two-hundred liter drums ejected from water three kilometers deep and traveled hundreds of kilometers just over the water's surface. Due to low clouds and the drums' small size, Skyguards did not detect the objects until they were fifteen kilometers from shore. Twenty-five drums landed on or near the SCED and IRE underground buildings. Air force fighter jets knocked the remaining drums into the ocean, which were later retrieved by boat.*

As he finished reading the report, Daniel tightened his fists to release the anger. *When did the Pacific Ocean become an atomic trashcan?*

Nielsen sighed. "What types of nuclear waste are we dealing with?"

Clemens straightened his tie as if once again trying to polish the facts. "The drums were filled with Class B waste belonging to IRE. A few hours ago, spent fuel was also found in the dump."

Daniel stared at the floor wondering how much longer the bones and joints in his hands could hold out. Class B waste caused cancer and poisoned the elements for three centuries. What on earth was spent fuel doing there?

Smiling, Clemens seemed proud. "Thankfully, those casks didn't expel."

"That's a good campaign slogan," Robert said. "Elect the People's Party to control radioactive waste! The spent fuel casks they allowed to be dumped in the ocean didn't expel!"

"Sour grapes, Senator Landry?" Clemens responded. "The situation could've been much worse. The attacks occurred in the early morning when people were home asleep."

Daniel looked at the president then turned away. The guy always seemed to be hiding something.

JoMarie glanced at Daniel as if sensing his question. Turning to Clemens, she asked, "Mr. President, do we know how the waste got there?"

Clemens smiled at his poster girl as she tossed her chestnut hair behind her shoulders and puckered her red lips into a tight bow. "The spent waste casks are being pulled from the ocean and are fully contained," she said. "They're being brought to Mount Yucca for immediate lunar transport."

Robert glared at Clemens. "That's a risky way for IRE to save money. Dumping casks filled with waste that lasts ten thousand years into an ocean of saltwater."

Daniel broke his silence but promised himself that he'd be respectful. "What if those containers that hit SCED had been spent waste?"

"'What if' is a hypothetical," the woman answered with a sniff. "Our priority is to find those responsible for the attack. DHS is checking for links to GlobeTek Finance."

If Daniel's composure had a physical quality, he knew it would have escaped from his pants and spilled on the floor like urine. He tightened the thin white lab coat around his chest like a barricade. The US government didn't care what happened to future generations as long as the cash from IRE kept pouring in. After all, a handful of Party members were majority stockholders.

Daniel trembled, trying to stay calm toward the US president. *Push away Dad's DNA.* "Ever since the Nuclear Regulatory Commission was stacked with People's Party members, radioactive waste has not been monitored."

Robert nodded. "He's got you there Clemens."

Clemens stared back at Daniel as if to regain dominance. "All the elements of nuclear technology come from Earth to begin with. I've heard stories about you, Griffin. Stop trying to push Phase II before its time. None of your doomsday predictions ever come true."

JoMarie clasped her hands on the table. "The big mistake most people make, Mr. President, is assuming that doomsday is a single day. More likely it's the end of a digressive journey that had all the signs posted and yet nobody looked."

The hologram of Princess Nabeeha folded her arms into a tight knot.

"*Galax.net America* is reporting that Islamic groups may be responsible for this attack. Such outdated stereotypes stir unnecessary panic and violence. Doomsday is looming close enough already. Why make things worse?"

Daniel fixated on Clemens. If anyone would spread such a rumor, it would be him…anything to enhance his own position in the world.

Motioning to JoMarie and Daniel, Clemens scowled. "We don't even know where to begin much less who to start pointing fingers at. And if some type of doomsday is forthcoming, that's what these scientists are supposed to stop."

Daniel noticed that Nielsen's face had turned a shade of red that meant he was getting impatient. He tried to humor himself in this political chokehold. During mission training, Donovan Lu had assigned names of paint colors to the varying shades of Nielsen's face that changed with his mood. Right now it was terra cotta, which was somewhere in the middle between electric crimson, his furious shade, and his normal pigment, which was winter peach.

Nielsen stood, the terra cotta shade deepening to rich mahogany. "Why are we here?" he asked.

Clemens looked at Nielsen. "To be updated on the mission by your charming self and your project specialists. Unless you'd rather have the dancing dog do it."

The poster girl giggled at Clemens' quip, making Daniel's breakfast churn. Casey was smarter than both of these fools put together.

Nielsen slowly lowered in the chair. "That show brought in millions of donated dollars, among other currencies. And while the SCED attacks are a tragedy, any further discussion is best suited for the investigators. JoMarie and Daniel, can you get us started on the mission update?" The USRG leader entered notes on his tablet as his skin faded back to winter peach.

JoMarie displayed the handout text on the HV, which Daniel noticed was also displayed on everyone's tablets. This meeting, of course, had to be about the precious compound.

"Earthstar's power system is operating as designed," JoMarie began. "Matt Bertrand and the IT specialists have streamlined the wiring architecture. Solar tubes in the exterior panels reduce the need for nuclear energy. The small quantity of nuclear waste from the reactors will be converted into plutonium for Earthstar defense systems."

"As for the remaining population," Daniel said as he felt his sarcasm starting to seep out, "we need to focus on, dare I say, Phase II. Much effort has been made in constructing Earthstar and less on dealing with what created the need for the compound in the first place."

"That's how Charlie's system works," Matt deadpanned. "You don't have to agree, just accept."

Daniel couldn't help but stare at Clemens. Matt was ignorant not evil, but Clemens and the People's Party were the latter. He knew these bastards were hiding something.

Fighting to keep his hypothetical urine puddle from spilling on the floor and embarrassing JoMarie, Daniel started tapping his shoes on the carpet. He couldn't believe how some progressives had changed into this. They walked away from the ecosystem and the poor, and then joined with a group once called right-wingers. Whatever happened, he knew that the People's Party had either directly or indirectly killed Hannah. Their policies had allowed polluted land to be sold without proper disclosure.

Daniel figured he'd go ahead and draw attention to a more personal battle. "Mr. Chistyakov, the desert camp proposal has been on the table for a few months. You know my daughter died at four years old from prenatal cancer brought on by pesticide exposure. I'd really prefer that this and similar tragedies not happen to others."

Responding with the blank look that Daniel was dreading, the UN leader cleared his throat. "I know about your daughter and I'm very sorry. Right now, the camp's cost is prohibitive on a large scale, but the plan is under review on a smaller one."

Daniel stared at his clenched fists, his fingers weary but not ready to stop pumping anytime soon. The walls of the Thinkers Room must be begging for mercy by now. As he scrolled through his camp proposal with his Epad, Pokey frowned and flashed a sad face. "The cost of Earthstar is insane compared to the investment in Phase II."

"I know you're frustrated," Chistyakov countered. "HEPCOM is struggling to get funds. When we have more figured out, I'll let you know." He aimed his large wrinkled hand at JoMarie.

"Can you present an overview of Earthstar's final construction processes? Our meeting with the defense engineers is in a half hour."

JoMarie displayed the compound's architecture on the HV as she eyed Daniel from her peripheral vision.

"The final structure is based on the Unity Station design but larger," she said. "The residential hubs are shaped like train cars that are thirty meters long, fifteen meters wide, and three meters high. Many options were considered and it was decided to connect eight of these hubs with four meter-wide corridors, shaping it like an octagon. Six of these modules are stacked on top of each other and are connected by vertical corridors with elevators."

"I assume the VIPs are still living in the center structure?" Clemens said.

JoMarie aimed her laser pointer at the structure. "Six hundred and fifty of the residents will live in the octagons. Fifty world leaders and their guests will live in the six-level center structure, where the commons are located. Those will have private baths."

Clemens smirked at Daniel. "I'm getting one of those."

The elitist bullshit was driving Daniel nuts—people living in octagons compared to those living in the center structure with a private bath. He shot a pained expression at JoMarie.

Please let me out of here, he tried to say with his eyes.

She smiled and shook her head subtly. *Not yet.*

JoMarie then displayed a close up of the VIP level. "Mr. President, I believe your room has already been reserved in level four below the military's two top levels."

Clemens grinned in what Daniel considered a pathetic victory.

"The possibility of the Earthstar project was exciting and the reality incredible," Chistyakov said. "Let's hope the thing stays in the air."

Daniel felt his neck tighten. "I'm sure the US government will pay whatever is necessary. They don't give a shit about anything else."

"The People's Party is dumping the trash the Dems and Repubs left behind," President Clemens said. "We're not responsible for nuclear waste problems. Those have been around for almost two hundred years."

"What about the attacks on GlobeTek Finance, Baton Rouge, the Empire State Building, and Chicago?" Daniel said as he felt the puddle spill. "What about nuclear attacks in Europe and China? The United States has prevented a few attacks, but most of the time we're surprised. Either the United States doesn't care or we have lousy intelligence." He turned to Chistyakov and asked, "How is our intelligence? You ought to know."

"I don't know what the US government knows about terrorists' inner-circles," Chistyakov said quietly, "but I do believe your DHS forces are quite adept at spying on us."

Looking down at his Epad, Daniel saw a text message from JoMarie that read, *Calm down ,please*. His shoulders dropped. He didn't want to seem ungrateful for her bringing him on the mission. Office politics, government politics, and any other type of politics came as naturally to him as eating cockroaches.

"Remember, Daniel," Chistyakov said, "the United States is paying for more of Earthstar's construction than any other country."

"Sure," Daniel said. Inner demons scorched his abdomen. They begged him to escape, to tell the world how he really felt about the People's Party treating human beings like sacks of wheat traded on the commodities market. Chistyakov knew, Robert knew. The party's ambitions smelled ominous.

"Mr. Chistyakov is correct," President Clemens said. "The United States is paying for most of Earthstar's construction, which you could've lived in and turned down. Since you decided to stay, things can't be that bad on the ground. Besides, how many people need to be saved, anyway?"

Chistyakov stared at the US president as if trying to figure out what lay beneath, if anything. "While I appreciate your contributions to the UN, the mission's primary effort was to save as much life as possible. Now that the compound is nearly complete, the humanitarian phase is becoming a luxury?"

"What are you complaining about?" Clemens said. "You and your top officials are included in the move."

Chistyakov's face softened but seemed unconvinced. "Sometimes I wonder."

Clemens yawned. "Go ahead and wonder. We can't transport every spider and horsefly to Earthstar. That's just reality."

Daniel was hit with a sickening possibility. What would make tree huggers turn into tree killers? And right wingers vacate religion to form a union with them? Perhaps some people in those groups were never what they'd appeared to be. They had the obvious bond of thinking that they knew what was best for everyone else. He suspected this thinking went further and much darker. Daniel shifted in his seat.

There's only one thing I know of that dark—megalomania.

A nauseating flush hit Daniel as he watched Clemens. The net site girl combed her manicured nails through the guy's hair and the president closed his eyes, reveling in her adulation. Relaxing his throat muscles to keep his gag reflex at bay, Daniel started tightening his fists again.

President Cheng's hologram stood, the fury in his eyes transmitting clearly from Peacebuilder. "I have nearly three billion citizens who have to live on the surface, Mr. Clemens. I suggest you be careful about deciding whether or not Phase II is irrelevant."

Clemens shook his head and scoffed. "Not irrelevant but not a priority either."

JoMarie stood and held up her tablet displaying the mission synopsis.

"If you'd read your handouts you would understand that we've been working on Phase II on weekends and nights. I'll brief you."

She sang her song and Daniel breathed a sigh of relief. Nielsen's skin shade stayed relatively human and all was well. She was pulling this off and closing with the high note they deserved. But he wondered if that mattered anymore. If his suspicions were correct, there were far bigger troubles ahead than mission politics.

* * *

Casey's stomach was weighed down after enjoying a second helping of dinner. His four legs wobbled as he headed back in the viewing room. A big breakfast and two dinners were too much for one day. He zeroed in on a lounge next to Cindera and crawled onto the cushion. Cindera motioned to the blue pouch on Casey's harness.

"Can I have a Warmwype, please?"

Stuffing his front paw inside his satchel, Casey yanked two moist cloths from the heated dispenser, passed them to her, and lay back down.

"Thanks," Cindera said as she set one wipe next to her and then rubbed the other from her shoulders to her tail. Shoving the wipe into a recycle can, the cat began rubbing the second cloth over her face.

Casey turned back when heard a man coughing behind him. President Clemens and his DHS agents were approaching the chairs. *Yuck*, he thought. The dog was on alert as he watched Cindera pretend to fuss with the cloth.

Clemens swatted his hand at Cindera. "Shoo! Out of the chair."

The tissue slipped from her paw and dropped on the turf. Blinking her eyes, she hissed and snarled. "There are plenty of other chairs. Go sit in one of those."

"I want this one."

"You can make a polite request and I may oblige."

"Good," Clemens said. "Can you get your ass off the chair?" He lifted his foot and smashed the tissue into the turf with his shoe. "Please."

Casey waved Cindera over to his lounge. As usual, Clemens was acting like a butthole. Better yet, he was one, and Casey knew that making him mad would make things worse. Cindera leapt onto Casey's lounge and settled in the arc of his stomach. The dog seethed at the bully. Humans—so many were savages. *I'm glad I was born a dog.*

Growling under his breath, Casey watched Clemens plop onto the lounge. The president started digging his fingers into his arms, scratching up and down as if he had a rash. Casey couldn't help but feel a smidgen of delight, spreading his mouth into his evil clown grin. He swore the DHS agents were smiling too. Clemens kept pinching the skin around his neck and shoulders. What a creep. Even Matt was nice compared to him.

Bending over the lounge, Clemens lifted his pant leg and started tearing his fingers inside his socks. Casey looked at Cindera. He knew she saw the same thing he did. As Clemens bent down, his face was covered in a thin layer of flesh-toned skin covering that was lifting off. Underneath, blue and purple bruises mottled his brow bone and eyes. Human vision wasn't astute enough to see such subtleties. Few things compared to dog and cat vision.

Clemens' beaten face reminded Casey of the enhancement lab. The dog's stomach cramped when he thought of that place. The lab's ghostly walls had smelled like antiseptic and the phony cleanliness had been nothing more than a ruse to hide the bloodshed. The wide ribbons of glass that bordered the top of the walls had cast an eerie light into the evil lab.

From his cage, behind the glass wall, Casey had scoffed at the researchers in their white starchy coats peering through microscopes, guiding the computer's assembly of the nanobots. The humming machines that created the bots groaned like the spirits of dead animals pleading for justice. He knew those bots would be implanted in animal and human brains to see if they could be made smarter.

The dog remembered more of when he was a captive. Caged up with other animals, he watched dogs, cats, and monkeys get mutilated in the grand experiment to benefit humanity's capacity for knowledge. Too bad they didn't spend more time on wisdom. The lab was not a fluffy white tribute to science but rather a torture chamber. Instead of making the animals intelligent, the operations usually made them psychotic or suicidal—and so far, that's all they'd done for humans.

Trying to push the thought away that Clemens was enhanced, Casey shifted on his lounge and looked down. Maybe the president had a skin condition from anxiety. After all, being such a big butthole has to take its toll. Cindera stood up, stretched, and then sat back down. She folded her front and back legs under her body. They both stared at the US president. Looking at the president's bruises again, Casey shrugged. Maybe the bruises were from Daniel beating up creepy Clemens after the UN meeting. It was about time someone did.

FRI 06/30/2130
CENTERS FOR DISEASE CONTROL
ATLANTA, GA

Shaune and Clark strode past security guards paid off to look the other way. Act Two was in its first stage of execution. The connections had been made, the science perfected. The metal door to the refrigerated warehouse clanked shut. Shaune rubbed his white gloved hands together and stared at rows of tall, steel freezers that filled the room like massive tombstones. For his purposes, that's what they were. He stopped and read the illuminated blue numbers on a freezer that displayed a temperature of minus 175 Celsius.

The faint hiss of their motors made them seem as if they had lives of their own, breathing and panting with a hint of sensual fervor. Or maybe that was his breath as he thought of Vara. Shaune knew going to that art show on Valentine's Day would be a good idea. He'd found his artist as planned and while she was a painter and not a sculptor, he was half-right. Hotter than a freshly shot pistol yet equipped with too much of a heart, she couldn't find out about his assignments until after the takeover. Maybe once Vara saw that his acts were for peace on Earth, she'd understand.

The warehouse even looked cold. Shaune shivered despite being warm in his hazmat suit. Numerous ceiling lights brightened the warehouse like icy stars. The stark white floor and ceiling and the bloodless, gray metal walls were austere and pure. The air was pure. Everything in the place was free of uncontrolled germs and contamination. It was ironic since there were enough bacteria stored in the room to remove the human population from the planet.

Shaune felt like he was on the top of Mt. Everest looking down on the world. With the help of a few culture tubes, he'd get to rule one of the nation's largest cities for a day, an honorary mayor of sorts. Act Two would conclude with a standing ovation from his soon to be peers. After his enhancement, he'd help rule a planet finally at peace with itself. Clark interrupted his daydream by waving at him from the freezers against the back wall. He walked toward his young advocate.

"Get over here," Clark said through his headset. "We can't dick around for long."

Shaune tripped on the glossy white tiles, unsure if his shakiness was from wearing the wraps around his shoes or from plain excitement. "You promised we'd have plenty of time."

"I don't want to get caught and neither do you," Clark said as he pointed to a drawer in the freezer. "That one's holding the product that'll get you one step closer to USA leadership. Similar bacteria were used in my April exercise, but your strain's more powerful."

"I remember that assignment," Shaune said. "You only killed five hundred people because you screwed up the dispersion."

Clark shot him an annoyed glare. "I don't want to be a leader anyway." He unzipped a pocket on his suit and pulled out a clear tube, which contained a small object. Walking to the DNA reader on the freezer's side panel, he pulled off the tube's cap. He pulled out a human thumb and pressed it on the DNA reader. Clark popped the thumb back in the tube and pushed the cap back on. The drawer in the cabinet slid open.

Recoiling a bit, Shaune laughed. Clark was brilliant at times and a buffoon at others. He stared at the glowing white label inside the drawer: *Streptococcus Exotoxin Version 4.*

"You sure this is stronger than the standard?" Shaune said.

"Not stronger, per se." Clark stood and zipped the tube back in his pocket. "What I meant by powerful was that the molecular structure's smaller than the conventional flesh-eating bacteria. This enables it to enter the skin more easily."

"Good," Shaune said. "I can't kill five hundred people. I have to take out at least twenty thousand."

Clark pointed inside the drawer and bowed. "This belongs to you. Remember when we plant this strain the release should be very controlled."

Shaune scrutinized the small, clear box filled with tubes.

"Are you sure there's enough?" he asked.

"Trust me, there is." Clark grabbed the box and showed it to Shaune. "Later, I'll be loading these bios into the nanobots, which will then be installed in the implants. You'll be awestruck by their power."

SAT 07/01/2130
FLC FAMILY TRUST AIRPORT
MORRISTOWN, NY

Shaune clicked the phone off on his Epad and fell into a chair. Bernard had called to tell him that he and Vara were coasting the Slojet toward the jet way. He wondered if Vara could ever be a long-term gig, if she could ever accept his rather dark assignments as being for the greater good. Poppy would be furious if he knew that his involvement with her transcended sex.

Clark had passed the strep bacteria to a USA runner who was transporting it to an LA lab. Then he'd travel to the city of angels with the implants and nanos. Finally, he'd load the bios. *Can't trust anyone else to do the job.* The Affiliates had ensured him that nobody would find out about the stolen "inventory."

Bowling over and starting to laugh, Shaune remembered when Clark told him how he got the thumb that gave them access to the strep. Poppy had hired thugs to kill a CDC employee and make it look like a suicide, and before the guys took him out they chopped off and preserved his right thumb. When the assassins called to say the job was done, they told Poppy that a fake thumb had been fused to the guy's hand. It wasn't until they'd attached it, that they realized the thumb was a different color.

The sun warmed the waiting room and Shaune felt relaxed, or maybe it was fatigue. He rubbed his face. What was he going to do about Vara? He wouldn't have met her if he'd gone to the Kat Shak like Bernard told him to. And he wouldn't have gotten so attached.

Shaune had been seduced by Vara's turquoise eyes from the moment he saw them. They reminded him so much of his own. Her thick, brown hair was plush and she was a damn good painter, making a lucrative living off her art, which was rare and respectable. Damn. She was thirty-four, had never been married, and had no kids. She was perfect even in the morning.

Now Bernard had brought her from Socorro and was encouraging the union. Shaune knew his butler didn't want him to be a USA leader, figuring that being with Vara would take care of that. But he couldn't back down. While his father was helping him with his acts, he was still a hateful prick that thought Shaune was a loser. That was something that he had to prove wrong.

Shaune looked up when he heard a tired sigh. Vara was walking toward him with her arms outstretched. He stood up and hugged her as she pressed her face against his shoulder.

"I'm so glad to see you," Vara said, her thick, silky hair draped past her shoulders and arms.

Rubbing her back, Shaune closed his eyes for a few seconds. His enhancement surgery was Monday. He'd be better, smarter, stronger, and even downright irresistible.

Pulling away, Vara kissed Shaune on the cheek. "I was so glad to hear we're going to the lake house. It'll be nice to escape Socorro and not hear about the base's investigation. The whole thing's been so horrible and the news never stops reporting on it."

Bernard raised his eyebrows at him as he picked up Vara's overnight bag.

Shaune balked a little remembering Paul's murderous act to steal the X-1000's for GlobeTek—and how Vara knew a couple women at the base who were gassed. "Whoever stole those planes was a real monster."

"Unbelievable," Vara whispered.

Seeing a flash of light from his Epad, Shaune looked at his forearm. A message flashed across it from Poppy. *Shit,* he thought. It was a somber reminder that his relationship with Vara was doomed.

MON 07/03/2130
UTOPIAN SOCIETY ALLIANCE HEADQUARTERS
NEW YORK CITY, NY

Shaune walked inside the enhancement lab's operating room. His body shuddered with a euphoria that could be compared to a hearty dose of morphine…or to the weekend he'd spent with Vara. The purity of the lab was spellbinding. The white walls were pristine and filled with miraculous science. Windows cast shimmering light into the room and he felt its energy absorb through his skin.

By tomorrow. nanobots would be installed in his brain and he'd be in a coma for a week as they planted their seeds. These computerized worker bees would pollinate his cerebral cortex with convertible stem cells. From there, his journey to omnipotence would begin. Each day, as more stem cells transformed into brain tissue, he'd grow smarter—far beyond what any human-born genius could envision. Through a window in the lab, he watched researchers guide the assembly of those bots with microscopes.

Some of the other patients hadn't fared so well in these surgeries, but Shaune knew he'd be different. Their psyches had been inferior, fragile. He, however, was destined to be a world leader and the enhancement would only hasten the inevitable. Maybe his newfound intelligence could be used to get Vara on his side and they could rule together. He listened to the humming temperature control fans inside the computers. They sounded like they were singing a glorious song, perhaps even a hymn. Shaune suddenly had an epiphany and paused. How fitting it was that this mechanical music resembled an act of worship, because in some respects he was about to become a god.

TUES 07/04/2130
EARTHSTAR COMMONS AREA
ALTITUDE 550 KM AT 27.200 KM/H

Pokey was singing "My Country 'Tis of Thee" and waving an American flag. Daniel plunged a straw through the lid of his root beer float and glanced at his Epad. He didn't want to be there. JoMarie was on her social page connecting with EPA coworkers down yonder and of course, her family.

For the sake of the two hundred and eighty disadvantaged people who were given a new lease on life, Daniel promised himself that he would do his best. Casey had bugged the hell of out Nielsen to go and of course, he got his way. The dog would be flying in with the mission leader for dinner. *That's what Nielsen gets for starting this.*

The light beam Daniel had seen in that long-range microscope in May still haunted him. He'd run the images through the AI programs with no success. The possibilities generated by the computer were the same ones he'd already thought of. A blasé woman at NASA had told him that yes, the beam was there, but whatever the light molecules were, they appeared inert and didn't seem to be doing anything bad.

Daniel sniffed out a chuckle. That was some scientific explanation—they weren't doing anything *bad.* The woman had added that while NASA was busy working with Russian and Chinese space agencies on Earthstar issues, someone would investigate the phenomenon when they were able. Knowing a blow off when he heard one, Daniel accepted that he was on his own.

He scanned the room. The sports bar reminded him of his favorite Saturday nightspot in college. An HV was attached to the wall above the bar and the rows of international flags and neon beer signs made for a pleasant ambiance. Except for the football-sized robots flying around with the words, "SAFETY GUARD" painted on their sides.

The six dangling legs and little wings on the bots made them look like overgrown insects. Daniel wondered what the long, thin back end of the body was for. They were security bots, so it was probably some type of weapon. Turning back to the HV, he tried to ignore them.

Daniel remembered back in May when he told JoMarie that he thought the People's Party had a scheme going on. She'd told him to present his data, but then they'd got so busy trying to make the Earthstar demagogues happy that he wasn't able to research the possibilities. He wondered if he'd just chickened out, paralyzed with the fear that he was nuts like his father.

A robot numbered SG401 flew in front of him and landed on the table next to his root beer float. It turned a camera lens eye at him. Daniel tapped JoMarie's wrist.

"These things are screwed," he said, making a face at the machine.

JoMarie looked at the bot and shrugged. "They're supposed to be helpful. I think they're pretty. Their appearance is modeled after the yellow-winged darter, a captivating orange and yellow dragonfly."

"My opinion is that they're nosy and ugly," Daniel said. "And this one seems to have latched onto me."

"Maybe it's practicing," JoMarie said. "Each world leader gets a personal Safety Guard and five service workers share one."

"Another waste of money."

"Actually it's not." JoMarie motioned to the other bots floating in the room. "They save money in the long run because the guards work for free and have an estimated thirty-year useful lifespan. They perform common tasks like minor cleaning, making sandwiches, and pouring drinks."

"I'm still waiting to be impressed."

"They can also self-sterilize and inject medication, as well as perform CPR," JoMarie added.

“That I’d like to see.” Daniel watched SG401 stare at him. He knew it had to be processing something in that weird little body.

“You knew the Safety Guards would be observing us during our visit as part of their training,” JoMarie said.

“This one’s a pest, snapping its mechanical claws and staring at me.” The robot started circling him. Daniel blew a raspberry and flipped his middle finger at it.

JoMarie laughed. “I’m not fond of them, either. After this week, the mission can focus more on Phase II.”

A man wearing a DHS lab coat over his suit walked toward Daniel. “Excuse me, are you Daniel Griffin from Unity Station?”

“Ugh, yeah,” Daniel said.

“I’m Kenneth Farrell from DHS’s Automated Surveillance Division. In case you’re unaware, the use of hard profanities is prohibited in Earthstar.”

“I didn’t know,” Daniel said, “but I also didn’t swear.”

“The *use* of hard profanities is prohibited, not just saying them. You gave your Safety Guard the finger. That’s the same as saying the word.”

Daniel could see JoMarie staring at the HV and trying not to laugh. “Okay. So what’s a hard profanity compared to what I assume is a soft one?”

“A hard profanity is forbidden by the UN. Soft profanities, as you call them, are permitted though not recommended.” Farrell lifted his Epad. “I sent you the forbidden words for your review.”

Daniel reviewed the list of c-words, d-words, and f-words scrolling down his Epad screen. “I guess I won’t get to say much.”

“Not if you lived here,” Farrell said. “For Earthstar residents, the use of prohibited words and gestures are tracked. After two warnings in a month, the third offense results in a fine—strike three as in baseball.” The guard pointed to the mechanism. “Also, SG401 didn’t appreciate that you were making faces at her. She doesn’t like to be teased.”

Seeing JoMarie looking the other way and now fully laughing, Daniel shook his head. “You’re telling me this machine has feelings and is assigned a gender?”

Farrell patted the top of the machine and Daniel flinched when it cooed like a dove. “Their AI programs,” Farrell continued, “give them the ability to respond to verbal and electronic commands. A Safety Guard protects her assigned resident or residents. They have the ability to sense danger and attack when detecting threats. They also monitor their residents and determine if they are violating rules."

Daniel felt a cloud of big brother pouring over him. "Why would any world leader want their behavior to be monitored? They sure don't do that on Earth."

"They don't here, either," Farrell answered. "But since they don't trust each other and are in such close proximity, it was an agreed upon concession—a way to keep each other in check."

"Who keeps the robots in check?"

"I do," Farrell said, "along with a group of international programmers."

Daniel watched SG401 clean the table in front him and toss the wipe in a trashcan.

Farrell watched the bot and smiled. "They're in practice mode, helping clean and identify forbidden activity."

"Nice." Daniel turned away and rolled his eyes.

"I authored the AI program that guides their functions. This is their first encounter in a real world situation. I got two kids at home and frankly, I feel like these are my adopted children."

"Congratulations," Daniel said dryly. "Do you have any cigars?"

Farrell's serious glare broke and he laughed. "No smoking up here except in a reserved area of the viewing room. The bot's official name is the M80. Some of my programmers call them Mateys, like a mate or spouse. They follow you around, record everything you do, then bring up bad stuff at their convenience. I refer to them as female because they sometimes have mood swings."

JoMarie turned to Farrell and shook her finger at him, saying, "Excuse me?"

"Only some women," Farrell said in obvious damage control mode. "And men are often much worse. There's no Matey as obnoxious as most of us guys. They're just a little unpredictable. That's what I meant."

"I guess that's better," she said.

SG401 landed on the table next to Daniel. Fixating on the bot, he said, "So it's a snitch, a nag, and carries a grudge. Will it watch me when I go to the bathroom, too?"

Farrell nodded. "Yes, until she determines you're not evacuating weapons or explosives. Then she exits and waits outside the door."

"It exits?"

"She respects privacy," Farrell said. "Her legs are equipped with various metal tools, lasers, and remote keys that can access any authorized area."

"I'll watch my language."

"No harm done," he said, shaking Daniel's hand. "I sent a business card to your Epad in case you have any questions. If you're interested in having Safety Guards on Unity Station, I can probably get you some at a discount."

"I'll pass," Daniel said.

JoMarie smiled at Farrell. "I think our mission leader Dr. Nielsen might like having some of those around."

Daniel glared at her and shook his head. *He'd program them into micromanaging mini-Nielsens. Please, no.*

Captain Farrell turned back as he walked to his post. "Have him contact me. I should also warn you not to make her mad. She's loaded with tranquilizer bullets and other drugs."

"They have the capacity to be vengeful?" Daniel asked as Pokey opened Farrell's eCard. He read a summary of the captain's credentials and Safety Guard information.

"Hell hath no fury," Farrell said. "During our test runs some people were zapped after cursing and swatting at them. The Safety Guards are only supposed to do that if the person they're assigned to is physically threatening. One dart will knock a person out for an hour. I had to tweak the programming a bit. I'm not sure if they're one hundred percent fixed, but improper dosing hasn't happened in a while."

Captain Farrell walked away and followed one of the oversized insects. He beamed like a parent at his newborn progeny.

Daniel spun around to JoMarie. "Why did you have to tell him that Nielsen might want those things on Unity?"

"I couldn't help it. Could you imagine them following the animals and Matt around?"

"That would be pretty funny," Daniel said as he imagined the dogs, who despite their human intelligence, instinctively barked at anything unfamiliar. "Luckily, Nielsen's probably too cheap to buy them."

JoMarie looked at Daniel with a pained face. "Even without the bots and world leaders, I could never live here and leave my kids and grandson on the surface. I'd even feel bad leaving my mom behind."

Visualizing Hannah in her crib and later in her Tinkerbelle bed, then finally in her urn, Daniel gulped down his ache. "As for me, I don't have anyone to worry about. But when I watch fieldworkers, housekeepers, and their loved ones boarding the shuttle in Florida, I want to believe that life will be better for them." His eyes locked onto the orange and yellow body of SG401 levitating by his shoulder.

A few minutes later, Daniel turned to watch the HV as it began displaying NASA's Kennedy Center. Cynicism rose in his throat as the US Air Force band played "The Star Spangled Banner," followed by the Russian Federation and Chinese national anthems, and capped by the eerie "Hail to the People's Party." The first citizen's shuttle was on the runway, ready to transport residents to Earthstar. Streams of fireworks exploded against an indigo sky.

"I hope the situation remains stable," JoMarie said.

Pondering the ruthless ambition required for Earthstar's birth, Daniel sucked up the last of his root beer float. SG401 grabbed the cup, floated across the room, and set it in a bus tray. His gaze followed the robot as it returned to him. *Why doesn't this thing find someone else to irritate?*

Daniel tapped his fingers on the table. "Are you suspecting that if the situation on Earth worsened to the point where the world leaders' buddies were in jeopardy, the disadvantaged citizens would be replaced?"

JoMarie shook her head sadly. "Yeah."

"That's been my thought all along."

"Mine too," JoMarie said.

Turning to the screen, Daniel watched two slim, wide-eyed African teen boys step inside the Earthstar transport shuttle with a man who was probably their father.

"Matt does have a point about Charlie D.," JoMarie said.

Daniel felt his eyes bulge a little. "You aren't saying he's right."

"What he says is fact," JoMarie answered. "The difference is that I believe people shouldn't be left to fend for themselves and die. He accepts that as part of the system."

"You scared me for a second," said Daniel.

JoMarie patted his shoulder. "You know me better than that."

On the HV, the shuttle's doors closed. The engines fired and the craft rose up into the sky. On the sidelines, family and friends cheered and waved. Daniel watched the shuttle depart from its home planet's grime, filth, and pessimism. Footage inside the craft displayed passengers clapping when they saw Earth's arc form under them.

Daniel bit his lip, skeptical and worried. "Those whooping it up on the surface haven't figured out that they're fish trapped in a terrestrial bucket, squirming to escape, only to be slapped by the fins of other desperate fish."

"And you wonder why you have a reputation for being a downer?" JoMarie said.

"Consider me a realist. The shuttle will be here in two hours. You ready to be a greeter?"

JoMarie nodded. "Yes and I feel a semblance of success. How about you?"

"A little," Daniel said, "but I'm afraid that the only reason we're here is to make the mission look good and schmooze the underprivileged folks who'll be living here." He remembered the Public Hall meeting and the protestors. Shifting uncomfortably in his chair, he noticed that SG401 was still watching him.

"To some degree that's true," JoMarie said. "But I plan on staying in contact with the people I gave my slots to. I want them to be happy here."

"Me, too," Daniel said as he looked around the pub. "Are Matt, Sharon, and Robert getting here soon?"

JoMarie pulled her Epad from her purse and read her mail. "They arrived five minutes ago and are getting cleared in security. Chistyakov is here and of course, President Clemens."

"With his *Galax.net* girl?"

"Probably so, but don't be too rude. She may end up as the First Lady."

Daniel laughed at the prospect. "First something, but First Lady? I doubt it."

"And on top of that," JoMarie said, "Dr. Nielsen and Casey will be here shortly before dinnertime."

"That will be interesting," Daniel mused.

JoMarie raised her eyebrows and smiled. "With Casey, it always is."

WED 07/04/2130
EARTHSTAR SHUTTLEPORT
ALTITUDE 552 KM AT 27,210 KM/H

Inside the shuttleport terminal, Daniel turned to one of the HVs. The shuttle was displayed as it prepared to dock in one of five landing ports. Like the smaller Unity shuttles, the craft slid inside the port's transition capsule and the outer seal closed around the fuselage. As the craft pulled fully into the port, the outer seal restored to a flat surface. Gravity, temperature, and oxygen levels were checked. The front seal opened and slid back from the shuttle then receded into the wall. Finally, the doors opened.

Daniel, JoMarie, and the other greeters watched passengers step from the shuttle. Their bodies wavered back and forth as if off balance. Daniel knew they were adjusting from Earth's gravity to a zero gravity shuttle and then back to gravity. Or maybe they were nervous. He would be. Safety Guards floated together forming a large cube in the check-in area. UN officers guided the new residents into lines where they would be introduced to the greeters.

Watching the new arrivals, Daniel bit his lip. These residents would have a final ID verification then a Safety Guard would be assigned to five people. He saw Matt, Sharon, and Robert walk in from the Central Hub. Cal and his NASA group followed, having been invited to attend after fixing the Earthstar laborers' spacesuit problems. Daniel was ready for a spacewalk, but this time he'd hold back on the singing.

Daniel walked with JoMarie to the greeting area of the terminal. Lines of people had formed in front of them and the others. He shook hands and talked with the new residents more than he expected to. A woman and her daughter shook his hand. He recognized them immediately.

"Mr. Griffin," she said, "I am Clair Nabu from Kenya. I have to thank you for donating your slots to me and Larisa. Ever since Larisa's father died we've been struggling to get by."

Daniel couldn't help but notice that the girl was in her early teens, around the age Hannah would have been. "I hope your experience and future here are wonderful for both you and Larisa."

"We'll do everything we can to take advantage of this blessed opportunity," Clair said as she flashed him a big smile.

"I want to be a lawyer," Larisa blurted.

"Keep in touch with me," Daniel said as he emailed her his business card. "And think about a science career. The USRG has scholarships for kids who get good grades."

A Safety Guard floated over to him. "Sir, the residents need to be checked in. Can you please let them through?"

"Oh, excuse me." Daniel narrowed his eyes at the annoying creature.

Ms. Nabu gave him a hug. "Thanks again to you and the USRG scientists, Mr. Griffin."

"Please, no 'mister' anything. It makes me feel older than I already am. Daniel is fine."

"Okay, Daniel. Thank you," she said as she and Larisa walked toward the check-in table. He couldn't help but worry about them.

A group of guards marched in and stood with their backs against the walls. Daniel's stomach tightened and he felt nauseous. This was more than the normal stomach anxiety he'd suffered since he was a kid. This was a Clemens' face on the side of a building reflex, a Clemens at the UN meeting reflex. He suddenly felt like running to Ms. Nabu and Larisa and shouting at them to get the hell off this jail, the compound, Earthstar—whatever. He hesitated when he saw SG401 from afar. He wiped away the sweat that was beading on his forehead.

Daniel remembered his encounters with corrupt police in Africa and the Middle East during his Peace Corps assignments in college. They were not protectors but werewolves. He'd suspected that on clear, cold nights they expelled bloody mist from their nostrils with each breath. These Earthstar guards were of the same cut.

Their void expressions and waxy, blank eyes told Daniel that these clone-like creatures did not distinguish right from wrong. That responsibility was left to their commander. He was convinced more than ever that the Earthstar visionaries and their cohorts, headed by the People's Party of America, were not as godless as many of his contemporaries believed. He saw it in President Clemens at the UN meeting in May and in these police. He was certain that the object of the party's praise and worship lay in the reflections of their Earthstar mirrors.

WED 07/04/2130
EARTHSTAR COMMONS AREA
ALTITUDE 520 KM AT 26,970 KM/H

Daniel sat down in front of his name card. He was placed to the left of Chistyakov, who sat at the head of the USRG table. Service workers from different countries were brought in to wait on everyone and were almost as annoying as the Safety Guards.

Daniel groaned when Casey jumped into the chair next to him wearing his awful tuxedo jacket. He was baffled that Nielsen had brought the dog as a showpiece for the mission. He was more of a distraction than anything.

Casey jabbed Daniel in the arm. "Tell President Chistyakov to stop staring at me."

Pulling his arm away, Daniel sipped on his water. "A lot of people are staring at you. You're a talking dog."

"He's giving me dirty looks." Casey pulled a can of his canine protein drink from a satchel clipped to his jacket.

Daniel looked over and saw Chistyakov now standing by the table watching them as he talked to his security officers. "I bet it's the tuxedo coat. He's probably getting flashbacks of Public Hall."

Slurping on his drink, Casey pushed his bottom lip out. "Baloney."

Daniel folded his arms. "You're just stuffed with melodrama."

Casey barked at SG401 as it floated around the table. "I'm not melodramatic. And I don't like those things either. They remind me of the giant horseflies that buzzed around the evil lab that I was held captive in."

"They do resemble some type of insect-lobster hybrid," Daniel said wondering if the Safety Guards had the same capacity for hate as some of the people they'd be watching over.

As Casey dumped a pile of green olives on his appetizer plate, Daniel studied the dignitaries mingling in the convention hall. Soon they would all have to endure President Clemens as the keynote speaker in exchange for a meal and Earthstar tour. Squeezing a lemon in his water, he resisted the urge to drink a beer, which might reveal too much of his candid nature.

Dr. Nielsen and JoMarie stood at the table's far end talking to Kenneth Farrell, who was demonstrating the Safety Guard's features. Stiffening in his seat, Daniel looked away. *Please don't bring those things over to Unity Station.* To kill some time before the speech, he checked his email and then went onto *Galax.net*.

Robert sat down across from Daniel and swatted at a Matey that was circling his head. "What's up with these flying bugs? This one's drivin' me nuts."

The bot was comical, flying, and buzzing around the senator. "Don't make her mad," Daniel said, laughing. "Their back ends are filled with tranquilizer darts."

"These things are armed?" Robert said. "Why didn't anyone tell me?"

"President Clemens probably forgot."

"I have some good news for a change," JoMarie said to the group as she sat in her designated seat next to Robert. "Dr. Nielsen just told me that Phase I will trickle to a soft close at the end of August. Starting next week we can start working part-time on Phase II. That's without the nights and weekends."

Daniel sighed. "It's about fu…." He stopped as SG401 glided toward him. It slowed down and levitated by his shoulder. "I mean, how delightful that we can finally work on Phase II and Nielsen is learning about these helpful Safety Guards."

Matt dropped into a chair on the other side of Casey and poured a glass of wine. "People are mere ingredients for elitist cuisines," he mumbled.

"Geez, Matt," Daniel said, "and I'm the one known for being a downer."

Casey tossed four olives in his mouth. "So, Matt, are you here to cheer us up as usual?"

"Like I've always said, canine, I didn't grow the lemon trees. I'm just forced to eat the bitter fruit."

"Stop that," JoMarie said. "We owe our constituents our best effort."

"I'm with you guys." Matt gulped down his water. "I gave up my slots yesterday with no regrets. I've been told that two people are coming up from Mexico. This place is too confining for me considering my independent nature."

"You don't want to admit that you did it for charity," Daniel said.

"Part of me did—and then there are the cussing rules."

Thinking of the wax-eyed guards in the shuttleport, Daniel tightened his jaw. "Those language regs are too much."

Chistyakov sat in his chair and raised his wine glass. "Isn't the compound magnificent? The power system is seamless. The USRG and NASA did a great job. Of course, they couldn't have done this without the Russian Federal Space Agency and the Chinese National Space Administration."

"Phenomenal for a few, but not enough," Daniel said. "We have to prove the protesters wrong." He wondered if they could.

Chistyakov set his glass down. "We all knew from the beginning that Phase I was a refuge for a few. As for you my friend, Phase II will make the difference. HEPCOM has approved a camp prototype outside of New Delhi for five thousand people."

Finally, Daniel felt a surge of excitement about the mission and hoped Hannah could hear this. "Thank you so much." He saw JoMarie nodding at him. She must've pushed this through.

"I hope the camps succeed," Chistyakov said. "I'll keep you involved in the process." The Russian leader took a sip of wine before turning to talk to his security team.

Casey cocked his head from side to side, looking at Chistyakov. "That guy doesn't like me."

"Would you stop?" Daniel said, noticing that Chistyakov had gotten quiet and was watching them. "He just thinks we spent too much money making you."

Brushing his paw over the glittery trim on his jacket, Casey smiled. "Some things are priceless."

"I agree, now relax."

Daniel started thinking about funding for future camps. "Mr. Chistyakov, will there be any help on the camps from Clemens?"

"Not a single American dollar," Chistyakov said as he glared at Casey's jacket. "Do I want to know who paid for that?"

Casey pulled a wallet from an inside pocket of his tux. "I did with my salary!"

Chistyakov leaned forward. "Salary for doing what?"

Pouting, Casey popped three more olives in his mouth and didn't answer.

Daniel could tell by Chistyakov's smile that he was teasing Casey a bit and decided to soften things before the dog started blubbering or, worse yet, got mad. He shook the Russian leader's hand.

"Five thousand people? Like the old saying goes, better than a poke in the eye with a sharp stick. In fact, much better. Thanks for giving the camps a chance."

"Speaking of pokes in the eye with a sharp stick," Robert said, "where's Clemens?"

"He's in his quarters with Hortensia, preparing for his dinner speech," Chistyakov answered. "Do you need to talk to him?"

Robert laughed. "I'd rather be poked in the eye with a sharp stick."

"I didn't know her stage name was Hortensia," Daniel said. "Too many syllables. I'm sure the first one will suffice."

"Daniel!" JoMarie shot back. She folded her arms and stared at him. "I'm gonna to talk to Nielsen about how great the M80s would be on Unity Station."

"It was a joke."

"Not a funny one. Maybe Unity does need some vulgarity controls." She grinned at him and headed over to Nielsen.

A faint buzz vibrated Daniel's ears. "Hey, it was there for the taking." SG401 lowered onto the table. Its pinchers opened and handed him a fork. He could only hope that JoMarie was joking about the Safety Guards.

He looked at the bot. "I didn't use a forbidden word. Did you see my fingers do anything? No. Did I say a cussword? No."

The Matey folded its mechanical arms and shook its eyes and antennae at Daniel. Casey had a quizzical look on his face as his gaze followed SG401.

Matt pointed to the machine's back end. "Because of people like you who'd try to get around the rules, programmers installed routines that gave the M80's the capability of identifying innuendos."

"Don't care," Daniel said as he stuck a fork in a couple of Casey's olives and ate them. Casey gave Daniel an offended look and poured shrimp from a nearby bowl onto a second appetizer plate.

"Now you're starting to act like that canine," Matt said. "With his smart mouth, one may start following him."

"Oh bull!" Casey mumbled with a mouthful of shrimp. "You have the smartest mouth of anyone on the mission!"

"But I know when to keep my trap shut unlike you and Daniel. If he'd behave, the Safety Guard would be resting under the chairs like the others."

Daniel laughed. Matt had a lot of nerve and so did SG401. "There's nothing about that giant insect that a good sledgehammer couldn't cure."

"Quite the opposite." Matt leaned past Casey and lifted SG401's left pincher arm. "The outer shell is constructed of a hybrid metal. Donovan told me about the M80s a few months ago. They're only destructible under the heat of a nuclear bomb and are another reason I don't want to live here."

The machine turned its tentacles to Daniel and winked an eye lens at him.

Daniel backed away a little. "I don't care what that bot thinks." Though he had to admit that he did.

"What worries me is that it thinks at all," Robert said.

Casey chased his shrimp down with his protein drink and a swig of water. "Like I've said a thousand times, I'm glad I was born a dog."

Pressing his hands together, Daniel frowned. "Those machines are what happen when a bunch of egotistical...." Searching his mind carefully for an allowed word he added, "Jerks are treated as if they're better than everyone else and start to believe it. Then they don't trust each other because they know how they are."

As Casey sliced himself a giant piece of cheese, he jerked his nose to two sleek young men wearing geometric ties. "That group sure doesn't seem to care much about the Constitution, especially that butthole president."

Daniel saw Sharon walk away from a group of doctors. She sat in the chair next to JoMarie's empty seat and poured herself a glass of fruit juice.

Robert plunged his fork into what was left of the shrimp. "Some of us politicians remember our humble upbringings."

"Not enough of you," Daniel said.

"Money and privilege by themselves are meaningless," Sharon said. "The more a person is at peace on the inside, the less he or she craves on the outside. All we need are staples like food, healthcare, and shelter."

Matt shook his head. "Don't be absurd."

Daniel leaned back, more at ease after SG401 decided to fly under the chair. Despite the hard exterior that Matt tried to project, he had a strong sense of right and wrong. The kid knew that this place was bad news.

Robert clanked his glass against Sharon's. "You're quite insightful, for a rich kid. Most of you aren't bred to do much."

"That's true," she said. "That's why I never got into drug scenes or wild lifestyles like my brother and some of my friends. I kept to myself and knew what I had to do."

"What was it that you "had to do," Sharon?" Daniel said.

"I felt guilty for my family's wealth. I wondered if the coat I wore or the limos I was chauffeured in were purchased by exploiting the destitute."

"Of course they were." Matt shot her a sarcastic look. "That's how everyone gets rich."

"No," Daniel said. "There are plenty of inventors and innovators that earned their money the right way. They just tend to avoid public office."

"Much of the time, Matt's right," Sharon responded. "The mission's my way of giving back to the world whatever my family may have taken."

"You can only own your choices," Daniel said, knowing where she was coming from. "Not someone else's. That includes your family."

"The kids are who I did this for." She smiled. "They're the future."

"I joined this mission to help the kids and poor, too," Robert said. "Everyone knew world leaders would be taken care of. My parents could've taken the spots I passed on, but they decided to stay home so two more people could have a chance at a good life."

Daniel shifted his hands in his pants pockets, trying to ignore the presence of SG401, which had floated back out from under his chair and was circling the table.

"Yeah, I hope the mother and daughter who took my slots have a good life here."

He looked up and again saw some of the human guards' blank faces and his heart sank.

* * *

The shuttleport was quiet. Daniel wandered from JoMarie and the others. He was glad she had been talking to Nielsen about Phase II, but hoped that the mission leader didn't buy into the Matey program. He stared out the windows, waiting for the ride back to Unity Station. He had to admit that the Earthstar tour was impressive. SG401 had finally relented when Farrell called all the bots back to a lab for diagnostic testing. Fatigued from Clemens' self-promoting speech and the magician assistant act from Hortensia, liberation was still a two-hour ride away.

Casey ambled to Daniel and sat next to him. The dog pulled a small bag from his jacket and threw a breath mint in his mouth. "Sorry about throwing up in front of everyone. I think I ruined dinner."

Daniel stifled a laugh. "You sure did. Nielsen should've never pushed you into giving a dinner speech."

"I hope he wasn't mad at me. Did you notice what color his skin was?"

"Winter peach. Or he might have been pale with shock combined with terra cotta. I noticed he left early with Chistyakov. Deep down he had to know he was taking a chance."

Tossing another mint in his mouth, Casey released a loud hiccup and lay on the floor. “I think I ate too many appetizers. Also, when I looked at Clemens he gave me stage fright.”

Daniel squatted down and pet Casey on the back. “Clemens scares me, too.”

For whatever passing appeal he’d felt about living in Earthstar after the mission, the wax-eyed soldiers and their creepy contraptions had pretty much settled the deal—no way.

PART III

TERROR BLEEDS THE SOUL

WED 11/15/2130
SKID ROW
LOS ANGELES, CA

Shaune sensed the bad energy the instant he walked through the door, making him want to escape as soon as possible. But he knew he couldn't. After all the Act Two planning, the day had finally come.

The century-old flat emitted a haunting chill as if sending a message that its lifespan was over and newcomers were not welcome. And that not only included people, but any rodent that happened to find itself impaled between the rusty clamps of the traps scattered throughout the mostly abandoned building. He didn't understand why the Alliance couldn't have rented something better than this shithole.

Tepid air seeped out of a ceiling vent that was stuck half closed. If he hadn't been wearing neoprene body armor, he'd be freezing his ass off. The damp carpet was a spongy mystery and he stepped across it with caution. And while the black, spray-painted windows were dismal, having them clear and being able to look outside was probably worse.

Shaune had to redirect his energy to a better place. His Epad read 23:40. Admiring his reflection in the warped living room mirror, he pulled a fake brown beard from a bag that Clark had brought when arriving a few minutes earlier. He was irritated by the sound of Clark's grumbling as he struggled to put on a wig covered in long red dreadlocks.

Taking a deep breath, Shaune groaned as he pressed on his beard. "Why is getting that mop on your head such a chore?"

The wig slipped from Clark's grasp as he tried to put it on again. "It's too small."

Shaune spun around and snatched the wig off the carpet. He stretched the inner cap to capacity and then forced it on Clark's head. "Use your soon-to-be enhanced brain! The clear part in front goes down over your forehead."

Wincing, Clark rubbed his face. "It's tight. I feel like my head's being squeezed."

"You'll live." Shaune turned back to the mirror. *Advocates are like women*, he thought. *Can't live with them, can't live without them.*

The target would be within Shaune's grasp in less than two hours. The abject poverty of Los Angeles was his best ally. The LA Xpress, Los Angeles' public transportation system, was a pile of shit and in that lay his treasure. This subway train was one of many that were shut down in the early morning due to lack of funding. Infiltrating the underground station would be a cinch, perhaps even a little boring. The security sucked and surveillance was almost non-existent. He was willing to endure the dreariness of it all, however, in order to rid the world of undesirables and move closer to USA leadership.

Turning to view his profile, Shaune was surprised by how his chiseled good looks still stood out. Trying to appear unkempt and unattractive was harder than he expected.

Clark walked up to the mirror, rubbing soot onto his face.

"What's that for?" Shaune said.

"I'm trying to look filthy."

"That black crap looks stupid, faked."

Clark stomped away from the mirror to the plaster coffee table. "If we were really going to be authentic, we'd have to pee on ourselves."

"Not interested," Shaune said. "How about staining our pants with apple juice?"

"Not bitter enough. The vagrants would know the difference."

Shaune looked at Clark and shook his head. He squirted gel on his hand and crunched his beard to make it look matted. *That's better*. He wiped the remaining gel on his torn jeans. "Let's stain our pants with some beer in the refrigerator."

Clark pressed soot on his fatigue pants. "What brand?"

"I requested Ámbar del Diamante."

"Oh," Clark said. "That's too expensive. They can smell different beers."

Shaune felt his face get hot. "Don't be an asshole. If they ask, we'll tell them we stole the damn beer."

Pushing the clumps of hair behind his shoulders, Clark nodded. "That might be okay."

"Now for the ale," Shaune said. He went to the refrigerator and grabbed a bottle of Ámbar del Diamante, unscrewed the cap, and took a few drinks. He tipped the bottle, dribbled beer down his T-shirt and beard then handed the bottle to Clark.

"Thanks." Clark grabbed the beer. He took a drink then poured some on his shirt.

Shaune wiped his hands clean with a Warmwype and then moved his face closer to the mirror. He pressed the USMC lenses into his eyes. "Got your extra peepers in?"

"Did that at home," Clark said.

Backing away from the mirror, Shaune blinked a few times to set the lenses. "Good. We'll need superhuman vision. Who knows what we'll have to walk through."

Clark laughed. "A lot of messed up, disposable people."

"Where's the final status report for the implants?"

"Printed it out from my computer this morning," Clark said. "There's a copy on the coffee table."

Shaune grabbed the papers and scanned over them. He was in awe of the implants. Despite knowing their properties intellectually, he was still mesmerized by their microscopic power. How could an object the size of a quarter hold millions of nanobots, each one filled with millions of bacteria cells? And the bots were cute when enlarged on the screen. They looked like ladybugs.

What was even more captivating to Shaune was how the bots would work after being implanted in the subway's climate control system. Once the air reached a set temperature, the bots would be released from the implants. Programmed to sniff out blood, they'd land. Their venom would soak from their tiny legs and through the skin. Nobody would ever know. He looked forward to tracking the nanobots' movement on his Epad once he and Clark got to his parents' house in LA Valley.

"How far can the bots travel from their release point?" Shaune said. "I don't see that here."

"Page three," Clark answered. "Once released, they have a twenty-four hour shelf life and can travel about a half a kilometer. These will end up all over the place because the cars will transport them into other substations."

"So they will release over three days," Shaune said, thinking about the incubation period.

"Yes. One third will release today and the rest in the following two days when the subway car heater turns on in the morning."

Shaune looked at his trembling hands. His adrenalin was revving up, just like it did the day of GlobeTek. "At what temperature do the bots release after the implants are set?"

Clark pointed to a paragraph in the middle of page four. "Were you too lazy to learn about your own attack? That was in the video you watched."

"I focus on logistics. The menial tasks are your department."

"Once the car holding the implants reaches eighteen degrees Celsius for more than five minutes, the implants start releasing evenly over three days."

"At what time will that happen?" Shaune said.

"About 06:00, after the heaters have been on awhile."

Shuffling in the kitchen and pushing the papers down the drain, Shaune turned on the garbage disposal as a precaution. Reviewing his Epad, he shook his head. Vara had emailed him four times and left two phone messages. She had to accept they were over. He couldn't be involved with someone who wasn't in the Alliance and never could be.

Putting on a tattered army jacket, Shaune turned to Clark. "Does this make me look fat?"

Clark shot him a smirk. "What kind of question is that?"

"I was trying to be funny," Shaune said. "She used to say that to me and I always told her no."

"Vara?"

"That's the one."

“Before you dumped her last month,” Clark said.

Shaune’s face flushed. He needed Clark to help execute this assignment and couldn’t blast him with his pencil taser, which was what he felt like doing. “These types of attacks, even if for the greater good, wouldn’t be her thing. USA leaders would never accept her.”

“Because she’s not a homicidal ruthless bitch?”

“That pretty much covers it,” Shaune said, playing with his beard. “Vara’s an artistic genius, but she has too much sentiment for the inferiors. Too bad she can’t overcome that character flaw.” Feeling a hint of regret, he frowned and wiped wetness from his eyes. *They’re probably still adjusting to the SEAL lenses.*

Pulling on his second-skin gloves, he opened the cryogenic freezer in the kitchen. Clark had hopefully loaded the bacteria into the nanobots right. He grabbed the container with the implants stocked with the bots. He zipped it up in his coat pocket. The box would keep the implants frozen until they were removed.

Tonight was supposed to be unusually cold, 4.5 degrees Celsius. Shaune imagined the heaters warming up the subway cars and the implants releasing the bots. “Too bad the incubation period is three to five days. I can’t wait to see what happens. This is the most sophisticated bio-attack on the public ever.”

“Which has me a little worried,” Clark said. “There’s not a precedent for biologically loaded nanobots being released in random distribution mode. DHS uses them for assassinations, but those bots don’t inject the bacteria unless the DNA they land on matches their target’s genetic coding.”

Shaune was becoming irritated. Clark was backpedalling. “I thought for most immune systems, the strain we’re using requires a hundred hits before infection occurs. Six million passengers ride the Xpress daily and only five percent will be hit that many times.”

Clark nodded. “Assuming it’s the same six million who ride the Xpress daily. I figure at least three hundred thousand people will receive enough hits to be infected. With all the advanced treatments out there, we’re expecting a fatality rate of ten percent.”

“That’s thirty thousand kills on a good day so my goal of twenty should be met. It’s more of a scare tactic than a killing spree.”

“If the expected death rate is higher, we could have a disaster on our hands.”

Shaune was struggling not to be infuriated. Clark was the one who convinced him and Poppy that this was the type of attack that should be done. Now he was acting like a wuss in case something went wrong. This was just as much Clark’s attack as it was his.

“If so,” Shaune said, “the effect of Act Two will increase exponentially, making the takeover even easier. I can’t think of a better place to do this than that sewer.”

Slipping on a jacket, Clark nodded. “I agree, but we’re in uncharted territory.”

Noticing Vara had sent another email, Shaune gripped his Epad tight. “And that’s what makes me a leader and not a follower. I take risks. I make sacrifices. The infection rate was so low in testing that I think our casualties may even come up short.”

Clark stood and checked his pockets. “Got my all tools. Time to find out.”

THURS 11/16/2130
LA XPRESS SUB STATION
LOS ANGELES, CA

Shaune raised his tattered boot in a slight kick. *Yes!* They'd made it past the weapon detectors and five LAPD officers guarding the Xpress. He laughed at seeing the cops in their head protection and gloves. Good thing they were so disgusted by homeless people that they avoided pat downs like the African Plague. His taser and Clark's tools looked like pencils and their second-skin gloves and body armor were completely unassuming.

Following a small group of men, Shaune and Clark headed down one of four escalators that led to the passenger loading area where the homeless were allowed to sleep from 23:00 to 04:00. With the night vision feature in his lenses, Shaune saw better than he wanted to once the two of them reached the bottom floor. He followed Clark as they stepped through several hundred men snoring and hacking in the shadowy cavern. It was hard to believe that in five hours, the beige tile floors and walls would be brightly lit, disinfected, and full of people waiting to board the cars.

A man wearing a red coat and an exposed Bulletaser was breaking up an argument between two hunched over figures that were pawing at each other in some type of scuffle. Shaune noticed that several other men and women were wearing the same coats with badges and carried weapons. He assumed they were unofficial guards that the cops allowed to be armed. Without much police protection, they were forced to self-govern. Lucky for them that would be changing soon.

Flinching as the lenses automatically sharpened his vision, Shaune was disgusted by the Xpress's early morning residents. Except for wearing clothes, which not all of them did, most of the men didn't even look human except for a few minor distinctions in race and age. Some of their faces were covered with overgrown, knotted hair. When their eyes were visible, there was a zombie-like blankness in them. Their bodies ranged from skeletal to bloated, revealing the end product of too many highs and untreated mental illness. Some seemed halfway normal, navigating on *Galax.net* with their Epads. Others were drinking and babbling with each other. In the far corner, his vision zoomed onto couples and women with children. *They must be the poor ones.*

Shaune slid against the wall next to Clark as they got closer to the train. The guttural sound of one guy choking on something was so vulgar that he wanted to shove an implant down his throat to shut him up.

"Clark, are you sure inhaling this crap isn't like ingesting toxic waste?" Shaune said. "I can taste the piss in my mouth."

"That's psychological," Clark answered. "When I was in med school, the smells were sickening to me until my brain learned to shut them out. Plus this is a bad station; the first one past skid row."

Shaune pressed his lips together and breathed through his nose. Smelling the air was a tad better than tasting it. "I can't imagine any place more putrid than this."

"Me neither," Clark said. "We have to turn left now. That's where the train's engines and climate control system are located."

Shaune fidgeted with his beard. "I'm already woozy from inhaling the stench of body fluids best suited for a toilet. Do the cops come in and flush these derelicts out at 04:00?"

Clark shrugged. "Normally 15 minutes before. Boarding starts at 05:00. To be fair, not all of these people are losers. Many of the families are down on their luck. They sleep here and take the Xpress to work and school."

"You think they're down on their luck now," Shaune said, "wait 'til they take the train in a few hours."

Nodding, Clark motioned for Shaune to follow him. "The sad truth is we're probably doing them and the world a favor. For the others who'll board this train at different stops, maybe not so much."

"The important thing is the effect on public morale. We need to create a mindset of fear so that when we take over next year, people will thank us."

"We'll get that," Clark answered. "Now we gotta move past the addict's section and toward the tunnel."

Shaune tiptoed around the men, many of whom were unconscious or sleeping. Clark pretended to stumble then flung a wad of paper currency from his coat pocket. Grinning as the men regained consciousness and leapt into a pile to tussle over the money, Shaune saw that a nice clearing had formed around the train. He headed toward the train cars and then climbed up a ladder that was attached to the first one.

A dwarf-like man with scrawny limbs and a pregnant-looking stomach was sleeping on the top. His long, gray beard draped down his torso, making him look like a hobbit. Clark crawled on the car and Shaune lay down to avoid drawing attention. As he scooted slowly toward the panel cover that led to the train's main air duct of the climate control system, a wind gust carrying the stench of urine and body odor blasted his face. Shaune struggled not to gag. "This place sucks," he whispered. "I'm getting sick to my stomach."

"We didn't have to come," Clark said. "Climbing in the beast's belly was your thing. And because of that I had to go with you."

Sticking his palm in front of Clark's face, Shaune was losing his patience. "Shut up and give me the tool."

Sprawled out like he was drunk, Clark pretended to fumble with something in his pocket. He pulled out the small drill and slapped it in Shaune's hand.

Shaune rolled on his side and set the screwdriver's tip on a bolt. The tool scanned the bolt, adjusted the tip's shape, and started spinning silently in reverse. One at a time the bolts were unscrewed: bolt one—done, bolts two and three—done. The last two came out just as easily. Gently pulling off five bolts, he clenched them in his left hand. Leaving on the last bolt, he shoved the screwdriver in his pocket. He turned the panel cover away from the opening to get a good view of the duct that delivered hot and cold air to the cars. The duct had a diameter of about twenty centimeters. The implants would fit nicely there.

He opened the box and pulled out the frozen implants. He studied them using the zoom feature of his lenses. In a few hours, the caps would rise up a bit and let the nanobots out. Peeling the skin from the implants' adhesive pads, Shaune pressed the first one inside the duct, and then implants two, three…ten.

Suddenly, a young man's bearded face popped up in front of him over the top of the car. Shaune jolted back and blasted him with his taser. The guy dropped on the floor like a trout out of water.

The man sleeping on the car sat up. "What the fuck *is* that?" he bellowed.

"A taser that looks like a pencil," Shaune said. "Some guy tried to grab my ass."

"Not the taser!" The man's voice trembled as he got more irate. "The beer! What's that beer? It's so familiar."

"Ámbar del Diamante," Shaune said.

"Yeah…that's it." The guy's lips spread in a partially toothless smile and he lay back down. "Drank that shit back in nineties. I used to be an actor, lived in Beverly Hills once." He mumbled a few more words before he started snoring again.

"Holy crap," Shaune said. "They *can* smell different beers."

Clark laughed. "That was hilarious. You did a great job handling him."

"The great job I'm doing with the bots will be more rewarding."

"You almost done? I have to run a final diagnostics test on the implants. The piss is starting to make me dizzy, too."

"Just pretend you're back in medical school."

Shaune traded places with Clark and lay on his side. Clark inserted a probe inside the duct and checked each implant. The probe displayed the bots as being on standby until the temperature hit eighteen degrees as planned. He turned the vent cover back over the opening.

"Your turn," Clark said.

Quickly pushing the bolts back in their holes, Shaune tightened them with the screwdriver. "We can't go until the cops clear everyone out, right?"

Clark lay back and yawned. "Not unless we want to be obvious. They'll clear the place in two hours."

"Way too long to smell this, plus I'm starting to get cold."

"Nothing we can do. My Epad alarm's set for 03:30. Let's rest a little."

Shaune closed his eyes. "Hey, if we take a take a deep enough breath, maybe we'll pass out."

"If we're lucky," Clark said.

* * *

Shaune woke up to the screech of fire alarms and cops shouting. He wiped sweat off his face. What the hell was going on? Clark shot up, disoriented, and rubbed his eyes.

Small fires were burning throughout the station. Aiming his lenses at the flames, Shaune realized that people had set trashcans on fire to stay warm. The police were shouting through megaphones for everyone to evacuate due to poor ventilation. Dysfunctional sprinklers dribbled water from the ceiling. Firefighters ran down the escalators and started spraying water on the burning cans. Police were herding large groups of women, children, and older men onto the escalators.

"We need to get out," Clark said. "My Epad's reporting high levels of carbon monoxide in here."

Jumping off the car with Clark, Shaune saw that the other guy hadn't woken up. He was probably better off anyway. They shoved through the crowd toward the escalators.

Suddenly Shaune bowled over. He grabbed Clark's arm. "What the shit is the temperature in here?"

Clark's face went white. Turning his Epad toward Shaune, he closed his eyes. "Almost nineteen."

Shaune slipped out his taser and started zapping people's backs. As they sprung up from the jolts, he pushed forward. He zapped a woman's side. She recoiled and fell against a wall. Reaching the escalator, he grabbed his Epad and navigated to the site that was monitoring the nanobots.

"The implants started releasing the bots twelve minutes ago."

"Oh fuck," Clark whispered. He took a deep breath. "Watch this." He clutched his chest and waved to a firefighter. "My aorta valve is shorting out!" Dropping to his knees he started choking. "I think I'm having a heart attack!"

"No you're not," an LAPD officer shot back pushing them away from the escalators. "Stop acting like a damn baby. The women and kids go first."

Shaune stepped back and grabbed Clark's arm. "Can we stop the bots release?"

"Of course," Clark answered, "from the computer at the apartment."

A firefighter spraying a hose ran down another escalator. "Everyone's going to be fine," he shouted through a megaphone. "Please remain calm."

If they only knew, Shaune thought. A part of him wanted to warn the guy not to go in the passenger area, but he couldn't. He really wasn't interested in killing firefighters, only the surplus people, and if some of the asshole porkers went then that was even better.

"What are we going to do?" Shaune yelled.

Clark's face was red. "You're the one who said just a fraction of a percent would actually die."

"Shut the hell up and push forward!"

The escalators were moving slowly, probably because of the load of people weighing them down. As the stairs finally crawled up toward the early morning air, Shaune peeked at his Epad. The status report display showed that one hundred and twenty thousand bots were gliding into the breeze over them. Not able to look anymore, he shoved his Epad in his pocket. If he lived through this, Shaune promised himself he'd call Vara back and make up with her. He pulled his coat tightly around him and tried to breathe through his nose.

THURS 11/16/2130
LOS ANGELES VALLEY, CA
UNITED STATES AIRSPACE

Shaune noticed that Bernard was unusually quiet as he piloted the Slojet into LA Valley. Clark was asleep a few seats back. The red glow of early morning commuters' brake lights on Interstate 405 crawled in both directions. Shaune glanced at his Epad.

Bernard turned from the cockpit. "You guys really screwed up. You should've paid a couple of USA assassins to plant those things."

"Wouldn't be the same," Shaune said.

Bernard circled the Slojet over LA Valley's runway, which led to a tunnel for the aircrafts. "We'll see what happens."

"Act Two will achieve its goals. That's what'll happen," Shaune said as his Epad started flashing on his forearm. He scoffed at Poppy's mug.

"Hey, Dad, what's the report on Act Two?"

"You know what."

Shaune reclined his seat. "Clark and I pulled off the most sophisticated bio-attack executed on United States' soil. Act Two was a success."

"Success?" Poppy said. "You and Clark may have been infected. This should have been left to professionals. You only had to plan it."

"I am a little worried." Shaune turned to Clark who was snoring with his mouth open as if ready to catch a pop fly from Dodger's

Stadium. "Clark said the strain would infect five percent of the people and kill ten percent of those—so only a half of a percent in total."

"You guys better hope that's the case," Poppy said. "This one has to be small compared to Act Three."

"I know," Shaune said, his sense of destiny solidified. "That one is already in motion and I got some helpers. I'm not into martyr terrorism."

Rubbing his eyes, Poppy yawned. "Remember, your Fat Man's gotta be much bigger than the nanobot attack."

"No worries." Shaune admired his thick fawn-colored hair and blue eyes in the reflection of the plane window. He understood why Vara had trouble letting go. Between his looks, money, and the pending leadership role she didn't even know about, he was a rare catch.

Poppy's eyes suddenly enlarged into two bulging olives. "Shaune, the kills must be controlled. Most antibiotics are useless against this strain of necrotizing fasciitis."

Shaune pulled a large water bottle from the wet bar, his throat still burning from the smoke in the Xpress. "That's the point," he said. "Should I call you Raymond since you believe I failed to inherit your diabolical genetics? Maybe you're not Poppy after all."

"Don't be a jerkoff," Poppy said plainly. "Regrettably, I am. Your DNA was tested before you were born."

"What I'm saying is that if all the infected people had to do was visit the corner drugstore or *Galax.net* to be cured, there'd be no impact. This strain isn't contagious."

"If we kill half of LA, we'll be sunk," Poppy said. "Remember the outrage when you torched the daycare center next to GlobeTek?"

Uttering a disgusted sigh, Shaune took a large gulp of water. "When did you become benevolent to the plight of mongrel offspring?"

"What did I say about being a jerkoff? We want fear, not fury."

"The fatalities should be twenty thousand, max, maybe a few hundred thousand injured—a drop of water in that sludge pot of a city. Remember when we tested scenarios with an AI program and then on the Brazilian kids? The kills came within the expected range."

Poppy's pupils receded to small pins as they struggled to grasp the simple explanation. "As you say."

Small rocks pelted the Slojet as it lowered to the ground. The jet levitated at the LA Valley checkpoint. "There's another damn meteorite storm starting up. We need to get underground."

"You're not flying the plane," Poppy said. "Let Bernard worry about that."

"We have to exit the jet for the drug and weapons search."

"Fine. Bernard and others will be observing if anyone's on your trail. I'm concerned about DHS after you left that statue at GlobeTek."

"I'll be here in LA Valley, and then I'm heading to Socorro on Monday for Thanksgiving." Shaune suddenly thought of Vara in a black leather teddy.

"After you left behind that statue at GlobeTek, I should ram a turkey drumstick up your ass when you get there," his dad said.

Shaune was tempted to hang up, but figured he could be risking his health. Even Poppy had limits. "Look Dad, I'm sorry. You're overestimating law enforcement. They're only gettin' a paycheck."

"Some of them have pretty big egos, maybe even bigger than yours."

"I doubt it. Bernard, open the door. I'm getting out."

"Why?" Bernard said. "The rocks are getting bigger. We've been given the clear to stay in the plane while it's being searched."

Realizing that he and Vara's long-term possibilities were nil, Shaune grumbled. "I'm gonna visit the chicks loitering by the coffee shop."

"You should stick with Vara," said Bernard.

Poppy's voice rose to a new tenor. "Shaune! Focus on the bigger plan."

"Dad, I need to go. I have a chance to get laid."

Poppy's tone was insensitive to Shaune's plight and even a bit frightening. "Screw whoever you want, but don't screw your tribe." The jet door slid open and Shaune stepped down the stairs. A young brunette in a miniskirt was pressing her body against the shop's door. He could see from the reflection in the plane's windshield that Bernard was giving him a dirty look. So everyone thought he was an asshole. What was new? *Time to move on.*

Shaune waved the woman over. "Of course not, Pops. Never."

MON 11/20/2130
UNITY SPACE STATION
ALTITUDE 417 KM AT 26,990 KM/H

Daniel stretched his arms and took a deep breath. He sat in a chair at the last table he'd unfolded for the Thanksgiving lunch then took a brain freezing slurp from an iced mocha. Over ten months of the mission had passed, three of those working on Phase II. Finally something was being done. The AI programs were doing a better job than in the early months, but Daniel wondered if it were cheaper to use human logic. The software was continually being upgraded, patched, and updated.

He thought of the prototype camp's success. The camp in India was working well and Chistyakov was expanding the program. There was still plenty of work to go around and plenty of unemployed people to do it.

JoMarie sat at the table with him. "When did you mail the entrée requests to the kitchen?"

"This morning around six."

"This morning?" She laughed. "What's that?"

"Dunno. Seems like midnight twenty-four seven."

"I had to ask about the email," JoMarie said. "I know how you are."

"I forwarded a list of the ninety-six responses I got out of the hundred and five who signed up. The ones who didn't answer will have to take what's left."

“That’s a high attendance rate,” JoMarie said. “Many of the scientists and maintenance crew aren’t American so I figured they’d be indifferent to Thanksgiving.”

Daniel checked his email and then put the Epad on his forearm. “I guess the free food and four-day weekend has something to do with it.” He frowned as his holiday spirit slipped. “What do you think of getting even more help from the masses to clean the environment? The harder we work, the more I realize that this mission can only do so much. The idea’s churned with HEPCOM for some time.”

“Sounds good,” JoMarie said. “Maybe you can organize it on a larger scale. Meanwhile let’s get the tablecloths and set out the silverware.”

Setting his mocha on his chair, Daniel pulled gold tablecloths from a box on the floor. He spread the cloths on the tables while JoMarie followed behind him with orange napkins and silverware.

“I wish we weren’t celebrating Thanksgiving on Monday,” he said.

“We have to,” JoMarie responded as she set a stack of tablecloths on a chair. “Most of the researchers are leaving tomorrow for family time.”

His aloneness coming to light, Daniel nodded. “Oh, yeah. I had no such plans, so I didn’t think about it. Plus, my December funk season will be here in a couple weeks. Maybe I can spend Thanksgiving organizing a workforce of billions, an early Christmas gift for Hannah.”

“I’m going home Wednesday morning,” JoMarie said. “You’ll be having dinner with me and the gang. And that includes the USRG animals. You need to make this holiday season different and be happy.”

“Mama Kim gonna be there?”

“Where else would she be?”

“You guys getting along better?”

“She’s fine for now,” JoMarie said. “She’s always cheerful around the holiday season.”

“I can’t stop worrying about power abuse coming from that damn Earthstar,” Daniel said. He grabbed silverware and helped JoMarie set the tables. “You know what I think of the leaders there.”

“They’re probably megalomaniacs like you suspect,” she mused. “But those have been around since humanity’s humble beginnings.”

"This bunch can do a lot of damage with twenty-second-century technology."

"You still don't know if there's a grand conspiracy or if they're egomaniacal at the individual level."

Daniel saw Jake and the two other counselors walk in the commons area. He realized that he hadn't had a session in over a month. He'd make an appointment after lunch.

"I can't help but think they have a plan," Daniel said as his stomach growled from the aroma of baking bread. "And after I eat, maybe I can figure out what it is."

JoMarie folded her arms. "Don't distract yourself from the mission and remember to pack your things."

Pokey released a reminder beep on Daniel's Epad. He looked at the memo and his shoulders dropped. His memory seemed to be eluding him lately or was it the other way around?

"Shit! I promised Nielsen a detail outline on the camp expansion for South America by Monday. Gotta work this weekend. I'm not giving him or Chistyakov any excuses to blow this off."

JoMarie looked up from setting the tables. "You're pushing yourself too much. If you're not coming for Thanksgiving then you need to come over for Christmas, unless you're gonna have dinner with your parents."

"I may visit them in January, so Christmas is good." Daniel centered a tablecloth on a table. "Maybe by then I'll find out what that light spearing out of the ocean is. Nobody else seems to care."

"Only immediate threats are being addressed," JoMarie said. "My guess is that it's military, so you won't find out much."

"I'm gonna track it anyway."

"Okay, but finish the tables first."

* * *

Robert exited the galley carrying a plate capped with a transparent dome. Casey and Rushton trotted past him and out of the dining hall with molded turkey legs in their mouths. Cindera and Kosmo followed with turkey sticks.

Lifting the lid off the plate, Robert took a deep sniff. "This smells like Thanksgiving dinner from when I was a kid. I'm glad NASA brought in volunteer chefs." Setting the lid back on the food he shook his head. "It's still strange to me how meat is grown in labs."

"I guess that's more humane," Daniel said. "Chasing something down or raising it for food does seem lowbrow." He looked at his Epad. Twenty minutes to noon. "JoMarie, do you know where the hell Donovan is? He and Matt were supposed to be here a half hour ago to set up the HV."

"Last night at dinner I heard them mentioning the pub. Can you call them?"

"Where are the Mateys when you need them?" Daniel pressed the icon on his Epad to call Matt. As he was sending his call, he looked up and saw Donovan run past JoMarie. Matt followed wearing a rumpled pair of pants and a t-shirt.

Daniel was instantly irritated. "Hurry up! People are lining up outside the door."

Donovan thrust a mock kung fu kick at Daniel and kept walking. He grabbed a pair of small speakers, his eyes darting around for wireless interfaces.

"Hurry up," Daniel said, stuffing his Epad in his pocket and following Matt to the HV. "The parade starts at noon. Did you guys get drunk last night?"

"Parade?" Matt laughed. "Are you getting old or what?"

Daniel turned to answer, and then heard Robert talking on his Epad as he walked toward them.

Robert's voice trembled. He motioned Daniel and JoMarie over. "Not another one, not again."

"What's going on?" JoMarie said as she ran toward Robert.

"Call from DC." Robert wiped his eyes. "We had a terrorist attack in Los Angeles with biological agents. AP's sending the story to *Galax.net*."

Daniel ran to the equipment. "C'mon, Matt and Don! Get this running!"

He helped Donovan and Matt position the speakers' wireless ports toward the HV's receptor. Researchers pushed inside the dining hall and stood around the screen. A *Galax.net News* icon rotated in the center. The image expanded then faded. Daniel ran back to Robert and JoMarie who were now standing with Sharon. He stared in horror at the text scrolling down the screen and listened to a male newscaster read the text aloud.

> *At least one hundred and fifty thousand people are dead and five hundred thousand are fighting for their lives from a biological attack in Los Angeles, California.*
>
> *An unknown strain of Streptococcal Exotoxin, also known as necrotizing fasciitis and the flesh-eating bacteria, was dispersed by nanobots stored in implants placed in the main ventilation system of the skid row subway train cars. the nanos were transported to other parts of the city where they infected more victims.*
>
> *It is still uncertain if this strain of the disease is contagious, but the standard flesh-eating bacteria are not. Anyone who has ridden the LA Xpress in the past month should be tested immediately, even if asymptomatic.*
>
> *Without the treatment of a rare antibiotic combination, this condition usually leads to death. Check Galax.net for local school gyms where emergency workers are testing for infection.*

Images displayed on the HV. Daniel covered his face with his hands and then slowly spread his fingers and looked through them. The screen's light pixels had evolved into evil, solidifying to images of varnished brutality.

An outside view of Cedars-Sinai Hospital displayed and then changed to the emergency room. Daniel turned away and JoMarie gripped his arm. Hannah had died in a hospital hooked up to wires, hoses, and machines.

Looking back at the HV, Daniel took a hard, painful swallow. A frail older man cupped his arm around his sore-covered wife. A muscular Hispanic man writhed on the floor, twisting his half-consumed arms as he begged for relief. The footage switched to the hospital morgue. Shrink-wrapped bodies were stacked on shelves. The wrapping machine whirred as workers in hazmat suits encased the dead in plastic cocoons.

"There's no forbidden Earthstar word obscene enough for this!" Daniel said.

Sharon's eyes were soaked from emotion. "Many survivors will struggle with simple tasks. Much of the lost tissue will never be restored." She looked down as if defeated already. "Frankly, we don't have the resources to help them all."

Fighting to stay calm, Daniel knew he had to remain in an elusive state between the conjoined worlds of bravery and paralyzing fear.

Fixating on the HV, Sharon's face hardened into a stoic frown. Daniel figured she must have switched into her physician mode. "My African Plague Intellipatches are loaded with the newest nanobots," she said. "They're very effective at traveling in the bloodstream and targeting only bacteria. Donovan's team really helped with the programming."

JoMarie eye's burned with resolve. "That's right. Those nanos work very well. We will not let evil win."

Less certain about success than JoMarie, Daniel's gaze veered to Sharon. "Do you know for sure if your patches will work with necrotizing fasciitis?"

Sharon pulled a tablet from her pocket and expanded the screen. "The patches should work on any bacteria, provided the right meds are loaded. I'm calling Cedars-Sinai and offering my assistance."

Robert hugged Sharon. "I'll see what I can squeeze out of Congress to help LA and with this group, I will be squeezing."

Staring at the HV, Daniel could sense the People's Party and Victor Clemens in the equation, but he wasn't sure why. He did know that for them, the 'surplus' population was an inconvenience.

JoMarie was watching Daniel as if she knew what he was thinking. She gently nodded as if to say his suspicions were possible. He scoffed when he noticed Matt slouched against the wall, half asleep. His generation needed to do a little better than that.

Donovan strutted to Sharon. "What do our Intellipatches do to bacteria?"

Sharon forced a half smile and gave him a high five. "Kill! Kill! Kill!"

"Let's go to LA and kill, kill, kill the necrotizing strep!" he said.

Daniel turned to the narrator's voice on the HV that started up again.

Doctors on the surface are pleading with LA Valley city officials to ship broad-spectrum antibiotics to the surface. Due to residents' fear of infection, the request was denied until more information about the strain is available.

Robert sat in a chair and stared at the floor. "How did we end up in such a grave state? How did our world end up like this?"

Daniel wasn't ready to make his concerns public knowledge. Even if the Party was responsible, the public had to be accountable, as well. He remembered an old quote: *In a democracy, people get the government they deserve.* Whoever said it was right. That was, if the United States was still a democracy.

* * *

Standing in the Thinkers Room, Daniel read the time on his Epad—18:54. His ulcer pangs had hit a new high and his Thanksgiving meal was left almost untouched. Robert and JoMarie would be showing up in six minutes to meet with him on Phase II.

The LA attack made Phase II even more urgent. The US public's morale was below zero, and the global outlook wasn't much better. Robert was a key person to bring to his camp. If the senator could get funding to treat the flesh-eating bacteria victims, maybe he could get a bonus for Phase II. Daniel would ignore JoMarie's looks if they emerged and say what he had to say. Thanksgiving was three days away and the United States and the rest of the world had less and less to be thankful for.

Robert walked in carrying a basket filled with Christmas cookies wrapped in plastic. He waved at Daniel and then sat down. JoMarie followed and stood between them.

"Daniel, pack your bags for an overnight stay. You and I are leaving for Los Angeles."

MON 11/20/2130
LOS ANGELES VALLEY CITY GATES
LOS ANGELES, CA

Walking next to JoMarie, Daniel looked up at Slojets circling overhead. A towering electrified chain link fence topped with razor wire barricaded the top of the underground city. LAVPD and LAPD officers paced the interior. A group of what looked like tens of thousands of people surrounded the fence.

In the distance, a tall male police officer waved at them.

"Is that our escort?" Daniel said. He watched JoMarie browse through her Epad's past calls. A man with a military crew cut, blue eyes, and square jaw flashed in her screen with the name "Officer James Harrison" at the top.

"I can't tell from here, but nobody else would be looking for us," she answered.

A group of kids started throwing rocks at the fence to make it spark. Street vendors and music made for a post-terrorist attack carnival. Daniel watched National Guard tanks trek the streets to control what seemed to be, with the exception of some rouge electricity, an anemic crowd. The spotlights from media and police Slojets reflected off people's faces, making them look like sickly porcelain masks.

"Is it possible to feel nostalgia for angry protests? I'd rather have people pissed off like they were at the UN."

“Be comforted that the crowd outside of Cedars-Sinai will be much nastier,” JoMarie said. “One good thing is *Galax.net*’s reporting that Unity Station researchers are working to mass produce the necrotizing strep Intellipatches.”

“So everyone knows about Donovan and Sharon,” Daniel replied. “But are they set up to fail? The broad-spectrum antibiotics are gone, so they’re stuck filling the bots with standards.”

“Sharon will make them work. Maybe their efforts will show the USRG’s goodwill.”

“Is that why Nielsen allowed them to leave the mission for Cedars-Sinai?” Daniel asked, feeling a hint of suspicion, “To make the mission look good, like being greeters on Earthstar?”

“Sharon insisted on going and Nielsen didn’t hesitate.”

“What about us? We could’ve visited LA Valley through *Galax.net*.”

“We’re here to tour LA Valley’s life support systems,” JoMarie said, her face blank and uncomfortable. “We’re gonna see if their technology can be incorporated into our mission.”

Daniel assumed that there was probably more to it, but JoMarie had no control over what Nielsen did. “So we’re here to work on Earthstar?”

“Yes and no,” JoMarie said. “We’ll discuss the whole thing later. But for now I can tell you this. Since LA Valley’s underground, using natural resources is a challenge. Nielsen sent us hoping to improve the terrestrial systems where resources are also limited. And if Earthstar can benefit, then that’s fine, too.”

“Sounds fishy.”

Letting out a frustrated sigh, JoMarie walked toward the cop and waved. “Most of the researchers are on holiday leave. He figured sending us now wouldn’t interfere with the mission. I’ll probably stay on the station this weekend and reschedule my time off.”

“I guess that makes sense,” Daniel said. “Still, Nielsen didn’t care if he ruined the time you had planned with your family.”

“No one forced me to sign up and there is work to do.”

“He could’ve been more considerate.”

JoMarie laughed. “One of his strong points.”

Daniel and JoMarie maneuvered through layers of law enforcement and shook hands with their police escort. *Definitely a military veteran*, Daniel thought. The US Army insignia tattooed on his forearm substantiated that. Just like General Griffin.

"Nice to meet you Ms. Sanford and Mr. Griffin," the officer said. "I'm LAPD Sergeant James Harrison, but please call me James. As you well know, LA's had a horrific week."

"Evil never ceases to surprise me," JoMarie said. "Any progress in the investigation?"

"Not yet, but whoever it is better move to another planet."

"We probably won't be that lucky," Daniel commented.

They approached the LA Valley entrance and James submitted his badge and DNA to an LAVPD guard. The guard nodded and then reviewed authorizations on a computer screen for Daniel and JoMarie's visit. Their DNA was scanned and the metal gates of LA Valley slid open.

"Most people hate the police right now," James said. "So you may get jeered for being seen with us."

As they walked inside the fence, Daniel noticed that the faces in the crowd seemed to have gotten whiter. Some were mottled with sores. Others had bandages wrapped around deformed limbs and a few were missing arms. Soon to be dead. *Maybe already dead.*

"The reason the public resents the police," Daniel said, "is because they see you as working for the other side. LA Val has more security right now than the nuclear power plants."

"I'm not in the mood to be a cop tonight, at least not a bad cop," James replied. "Most of us feel like public enemies."

"I understand that feeling." Daniel stared at the ground.

"You're following orders to stop riots," JoMarie said to James. "If you weren't here, people would try to storm LA Valley. Thousands more would be killed."

Daniel noticed that the LA Valley signs that flashed on HV soap operas and nighttime dramas had gone dark. He looked up as they walked under the huge solar panel structures that bordered the two kilometer-square sky window that topped LA Valley. LAPD units were parked under the structures. Police were sleeping in a few of the cars. Slojets shot armor-piercing tranquilizer darts at people wearing rubber suits who were trying to scale the fence.

James led them to a security station outside one of the city's underground entrances. "I tell my kids, who I don't see enough, that police work is for the public benefit. What good does that do them?"

"I'm sorry," JoMarie said. "Serving the public can be a pretty tough life."

Motioning to a security guard, James frowned. "I don't mean to complain. This is my third day sleeping in a patrol car. Usually I like being a cop. Maybe by morning I'll feel like a public servant again."

Daniel turned to the crowd. They knew that broad-spectrums were below. Everyone knew. "They're afraid of being next. People are dying by the thousands every hour."

James nodded. "Yeah, and I'm guarding their cure."

"Protecting the elites, in their eyes," Daniel said.

The crowd began to chant. "Let the people live! Save us! Save us!"

One woman's voice seemed to chime above the rest as if she had a megaphone. She was staring at Daniel and pumping her fist in the air.

Daniel tapped JoMarie's shoulder. "I'll be back in a minute."

"What are you doing?" JoMarie winced at him.

"I couldn't do this at the UN but I can now. I have to say something."

JoMarie sighed. "What for?"

"Let him go," James said. "He has to be back in fifteen minutes. It'll take that long for us to get final approval for the tour. Maybe he can calm her down. She's been leading chants all night."

Maneuvering around the cops and toward the protesters, Daniel whipped around to the screech of sirens and brakes from across the street. A bus with an LA County logo pulled alongside a group of apartments. A queue of people wearing hazmat suits jumped onto the curb and headed in the buildings. Some were carrying gurneys. Other workers followed carrying a portable shrink-wrapper.

Daniel approached the fence where the loud woman was standing. She looked healthier than the rest of the crowd and more impassioned. He reached the fence and stopped. Appearing to be in her early or mid-thirties, she had long black hair, and her eyes were brown and almond shaped.

Maybe she's one of the Chinese protestors who hated Clemens after his comments at the May UN meeting.

Her gaze locked onto Daniel as she shouted. "You can make the difference! Use your head. Use your freedom of choice!" She paused and her voice trembled. "Use your conscience."

Other people started gathering around the woman. She waved them back. In their white-mask faces, Daniel could see a hopelessness that he couldn't bear to look at.

"There's nothing I can do about this horror!" Daniel yelled back.

"Yes, there is!" she said.

"The masses need to take their world back. I'm an EPA scientist whose job is to be a part of healing the ecosystem. I can't make people participate in governing, even if it's in their best interest."

"Pardon me for my rudeness," the woman said, her voice softening. "My name is Gwyneth. Let me rephrase. You must take the right action. Do the right thing."

"I'm here to tour LA Valley's life support systems for the Global Restoration Mission. We also have people at Cedars-Sinai developing more advanced Intellipatches."

"You sure the tour isn't for Earthstar?"

"That's not why I'm here and not why I'm on the mission."

Gwyneth's boot jabbed a sleeping mound behind her. "Earthstar, ugh! An escape for the people that caused this mess. Stephen! Wake up. I'm talking to Daniel Griffin, the USRG scientist."

Daniel backed away from the fence. "How did you know who I was?"

"Anyone who's following the mission knows," she said. "A *Galax.net* search results in thousands of hits on you. More on Casey Caldwell, though."

Rolling his eyes, Daniel sighed. "I never do a search on myself so I wouldn't know that. As for Casey, I'm not surprised."

A stout, muscular Asian man with a blonde buzz cut popped up from under a sheet. He squinted and stood up, disoriented, then he stretched and stood next to the woman. He yawned and folded his arms.

"Hey, I'm Stephen. Why did you become a scientist?"

"To improve the ecosystem's stability and to make Earth a safe place to live."

"Tell me I didn't wake up to hear a blurb from an EPA pep rally. Why are you really here tonight? Sounds like you're supporting oppressors."

"My daughter was killed," Daniel said his muscles stiff, defensive. "Nobody cared about selling land saturated with the poison she was exposed to."

Looking him up and down, Gwyneth nodded. "Your passion will lead you down the right path."

"I'll either take the right path or die on the wrong one. While the Global Restoration Mission is being questioned, for me there is no question."

The woman stared at him. "Your daughter is Hannah."

His face tightened as he replied, "I'd say 'was' is more accurate."

Looking at the ground, Gwyneth grabbed the fence. Daniel noticed there were no sparks. "As far as this world is concerned, you are right," she said. "Remember her during the mission to keep you grounded. We don't want you serving only power mongers."

Daniel hesitated. That was all he did half the time. "I believe our leader, as much of a jerk as he can be, is trying to do the right thing."

"That's Dr. Nielsen?"

"That's him." Daniel laughed, wondering if there was a strong word association between Dr. Nielsen and jerk on *Galax.net*.

Gwyneth and Stephen began whispering to each other. Daniel turned away and shook his head. Some opus maker he was.

"I know about Dr. Nielsen and your mission," Gwyneth said. "For tonight, do what you're told. But if you remember nothing else of what I've said, remember this. Your actions will one day have to be based on your own judgment, even when you're opposed."

"You move to the left, you're a villain." Daniel shrugged. "You move to the right, you're a sellout. With all the doom in the world, it's hard to know how to make things good."

Gwyneth's eyes cast a strange glow and her hand touched the fence again without incident. "Doom is subjective. The only things not subjective are the Golden Rule and common sense."

Staring at her eyes as they seemed to change color, Daniel pressed his stomach as it cramped up. He felt trepidation with a bit of childlike curiosity. This woman knew more than she was letting on. "What do you mean?" Daniel demanded. He hated half-ass answers.

"Doom is subjective in your world." She coughed then hesitated. "Excuse me, I mean the world."

Backing away from the fence, Daniel widened his eyes. *What are they?* "Where are you from?"

"The Mohave Desert out by Johannesburg," Gwyneth answered. "I research there with my younger brother, Stephen. We're biologists, always out in the field studying different life forms."

Daniel kicked the dirt and a dust cloud rose around his legs. There was something strange here. "Okay, Gwyneth. As a scientific peer, what does your logic tell you? Am I a public enemy or servant?"

"That will always be up to you."

"I feel like the enemy for even visiting LA Valley."

"Your LA Valley controversy will soon be the least of your problems. One day you'll take a stand against your peers and superiors."

"I could never turn on JoMarie, if that's what you mean," Daniel said. He didn't want to know about some shitty future if that was what this woman was predicting. "She's my boss, but she has also been like a mother to me. Or, as she likes to joke, a youthful aunt."

"There will be no confusion."

Daniel felt someone tap his arm. James and JoMarie were standing behind him.

"Are you ready for the tour?" James said. "I had a feeling you might get stuck here."

Gwyneth either smiled or sneered. "Go on your tour and remember what I said."

Daniel waved a clumsy goodbye to her and Stephen. He walked between James and JoMarie toward the checkpoint.

"That woman gave me the creeps," Daniel said as he took one last peek at the odd twosome. Gwyneth was now mingling with the crowd, hugging people and putting her hand on their foreheads.

Looking back at JoMarie, Daniel's voice trembled. "She seemed to know the future and said I'd turn on my peers. Then, when her hand grabbed the fence, nothing happened."

"She's trying to scare you," JoMarie said. "There are a lot of angry scientists who think we sold ourselves."

“That one’s strange,” James said. “I don’t think she’s dangerous, just a pain in the neck. She probably coated her hand with something to mess with people’s heads. I can do a run on her. What’s her name?”

“Gwyneth. She told me she was a biologist in the Mohave Desert.”

“Does she have a last name?” James asked.

Daniel typed the key words “Gwyneth, Stephen, biologist, Mohave” into his Epad. Ten million hits popped up that had nothing to do with anything. He sighed. “I was too spooked to ask.”

“I wouldn’t worry,” James said.

As they returned to the security checkpoint, they walked toward a blonde woman in her mid to late thirties who was standing next to a dark-skinned man who was wearing an LAVPD uniform.

The woman’s long legs and wavy, shoulder-length gold hair immediately grabbed Daniel’s attention. She was wearing a brown pantsuit under a lab coat. Her fingers squeezed around the handle of a black briefcase. Staring straight ahead, her mouth was stiff, her eyes hardened. The sensual element of her persona quickly evolved into that of a peer, perhaps a superior.

“My name is Dr. Jeanette Sparkman,” she said to JoMarie. “I’m chief researcher at Cedars-Sinai Medical Center. I’m here on instruction from Drs. Caldwell and Nielsen.” She drew an Epad from her coat pocket. Her driver’s license and US citizen card were displayed on the screen.

JoMarie looked at Daniel and then smiled. He was so awful at hiding his emotions.

“LAVPD officer LeRoy Briggs and I,” Dr. Sparkman began, “will be accompanying you on the tour. I practiced medicine and lived in the valley for six months. We’ll visit the life support area, which is located in the municipal building. Hopefully, you’ll get some ideas for healthy living in outer space and resource management on the surface.”

James’s Epad rang from his forearm. He tapped the screen to answer. Daniel saw an older man wearing a police cap appear on the screen.

“Commander,” James said, “I’m escorting the Unity scientists to tour LA Valley’s life support. Did you need someone to cover me while I’m gone?”

“No,” the man grumbled in speaker mode. “There’s enough of you there to invade a small country.” The commander’s Epad disconnected without a goodbye.

“My boss isn’t happy with so many LAPD cops watching the gates,” James said. “He thinks we should be controlling the looters downtown and everywhere else.”

“Me too,” Daniel said.

“We don’t have a choice. We’re here under instruction from the feds.”

Victor Clemens flashed in Daniel’s thoughts. “Not surprised.”

* * *

Daniel and JoMarie followed the rest of the group as they walked into a lit tunnel that led to a large steel door. Officer Briggs pressed his thumb on a glass panel and entered a pass code on a number pad. The doors slid open and then shut behind them.

The room-sized elevator plunged down. Pokey’s eyes bulged at Daniel. The hissing hydraulic sound was unsettling. A camera stared at them from the ceiling and the display showed their declining elevation by meters. In what felt like a few seconds, they dropped to minus one hundred, then two hundred and fifty meters. The elevator doors opened at five hundred meters below sea level. Daniel followed the others into an enormous cavern. The air was cool and moist, perhaps a bit sticky. Even though he’d gone on a brief virtual tour during the shuttle ride from Unity, he was stunned at the technology and government resources that must’ve been used to make the underground structure happen.

After briefly trekking down a sidewalk, Daniel and the others entered a parking lot staffed with LAVPD cops. The lot led to a concrete road that disappeared into a tunnel. They walked to a small car. Officer Briggs waved at one of the cops who slid back the gate blocking the road. Daniel, JoMarie, and James squeezed in the backseat. Briggs and Dr. Sparkman sat in the front.

Officer Briggs pulled onto the road and drove through the tunnel. A few cars passed in the other direction. The tunnel was well lit but steep and had no end in sight. Daniel closed his eyes as waves of claustrophobia hit him. He thought the space station was confining until this. At least Unity Station had windows. After a few minutes, the car pulled into a parking structure. They stepped out of the car and headed toward an elevator.

MON 11/20/2130
LOS ANGELES VALLEY
LOS ANGELES, CA

Daniel walked with the others down the city sidewalk, staring in awe like a child at an amusement park. *Damn,* he thought. *Just like a regular city.*

Glass domes and buildings stretched up toward sea level. Slojets glided between the structures. The solar lighting that brightened the city by day was dimmed and streetlights were on. A limousine was driving toward them on a road divided by a concrete island filled with date palms and flowers. Hanging from the windows, intoxicated passengers whooped and shouted at pedestrians. He felt like he was in different world, and in some ways he was.

Night clubbers sipping from champagne bottles strode past them. Daniel noticed that jewelry was pressed against their eyes, casting unsettling reflections. *Galax.net* photographers followed the clubbers, pushing past Dr. Sparkman and Briggs. He recognized several celebrities propped against a nightclub wall wearing barely a patch over all the mandated spots. His arms started itching as if he was allergic to the overkill.

"This is an expensive getaway."

JoMarie's gaze followed another limo as it drove by. "I've seen Housewives of LA Valley, but this surpasses their most advanced staging capabilities."

Dr. Sparkman slowed and walked with Daniel and JoMarie. "LA Valley cost a fortune to build because it was originally intended to be a bunker for world leaders. The fortification required for earthquakes was mindboggling."

Daniel watched the doctor as her hips gently swished under her lab coat as she walked. He forced himself to look up as the doctor motioned to the sky window. Part of him felt like an asshole for thinking about hips and sensuous figures while people were dying en masse in the city, yet he'd been alone for so long that the ache of isolation rose at unexpected times and often not in the most dignified forms. He stared back at the doctor, focusing on her strong yet feminine shoulders. *Can't get in too much trouble doing that.*

"I hope you both get useful information about the maintenance of oxygen quality in closed quarters," Dr. Sparkman said. "At seven hundred meters down, the vehicles must run on electricity. No emissions are allowed so dual-powered vehicles switch over before they are allowed in. That includes the hybrid Slojets."

Smiling, James commented, "That makes them slowpoke jets."

"They don't need to be fast," Officer Briggs said. "I haven't seen a high speed chase yet."

Daniel fixated on the cobblestone sidewalk to keep his eyes at bay. The sound of tires whooshed past him and then slowed to a stop. He looked up and saw a maintenance truck idling next to a trash receptacle on the sidewalk. Mechanical arms extended from the side and picked up the receptacle, dumping the contents inside the tank on the truck's bed.

Dr. Sparkman brushed Daniel's arm and he nearly stumbled off the curb. *Nice shoulders,* he reminded himself.

JoMarie smiled a little at Daniel. Then her mouth fell into a solemn pout. "Time's running out for a lot of sick people."

The doctor nodded at JoMarie. "After meeting Sharon this afternoon, I have a good feeling about her and Donovan."

Feeling himself starting to blush, Daniel took a deep breath. "Not that I'm complaining but why are JoMarie and I here when we could do a virtual tour?"

Dr. Sparkman motioned to the buildings. "Dr. Nielsen believed that visiting the city would give you a sensory feel of another environment that has no natural support for life. As I understand it, your group approaches problems using a combination of creativity and technology."

"Something like that," Daniel said, suspecting that Nielsen's official reason was "bull feathers," as Casey would say. Sniffing out those feathers came naturally to Daniel. Just like his ability to sense that the meteor storms were more than they appeared to be. Growing up in an insane household had taught him to see the underbelly of the most well thought out illusions. In some respects, he felt strangely gifted.

The LA Valley Cedars-Sinai logo glowed above them. He zeroed in on the doctor as she waved to a hospital police officer. Briggs shot Daniel a curious smirk. Daniel tried to act nonchalant as if his gaze had dropped from the sky like an unexpected raindrop and fallen upon Dr. Jeanette Sparkman by accident. He felt like an idiot being caught staring at the doctor again.

Checking his Epad, Daniel saw that Casey had sent a text message complaining about being stuck on Unity for Thanksgiving weekend with Nielsen. Daniel shook his head. *Boohoo.* Pokey displayed the headlines. The flesh-eating bacteria death toll was approaching two hundred thousand and five hundred thousand were infected. He thought of Hannah in an urn, over and over, two-hundred thousand times over. He bowled over and had to stop to catch his breath. He looked up and realized the others had kept walking except JoMarie who stood in front of him.

"You okay?" JoMarie asked.

Blowing a stream of air into the coldness, he nodded. "Okay for me."

"Good enough," she said.

He and JoMarie trotted ahead and caught up to Briggs, James, and Dr. Sparkman who had stopped and were waiting for them. They approached the utility building and walked in a lobby. An elevator took them below the city. The doors opened and they walked in a heavily guarded room.

The guards performed DNA and thumbprint scans on the group. What looked like two ominous castle doors slid open and closed behind them. As they walked inside, more sets of doors lined the walls of this vast room: Electric Support, Water Support, Dehumidification, Carbon Dioxide Filtering, and Oxygen Purification.

"We'll tour the electric systems after we watch an overview of how life support works in LA Valley," Officer Briggs said.

Daniel followed Briggs and the others through the large Electric Support doors that slid open. They entered through another doorway labeled Media Department and walked down a brightly lit hall to a spacious executive room with a large HV hanging on the wall. He sat down next to JoMarie at a long, narrow table. James and Dr. Sparkman sat across from them. Briggs darkened the room and turned on the computer linked to the HV.

Struggling to focus, Daniel tried to take notes on his Epad but found his gaze veering back to the doctor. Her clear emerald eyes, even in the dark, were captivating, but she was very austere and he hoped not too stodgy. He turned to LA Valley's nuclear power facility displayed on the HV. Transferring electricity wasn't a big deal in LAV nor was it a big deal for Earthstar. There was nothing new here.

The part on oxygen purification was relevant in fighting WMD attacks in all levels of life. Finding structures where clean air was available or could be quickly purified was a universal concern. Suddenly Daniel felt tired. The second wind brought on by touring LAV and meeting the doctor was dissipating. He wondered why that protestor, Gwyneth, said he'd turn on his peers. He couldn't imagine what she was talking about.

He yawned and forced his attention on the presentation. Everyone knew how to fix polluted air. The "giving a shit" part was missing. Including greenery in closed quarter schematics was important for oxygen production and carbon dioxide absorption. Maybe the space stations could use more plants. Maybe Earth could use more plants since a lot of them had been destroyed or died on their own. He hoped Nielsen was right, that exposure to the sensory environment would result in solutions, like his spacewalk did. Maybe tomorrow, when he was more alert, the ideas would come. Leaning back, he frowned and again thought of Casey's oft-used exclamation, "Bull feathers!"

LAV's water treatment facility extracted water from the ground and purified it—another good idea but impractical for Earthstar. What about the surface residents' water infrastructure? Daniel shook his head. More wasted time.

Daniel sniffed out a quiet laugh when he noticed that JoMarie's eyes were half closed and her head tilted toward her right shoulder. He'd woken up on Unity Station at 05:00 UTC nearly twenty-seven hours ago. Daniel blinked several times to relieve his dry eyes. Turning to admire Dr. Sparkman while hoping he wouldn't get caught again, he realized that she'd left the room. He couldn't blame her. She had to be more bored than he was.

After the presentation, Briggs turned the lights on. "We need to go. We won't be able to tour the electric plant."

"Where's the doctor at?" Daniel said.

"She's in the lobby answering a call from Dr. Caldwell."

Daniel smiled. "I hope our assistance helps LA."

"Me, too." Briggs nodded with a somber frown.

JoMarie released an extended yawn that sounded like an off tune musical note. "That presentation was good. Thank you, Officers Briggs and Harrison, for taking the time during this tragedy to give us the tour."

"You're welcome," James said. "Daniel, did you find anything useful?"

"Oh, yes," Daniel lied. "We got some good info on air quality."

"I sent you emails with links to reports with more detail on how the city works."

"Thanks." Daniel followed everyone toward the lobby area. Claustrophobia and fatigue were pushing his body to find some type of bed—a floor, a pile of grass, even floating next to the hairy back end of a golden retriever seemed acceptable. He didn't care. As he walked in the lobby, he wondered why Dr. Sparkman seemed shaky and upset. She was blinking fast and her mouth was tight and tense, even more than earlier.

Daniel cleared his throat, which was becoming irritated from the moist air. "The climate is cool and damp. One might even say musty," he coughed out.

Dr. Sparkman stared at her Epad, her other hand gripped on the briefcase. She didn't seem to hear him. "Sharon told me that people are rioting outside LA Cedars," she said. "We have to pull an all-nighter, maybe several to get the Intellipatches out."

"You're going to do wonders," JoMarie said.

Putting her Epad in her coat pocket, the doctor frowned. "Maybe, but only if we can get the patches produced fast enough. Sharon and I will see you in the morning when you visit the hospital."

Daniel recoiled. *Am I not reminded of Hannah's death enough?* Then he felt a slight grin creep across his face. There was one bright spot in this dismal scene. He would get to see the doctor again.

* * *

They drove out of the parking structure toward the tunnel. Daniel sensed a change in mood not just from Dr. Sparkman, but from James and Briggs. The shift reminded him of the day when doctors told him and Cherril that Hannah was terminal. Such hesitation seemed to precede the revelation of a dreaded truth.

Officer Briggs accelerated the car.

"What's wrong?" JoMarie said.

"There's a system problem at LAVPD headquarters. I don't know what's up yet."

The lights lining the road were flashing red. Daniel knew something was being kept from him. JoMarie was being elusive about why they were there, as the info they'd gotten was available on *Galax.net*. The sensory perception story was questionable at best. Pokey was shaking his head. Even his Epad knew that Nielsen was full of shit.

Officer Briggs parked the car in the lot and started running down the sidewalk toward one of the elevators. Daniel and the others followed. Briggs pressed his thumb on the reader. The display read, *"System activity is temporarily suspended."*

Pokey's image on Daniel's Epad spun like he was going down a toilet. Then the screen turned blue and crashed. "Something's cut off our computer access," he said.

"Please don't let us go to jail, LeRoy," Dr. Sparkman said to Briggs. "Get us out of here."

Officer Briggs shouted at elevator. “Get the doors open, Leticia!”

The elevator doors opened and everyone shoved their way in. The doors slammed shut and Daniel felt more trapped than ever. “What do you mean, ‘go to jail?’”

“Don’t worry,” JoMarie whispered.

“What do you know that I don’t?”

James pushed on his Epad screen, which Daniel noticed was also blue. “Don’t worry about what she knows, Daniel.”

“What the hell’s going on?”

“You guys will be fine,” James added then turned to Briggs. “A concentration of illuminated specks is concentrated at the north exit. Those are LAPD officers. Go south.”

Officer Briggs pressed the south button and the elevator shot sideways.

Pressing his back against the wall, Daniel struggled to stave off motion sickness.

“What did Nielsen get us into?” he asked JoMarie.

JoMarie’s eyes twitched as if she was nervous. “I’ll explain everything soon.”

Daniel started at his blank Epad. “Who’s Leticia?”

“My partner at Central,” Officer Briggs answered. “Thankfully she was able to override the security so we can get back above ground. We won’t be exactly where we started but within a kilometer or so.”

The digits on the elevator’s clock advanced at a cruel, unhurried pace. The elevator status screen flashed, “LA Valley South Entrance” and the doors slid apart. They walked a few meters. The area exploded into brightness and Daniel stumbled back. There had to be ten cops pointing assault weapons at them.

An older cop with a USMC tattoo on his arm walked to James. “Somebody entered LAV’s hospital without authorization. You know anything about this?”

“We got lost, Lieutenant Thane,” said James.

“Don’t go there,” Thane said. “After forty years on the beat I’m a human bullshit detector.”

“This is Dr. Sparkman,” James said as his shoulders went limp. “I escorted her to LAV to get medicine for the terror victims.”

Daniel leaned against the wall. *Bull feathers indeed.* "We were props," he said.

JoMarie patted his shoulder. "We did nothing wrong."

Thane stomped his boots against the concrete floor like a furious drill sergeant. "Open the case."

Daniel felt bad for the doctor as she fumbled with the lock mechanism. She wasn't stoic and stodgy at all. She was like him, willing to do about anything for what she believed was right. She'd been scared shitless the whole time. As she lifted the lid, he saw bags of yellowish powder packed in the case.

Thane examined the bags in the light and then slammed the case shut. He released a military groan that sounded like something he'd give to disobedient minions in the corps.

"Officer Harrison, what the hell do you want me to do?"

"Do what you want to me and Officer Briggs," James said. "We had to choose between the blood of the LA victims and our freedom." He slumped to a sitting position on the floor. "Don't punish the doctor. We had to do it."

Thane stared at the case. He sat on a bench and motioned for his officers to leave the tunnel. The quiet burned Daniel's ears and he wished something would happen. Slojets and helicopters rumbled in the background. Pokey was back on and his clock read 00:17 Pacific, November 21.

"Dammit, James!" Thane said as he paced back and forth. "You can be glad I'm an old fart near retirement and have nothing to lose. I'll delay the violation report by jacking around with the processes. You know, like leaving a couple data fields in my report blank the way us aging cops can do sometimes."

Thane put his arm around Dr. Sparkman's shoulder. "I'll take you and the others to Cedars in the jet waiting outside. I think I have an injured officer. LAV officials know that their meds were relocated, but they won't dare come up and get them now. Let's go."

* * *

Daniel was blinded by spotlights that seemed to be coming from everywhere. He climbed into the LAPD Slojet after James, Briggs, JoMarie, Jeanette Sparkman, and a couple other police officers. The defeated faces he'd seen behind the fence were no doubt somewhere in the chaos, waiting for their cure—and he hoped soon that they would get it.

Thane hopped in the pilot's seat and called headquarters. "Lieutenant Devon Thane, 3541. I have an officer who tripped in the LA Valley entrance when looking for Officer Harrison. His ankle might be fractured. Martin Luther's full but Cedars-Sinai okayed us. Harrison was found in an unauthorized area with LAVPD Officer Briggs. I'll submit paperwork for disciplinary action within an hour."

The jet ascended above Los Angeles over the LA Valley barricades. Daniel wondered if Gwyneth and Stephen, wherever they were, would be pleased.

Dr. Sparkman stared at her briefcase. "Not a single person in the Valley's been infected. They don't ride subways."

Daniel smiled as an affinity started to brew. "You took their broad-spectrum antibiotics. You stole them. That's pretty cool." He leaned back in his seat. *Actually, that's pretty hot.*

"Just their surplus," she said. "There's plenty left for them."

Daniel turned to JoMarie who was looking out the Slojet's window. "You knew we were being used by Nielsen so the doctor could get into LA Valley?"

JoMarie nodded.

"Don't they trust me? Don't you trust me?"

"Nielsen thought you might accidentally slip," JoMarie said.

"He's such an asshole."

JoMarie shrugged a little. "Maybe he's still punishing you for ignoring his emails and phone calls."

"So he's a punitive asshole."

"Dr. Nielsen's a brilliant humanitarian," Dr. Sparkman said.

Daniel realized that JoMarie was falling asleep and figured he should leave her alone. He looked at the doctor and bit his lip, not wanting to appear disagreeable. "Let's say my view of Nielsen is based on personal experience. Why was a plan hatched to use us, Doctor?"

Her face relaxing, she managed a tight-lipped smile. "I needed to get down there without arousing suspicion. I couldn't go alone so we came up with the tour. Some of city leaders were wary of any visits during all this chaos, but the LA Valley mayor and a couple council members are hoping for the few open slots remaining on Earthstar, so they relented to Nielsen. He's got connections to the UN."

"I figured it wasn't his personality." Daniel smirked, hoping it looked like a return smile.

Dr. Sparkman glanced down at the case. "No, he used his reputation. He was willing to compromise that to save lives, so I became an official guide for the Unity scientists, sent by USRG leader Noah Nielsen."

"How were you able to enter the hospital and not be seen stealing the meds?" Daniel said. "Their security must be monitoring every flick of a finger, every wiggle of a toe."

"I was seen taking the meds," Dr. Sparkman answered. "But that security equipment is operated by people who have family in LA. I entered through a tunnel from Electric Systems Support that connects to the hospital's power generator. With the help of a few guards, I got the meds. I may go to jail or maybe not. I was scared at first. Now I don't care."

"You could've stayed in LA Valley," Daniel said. "They need good doctors. Life would have been so much easier."

"My prosperity would've been founded on ignoring the pain of those who need my help the most," she said as she patted her case. "There's at least a quarter million lives in here."

"Unbelievable." Daniel felt guilty for initially seeing only her physical qualities. Inside this attractive woman was a brain and soul.

The doctor pushed her hair away from her face. "Even people of science sometimes forget the sovereignty that microorganisms have over life. The most powerful forces in the universe are invisible to our naked eyes."

Staring at the doctor, Daniel felt privileged to have unwittingly been a part of her scheme. "We work with that every day," he said. "It's hard to convince people of things they can't see. Sometimes I feel the job's thankless."

She held the case's handle tight. "Seems strange to a lot of people, but my reward comes during ER shifts. Ten years ago, when I was a resident at Cedars, I remember a dying teenage boy injured in a car accident being brought back to life. Last month, when I volunteered for ER duty, he came in with his wife and I watched his daughter being born. That's payoff."

Daniel realized that the Slojet was lowering toward the hospital roof. SWAT teams were holding back the shouting mob on the ground. Tanks cruised around the building's perimeter.

"So now that our assignment is over, what do we do?" Daniel asked.

"Go to your hotel room," Dr. Sparkman said, "and get a good night's sleep for your tour tomorrow. Senator Robert Landry and Matthew Bertrand arrived tonight and are staying at the Beverly Wilshire, as are you. I'll meet you and JoMarie in the Cedars research lab in the basement at 10:00 tomorrow."

The Slojet lowered on the hospital's roof. Lieutenant Thane gripped James' shoulder. "I'm sorry. In a couple hours, my report errors will probably be fixed. You and Briggs may have arrest warrants once they know the whole story. Maybe I'll have one too." He pointed to the crowd below. "The upside is you'll be low priority."

"I've already called for a cab home and am heading north to my in-laws," James said.

One of the officers stepped out of the Slojet, bent over, and faked a limp. Officer Briggs held the limping officer's arm and exited the plane to the awaiting EMTs. Dr. Sparkman stood and started toward the jet's exit and JoMarie followed.

Daniel felt his eyes brighten as he followed the doctor and JoMarie onto the hospital roof. He looked down at the piles of people. The screams and shouts were much worse than outside of LA Valley. As the doctor turned to walk inside the hospital, Daniel tapped her shoulder.

"Good luck with the patches," he said.

Lifting the attaché case, Dr. Sparkman winked. "Sometimes success takes more than luck."

"Sure does," Daniel said as he winked back. JoMarie stood next to him and caught his gesture. Putting his arm around JoMarie, he added, "Nothing that a little collusion, or shall we say teamwork, can't cure."

TUES 11/21/2130
CEDARS-SINAI HOSPITAL
LOS ANGELES, CA

Feeling a shudder run through him, Daniel breathed deep to relax his throat and stomach. The emergency room was death in the making. People in various states of consciousness were lying in hospital beds, on chairs, and on the floor. Most of their limbs and torsos were wrapped with skin gauze. A few had horrific gaping wounds in their flesh. He followed JoMarie as she stepped around people curled up against each other on the bloodstained floors. *Galax.net* cameras were aimed at a reporter who was standing in the middle of the waiting room and interviewing a hospital spokesperson.

The odor of sickness and antiseptic was dizzying. The squeaks and beeps of machines and, worst of all, the wails sliced him like broken glass. He tripped over a young man lying against a wall. The man opened his eyes and lifted himself off the jacket he had shoved under his head. The guy's forearm was as narrow as a bone and wrapped in mesh.

"I'm so sorry, sir," Daniel said.

The man nodded. "I'm okay." He looked at Daniel and JoMarie. "Aren't you two on that global mission?"

"Yeah." Daniel rubbed his aching stomach. "My coworkers are in the lab downstairs doing everything they can to stop this madness."

The young man's eyes lit up for a second. "You two work with the talking dogs and cats? I'm a friend on Casey's social page."

"I work with Casey. Glad to know you're on board with us."

"Good luck," the guy said as he laid his head back on the jacket and closed his eyes.

Daniel grabbed JoMarie's arm as his legs began to wobble. "I can't deal with being recognized like that. And the guilt is overwhelming."

"He's on our side." JoMarie pressed the small of Daniel's back leading him out of the emergency room. "Casey has quite a fan club."

Daniel stopped walking. His body became stiff and he gasped, "I can't handle being here."

"We can stand and relax for a few minutes."

Staring at the floor to regain composure, Daniel struggled to slow his breathing. "Too much déjà vu."

Gently pulling him toward the stairwell, JoMarie talked softly. "Let's take the stairs so you can calm down."

"Thanks," Daniel said, grateful for her patience. "I can't walk through this place alone."

Gripping his arm, JoMarie guided him further. "Getting away from the emergency room will help. And remember, you'll see Hannah again someday."

Daniel was comforted by JoMarie's grip but not so much by her words. He wasn't sure about an afterlife. Not that his opinion mattered. The whole system, whatever it consisted of, was out his control. The door to the stairwell slid open. "I don't know if I believe that."

"You really think that all there is to life is what our mortal human eyes and brains can see?" JoMarie said.

"I don't know but I hope not."

"I know not," she answered with a certainty that Daniel wished he had. They entered the stairwell and he gripped the railing.

JoMarie walked slowly with him as he headed down the stairs. "Keep remembering how many people are on our side."

Daniel, with his eyes half closed, started stepping down the two flights of stairs that led to the lab.

JoMarie glanced at her forearm and read *Galax.net* from her Epad. "LA's now lost two hundred twenty thousand people. Five hundred and fifty thousand are still fighting for life. We're in the eye of the hurricane, my son."

Keeping his hand tight on the rail as he progressed down, Daniel focused on his shoes to stay balanced.

"Back in January, I would've asked why we went to LA Valley, why we're in this hospital. But I realize this is also our job. After we spoke at Public Hall, we became symbols of the mission and of the future. This has moved beyond science. Just like the talking dog in the Elvis tux."

"Exactly like the dog in the tux," JoMarie said.

Daniel stared at his feet as they precipitously moved down the stairs. "That's why the press asks us questions we don't know the answers to. We're seen as gatekeepers to the future." A waft of antiseptic smell came from nowhere, reminding Daniel of Hannah in ICU. Pushing the visual away, he realized that he was being self-indulgent and unfair to his daughter's memory. She'd often been happy. He remembered her running in the park, playing computer games, and being smart as a whip with a wry sense of humor.

JoMarie wrapped her arm around him as they walked. "You understand now."

Daniel sighed. "No thanks to Chistyakov, who told the public we'd compose the magnum opus that would save humanity."

JoMarie let go of Daniel's arm as they reached the bottom of the stairwell. "Expectations are high but people live off hope when times get tough. They don't have much else."

Daniel walked with JoMarie down a long, white, brightly lit corridor. He knew that somewhere on this floor, the less fortunate were being encased in bio-plastic cocoons en route to the crematories. Still, he felt motivated. JoMarie's wisdom and his own realizations were bringing him to a better place. Maybe those sessions with Jake were doing something after all.

As they approached the door to the infectious diseases lab, Daniel waved at Robert and Matt who were leaning against the wall. Their expressions were trancelike, as if they were not able to grasp what was happening. Robert's cowboy hat was MIA.

Dr. Sparkman walked into the hall wearing the same clothes from the night before. Her face was tired, her hair unkempt from working all night. Despite that, Daniel suddenly felt giddy. He couldn't believe he was having these feelings in a lab so close to a morgue.

"Please everyone," the doctor said coolly. "I need to update you on the situation."

They followed her into a sparsely furnished white room. Daniel couldn't help but notice the curvy figure under her lab coat or maybe he was imagining things. Maybe she was shaped like a tree trunk. He was starting not to care.

Sharon sat behind a glass wall in an adjacent room bent over a microscope wearing the intense expression he knew so well. She was in her glory, making a difference and trying to cancel out her family's notorious greed. Donovan and two assistants were with her, testing the Intellipatch's nanobot drug distribution system.

Dr. Sparkman sat on a chair in front of a round table. Daniel and the others sat with her. She presented images of two DNA strands on a wall HV.

"On the left," she said, "is the conventional necrotizing fasciitis. This strain of the flesh-eating bacteria spreads throughout the body like wildfire, but most antibiotics can cure it if found early. About ninety percent push through if treated."

She motioned to the other strand. "The one on the right is what was used in Los Angeles. It has a much higher death rate."

"The bacteria are mutating?" Daniel said.

"No, that's *Galax.net* spin. The one used in LA was developed in a lab by the CDC." She paused then added, "For the military."

"Geez, I didn't know about this biological weapon," Robert said with a pained look on his face.

What little faith Daniel had in government faded into the blue nothingness that glowed on his Epad screen after Pokey was flushed down the eToilet in the LA Valley elevator. "Robert, are you telling me that the United States develops biological weapons?"

Looking at strands displayed on the HV, Robert sighed. "They're only for use on targeted individuals."

Daniel narrowed his eyes. "But they exist."

"They're more effective and much cheaper than a full-scale war."

Cracking his knuckles, Matt nodded. "Charlie D. rises again."

“Please,” JoMarie said. “Stop that, okay?”

“Sorry JoMarie,” Matt answered. “As I’ve said before, I didn’t grow the tree. I’m just forced to eat the bitter fruit.”

Ignoring Matt, Daniel tapped Robert’s shoulder. “You didn’t know of *this* biological weapon? That’s nice. Well, two hundred and twenty thousand people have died and five hundred fifty thousand more are struggling to survive. Surprise! Now you know about the weapon.”

“Look,” Robert said, “there are some people who should be taken off the planet. As bad as bio-assassinations are, the other options are much worse.”

“I get that, but....”

“Let me finish,” Dr. Sparkman said as she paced in front of them. “After contacting the CDC, we found out that the bacterium is the Streptococcus Exotoxin V4, also known as SEV4. Nobody apparently knew it was missing despite their supposed seamless tracking system. The strain is not contagious.”

“Then why are so many people dying and sick?” JoMarie said.

“With the conventional patch treatment,” Dr. Sparkman answered, “we’re finding this strain has a thirty plus percent death rate if a person is hit by more than a hundred nanobots. Over three quarters of a million people got that many hits and more.”

“What do you expect?” Daniel said. “Not too many people in LA can afford cars.”

Dr. Sparkman frowned. “True. The Xpress was used by six million people over three days averaging the same five million people per day. These passengers have the highest infection rate.”

Staring at the DNA strands on the screen, Daniel’s hope for the future dissolved into the bloodied emergency room floor at ground level. “So the CDC acknowledged having this shit?”

“Yes,” the doctor said. “There’s an unpublicized, frantic investigation to find out what happened to the missing inventory.” Her face reddened and she clenched her fists. “What type of monster would use nanobots for this? It’s beyond my comprehension.”

Matt sneezed, barely covering his mouth. “Doctor, I’m sorry to interrupt but I have a question about the African Plague. I’ve had this cold since January.”

Sharon's voice blared from an intercom, "For crap's sake, Matt! You don't have the Plague. Cindera was messing with you. You're probably allergic to animal hair."

Looking at Matt, Dr. Sparkman said, "You should get allergy tested. You'd be long dead if you were infected with the plague and not treated. As for the Intellipatches, the first run of fifty thousand will be distributed today by the company that makes our standards."

"Are these patches loaded with the meds from last night?" Daniel said.

Finally breaking the faintest of smiles, Dr. Sparkman dropped in a chair. Daniel felt empathy as she stuffed her hands in the pockets of her wrinkled brown pants that looked as tired as she did.

"Yes. We'll end up with over a quarter million patches from last night's visit. For the others, we'll have to use standard antibiotics. But with the new technology Sharon is providing our patch manufacturer, we expect they'll work very well."

Looking in the doctors' eyes, Daniel felt compassion for her. She was stuck cleaning up someone else's garbage…just like him. "Doctor, how many more people are expected to die?"

Hesitating, she stared at the HV. "About twenty-five to fifty thousand. The range is hard to know for sure."

Frowning at Robert and noticing that JoMarie was giving the senator a similar look, Daniel started to take deep breaths to avoid losing his temper. "Robert, how did this virus get removed from its home at the CDC and end up in the subways?"

"I can't believe that it did," Robert said. "There are so many layers of security, it's ridiculous. I have to conclude that we're dealing with an inside job, deep in the core. The idea's downright terrifying."

Daniel smelled the Oval Office or something very close.

"Let's not focus on political issues," Sharon said on the intercom. "I'd rather talk about the solution. Thanks to Dr. Sparkman and a few colluding police officers, we'll treat a quarter million people with the broad-spectrum antibiotics. The others will get the standards. We can't save everyone, but a large majority will make it. Also, thanks to JoMarie and Daniel for helping."

"Why didn't you tell me the truth about LA Valley?" Daniel said, shooting a scowl at Sharon. "That I was a stooge used to help Dr. Sparkman steal antibiotics? I would've been glad to help."

"It was Nielsen who decided that less was more and I agreed," Sharon said with a sly smile. "It's not that we don't trust you. You're such a bad liar. We thought you might slip to Casey. And once that happened, *Galax.net* would know."

"Thanks for the vote of confidence."

"You're so forthright, but here's what you helped us with." Sharon displayed cells squirming toward others and consuming them.

Daniel stared at the screen. He had to stop himself from being unscientific, from wondering if this scheme of life was bigger than human physics and science.

"Here are the SEV4 bacteria infecting healthy cells," Sharon said. "Once the broad-spectrums are loaded into the micro-beads, the nanos will transport the beads to the infected cells and release the medicine. The standards, though not as effective, will be loaded in the beads as well."

She turned to Donovan. "What do our Intellipatches do to necrotizing strep?"

Donovan raised his fist. "Kill! Kill! Kill!"

"Okay," Dr. Sparkman said, "now that we've got our bacteria killing techniques perfected, we're ready to take a tour of the children's wing."

"No!" Daniel shouted, surprised at his reaction. "I'm sorry Dr. Sparkman. I can't see kids and babies like that."

"Let me escort you," the doctor said. "I think the kids and you will benefit." She passed out masks and gloves. "Put these on. You don't want to expose them to germs."

JoMarie looked at him. "C'mon, Daniel, let's tour the wing with the doctor and Donovan. Sharon's taking Matt and Robert. Would you rather go with them?"

"Ugh, no," Daniel said.

The doctor touched Daniel's wrist. "And please don't call me Dr. Sparkman. From now on, to everyone on your mission I'm Jeanette."

Nearly fainting from her touch, Daniel made sure he fixated on her shoulders. "Sure, whatever you say, Jeannette."

* * *

Tears burned Daniel's face like the day he tripped and fell in a patch of stinging nettles while inspecting an old IRE dump in Nevada. He turned from the boy whose right temple and forehead were consumed by SEV4. The end product of consumed flesh was hidden but the skin gauze that dipped inside the child's skull was enough. The child was an African-American boy, maybe five or six. One of Sharon's Intellipatches was inserted under the skin on his neck.

The boy rubbed his healthy temple and pointed at JoMarie, saying, "She looks like my nana."

Jeanette brushed her gloved hand over the boy's hair. "The lady is JoMarie and the man is Daniel. Can you tell them your name?"

"Todd Hansen." He scooted up to a sitting position. "I started first grade in September. I go to school all day now."

"All day?" Daniel said. "That's great."

JoMarie shook his hand. "You're quite the grown-up."

"I'm really trying. I've learned how to read and write. My teacher told me I read like a third grader."

"With smarts like that," Daniel said, "you can have a good job someday."

"I want to be a tree doctor because it seems like they're all dying." The boy stared past him and JoMarie. His eyes glistened as if he'd retreated to a mental oasis he'd remembered from HV or a book. "Where I live there's only a few trees because they either die or are cut down. Our outside is covered in hot black playground stuff."

Daniel pulled out his Epad. "Do you have an email and phone number?"

Todd gave him a stern look. "I have both but don't call me past 21:00 on a school night. I might be sleeping."

"Make sure you get permission from your mom to talk to me," said Daniel.

Todd told Daniel his email address. "I'll ask my daddy instead. Mom's probably busy. She just got to heaven a few days ago." The boy blinked away tears. "Dad's been there a little longer."

"Todd's mother died of SEV4 on Sunday," Dr. Sparkman said. "She and Todd took the subway to go to the movies on Thursday. In May, his father was robbed and murdered in the parking lot of a mall."

"Where does Todd go after he's recovered?" JoMarie asked.

“His two living grandparents are in poor health, so he goes to Golden State Orphanage here in LA. The care’s not bad, but there are so many kids. He has an aunt and two cousins in the area. Hopefully his family will visit him sometimes.”

Daniel was silent. The tears he could never blame on the nettles were back. The few times he’d cried in his adult life were during his divorce and what would have been Hannah’s fifth birthday. Maybe his daughter was better off not surviving if this was the world she would have to live in. Feeling selfish for wishing she were alive with him on this dying planet, he was ready to return to the hotel. He’d had enough PR for one day.

TUES 11/21/2130
BEVERLY WILSHIRE HOTEL RESTAURANT
LOS ANGELES, CA

JoMarie dug into her pasta with a fork then looked at Daniel and Robert. "Every terrorist attack this year was preceded by a meteor storm in the immediate area, often by a week or less. LA was hit with a storm in the early hours of November 16. They're appearing to be more targeted and the social networks are going crazy with theories and predictions."

Daniel nodded. "You're finally coming on board with me."

"With a few reservations," JoMarie said. "The problem is that we don't know enough to do anything."

Daniel stared at the basket of cookies Robert had brought from Unity Station. His anger toward the senator had faded. The guy hadn't killed anyone in LA, but someone in the government had. As trite as the basket was as a holiday symbol, it was still comforting.

Robert read his Epad. "How in the hell do we deal with something like that?"

"When the meteors hit again," Daniel said, "DHS will have to investigate until their eyes are crossed and their computers short out."

"DHS has to do what they're told," Robert responded. "Clemens already thinks you and I are jerks, so we probably won't get much out of him and his party."

Daniel felt a stomach pang from hunger or his upcoming December funk. He popped two antacids in his mouth. The quesadilla on his plate now seemed like a risky venture.

"I believe negative mental energy is released by the perpetrators," he said. "This energy could be coming from terrorists, polluters, or even people in general who apathetically overuse Earth's life system. Something in nature senses a threat."

Giving him a blank look, Robert squinted in deep thought as if wanting to believe Daniel but couldn't muster a vote of confidence.

"Okay," Daniel said, "I gotta more practical example. Flower petals closing at sunset to protect the plant from the cold. This can be expanded to, and I know it's a stretch, meteorites trying to protect and warn Earth about an upcoming danger."

Robert picked at his chef's salad and then looked at Daniel. "You're saying that when terrorists are planning or causing destruction, Earth detects the upcoming danger and sends a warning?"

Daniel knew the idea was far-fetched but had nothing better to offer. He started wondering what role, if any, the light beam spearing from the ocean played in this. He wasn't going to cause more paranoia and bring that up too publicly until he had better information. He shoved a piece of the quesadilla in his mouth, chewed a few times, and swallowed. Since dogs were now gossiping like people, he was going to start eating like a golden retriever to save time.

JoMarie dipped a cookie in her almond milk, "We as a species have really messed things up. Earth has always had a system in place to rejuvenate and restore." She looked at Daniel and Robert. "Maintain life and restore—that's what the system wants to do."

"Will that restoration come fast enough?" Daniel said, showing Robert a display of Earth on his tablet. "Just a few centuries ago, Earth produced one hundred and fifty billion tons of organic matter. By 2100, humans reduced this to one hundred and twenty-five billion by destroying capacity. People consume sixty-five billion tons and have ruined twenty-five billion. So, ninety billion is taken by us, leaving sixty billion for everything else."

Robert looked pained, the creases in his mouth deep and worried. "What does all this mean in English?"

"Earth's ecosystem is bursting at the seams," Daniel said. "Humans have removed sixty percent of the food from the pool. Then as a cherry on the sundae, terrorists cause destruction through bombs and bio-attacks. These meteor storms aren't random and I suspect are driven by human thoughts. Whatever the case, something else is going on."

"Cookie, please," Robert said.

JoMarie pulled two cookies from the basket and gave a Santa Claus to Robert. She handed a gingerbread man to Daniel, saying, "I think you need one, too."

Nodding, Daniel grabbed the cookie and took a drink of tea. He wondered if a shot of whiskey to chase the gingerbread man down would be even better. "With current rates of consumption and food technology, a human population of nine billion is the max for a diverse species mix on Earth. Then we have industrial waste."

Robert ate his cookie and took a sip of tea. "I would've preferred that personal responsibility prevent this mess."

Daniel shook his head. "Oh, heaven's no. That's too strenuous for consumers and too pricey for companies like IRE. Yucca II was over-filled with industrial gunk so they dumped the radioactive waste in the ocean rather than spend the money transporting it to the moon. Had that waste not been retrieved, it would have killed sea life and found its way in our rivers."

"It would be ironic," Robert said, "if something as simple as water is what ends up taking us out."

Staring at his gingerbread man, Daniel bit the head off. "It might. Only three percent of Earth's water is fresh and easily usable. That includes clouds, lakes, and rivers. So what've we got left after polluting that?"

Robert looked at him blankly. "Dirt clods?"

Daniel raised an eyebrow. "Radioactive dirt clods."

JoMarie's Epad rang. Daniel saw Nielsen's face in the screen. He shook his head at her. Don't answer. *Worse than Casey.*

Smirking at Daniel, she answered the call.

As JoMarie talked, Daniel noticed her face growing pale. He'd tried to warn her. Nielsen's calls were always shitty. When good things happened, mum was his British word. Nielsen had already ruined her holiday weekend and now he called at dinnertime. Seeing JoMarie's dismal face caused Robert to become quiet and gloomy. Nielsen had even screwed up a US senator's dinner. What a cad.

JoMarie's face became even more drawn. Daniel's discomfort advanced to panic. She normally wasn't affected much by Nielsen's calls. Could this be something really bad? Hannah's urn revisited him, two hundred and twenty thousand times over with up to fifty thousand more urns to go. How much space does almost three hundred thousand urns take up?

Tell me everything's going to be okay, JoMarie. I want to get to know Jeanette. I want to honor my daughter's memory and get this mission done. Sucking in a deep, meditative breath, he refused to let Nielsen's shit get to him.

JoMarie clicked the phone off. She grabbed Daniel and Robert's wrists.

Her words were slow, like the bomb that sailed toward Daniel in Public Hall—slow in its gait but sure to reach its destiny. "I need to go upstairs and call Ed," she said to Daniel. "Can Robert and I go to your room in a half hour and discuss Nielsen's call?"

"Of course," Daniel said. "Should we wake up Matt?"

"No," JoMarie whispered. "He's probably best left alone for now."

Robert patted her arm. "Is everything okay with your family?"

Daniel had never seen JoMarie look that way before. Her face was almost lifeless, like the people outside the gates of LA Valley.

"In the immediate sense, yes," she said. "Nielsen told me almost one billion people have died from the African Plague in the past ten months. Even with the Intellipatches, the strain is getting more resistant. That death count was far higher than anyone had estimated. He and Donovan did some population forecasting using an AI program. They analyzed global death trends and causes of death."

She took a deep, loud gulp that Daniel felt going down his own throat. "We need to get back to Unity Station. Their final conclusion is that humanity is entering the early stages of extinction."

WED 11/22/2130
FLC FAMILY TRUST RANCH
SOCORRO, NM

Three doctors and a nurse stood over Clark, who lay in a hospital bed. A morphine patch released meds into his body. Shaune paced in the makeshift hospital room set up in one of the ranch's extra bedrooms. He turned to Poppy to say something and then stopped. His dad hadn't stared at him with such anger since he set the ranch's barn on fire in third grade.

Poppy stomped around in a little, stupid circle. He shook his fist at Shaune. "You fool!"

Shaune could tell by Poppy's swelling face that he was mad, really mad, and wanting to say much worse. He was trying to control his temper as if everyone in the room didn't already know he was psychopathic. His voice was upping in pitch but not to the octave of the insane hyena cackle that Shaune was used to.

Balking a little, Shaune whispered, "The bots wouldn't have been so infectious had Clark programmed them right."

"Do you know what trouble he had to go through to get those bios?" Poppy snarled at him.

"I know about the runaway thumb, if that's what you mean," Shaune said, wincing at Clark, whose right arm had been amputated. Half of his jaw was covered in Dermawraps and bandages.

Poppy walked up to him. He shoved his face up to Shaune's nose, practically grazing his skin. He motioned to Clark who was asleep. "The guy's arm is eaten off because you had to go in the subway and expose yourselves to the nanobots. In a few days, right here in this room, we'll have to attach a donor arm."

Shaune backed away from Poppy's stale breath. "I hope his new one matches the other."

Poppy squeezed his eyes into hateful little slits, clearly no longer caring whether his true soul was revealed to the USA medical team.

"We hope when Clark returns to the CDC after his aunt's funeral, who we also had to kill to make this authentic, nobody will notice his arm's a little shorter or longer, or a slightly different color."

Looking at Clark, Shaune furrowed his brow. "Next time I'll outsource."

"Finding a donor arm is harder than you think."

"Could you use his aunt's arm?"

Poppy's tightening eyes were getting a bit uncanny. "She was sixty-five years old and almost three hundred pounds, you idiot."

Shaune felt Poppy's limit approaching. "I am truly sorry. Act Three will bring a standing ovation. I promise."

"Good, because you risked the USA's entire plan by going in that damn subway to build your ego."

"There may have been a few mistakes, but Clark and I did a great thing."

"He's lucky we decided to treat him after the shit you two pulled. Be glad enough of those little bastards didn't find their way up your ass."

"You knew what we were doing." Shaune frowned. "Besides, I got hit twenty-six times."

"I thought that between you and Clark, a single brain could be put together. You didn't have a realistic projection of the casualties."

Shaune was starting to get pissed. "We pulled off the most technologically sophisticated terrorist attack in human history."

"And killed hundreds of thousands of people instead of the twenty thousand you were supposed to, idiot! The public's furious and the People's Party's approval ratings have plunged!"

"So the scare was bigger than planned," Shaune said.

His dad's skull seemed to bulge at the temples with each breath. "There's even talk of recall elections to bring the Dems and Repubs back. That's a new low for us."

"By the time anyone attempts that, our deal will be done," Shaune replied, trying not to laugh at his big-headed father. "They won't and they can't."

"You better hope," Poppy said.

Shaune ignored his dad's thinly veiled threat. He needed to call Vara. He needed to see her. She had to be a witch who'd put some damn spell on him. For some sick reason, he wasn't able to have sex with that hooker in LA Valley.

"My final assignment will make up for whatever mistakes I've made."

The bedroom door slid open and Mummy walked in. She grabbed Clark's remaining hand and shook it. "Good job for the cause."

"Good job? Are you crazy?" Poppy said. "They killed half the people in downtown LA."

WED 11/22/2130
VALUE PAK GROCERY STORE
MISSION VIEJO, CA

Guiding her electric cart down the grocery store aisle, Sanya picked through a basket of gourds. The flesh-eating bacteria attacks weighed on her. Her uncle worked in downtown LA and rode the Xpress every day. When she found out that morning his tests came back negative, she was able to shop for Thanksgiving dinner without a heavy heart. But now she had only a few hours to pick up the food she needed and start defrosting the turkey meat.

Pressing the "Purchase Food" button on the Grocers' Net was too impersonal when preparing for a Thanksgiving dinner. The site crashed a lot during the holiday season and was more trouble than it was worth. Plus, she needed to get away from the news and reality. Jessie ran to the cart and dropped boxes inside. Sanya watched her take off down another aisle. Her youngest daughter was growing up so fast.

Sanya smiled at a can of cranberry sauce as if it was an old friend, and in a way it was. Cranberry sauce had been a timeless symbol of holidays and family since she was a small child. Taking off work Thanksgiving week was a godsend. Since the SCED attack in May, DHS agents had been popping up in IT and bothering the programmers. They had access to the company computer system and helped themselves to conference rooms and files. When she was busy they'd interrupt her, asking questions in accusing tones. She thought of the email she'd received from Aaron that morning telling her security was a nightmare after the LA attacks and coming back to work on Monday would not be fun. She uttered a sigh. *As if I had any expectation it would be.*

Jessie ran up and tossed two cartons of ice cream in the cart.

"Enough with the sweets," Sanya said. "Since you're in ninth grade, I've decided you can help me get the turkey ready."

Jessie braced her hands on her hips in that teenage pose. "But Marika can get herself ready without us."

"Don't make fun of your big sis." Sanya laughed and reached for a jar of gravy. "You know what I mean."

Suddenly, Sanya's body became heavy as if she was being pulled into quicksand. She was standing in SCED's Admin control room. Flames exploded and surrounded her. Her coworkers were pushing through emergency exits as alarms sounded. Blinded by fire she started screaming.

Her hip knocked against metal and someone grabbed her arm. The fire faded into the store's bright lights as she stared into the ceiling. Looking around in a daze, she realized that she must've knocked the stack of cans next to her off their display because they were now rolling across the floor.

Jessie was holding Sanya's arm and starting to cry. "Mom, what's the matter?"

A woman wearing a store badge ran toward her. "Did you need me to call for medical help?"

A small robot darted from the double doors behind the meat counter. Its mechanical fingers began setting the cans back onto the display.

"No," Sanya answered. "I'm fine. I'll go rest in the car. Thanks." She shoved a one thousand dollar cash card in Jessie's hand. "Can you pay for this?"

"Mom, let's go to Urgent Care."

"I need to sit down." Sanya's throat tightened but allowed her enough air to retain a dull consciousness.

The store employee shook her head. "Are you sure you don't need help?"

"Please, I just need some rest!" Sanya said. Her mouth dry and burning, as if still filled with fire, she swallowed and struggled not to choke.

"Okay." The woman shrugged and walked to the vegetable counters.

Sanya jogged toward the front of the store. She felt like everyone was staring at her. She focused on a row of glass refrigerators in front of the checkout stands that faced the aisles. Florescent lights bore down over her in dizzying white glows. She felt relief as she closed in on the exit. The automatic doors slid apart and she toppled over her feet rushing to freedom.

Breathing hard, she ran inside the parking structure. She stumbled into one of the elevators and rose to the third level. She ran to her car then pressed her thumb on the DNA reader on the driver's side mirror. The lock released and she pulled open the door. Falling into the driver's seat, Sanya dug through her cluttered purse for meds. She found her anti-anxiety patches and slapped one on her upper arm. She set the purse down and lay back. Papers and receipts seemed unfamiliar. Even the car felt different, as if not hers.

Her face throbbed with nausea. She tried to think of Thanksgiving and Christmas dinners and the fun times cooking and decorating. Leaning her head back, Sanya silently screamed at the enemy living in her head. Unfortunately, that enemy was her brain. The sound of knocking on glass startled her.

Sanya blinked. Jessie was standing next to the driver's window with a cart of bags next to her. "Mom, can you help me load the groceries?"

Taking a deep breath, Sanya felt less panicked. She was back in reality, at least for now.

"Let's go to Urgent Care," Jessie said. "You don't wanna be sick tomorrow."

Sanya got out of the car and helped toss bags into the trunk. "I need to lie down. I had an awful daydream, a vision."

Jessie brushed her ruddy bangs out of her face. "Like the one you had about Dad?"

"No, this was scary, not sad," Sanya said.

"What was the vision about?"

“I was in SCED while it was on fire. Just my imagination playing tricks on me.”

Jessie hugged Sanya’s waist. “Is something going to happen to SCED again? Can we catch the flesh-eating bacteria?”

“No, honey. The strain’s not contagious.”

“I’m scared. Meteors hit the beaches and SCED yesterday. People are saying there’s gonna be another terrorist attack. Why’s this stuff happening?”

Sanya brushed her hand over Jessie’s hair. “I don’t know about the meteors but terrorists can only scare us if we let them.”

* * *

Marika slid two cartons of milk across the refrigerator’s top shelf and shut the door. “Is there any reason to believe something will happen to SCED or IRE again?” She stared at her mom. “That dream back in May sorta came true.”

Sanya shoved the thought to the back of her mind. “I doubt it. After LA, it seems like these monsters have changed their tactics.”

“If the terrorists hadn’t hit in May, nobody would’ve known about the illegal waste,” Marika said. “Things would have been worse if the waste had stayed there.”

“At first I thought that attack could have been an inside job,” Sanya said, “though I couldn’t imagine how it was done.”

“Why’d you think that?”

“SCED had a lot of disgruntled employees after last year’s retirement scandal. But after the strep attack hit Los Angeles, I nixed that idea.” Sanya hugged Marika tight. “And don’t worry. Today’s vision was caused by stress from those damn DHS agents that have been poking around the IT department since May.”

Marika was silent and grabbed the kitchen cleaner. She shuffled away and sprayed the counter, wiping the same area with the cloth over and over. Sanya felt bad. Her girls had always struggled to cope with her visions and nightmares.

Sanya massaged her tight neck muscles. “I need to walk in Laguna Reserve for a few hours.”

“Good idea,” Marika said. “Maybe all of us can go to the forest section before Christmas.”

“We sure will, sweetie,” Sanya replied as an unexpected laugh escaped her. “I hope the meteors don’t come after me. I’ve had enough for one day.”

Still spraying cleaning solution over the counters and wiping the same areas, Marika seemed withdrawn, upset. Sanya understood why. “Sure, Mom,” she said flatly. “See you in a while.”

WED 11/22/2130
CALIFORNIA BOTANICAL RESERVE
LAGUNA BEACH, CA

Broken clouds filtered the sun's hot breath. Orange County was either hot and muggy or bitter damp cold. She was grateful today was an unusual happy medium. Sanya sighed as she felt a cool breeze brush over her skin. Her anti-anxiety patch smoothed the misery that had hit a couple hours earlier. The flames at SCED had extinguished in her mind for now.

She strolled down the park's sidewalks that arched like soft taffy over the shallow hills. The fifteen square kilometers of the reserve were gifted with California's diverse ecosystems—Desert Divine, Chaparral Shangri-La, Enchanted Forest, and Coastal Collage, among them. Her house was a twenty-minute drive away and this was only her third visit since the park opened two years earlier.

Sanya looked up at the colossal, transparent walls in the distance that had to be ten stories high. During the holiday season, Enchanted Forest was sealed. Machines sprayed snow over the statuesque pines, a reminder of her happy childhood in Lake Arrowhead.

Oak branches scratched together in the breeze in Chaparral Shangri-La. Towhees fluttered from tree to tree and then landed in their nests. Hummingbirds hydrated their petite frames as they landed on honeysuckle flowers. The new breed of perennial California poppies splashed vibrant orange through the grassy areas.

Sanya crossed the bridge that led to the Desert Divine section. Palm trees set in crushed granite towered over blossoming cacti that were covered with plate-sized magenta flowers. A pond centered in Cowabunga Cactus garden attracted crows and seagulls that didn't honor the boundaries between the park's ecosystems. She watched the birds swoop down toward children who were tossing crackers on the grass for them.

Watching the kids feed the birds was cathartic yet sad. She yearned for the days of innocence that vanished after turning thirteen when her first vision hit her. That was when she was forced to accept that she'd dream, think, and visualize what was imposed on her. One of life's privileges for most people was the ability to navigate their thoughts at will. This inalienable right had been snatched away from Sanya in middle school.

The clouds began to thicken and blocked the sun. Sanya walked on the sidewalk that circled the pond then returned to Chaparral Shangri-La. A few minutes later, she sat on a large bench built around the trunk of an oak tree. She ran her fingers across bushels of tiny, yellow wildflowers. College-aged kids on holiday break talked and laughed, read books, and fidgeted with their Epads and tablets. A young man with long brown hair sat on the grass and began playing his guitar. Sanya closed her eyes. Through the surrounding voices, giggles, computer beeps, and strums, she brought herself to the only moment she could enjoy—the one unfolding before her.

THURS 11/23/2130
SANYA VASQUEZ'S RESIDENCE
MISSION VIEJO, CA

At 00:15, Sanya sat on her bed and grabbed the December 2130 hardcopy edition of *Modern Woman* magazine from her end table. She swallowed an energy pill and sipped on a mug of cranberry tea. The potatoes would be peeled by 01:30 and then she'd prep the stuffing and vegetables. After watching a movie, she'd put the turkey meat in the oven at 04:00 and send the girls a text message on how to finish the last steps. Finally, she'd take a sleeping pill at 04:30 and set her alarm for 09:30.

Flipping through the magazine's pages, Sanya stopped at Doctor Katrina's column filled with letters from disgruntled women and a few men. She slid back on her pillow and read a letter from a woman who struggled to trust again. The text faded into gray, blurry stripes.

* * *

Violet clouds barricaded the sky like iron doors. Wearing her short pajama bottoms and a flannel shirt, Sanya dropped in the ocean, plunging down until her feet pressed into silt. Somebody she loved was hurting. The ocean bottom split below her and lava ejected around her. She catapulted into the sky from the force.

Soaring above the ocean, Sanya screamed when she looked down and saw muddied mountains rise past the water level. She rose further in the sky then began to plummet back toward the massive waves of water and lava below. Closing her eyes, she succumbed. This was where she was going to die.

The metal chair's cold seat burned Sanya's bare legs. She studied the operations control room in the SCED admin building. The first five screens displayed readings of eruptions and earthquakes happening in the Pacific Ocean. Lights on computers flickered.

As Sanya stared hypnotically at the screens, she saw her co-workers scramble past her and through her. She winced as their pink and red organs and skeletal structures squeezed beyond her. A green ribbon whipped like a rope up and down on the seismic monitor. The line veered off the screen like a gleaming snake beyond the measurement capacity of the 10.0 Richter scale.

Once again, Sanya felt like she was an alien in her own world. Though she recognized the frantic people as her coworkers, the figures still seemed to be strangers in an alternative reality. She watched screens six and seven display people evacuating from the Energy Systems building. SCED's ten reactors and IRE's spent fuel cooling units were shaking. Boiling lava burst through the Energy Systems building like ocean water overtaking a ship. As the ground shook, the cooling towers began sliding into the ground like dissolving sand castles.

She stared at the dense walls armoring the control room. Molecules and atoms receded into some other realm and Sanya was able to see through them. Nightshift workers dashed toward the building exits. Robo-guards from the IRE warehouses broke through the security glass in the lobby. They stomped down halls and blocked emergency exits, handcuffing workers to their metal arms. Screams ripped the air as people fought to escape. The guards were malfunctioning. Sanya licked her dry lips.

Glowing rock started spilling down the halls. Confused robots and their struggling prisoners dissolved in a stone broth. Sitting in a chair in front of screen eight, Sanya shoved her thumb on the keyboard's DNA reader. SCED's employee general menu displayed.

"Good Morning, Sanya Vasquez, Programming Manager. Access level eight of ten. Welcome to San Clemente Electrical Distribution."

Her eyes darted over the company's general menu: Information Technology, Energy Systems, Human Resources, Accounting and Finance, Plant Security, Research and Development, Quality Management, Facilities, Public Relations.

Sanya hung her head down, her heart pounding. Her shaking index finger touched the screen to activate the security module option. She navigated through different sub-menus. She found a link to a detailed map of the security floor. Testing various screen commands, she clenched her fist as live footage displayed.

Aaron sat in the chair at his desk. Lava was rising from sublevel two, through sublevel one, and then ground level. He knew the rock would rise past the fortified walls to the twentieth floor or the building would collapse. With lava now rising in the admin building and no escape, this room would be the place where he was going to die. He'd be gone before the magma found him and he knew that. He bowed his head and closed his eyes. *I have to say goodbye*, she thought.

Sanya watched Aaron mouth his last words. She headed up the stairwell toward his office. By level six she was panting and starting to cry. Then came levels seven, eight…ten. By the time she climbed toward level fifteen, her muscles were soft and blisters had erupted on her skin. Her vision was blurred by heat and smoke.

At level seventeen, she could barely see though the smoke and white heat. Her body was numb. She forced each leg to a higher stair, knowing how close she was. At level nineteen, her legs folded under her and she crawled to level twenty. Finally reaching the corridor that led to Aaron's office, she fell limp. Straining her eyes to focus, she saw through the walls. The room was engulfed in white flames. Sanya felt a gust of heat blow over her. She looked up and her eyes started burning. And so did the rest of her.

* * *

Marika and Jessie were staring down at Sanya. She shifted on her bed and realized her sheets were damp with sweat. She knew what had happened.

"Mom, you were shouting for Aaron," Marika said.

The bedroom was quiet and cool. Sanya blinked several times and groaned. *Damn,* she thought. *Not waking the kids again.* She wiped her forehead with her sheet. "I had a nightmare about SCED and IRE being swallowed by the earth, exploding and imploding at the same time. Aaron was there."

Her daughters looked at her with routine fright.

"I'm sorry, kids."

"Mom, this isn't about us," Marika said. "You need some type of medical treatment. Maybe Dr. Jaffrey can help."

Sanya covered her face with palms. "You're right. I can't live like this."

Marika sat on the bed. "I don't see how you have for so long."

Sanya grabbed her Epad off the nightstand and shouted in the receiver, "Aaron, work." As the phone rang, she closed her eyes.

"Hello? Hello?"

Aaron's face transmitted on the screen and she forced a calm expression. Sanya noticed Marika shooting her a sly smile while Jessie giggled.

"Hey, Aaron. Happy Thanksgiving."

"Sanya!" Aaron laughed in his gravelly voice and flashed the smile that she had to admit she still swooned over. "What are you doing awake?"

Sanya rubbed her face. *Crap, why am I calling?* "I was having trouble sleeping. You know my insomnia."

"I remember," Aaron said. "Bad dream again?"

Her voice cracked through awkward fabrication as her daughters smiled at her. "Yes. I'm calling because think I forgot to turn off my computer when I left for vacation. I know they're supposed to automatically shut down, but I was worried."

"I gotta give you credit," he said. "On Thanksgiving, most employees wouldn't care if their computers were singing program codes to terrorist satellites."

Sanya shook her head. "Some would."

"Not most," Aaron said. "But don't worry. The network scans the company PCs for active units. Any unit that shows no sign of use for more than two hours is shut down. Didn't you get the updated security memo after the May attack?"

"I read most of them, but I lose track of all the changing policies," Sanya said, hoping her half-truth was a bit convincing.

"The old rule was every four hours." Aaron paused and stared straight at her. "Now, it's almost 03:30. Are you sure you didn't call to talk to me?"

Sanya thought for a second and looked at Marika, who shrugged. How could she get out of this? "I work with computers and am well aware that no system's foolproof. I handle a lot of information that unauthorized people could use to their advantage. And of course, I'm comfortable calling you with concerns."

Marika and Jessie nodded with approval at the hatched up story. Sanya hoped she wasn't as obvious to Aaron.

"Okay, sweetie," Aaron said with a chuckle. "Whatever you say. I'll do a system check on your machine. Are your mom and dad com-ing' over tomorrow?"

"They sure are," Sanya answered. "What are you doing?"

"Going to my sister's in town then to San Luis Obispo on Friday to see the kids."

"Well, have fun. I'll see you Monday. Happy Thanksgiving, Aaron."

"You too. If there's anything else you need, let me know."

"Sure will. Goodnight." Sanya set the Epad down and smiled so hard her face hurt.

Marika hugged her. "Everything's okay. You talked to Aaron and he's fine. How about Jessie and I sleep in here tonight like the old days?"

Buster leapt on the bed and spun his tail in circles.

"This king-sized bed can hold all of us," Sanya said as she changed her Epad alarm to 07:00. "Let's put the turkey in the oven and take care of the rest in the morning."

Sanya and the girls walked down the hall toward the kitchen. Maybe she and Aaron could work things out. She just had to let go of her fears.

* * *

Sanya woke up with Buster's back shoved against her face. Somehow he'd contorted his body between Marika and Jessie. Twisting around the dog and into a sitting position, she grabbed the HV remote and pressed the power button. Nothing. She flipped the power button again. Her heart began pounding with dread. Nothing. She ran to the HV and pushed the power button. Nothing. Looking at her sleeping daughters she noticed that the clock was black. That meant SCED electricity was out. The generator's default setting was limited to the kitchen.

Afraid to look at her Epad, Sanya slammed it face down on her end table. As she ran in the garage, she heard Buster trotting behind her. She flipped the generator's switch to expand the power through the whole house. As more electricity started to flow, the gauges began to brighten with numbers. Battery registers changed from yellow to white. She ran back in the house and in the family room. The HV's dark screen was serene like the deep ocean water in her nightmares. Looking at the remote control's power button, Sanya figured the small red button was probably the path to despair. Her index finger trembled as she barely pressed it.

The images formed instantly, stabbing Sanya in the chest like a thousand daggers. From the eye of a Slojet, SCED and IRE had transformed into piles of steaming rubble. Black and orange glowing rock lined the coast. Tides crashed over the hot lava creating plumes of steam. In the background, a newscaster wouldn't shut up.

"Two hundred people are believed dead. Electrical power has been cut off for ten million customers in California. Battery reserves are holding strong. Investigators are checking to see if this attack is linked to the one in May."

Sanya shoved her face against the couch pillow and screamed. The searing agony of being right, of being cursed, flooded her body. How could this have happened *after* the dream? The curse was expanding, growing like a crazed demon taking over her brain. Buster whimpered and licked the sides of her face.

Rolling on her side, Sanya faced the HV. Marika walked in and sat on the couch. Jessie followed and stared at the HV, and looked down. Both of the girls had tears in their eyes. They must have seen the news on their Epads.

"Let's finish getting dinner ready," Sanya said, gasping as she sat up. She couldn't deal with this. Had to pretend it wasn't real. Falling back on the couch she started sobbing.

Marika wiped tears from her face with her hand. "Don't worry. Jessie and I will take care of dinner."

"I can only hope Aaron was home when this happened." Sanya's heart ached. She should've never broken up with him. Her kids liked him, she loved him. The fear of betrayal and knowing too much had pulled her away. She shoved her face back in her pillow.

After a few minutes, Sanya forced herself off the couch and followed Marika into the kitchen. She peeked in the oven. The turkey was fine. *Who gives a shit?* She walked to the sink and hung her face over the drain. Her Epad was in her room and it was surely getting calls. Soon the home phone would start up. Marika and Jessie solemnly whipped potatoes and cut vegetables as if also pushing away the reality.

Sanya reached for a mixing bowl inside a top cabinet. A steel pan slid past her, bouncing on her foot then onto the floor in a series of shrill yelps.

"Son of a bitch!" She kicked the pan into a wall. Her toes, covered with soft slippers, ached in relief.

Marika turned from the Vegaslicer. "Mom, there's nothing you could've done!" Her voice lowered to a teary whisper. "Get some rest. When grandma and grandpa get here, I'll wake you up."

Sanya had always prepared the Thanksgiving meal from scratch. That was a gift to her family. Her mom took care of Christmas. Today, she was failing, unraveling.

"If anyone calls except Aaron, say I'm sick over what happened. I'll call them back." She staggered down the hall toward her bedroom. Why was she born this way? Why was she born? *Welcome to the lake of fire your grandma warned you about.*

Sanya lay on her bed next to Buster who was awake and resting his head on one of the pillows. She shut off her Epad without looking at it. Marika and Jessie had a tough life in some ways; no father beyond sporadic child support payments and a mother weighed down by episodes of tormented dreams and visions. She was proud of both of them. They were responsible young women who cared beyond themselves.

Staring at the ceiling, Sanya couldn't stop her panic. Other dreams had always struck her after or during a tragedy. When her brother died, she'd felt guilty for not helping him. The nuns at church warned her about evil forces that could bring on self-loathing. They told her that she'd been powerless to help her brother. God's goodness was stronger than evil, they told her. She wondered if she didn't have enough faith.

Buster's pale brown eyes stared at Sanya with that loyal compassion that animals had. He knew she was doing her best, and she had to believe that so did God.

* * *

"These damn things always shrink after they're washed," Sanya muttered. She stretched the corner of a fitted sheet over the mattress in the guest room. Her parents deserved a decent place to sleep after they'd driven all the way from Flagstaff.

Her nostrils burned like she'd inhaled cleaning fluid. She'd thrown up twice after dinner and the release of anguish had been exhilarating. She knew she'd have to call her surviving co-workers and stop feeling sorry for herself. SCED could start an assistance drive for displaced employees. She was one of the lucky few who had some spare money.

A flashback to Aaron's face in the Epad weakened her. He'd been among those confirmed dead. An aching wail fell from her mouth. She grabbed a tissue and wiped her face. Not another person she loved, not after her brother.

Marika tapped on the bedroom door and walked in. Her eyes were wide, her lips trembling. Why was her baby afraid?

"Mom, some people want to talk to you."

Standing up, Sanya grabbed a tissue from the nightstand and wiped her nose. "Sure, honey. Let them in."

She looked up and the figures walking in the room looked familiar: two men in suits and a woman in a suit. *Who are they?* Then she remembered—they looked like some of the DHS agents picking around SCED.

Her heart skipped as she felt her arms yanked behind her and restraints locked around her wrists. The agents shot her icy stares that made her shudder.

"Sanya Vasquez," one of the men said, "you are under arrest for conspiracy to commit terrorist acts against San Clemente Electrical Distribution and International Refuse Eliminators. You have the right to remain silent. Anything you say can and will be used against you in a court of law. You have a right to an attorney. If you cannot afford one, one will be appointed for you."

Sanya tightened her hand around her wipe and said, "What are you talking about?"

"Do you understand your rights?"

"What's happening?"

"Do you understand your rights, Ms. Vasquez?"

Sanya cleared her throat and swallowed. "Yes."

She was led down the hall by the woman while the two men trailed behind them. Like a criminal, she was being torn from her home where she raised her girls. Pictures on the walls passed her by. Another suited man held open the front door.

Sanya's mom and daughters followed her outside and stood on the front lawn. Police cars were crowded around her home. Her dad was in the driveway arguing with an Orange County sheriff as Sanya was led into the backseat of a sedan.

Neighbors and their visiting families stood on tidy lawns, their faces drawn into curious scowls. Slojets spiraled in the skies. The car backed out of the driveway and turned to the street. Buster stared outside from Jessie's bedroom window. Sanya licked a drop of blood that leaked from her nose onto her upper lip. Indeed, the beasts were often the lucky ones.

FRI 11/24/2130
MARCH PLANETARY PATROL BASE
MORENO VALLEY, CA

The Unity shuttle circled over the March Base runway to prepare for landing. Daniel admired the structures below through the low morning haze. The military installation stretched several kilometers down the California Interstate 215. Lunar transport ships were aimed upright, ready for takeoff. Ships built for human voyages to Mars and unmanned ships for Venus were displayed under large, transparent aircraft hangars. A tall, hexagon structure made up the base hospital. Nearby was a shopping center. An aircraft museum was set in the northwest end.

Daniel had heard that the surface buildings were only a portion of what existed here, that underground warehouses held secret weapons and bunkers that far surpassed LA Valley. In the base's center was an observatory that he'd always wanted to visit. He'd have to take the grand tour.

No one else on the shuttle seemed interested in the base. Daniel couldn't help but be fascinated. Maybe it was all those military toys and games his dad had bought him over the years. Casey and Cindera were asleep in their seats. Matt was playing chess.

"Doesn't this base impress you?" Daniel said to anyone who might listen. "You should be chomping at the bit to see what goes on here."

Matt froze the holographic pieces fighting on his game board and looked at Daniel. "Not on the day after Thanksgiving. I'd just got home last night to visit my dad and grandparents. Nielsen's assistant calls and tells me to go to DC and board this damn shuttle at 05:00 today. Has Nielsen any shame?"

"He's not gifted with a surplus," Daniel said, thinking of the LA Valley trick pulled on him. "I was supposed to be on Unity this weekend working on a camp report. Now JoMarie has to finish it. Still, this place and its history are pretty cool."

"I don't care," Matt said. "We finish one PR assignment in LA and then we're shipped back to California. Nobody says a word but 'go.'"

Daniel's stomach fell as it always did when the shuttle dropped for landing. He tensed his muscles to soften the descent.

"In all fairness to Nielsen, we need public support for mission funding. When investigators from the base contacted him, he agreed to let us come here for a few days. I guess a general here is heading part of the investigation. He liked the work JoMarie and I did in investigating the 2127 eco-attacks in the Bronx and Philadelphia."

"Then you and JoMarie should've come," Matt said.

"Nielsen wouldn't let her go," Daniel answered. "So it's you, me and the animals. Plus the general liked the mission's advances in AI programs for scientific analysis."

"The jury's still out on that," Matt said.

"Either way, we're gonna talk to the woman arrested in the San Clemente attacks. DHS wants to know if it's linked to GlobeTek Finance and who knows what else."

Matt sneered. "Does it matter?"

"Yes," Daniel said. "We have a collapsing ecosystem, people dying of African Plague in epidemic proportions. Plus, humans could be entering the early phases of extinction."

"I read Donovan and Nielsen's report; just a bunch of end-timer bullshit. I'm surprised they'd buy into that."

"We can't downplay what they found."

"I can and will." Matt rolled his eyes. "Having the weekend off to see my family wouldn't have changed the planet's destiny."

Daniel reclined his chair. "DHS wants to interrogate the woman before her defenses build up. We may also be able to figure out the technology used in the SCED attacks using a new AI program called Humanspeak that Donovan's been working on."

"Sound like underground imploding devices were used."

"But DHS would know that," Daniel said. "We might also get to interpret the suspect's brainwaves. I'm a little excited. If we're successful in solving this case, we'll get the credibility we deserve for the work we've done toward improving Earth's ecosystem. That means more funding for research."

Matt scoffed at Casey, who was sleeping belly up across three seats. "Wasn't LA Valley enough?"

Daniel felt a hint of self-interest thinking of Jeanette. "That wasn't so bad. I unknowingly helped steal lifesaving drugs for the SEV4 victims."

"You're only glad because you got to meet that doctor."

"That was a pleasant surprise too," Daniel said, remembering that he had to email Sharon and find out more information on Jeanette without appearing obvious. Probably too late for that, he figured. "The public expects us to be interactive, not aloof, tight-jawed scientists working on a space station."

"DHS is wasting our salaries. I still can't see the purpose that Casey and the feline are going to serve besides eat, sleep, and you know the rest."

"They're more intuitive than people, and their five senses are more highly developed."

"That's Sharon's interpretation."

"It was good enough for DHS."

"We're not criminal investigators," Matt protested. "Our mission is to find solutions to the ecosystem's crisis. Now we're stuck hunting down suspected terrorists." He set his game under his seat. "I've been looking forward to this four-day weekend since Labor Day."

"USRG soldier!" Daniel said, unable to resist needling Matt. He shook his finger. "If Uncle Sam wants our help with an eco-attack, there's not a whole lot we can do to stop him."

"Screw Uncle Sam," Matt said. "He's most of the reason we're in this ecological mess and I think mindreading is a crock of shit."

"That sounds like court martial talk, soldier. We need to sanitize our language."

Cindera opened her eyes and stretched. "Don't be stupid, Matthew Bertrand. There are physical realities in our universe we can't experience because our senses lack capacity. Do atoms not exist because your naked eye can't see them? Just because a fetus is unaware of having a mother doesn't mean it doesn't have one. Maybe mindreading technology has opened a new door to our awareness." She scratched her chest and blew on her left paw.

"Our senses lack capacity?" Matt snapped back. "Am I mistaken or are you a cat and I, a person? Is there some oversight I'm not aware of?"

"Indeed there is," Cindera said. "I am a cat and you're a person. If I were a person, I wouldn't like you because I don't know one who does. I at least tolerate you."

Daniel laughed. "She's pretty sharp."

"Her smart mouth doesn't bother me." Matt stared at Cindera. "Go turd in your cat box."

Cindera's gold eyes reflected the sun, giving her pupils an emerald glow. "I used a commode even before my operation. For you, however, when I get back to Unity I will visit your room and find an obscure place to deposit my gift."

"Stop acting so pompous."

"She was trying to help," Daniel said. "You're an intelligent boy and I do mean boy. You need to grow up."

Matt slid down in his seat. "She's giving me a 'cattitude'. My IQ's one sixty, a genius no less, much higher than that beast's, and she's patronizing me!"

"My IQ's one eighty-five," Daniel said, wondering why his genius capacities didn't help him be more savvy with women. "Frankly, I feel like I don't know shit right now. Stop antagonizing Cindera."

"So your smart ass IQ's one eighty-five," Matt said as he dug in his backpack and tossed a square of plastic at Daniel. "This is a deluxe Rubik's cube with twenty-five squares per side. First time, I figured out the solution in twenty minutes."

Daniel grabbed the cube and stared for a few seconds. The flaw was obvious. He spiked the cube at Matt, hitting him on the arm. "You're full of crap."

"Too wise for your cerebral owl?"

“You didn’t solve this thing. This cube has twenty-six squares of three colors and twenty-four of three colors. You can’t get one color on all six sides. The cube’s a trick.”

Matt looked sheepishly at Daniel. “That’s what took me twenty minutes to figure out.”

FRI 11/24/2130
USRG BASE QUARTERS
MORENO VALLEY, CA

Daniel read between the lines. The plain but comfortable furniture in this three-bedroom, two-bath apartment indicated they'd be staying awhile. Part of him was glad to be there, but he dreaded another delay for Phase II. He looked at his Epad and revisited the emails JoMarie had sent him during the shuttle ride. She'd informed him that General Andre Jackson would be directing the USRG's role in the investigation and would be contacting them soon after they arrived at the base. She had attached investigator files, which he'd skimmed through. He looked on the coffee table. There was a hardcopy file on Sanya Vasquez next to a computer tablet.

Matt plopped on the couch, wearing a scowl that Daniel knew was a precursor to what he'd be dealing with. If only JoMarie could've come instead. He liked Matt, but the guy had growing up to do.

"Did you review the DHS reports JoMarie sent us?" Daniel asked.

"Yeah," Matt said, pinching his mouth to one side. "We can't assume a forty-five-year-old Catholic woman is less likely to be a terrorist than an adolescent Jihad boy. Most sects have killed for their imaginary gods."

Daniel paced around the room. "Most religious killing is selfish ambition justified as holy. If there is a creator of the universe, I'm sure it can kill anything it wants and in effect, un-create, without the help of humans."

Setting his feet on the coffee table, Matt groaned. "The suspect was arrested after Thanksgiving dinner while putting a sheet on a bed. Based on what I've read, she's either presenting a masterful front or Uncle Sam needs a dose of powdered reality sprinkled on his apple pie."

Daniel tried to connect the dots. "There's a lot of unanswered questions. That's why DHS wants us to analyze her."

Cindera jumped on the coffee table and rubbed her front paws together. "As someone who is refined in the art of human nature, I suggest we extract the truth without resorting to the harsh methods that have been pulled in the past."

Casey trotted in the living room from the bedroom he was sharing with Daniel. Walking to Cindera, he said, "Pardon me? We canines have our own take on human nature. From a psychological standpoint, people are quite simple."

"I'm sorry," Cindera answered. "I meant no offense."

Casey nodded and sat on the rug. "Understood."

"That's why you two were brought here," Daniel said, ignoring Matt's grumbling. "You two can help figure out the best approach to getting information out of Sanya Vasquez."

"I say we bring Charlie D. into the equation," Matt said. "Bring out her survival instinct and fear of death. Use her kids and parents as weapons."

Turning to Casey, Cindera aimed her paw at Matt. "Is that what you meant by simple?"

Casey bared an alligator grin, "He shines with simple."

Cindera lay next to Casey on the rug and closed her eyes. Casey rolled on his back and started snoring.

"See, what did I tell you?" Matt said. "They've already started doing nothing."

Wincing a little, Daniel pushed out his bottom lip in deep thought. "They're nocturnal."

"Okay, defend them as usual. You're their daddy and Sharon's their mommy."

The word 'daddy' hit Daniel unexpectedly. A stinging sadness flowed through him as memories of Hannah swooped over his head. "At least I'm someone's daddy."

"I'm sorry. You know I'm teasing you about the prodigies."

"That's okay. I know what you meant."

Seeing the animals in such a peaceful state, Daniel envied how they could go to sleep at will. "I'm gonna pretend I didn't hear that Charlie comment. You know how that riles JoMarie."

"I'm telling you what works."

Shaking his head with a slight laugh, Daniel turned on the tablet and expanded the screen to the forty-centimeter max. Unable to sit down after being in the shuttle for three hours, he shifted back and forth on his feet. Opening the report file, he read sections from the Orange County, California Sheriff's report.

"Sanya Vasquez was arrested after her co-workers called the Orange County Sheriff Department's hotline. The callers told police that Sanya knew details about yesterday's SCED attack before it happened."

Daniel scanned through the pages. He couldn't imagine a divorced woman with her good job history and two kids being a part of something like this. At first he thought she might've needed the money, but her credit reports came out good. She was a computer programming manager who got paid well. Shaking his head, he found an interesting snippet.

"SCED phone records show that at 03:25 Thanksgiving morning, Sanya called the security director, Aaron Willis, who was also her ex-fiancé. The company records all its security calls. She told Aaron that her computer might've been left on. Her tone of voice seemed happy and she made small talk with him. SCED was destroyed an hour and a half later."

"Sounds like she was making up a reason to talk to him," Matt said. "According to the report, the day before the drums were shot over SCED in May, she went to guy's office. She'd fallen and hurt her hip in SCED's lobby during a meteor storm that hit San Clemente. According to statements after her arrest, that morning she'd had a nightmare about floating in the ocean and seeing casks filled with spent fuel. That was the day after the SCED meteor storm."

Daniel navigated through the file. *Of course, the meteor storm again*

"She works at a power plant that generates radioactive shit and has bad dreams about her job. Who doesn't?" He moved to another page in the report.

"The day before Thanksgiving," he continued, "a long-time friend called Ms. Vasquez's home phone because she wasn't answering her Epad. Her fourteen-year-old daughter Jessie answered. She told the caller that her mother went to the Laguna Reserve after getting sick in the grocery store, where she had a vision. In that vision, she saw fire around her at SCED. The friend knew of Ms. Vasquez's alleged psychic episodes and left a message for Sanya to call her.

"Being at the grocery store makes me sick too," Matt said.

"That's because you hate grocery shopping," Daniel noted. "Employees interviewed at the store verified that Sanya had collapsed and ran out, leaving her daughter with a cash card. DHS thinks she could've faked the vision to support her story."

Looking for more detail, Daniel tapped his finger on a link.

"Here it says that Aaron Willis was an avid environmentalist in his youth and had been politically active in promoting solar energy. Ironic, considering he ran security in SCED's nuclear division."

Matt squinted. "I picked that up, too. SCED has sizable solar, wind, and natural gas divisions. Aaron talked like a hick, but he was a genius according to interviews with his friends and family. Kind of like Robert, I suspect."

"Probably," Daniel said, reviewing more text. "Aaron Willis was arrested twice for hanging banners on cooling towers. He pled guilty to misdemeanor counts of trespassing and was put on probation. That was twenty-five years ago. He was an excellent employee according to SCED evaluations. He was divorced with two grown kids and two grandkids." Daniel shook his head. "I don't know."

"Was this woman on good terms with her ex?" Matt said. "Or was him being melted alive an unforeseen bonus?"

Grunting out a chuckle, Daniel thought of Cherril. She probably would've melted him alive in a building if given a chance. And right after Hannah died, he probably would've let her. He glanced at his Epad notes. "According to interviews with SCED employees, she was friendly with Aaron and had lunch with him sometimes." Daniel sat and fidgeted through the hardcopy reports. "DHS believes he could've known the attack was coming."

"A suicide mission?"

"He wasn't scheduled to work and volunteered to fill in on Thanksgiving. Pretty generous."

"Martyrs are so stupid." Matt raised his palm toward the ceiling. "Oh, wait! They're going to a special place in post-mortem paradise." He turned back to Daniel and set his hand down. "In other words, nowhere."

Daniel gripped the tablet hoping Matt was wrong for Hannah's sake.

"Neurological testing in high school," he began, "showed Sanya Vasquez had limited psychic episodes. They were similar to a near-death experience where people's consciousness seems to separate from their bodies. That gave her the ability to see events occurring in places where she wasn't physically present." He handed Matt the tablet. "Did you see page ten of section one?" Matt said, changing the tablet page to the first section. "On Thanksgiving, when Sanya was getting all those calls while napping, her twenty-one-year-old daughter Marika answered the phone. The girl was crying when she talked to the callers. She told two of her mother's coworkers, who she also knew, that her mother was devastated after having an early morning nightmare about SCED and finding out her dream came true."

Daniel sighed and marched in place, not ready to acquiesce to the couch or recliner. "Sanya's daughters knew Aaron and liked him."

"Do they know anything else?"

"Hard to tell," Daniel said, "but the nightmare is on top of the grocery store vision the day before. That's why her defense is that she's psychic. The interrogations should determine that validity of that."

Daniel wandered into the small kitchen and checked the refrigerator that was filled with food. He looked for something that could pass for lunch. He grabbed a wrapped sandwich, a diet root beer, and bag of cheese puffs. Admitting defeat by hunger and fatigue, he sunk in the couch next to Matt. He tore open the bag and grabbed a handful of puffs.

Matt stared at Daniel's soda. "Can I have a drink? After I got meds for my animal allergies, I'm not coughing as much."

"A sip. Then get your own. The sodas are ten steps away in the refrigerator."

Taking a wet slurp from the bottle, Matt frowned. "Sanya's role in the attack became suspect when one co-worker called back. She started asking questions about the nightmare. The daughter, still crying, told the caller about malfunctioning robotic security. This was not public information."

Daniel took the tablet back and scanned over section one. "Marika said she and her sister Jessie woke up after hearing screams from their mother's bedroom. They ran to her room and Sanya told them about her nightmare. The similarities between what SCED co-workers were told Wednesday and Thursday by the daughters and what actually happened is on the money. DHS isn't buying the psychic victim theory."

"They have to do more than reject the psychic theory," Matt said. "They have to have their own."

"They think she's using reverse psychology," Daniel said. "Her defense is that psychics have been falsely accused of crimes in the past. DHS thinks she could have psychic capacity and is using it as a front to cover her lie."

"And there's evidence that she's done this before?"

"There's nothing in this report I've seen that indicates that."

Casey's eyes popped open. Daniel remembered how the animals often appeared asleep, but were taking in scents and listening to every sound in the room.

The dog raised an eyebrow at him. "Her co-workers and friend called the cops on her?"

"Yes," Daniel said. "They called the Orange County Sheriff's hotline. The info was passed to DHS."

"According to this report," Matt said, "the daughters are distraught and blaming themselves. They're staying with their grandparents at a nearby hotel. I'd feel like crap, too, if I were them."

Daniel had his share of nightmares in the past and had woken up if not screaming, then gasping for air or panting. How likely was it that Sanya Vasquez was faking the visions, pretending to have nightmares and screaming, and then lying to her daughters?

Cindera stretched and hopped on the couch. “This dream must have upset her. Her daughters said they heard her screaming.”

“Maybe they’re in on this,” Matt said.

“No, Matt,” Cindera said. “I think her coworkers and friend assumed the worst.”

“I’m looking for evidence. I haven’t seen much yet toward guilt or innocence.”

Finishing off his soda and sandwich, Daniel put his legs on the coffee table. “Hundreds of people were dead. SCED was destroyed. I’m sure those who called the hotline were trying to help the investigation.”

“Innocent until proven guilty,” Casey said with his lips pursed out.

“We don’t know for sure if Sanya is innocent,” Daniel responded. “What’s interesting to me is, like the May attack, the destruction occurred when there was a reduced staff. At 04:00, Aaron Willis let one hundred people go home early for the holiday, allowing the surveillance to run on partial autopilot until the new shift started at 06:00. This leads to the possibility that killing people may not have been the attackers’ objective. The purpose of the SCED and IRE attacks could be....”

“The destruction of the plant,” Matt finished. “So, the plot of environmental terrorism becomes more probable. Aaron becomes more likely to be involved. He was also on duty during the attack in May.”

“There’s no environmental group I’ve heard of,” Daniel said, “that could or would do something like this. I can’t say if Aaron belonged to a rouge group, but such a club would have to have to be connected with the world’s most advanced physicists and weapons’ engineers.” He thought of the beam coming from the ocean. “Or something else.”

* * *

Daniel looked up when the door to their quarters slid open. Remembering his dad in uniform, he recoiled a bit. General Andre Jackson walked to the couch. His head was a few pegs down from the ceiling. The blue uniform and four silver stars on his shoulders signified he'd seen a lot and was results-oriented. His dense, blackish gray hair was cropped and his eyes were blacker than his glossed shoes.

"Hello, Daniel," the general said, shaking his hand. "Thanks for taking time off your mission to help us. I know of your father, General Griffin. I bet you're proud of him. He's done a great job serving his country."

Daniel felt like saying that his dad serving his family with something besides a backhand across the face might have been nice, too. "Thanks, General Jackson. I know he served his country well during his career."

The general saluted him and added, "And if the son is like his father, you'll do the same."

Daniel saluted back and nodded. He thought of the different types of patriotism, some expressed through peace and others through war. "I hope to have the opportunity."

"You will," the general said. "I talked to JoMarie Sanford last night and am glad to hear that you'll be staying as long as necessary."

Daniel looked around the apartment again. Just as he'd figured. "The extended stay has been approved by Dr. Nielsen?"

"Not really. He has some dismal predictions about humanity's future that he expects you to turn around. I explained that if we can stop the monsters that are destroying power plants and engaging in biological warfare, then our odds might go up."

"I agree," Daniel said.

"He was willing to have you stay for a week," the general said, "but when he found out it could be for up to a month he got quite perturbed."

Wondering if Nielsen's skin tone had turned terracotta or electric crimson during the talk with the general, Daniel laughed. "British intellects don't get angry, they get perturbed."

The general nodded. "With your knowledge of the environment and AI program analysis experience, we hope to get closer to some explanation because right now we have nothing. Also I understand that the enhanced animals are very astute."

"They assist in analysis," Daniel said. "They're also living lie detectors."

"Good. We'll use all of your skills then get you back on the mission as soon as we can. I'm leading the US Air Force's part of the investigation because the first attack involved using waste casks as a projectile in US airspace. DHS is involved, as well. We'd like you to interview the suspect as soon as possible."

"Yes, sir. Anytime you like."

"How about now?"

Daniel paused. "Okay. We haven't prepared any questions."

"That's all right," the general said. "The questioning is intended for you to assess any scientific evidence in her statements that may lead us to what she knows. Just start talking and get a feel for where's she's coming from. An officer will escort you to the interrogation room in a few minutes."

The general stared down at Matt. "Ms. Sanford didn't tell me you were bringing the interns."

"Nielsen sent him and he's a full-fledged physicist," Daniel said. "This is Matthew Bertrand. He's the USRG project specialist in charge of energy systems."

General Jackson's gaze scaled Matt from head to toe. "He looks a little scrappy to be doing such a man's job."

Matt scowled. "I'll have you know that I've worked for the Pentagon."

"Did you fetch donuts? I could use a few."

"I assisted in the development of missile defense technology," Matt answered.

Daniel tried not to laugh as Matt gritted his teeth. This is probably what he needed.

"Okay kid," the general deadpanned. "We'll see what you're made of."

Casey trotted from his bedroom wearing his DHS vest with Cindera following him.

"General, may I be permitted to observe the suspect? My name's Casey Caldwell, the founding member of the Enhanced Canine Anti-Terrorist Team. I can identify body language and voice tones that fit patterns associated with false statements. I also smell things you can't even imagine."

Daniel smiled as the general quizzically stared at Casey. He felt a paternal bond. The dog had gotten him in plenty of trouble by repeating things, but he always he meant well.

"I bet you can," General Jackson said to Casey. "I heard you could talk, but you sound better than I expected. Nice vest."

"Thank you. I also have more formal attire if needed." He motioned to the cat. "This is Cindera, my co-worker."

Cindera extended her paw. "I would be honored to help in the investigation."

The general released a cavernous laugh and shook her paw. "We need all the help we can get. And I think you animals may give us insights we wouldn't think of."

"I'll make sure I tell Vladimir Chistyakov that," Daniel said. "He's quite the skeptic when it comes to enhancements."

"Oh the UN leader?" the general answered. "Ah the Russian doesn't appreciate how creative us Americans are in our knowledge gathering."

He walked to the front door. "The suspect has probably never encountered a talking animal, since they're so new to the public domain. It might startle her into a little truth talk."

The door shut behind the general as he started down the hall.

"Seems like an asshole," Matt said.

Daniel magnetized his Epad to his forearm. "You better hope these quarters aren't bugged. The general seemed to like Casey and Cindera, but Mr. Bertrand, I think you'll have to earn your stripes."

FRI 11/24/2130
MARCH BASE INTERVIEW ROOM
MORENO VALLEY, CA

DHS's terrorist had a face, but it was nothing like Daniel expected. Sanya Vasquez sat separated from him and the others by a wall of bulletproof glass. They shared a table that had a large slot where paperwork or other information could be exchanged. Her collarbone protruded from under her olive skin. Her face was stiff and her mouth hung slightly open as if still in shock that she was a prisoner. Dark hair tinged with blonde streaks hung wearily around her face. Her bloodshot green eyes seemed resigned.

Matt sported a sneer, perhaps a sign of an interrogation technique he had in mind to impress the general. Daniel hoped not. He wasn't in the mood for surprises.

Casey looked at Daniel and then the woman. He cleared his throat. "Hello, my name is Casey Caldwell. I'm a project specialist for the Global Restoration Mission."

Jerking back in her chair, Sanya Vasquez's eyes widened. Daniel saw that the woman couldn't believe what she was hearing. She hadn't been exposed to talking animals yet. He hoped they could be in charge, at least for a while.

Sliding his Epad from his USRG vest pocket, Casey smacked his lips. "I'm one of a handful of animals in the world with speech capability. I'll be listening to your statements and gauging their truthfulness."

"Ms. Vasquez," Daniel said, "these animals have enhanced intelligence. Although Casey's no longer classified, he's new to the public eye. Don't underestimate him. He's very experienced at his job."

Jotting notes on his Epad, Casey raised one eyebrow as if trying to look inquisitive. "If I have any questions, I'll interject."

"Whatever you say," she whispered.

Daniel tried not to laugh at the Sherlock Holmes look on Casey's face. "I'm Daniel Griffin. Like Casey and the others, I'm a scientist on the Global Restoration Mission. My expertise lies in studying the effects of industrial waste on Earth's ecosystem. I've also worked on eco-terror cases involving employee sabotage."

"And you think I did this?" Sanya said.

"I don't know yet." Daniel motioned to the others. "The young man sitting by Casey is Matt Bertrand, a nuclear physicist. And the cat is Cindera Caldwell."

Staring at Casey, Sanya Vasquez nodded.

"Ms. Vasquez," Daniel said. "Do you have any information about the source or method that caused the May and November attacks on SCED and IRE?"

"Please use my first name," she said. "I've had enough ridiculous formalities. I'm a terrorist suspect who doesn't know anything about how this happened or who did it. Nothing."

Daniel drummed his fingers on the table, not knowing what to call the SCED event. "Okay, Sanya, how did you know beforehand about the horrific destruction that destroyed SCED and IRE, killing two hundred people?"

Sanya's voice was flat as if coming from an automated phone system.

"Wednesday, I had a vision at the grocery store," she said. "I was getting groceries when suddenly I was surrounded by fire in SCED's operations control room. Then, Thanksgiving morning, I had a gruesome nightmare about SCED and my ex-fiancé, Aaron. When I woke up, I called him because he was working the graveyard shift. When I found out everything was normal at the plant, I figured my nightmare was from stress."

"Do you understand why the authorities have trouble believing you?" Daniel said.

"I struggle to believe it myself," Sanya answered. "I've never had a premonition before. I don't know who or what caused this and couldn't begin to imagine why." She sighed. "I already explained this to DHS."

Matt's grimace transformed into words. "And to think they didn't unlock your cuffs and send you home! 'Oh, a vision. I'm so sorry, ma'am, how could we have overlooked that one?'"

He gave her the bad cop stare Daniel had watched him practice in their quarters. "Perhaps you're a psychic terrorist who's using her predictive abilities as a bullshit alibi. Do you know anything about the LA attacks?"

Daniel wrung his hands. "Sanya, we need more information to conclude you're not involved."

"No, you don't," Casey said. "My instincts tell me she's on the level."

"Thanks, Casey," Daniel said as he motioned him to a chair. "But we need tangible information, too."

"My hunches are better than tangible information," he huffed.

Sanya buried her face in her hands. "I'd never allow my friends and co-workers to die! And I sure wouldn't infect people in Los Angeles! I can understand asking me about SCED but DHS is grilling me about LA too."

Daniel decided to steer his questioning toward Aaron Willis. "Do you know anyone who would've done this, anyone angry at SCED or society in general?"

"We had a retirement scandal last year, but the company settled."

"The retirees that sued the company have already been investigated and cleared."

"Then I have no idea."

"Are you sure?" Matt said.

"She told you she has no idea!" Casey barked out.

"According to your medical records," Daniel said, ignoring Casey's outburst, "your abilities are limited to trans-physical perception. You're saying this has expanded to trans-time perception. Your mind can see things that will happen in the future as well as in other places. That's a big change."

Sanya's face reddened. "Don't I know that? Shortly after I turned thirteen, my brain seemed to grow a satellite that traveled the world, transmitting information to me about people I loved. I've never had a premonition until now."

Matt's raucous snort assaulted Daniel's ears. "Your story's a crock of shit."

"Okay, Matt," Daniel said. "Let's stick with asking questions, not giving opinions."

"Yeah!" Casey squinted at Matt. "Haven't you ever heard of a little document called the Constitution? I have it memorized. Maybe you should do the same."

Matt folded his arms. "That stupid remark's not worthy of an answer."

Sanya stretched her hands toward the glass. "Please understand, with SCED things changed and became much more terrifying. I used to only see events that affected my personal life, like my husband's visit to a hotel with his mistress and my brother's death."

She leaned forward and her voice started breaking. "I live in fear every day that my next vision will be about of one of my daughters. That's why I broke up with Aaron. I didn't want to know if he'd betray me or when he was going to die but I found out anyway. Sometimes, I feel my own death would be a relief!" Grabbing a tissue from a dispenser on her side of the table, Sanya wiped her face.

Matt smiled at Daniel and then winked at Cindera.

"Being the fair person I am, let's consider a few things. Perhaps there are physical realities that are undiscovered. For example, just because atoms are invisible to my naked eye doesn't mean they don't exist. Just because a fetus is unaware it has a mother doesn't mean it doesn't have one. So maybe there are some physical phenomenon's we don't know about."

Daniel rolled his eyes. Casey and Cindera smiled. Matt was trying desperately to earn his stripes.

"What about your ex?" Matt continued, "the radical environmentalist, Aaron Willis? We know about his criminal history and the rogue group he belonged to."

Casey gave Matt his mad dog look and turned to Sanya. "Ignore that comment. Maybe your subconscious mind overheard something that later materialized as a dream or vision."

"Aaron was in the Sierra Club," she said, giving Casey a confused look as if still unable to believe that she was talking to a dog. "He had no objections to SCED and wanted to be part of the system that kept things safe."

"Good plug, but perhaps you were wrong," Matt said as he paced on their side of the room. "And you know I'm not talking about the Sierra Club." He motioned to Daniel, Casey, and Cindera. "They belong to that one. Tell us about the other group."

Having empathy for Sanya, Daniel wanted to back off a little. She'd lost her ex-fiancé and was probably traumatized. Matt was engaging in some sort of a switchover that Daniel was struggling to follow. Casey was trying to do a good job, but his distracting comments cancelled a lot of that out.

Daniel jotted notes on the tablet. "Please tell us what you know about Aaron and his feelings toward SCED."

Sanya rested her elbows on the table and leaned her chin on her palms. "Aaron loved nature and cared about SCED and his friends."

Casey walked to the window separating them. He stood on his two back legs and put his front paw through the slot in the glass. Cindera jumped on the table and grinned, and then walked toward the slot.

Pulling another tissue from the dispenser, Sanya dabbed her eyes. "Should I assume the cat talks, too?"

"Yes, you may," Casey said as Sanya rubbed his paw.

Cindera extended her gray paw next to Casey's.

"My name is Cindera Caldwell, Casey's adopted sister. I had you humans figured out before my enhancement surgery."

As Sanya rubbed their paws, a smile brightened her tear-stained face. "Good Lord! What other secret weapons does the government have?"

"That I can't help you with," Cindera said softly, "but I believe Casey is right. Your unconscious mind knows more than the conscious part."

"All my psychic abilities know how to do is dream and visualize about awful events. Aaron was not a fanatic and neither am I. He never belonged to a group that would attack SCED and IRE. Many of my friends are dead and the ones that are alive think I'm a terrorist!"

"Ma'am," Casey said, "somehow you know more about the SCED attacks than any known person on Earth. Over time, more recollections may wash to shore."

Remembering that General Jackson was recording this, Daniel motioned for Casey and Cindera to sit down. They needed to be more technical. The animals returned to their seats and he redirected to Aaron again. "If your ex was planning something when you were dating or when you worked around him, you could've picked the information up."

Sanya frowned and shook her head. "This has nothing to do with Aaron. In seventh grade, when I was home sick, a scene popped in my mind. It was my best friend getting hit by a car and dying on the street. I found out later that what I envisioned had happened."

"Aren't there meds you can take to alleviate visions?" Daniel asked.

"The meds I took to stop these images made me violently ill. Doctors stuck a chip in my head that is supposed to report any abnormal brain function." She sniffled and laughed. "I'm supposedly normal."

Daniel watched her stare blankly down as she talked. He understood why DHS suspected her, but this was more complicated than a typical terrorist attack. This was beyond known science and he wasn't sure they were going in the right direction. But if she were psychic, maybe she could provide information on her visions and DHS could interpret the content.

"In college," Sanya said, "I had a nightmare about my brother dying in a car accident. I woke up to my Epad ringing and my parents' number flashing on the caller ID. Dad's face was crying in the screen. From then on, I've intermittently taken tranquilizers and used antidepressant patches."

Daniel didn't know what to do. He had no idea what the truth was at this point. He called out to General Jackson. "What polygraphs have been given?"

"Just the shitty ones," the general deadpanned from an observation room though a speaker. "Of course we gave her our best. The responses lacked deception with 99.99 percent certainty. Our testing for predictive ability came out inconclusive."

"Got it," Daniel said. He'd hoped to survive this trip without relinquishing too much of his tongue from biting down too hard. He'd had enough practice dealing with his dad's sarcasm.

"Big deal." Matt shrugged. "So she passed the polys. We could be dealing with a group that can instigate geological catastrophes. Who knows what control they have over their nervous systems?"

"That's what your AI programs and expertise are for," the general said to Matt.

Cindera gazed at Sanya. "I'm sorry for your pain."

A tear filled Casey's eye. He walked back to Sanya and extended his paw in the slot again. Sanya smiled and patted his thick, furry pads.

Matt leaned back in his chair. "What effective interrogators you are! Can I join the group hug?"

Daniel heard the general and other people laughing a bit at Matt's comment. He started to feel weighed down. He remembered this mental fatigue when school-aged kids would tour the EPA labs asking nonsensical questions and not listening to his answers.

"We need to figure this out so we can get back on the mission," Daniel said.

Casey pulled his paw back and pointed at Matt. "He has no empathy and is acting like a butthole."

"He's not acting," Cindera said. "Sometimes he is so crass!"

Shrugging, Daniel smiled. "That's what we love about him."

"They have to stop their absurdity," Matt replied. "Their cozy psychology is getting them nowhere."

"Even if she knows something," Casey shot back, "tormenting her is not going to work."

"Tormenting has worked for centuries." Matt motioned to the general who was standing in front of a glass wall in the observation room. "He knows that. We're not here to provide self-esteem to an accused terrorist. I'm not saying she's guilty. If we're going to interrogate her, can we at least implement this preposterous strategy effectively?"

"Keep your opinions to yourself," Daniel said, feeling as though his body was getting heavier like concrete ready to crash through the chair at any time. "Until we have something called evidence we can't make a judgment."

“I agree,” Matt said. “I was being a devil’s advocate. Believe me, this group needs one.”

“No,” Casey said. “You’re just being a devil.”

Matt started to respond but General Jackson’s voice blared from the speaker. “We’re done for now. First line of questioning is over. Daniel you’ll be back tomorrow for a briefing on what the next step is.”

SAT 11/25/2130
USRG BASE QUARTERS
MORENO VALLEY, CA

Daniel walked in the living room holding a large tray piled with sandwiches, paper plates, snacks, coffee, and Casey's protein drink. After sleeping twelve hours and seeing sunrises and sunsets, he was starting to feel a bit human again. He'd just talked to General Jackson and had a glint of hope.

Matt was sprawled across the couch. "How'd we do yesterday?"

"General Jackson didn't seem impressed with you and me. They seemed more interested in the animals' take on Sanya's tone of voice and body language."

Setting the tray on the coffee table, Daniel sat in the recliner next to Matt. "Tomorrow, Sanya will be visiting what's left of SCED. The idea is that direct exposure to the scene may stimulate any psychic tendencies she may have. You and I are going with the general and DHS. When we get back, her brain will be interrogated, mapped. Whatever you want to call it."

Matt laughed. "Oh, that."

Casey charged from the bedroom wearing his DHS vest. "Bomb's away!" he said as he jumped on the couch and landed on Matt.

"Shit, canine!" Matt twisted away from the dog and sat upright. "You almost cracked my damn ribs!"

“Better luck next time,” Casey said as he stared at the tray. He snatched his protein drink and then stacked two croissant sandwiches, a pile of carrots, and some apple slices on a paper plate. “Daniel, I heard you talking from our bedroom. I’m concerned about this interrogation.”

Daniel opened the base tablet. “General Jackson gave me a heads up on the equipment.”

Cindera leapt on Daniel’s lap and frowned. “I don’t like the sound of this, either.”

“You and the pooch are such lightweights,” Matt said. “Nobody wants to harm her. I expected answers yesterday, not a sadistic fix. You guys ass kissed her and got nothing. Besides, the testing probably won’t work, anyway.”

“I think it could,” Daniel said as he popped open a coffee drink. “Tomorrow she’ll be attached to a computer that’ll translate her thoughts into images, which will be projected on an HV.”

Matt walked in the kitchen and grabbed a bottle of iced tea from the refrigerator. “This sounds like the kind of crap that Donovan and his Chinese government would use on dissenters.”

“Maybe,” Daniel responded, “but apparently it works. An implant will be inserted inside her skull that will release millions of nano-bots into her brain. The bots will record her neurotransmitter activity. She’ll hold objects taken from SCED while being read details of the plant’s destruction. The implant will receive her neurotransmitter info from the bots and then send the results to an AI program.”

Matt sat on the couch and appeared to be in deep thought. He pulled the cap off his tea and took a drink. “Hmmm…sounds like DHS BS.”

“I was also skeptical at first,” Daniel said. “But think about it. The conscious part of our brain uses only what’s needed for immediate problem solving. The unconscious part retains far more.”

“So what does this mean?” Casey said with his Sherlock Holmes eyebrow raised.

Shaking his head, Daniel laughed. “Stop that and consider this. The brain mapping will give investigators information that even Sanya may be unaware of. After she’s been read or asked something, a brain response is generated into an image less than a second later.”

Casey raised his paw at Daniel. “They’re using nanobots in the brain? I hope they work better than ten years ago. You know how many animals I watched die in that lab I was in? I’m glad it was raided before they got to me. Lucky for you, I’m a product of Sharon and DHS’s handiwork.”

“That lab was illegal and incompetent,” Daniel said. “These are much more sophisticated nanos that aren’t being used to grow brain cells for enhancements. They’re only reading the brain. Once the testing’s finished, the bots return to the implant that is removed. Keep your mind open and eat your lunch.”

Daniel stopped for a second and watched Casey tear a chunk off his croissant. He hoped the nanos were safe. His love hate response to the military and investigative agencies came from his dad. He loved the science but balked at the brutality that was sometimes imposed. While General Jackson was gruff like his dad, Daniel was relieved he didn’t seem to come with the insanity, especially since he was overseeing them.

The dog shoveled pumpkin slices onto a plate. “Would you want robots dancing around in your head?”

“I would’ve let my brain explode into confetti if having my thoughts read could’ve saved Hannah’s life,” Daniel said, grabbing a piece of celery and chewing in deep thought. “Sanya’s doing the same thing. She’s taking the risk and hoping to save her daughters and others from future attacks.”

“I understand the motive which is being exploited by DHS and the military.” Casey pinched his paw around a pumpkin slice. “I’m asking if it will work and at what price?”

Daniel knew the animals would have problems with this. They were usually exposed to human science from an unmerciful receiving end.

“Brain activity’s been measured for over a century,” he said. “Interpretation’s always been the problem. That’s been corrected with better technology. We can now pinpoint exact coordinates of the brain where unconscious thinking occurs. We must know how this attack was carried out.”

Matt squinted and rubbed his jaw. “We may not find out. People, especially diabolical ones, are adept at manipulating their body functions. I've been able to make myself burp and fart since I was four. I used such methods to get attention."

"A heap of kudos to you," Daniel said, "but preventing such gaseous activity is more difficult than initiating it, yes?"

Blushing a little, Matt nodded. "Yeah, I got in trouble even when it was an accident. Nobody believed me."

"Not surprised," Daniel answered as he grabbed a vegetable cheese sandwich and took a large bite.

"The unconscious brain response is involuntary," he said, "like kidney or liver function, operating separately from a person's awareness. Early testing started around the year 2000. Criminal suspects were read non-public information from a crime scene. If the brain emitted a recognition response, investigators knew the person was present at the scene. That gave them the green light to gather more evidence."

Casey raised his paw again and aimed his half-eaten pumpkin stick at Daniel. "Excuse me, but is brain reading constitutional?"

Daniel frowned. "I don't know. Why don't you ask General Jackson?"

"I shall."

"The technology improved in the late twenty-first century," Daniel said, knowing he was running against the wind with this audience. Cindera's faint snores indicated that she had fallen asleep...maybe. That was fine. He didn't need another critic in the room.

"In the 2060's, test subjects were shown common items such as apples and trees. They were told to close their eyes and visualize these objects in their minds. After cultural factors, gender, and brain types were taken into account, people were found to have predictable response patterns."

Casey raised his paw. "Only one more question, Daniel."

Matt heaved a loud sigh and glared at Casey. "Would you stop interrupting him?"

Daniel patted Casey's back. "Yes. That was constitutional. The subjects were paid and signed liability releases."

Casey lowered his paw and slurped in loud deliberate inhales from a straw stuffed in his drink.

The sound of Casey sipping his drink made Daniel crave more adrenalin than his small coffee had to offer. He walked in the kitchen and grabbed an Adreno-Blaster from the refrigerator. As he walked to the couch he continued. "That's where things started to get interesting."

He sat on the coffee table with his Blaster. "By the 2080s," Daniel said, "magnetic caps with electrodes were pressed into the subject's scalp. Neurological responses were recorded as the subjects watched HV. The cap transmitted the results to the AI program. After testing tens of thousands of subjects, a common response range was able to be identified for each scenario. An enormous database was compiled."

Casey shook his head. "This is so bad."

"The bad part is that it probably doesn't work," Matt said.

"DHS was trying to find terrorists and other criminals," Daniel answered back. "So the science kept moving. Artificial intelligence software advanced to where brain activity could be mapped as people read short stories. The program would scan its database, search for matches, and generate a proposed scene. The subjects would communicate the differences and similarities between the software's findings and what they envisioned."

As Daniel sipped on his Blaster, he had to admit that he didn't trust the political system, and the military was an extension of the government, which for the most part was the People's Party. His enthusiasm became limp and a little sad.

"I'm worried this is going to hurt Sanya," Casey said.

Cindera's eyes popped open. "Me too." She leapt on the table and hooked a piece of chicken with her paw.

Daniel kept drinking without effect. "The problem is that as evil becomes more complex, so does its solutions."

"You humans get distracted with trivial things and the big stuff falls to the wayside," Casey said, extending his arms. "That's why your species is in such a pinch. You worry about the size of your house or paycheck. We dogs live in houses we can barely turn around in. The walls are made of plywood or plastic and the windows are patronizing cutouts with no glass. After studying most of your type, I'm glad I was born a dog."

Matt snorted. "You're so altruistic."

"Matt has a point," Daniel smiled. "Is that what your bedroom's like at Unity Station? Cutouts for windows? That would create quite a breeze in outer space."

"Now you're wisecracking me," Casey said. "All of us animals are cramped in a single room. That's why I moved from there to share a room with you."

Not wanting to argue endlessly, Daniel acquiesced. The Unity animals were spoiled even for humans. "Fine. That's how we got to this place with the science. In 2118, research leapt exponentially when the electrodes and cap were replaced with nanobots."

Casey somehow managed to shrug. "But Daniel, how can injecting bots in brains to read thoughts not hurt people?"

"They made you smart."

"How many other animals were killed before that? Hundreds of thousands. And how much research has been done on humans?"

"These bots are new, very expensive, organically compatible computers. I think yours were made from cheaper materials. Plus they're just recording information, not making changes."

Casey frowned. "Of course, but really this boils down to eugenics in a prettier dress."

"In a good way," Daniel said doubting his own words. "Like Sharon and Donovan using the bots for the necrotizing strep Intellipatches."

"Those are different. They transport medicine through blood and are eliminated through sweat and urine. Will the bots will be inside Sanya's brain, Yes or no?"

"Well, yes," Daniel said warily. "But because they're made of materials compatible with the designated body part, they navigate the tissue without incident."

Casey's shrill howl startled Daniel.

Matt turned to Casey. "What the hell's wrong with you?"

Casey protruded his lips. "Skull implants releasing nanobots that travel through brain tissue? Sounds like invasion of privacy and a health risk."

"I know you're concerned," Daniel said. "But we're desperate and Sanya has information about the SCED attacks that no one else has. And she's doing this voluntarily."

“Sanya’s in jail,” Casey said, curling his lips. “That’s not voluntary. And in case you forgot, there’s a little concept in our legal system called innocent until proven guilty.”

“No one’s saying she’s guilty.” Daniel shot Casey an irritated glare. “Let me finish.”

Matt tossed a celery stick that bounced off Casey’s back. “Shut up and listen to him!”

Casey grabbed the celery, throwing it back at Matt.

“I’m almost done so relax,” Daniel said, picking up the celery and dropping it on the snack tray. He read from the tablet.

“Once the AI program interprets the bots’ mappings, a still image called a ‘thought slice’ is generated every one thousandth of a second. The pictures are run together like old film reels, giving us footage of someone’s thoughts. Finally, the two-dimensional medium is run through a converter and we have holograms.”

He handed Casey the tablet. The dog started using the touch screen to navigate through the AI studies. “I can’t see anything good coming from this.”

“Casey’s right,” Cindera commented. “The process and the invasiveness sound disturbing.”

“One person fainted after testing,” Daniel said, “but nothing serious. I’m done talking about this. We’ll find out tomorrow.”

“Sounds impressive…if it works,” Matt said. “Maybe I can find out what the few attractive women working on Unity Station think of me.”

Casey stared at Matt. His eyes protruded in fiendish pleasure. “You would be more productive utilizing your free time building flatulence skills. I know what they think.”

“Mind you own business,” Matt said.

Daniel couldn’t help laughing. With no time off to have a life, he figured he might as well see the humor in the absurdity. Jeanette seemed like the type of person who’d need a humorous companion with the serious job she had.

Her ears flattening and clearly not seeing any humor in Matt, Cindera hissed. “Your obtrusive ego is our business.”

“Knock off the arguing,” Daniel said. “JoMarie’s coming to the base tomorrow. I want to give her a good report on your behavior.”

Cindera braced her paws on her waist. “Sounds like one step too far and for what—to snoop into people’s brains?”

“The testing was developed to help society,” Daniel countered. “People believed to be vegetative were brain-mapped. Doctors discovered that some of these people could engage in complex thinking.”

Casey handed the tablet back to Daniel. “Bull feathers.” He dipped his napkin in a cup of apple sauce. As he started chewing, Daniel balked a little but that knew napkins, especially dirty ones, were one of the dog’s favorite snacks.

“Are you sure you want to do that?”

“Stop trying to change the subject,” Casey said as he took what looked like a painful swallow. “Intelligence enhancements or ‘fill in the blank’ are for the good of humanity. Isn’t this about achievement and ego?”

“Probably,” Daniel said. “What do you suggest we do?”

Casey grabbed another napkin and wiped his face. “Acknowledge the truth.”

“Don’t pay attention to the canine,” Matt said. “Although far-fetched, these possibilities sound fascinating. I wonder why I never knew about this before.”

“Much of the info was classified,” Daniel replied.

“Or,” Cindera said scratching her temple, “while the science was being perfected, Matt was busy in a college lab building nuclear bombs.”

“I’d never do that,” Matt said, “although I’ve assisted the Pentagon on occasion. I’d rather clean up the global mess.”

“Did I just hear what I think I heard?” Cindera said.

“No,” Casey laughed. “That’s the good twin. The real Matt is underground designing CDC weapons with General Jackson.”

“Save your energy for tomorrow,” Daniel said. “After Matt and I return from SCED, we’ll all be observing Sanya’s testing. Then her unconscious mind will be revealed.”

Daniel’s hands trembled as he finished his Adreno-Blaster. Looking to his audience, he hoped he was right. “Maybe then we will discover the truth.”

PART IV

GOOD VERSUS EVIL

SAT 11/25/2130
UTOPIAN SOCIETY ALLIANCE HQ
NEW YORK CITY, NY

Shaune pressed his fingers into the backseat of his limo. The night was dark and brooding. The moon was a curved white strip in the sky, tilted back like a sexy woman beckoning him. Massaging the supple leather of his seat reminded him of Vara. Shoving his hands in his coat pockets, he tried to forget. She'd spent the night at the ranch after his parents had left for the New York lake house on Thanksgiving.

What the shit am I going to do?

He had to face the reality that she didn't have the heart, or lack thereof, for the Alliance. He looked up at Bernard in the driver's seat. Until Vara came along, the old butler was one of few people who'd ever really looked after him. *Fuck the USA. Once I complete Act Three, they'll have to accept Vara.*

Turning to his side window, Shaune watched street lamps pass by like geriatric faces guarding the sidewalks of New York's old business district. Sitting atop oxidized posts, the lamps' dim, solar-powered eyes seemed resigned.

"What did they used to call this shithole?"

"Wall Street," Bernard answered. "It used to take up eight blocks before it was consolidated into three."

"Looks like this place is missing some walls."

Bernard looked at Shaune in the rearview mirror. "Many of them were brought down in August 2078. I'd just started working for your family when terrorists attacked the area with dirty bombs. That's how your grandpa got three blocks so cheap in 2081."

Shaune laughed. "He's the one that probably blew them up."

"He may have. Nobody was ever arrested."

"I look forward to the day when these streets will be restored."

Nodding Bernard commented, "Too bad your grandpa didn't live long enough to see his plan fulfilled."

"The time's finally come." Shaune rubbed the healed incision on the back of his neck. "It's been over four months since my surgery. I don't feel as smart as expected."

"You have to wait six to twelve months for the full effects," Bernard said.

"I'm not a patient person. When's yours scheduled?"

"Not until after the takeover."

"You don't sound that happy. You should be excited that your fifty years of loyalty has paid off."

Silent at first, Bernard stared straight ahead. "I keep telling myself that."

Shaune grabbed a bottled martini. He winced as the car tires hopped in and out of deep asphalt ruts. Sipping his drink, he studied the old skyscrapers. These structures once housed the big fish that ate the little fish, only to find themselves consumed by the atoms of time—with the assistance of a few bombs.

"I'm intrigued by how decomposition strips objects of their dignity," Shaune said. "Like the ex-beauty queen whose crown passes to younger generations." He felt a sting of irritation. "Like the tiara-capped bitch who spurned my advances in Atlantic City two years ago."

"Most women do that," Bernard said. "Always looking for a fancier canoe to jump in but Vara isn't that way."

"No," Shaune said. "Too bad she doesn't have the right mindset."

Bernard laughed. "Not in the least. Her empathy that the USA loathes so much is probably what attracted you to her."

Shaune closed his eyes and pushed his fingers against the soft seat. "Maybe, but my patriotic duty to humanity's future has to take precedence."

Forcing his eyes open, he motioned to a slender, pyramid-shaped building. “In the mid-twenty-first century, that structure was a work of art, a tourist attraction. Now the fallen angel is a rodent-infested cadaver.”

“I know how the building feels.” Bernard sighed.

The mess of buildings seemed to blend into each another like piles of trash. Shaune pinched his brow. “We need to bring surplus labor from the hot continents to get this slop cleaned. Work them cheap, kinda like my dad does to me and everyone else.”

The limo plodded through the ruts onto another block. Bernard looked in his mirror. “Don’t plan on getting a raise soon. You’re still in big trouble for the flesh-eating bacteria attack. I warned you about those bio-weapons.”

“My dad’s whining over nothing. Act Three will seal my leadership in the Utopian Society Alliance.”

“Good. I’m getting tired of carting you around on these assignments.”

Imagining the glass structures soon to be built in this old district, Shaune’s conviction grew stronger. “The outcome will be good for all people—at least the remaining ones.”

“You don’t think there will be resistance to the takeover?” Bernard said.

“Their efforts will be fruitless,” Shaune shot back. “This mess of city blocks will one day be the terrestrial headquarters for the USA—a true Great Society. Franklin Roosevelt would be proud.”

Bernard turned back to Shaune for a second. “I doubt it.”

“Okay,” Shaune relented. He reviewed the tablet sitting on his lap containing the bomb presentation. “Maybe not proud but impressed.”

* * *

Shaune walked through the double doors of the underground meeting room. White walls and marble floors dressed the interior “for visual purity,” he was told. He massaged his tablet and started to think of

Vara again. Bernard followed him inside and then wandered off to talk to Mummy and Poppy. Shaune scrutinized the eighteen Utopian Society leaders and other high-ranking members totaling about fifty.

Most of the leaders had executed megakills in foreign countries, but not like the one he was going to pull. He studied the ten men and eight women leaders of all races and ages. People from Russia, the Asian nations, Europe, South America, and Africa had bonded for the cause of seamless global leadership and order. Clark was supposed to be the nineteenth leader and Shaune the twentieth and final one. But Clark had screwed up his assignment and didn't kill enough people, so his post was up in the air. Plus his new arm was still healing.

A mini robutler perched on the hors d' oeuvres table poured him a glass of champagne. Shaune grimaced when he saw squirming baby rats in one of the bowls. He suddenly felt squeamish, struggling to shed the aching conscience he was told came with early kills.

Shaune gulped up the tangy liquid in his glass. A new being had stepped into his body, performing the necessary tasks. Maybe a conscience did have a physical element that had to be excreted from the skin like perspiration or purged from the body like tainted water. The USA leadership classes had taught him that for practical purposes, that's what a conscience was.

Shaune stared at the gallery-sized painting of Grandpa Frederick hanging on the wall behind the small stage. He remembered his thirty-fifth birthday two years ago. He'd told Poppy about his desire for Utopian Society Alliance leadership. His dad told him that he must perform acts of destruction to prove allegiance. To ensure the proper mindset, he'd be required to have the neuro-enhancement surgery and complete leadership classes.

Wincing at the rats, Shaune knew that world rule was always the lofty goal of some type of group or government. But the USA would soon achieve what the Third Reich and other seeking souls had tried to do but failed: rule the world as indestructible superior beings.

He finished his champagne and handed the glass to the robutler. Walking to the front of the room, Shaune stood in front of the podium and adjusted the microphone. He turned on the large HV hanging on the wall behind him. Payday was closing in. The leaders and members took their seats. Bernard walked past the podium and sat behind him. Poppy was in the front row with that sneer of his. Mummy sat next to his dad smiling and seemingly proud. She at least liked him sometimes.

"So son," Poppy said wearing his new USA vice president pin, "you ready to show us your next ingenious plan?"

Looking straight ahead, Shaune didn't answer. *What a prick.*

Shaune gripped the travel itinerary that Bernard had printed out for him. He set it on the podium surprised he hadn't been hassled sooner to reveal his plan. He guessed the USA leaders trusted his judgment. Though some of them envied his Act Two in LA and were upset because they didn't think of it first.

Shaune studied his audience feeling confident, ready to rule.

"The purpose of Act Three," he began, "is two-fold: First, to be honored by joining you as a leader and second, to maintain domestic support for the People's Party when a similar attack is prevented near Christmas in Florida. The GlobeTek Finance and LA strep attacks have been effective in sustaining US public fear of megakills while maintaining our power base."

"Someone seems to be onto us," Poppy said. "IRE's destruction in San Clemente was not an accident. Our investigation's coming up with nil. We need to address this."

Shaune shook his head. "No we don't. The attacks in May and Thanksgiving were an obvious effort to cut off our money supply. But we're so close to takeover that someone destroying one IRE warehouse isn't going to affect the bigger plan."

"I hope so," Poppy answered, his squatty frame filling his seat like a sack of potatoes. Shaune silently thanked his mother for being six feet tall.

"Can I introduce you to Act Three?"

"Please do, dear," Mummy said.

Shaune used his tablet to display a suitcase on the HV. He ran his finger over the tablet's screen and the case opened. On a smaller sub-screen was a diagram of a suitcase bomb.

"When completed, the weapon will be the most powerful compact nuclear weapon in existence. Weighing in at twenty-five kilograms, this baby's capable of taking out a portion of a large city."

"Will you be able to carry it?" Poppy said.

"Of course, I've been doing pushups for weeks," Shaune replied.

President Victor Clemens stood. "What's the bomb's range? Can you show us?" Hortensia rubbed Clemens' shoulders as he sat back down.

Shaune scoffed at the president and his stupid woman. He couldn't believe she was going to be a USA leader like him while Vara was unacceptable. Clearly, Clemens' woman still needed her enhancement surgery. He displayed a computer-animated clip showing the release of the bomb.

As the HV displayed a computerized mushroom cloud rising over an image of Shanghai, Shaune motioned to the screen. "An instantly fatal dose of radiation will be produced within a three kilometer radius. Anyone within a range of ten kilometers will die, but more slowly."

Poppy's voice reeked of fake politeness. "China's quite capable of destroying all life with its weaponry. How do you know the Chinese military won't blame one of the major nuclear powers and attack them? This includes the United States in case you forgot."

Loving that his father persisted in asking inane questions he could answer, Shaune smiled. "I have recruited a nineteen-year-old suicide bomber who's a leader of the Jihad Warriors in Pakistan. In exchange for an eight-figure payment to her family, she'll perish with the bomb in the Shanghai business district a week from Friday as everyone's going to work."

"Do the Warriors know about this?"

"That's the best part," Shaune answered. "Suicide emails from the bomber will be released post-mortem to Chinese authorities. The woman is deep inside the group. She has info that will convince the Chinese that the Warriors are responsible."

"Casualty estimate based on detonation point?" Poppy said.

"As instructed, a grand total of at least a million will be dead in two weeks."

Mummy folded her arms. "The radiation won't get anywhere near Warwickshire I hope."

"No, the bomb's not strong enough to impact England. The ones that follow in the war between Pakistan and China might."

"I hope not," Mummy said as she waved a handkerchief in front of her face. "Warwick Castle's my refuge from this callous world. I can't wait to fly there after this meeting!"

"I'd never do anything to hurt Warwick," Shaune said.

Poppy leaned back in his chair. "This weapon's got to be released very soon. I've been telling you to get the damn thing finished for over a month. I only want you to be the best you can be."

Shaune squinted at his asshole father, narrowing his field of vision so as not to see him in his entirety. He knew his dad was mocking him, pretending to be interested in what he was saying. "The bomb will be set free on December eighth. I'm flying from England to Shanghai on the seventh to deliver the bomb."

Poppy shifted in his chair and leaned forward. "Why blame Pakistan jihadists?"

The members in the audience nodded and mumbled a little.

Shaune smiled again, another easy question. "To achieve the gigakill, I've decided to capitalize on China's piss poor relationship with Pakistan."

"That's a fantastic idea," Mummy said. "I don't blame the Chinese after those savage Jihad Warriors blew up a big chunk of the Great Wall."

Shaune clenched his fist under the podium. His mother understood, of course. His dad was an intellectual fencepost better suited for a woman like Hortensia.

"Since 2117, some Pakistani officials have been providing the Warriors with a safe haven. Once my communications are received China will think the Jihad Warriors are responsible who will of course, deny the accusations. Since they're known liars, China won't believe them."

"Why not Saudi Arabia?" a voice belted out. Shaune recognized the person asking the question—Paul, his GlobeTek pilot. He was a prick, too. *If only he'd been hit by the nanobots instead of Clark.*

"We haven't needed their oil for decades," Mummy said. "We'll be in Earthstar and can set the Jews up."

"I'm still the United States' president and quite a patriot," Clemens said. "I can't allow a holy war. We don't want annihilation, just the world's fear of the possibility."

"True," Shaune said. "Those who survive will thank us someday." He dimmed the HV and scanned over at his audience hoping for some response. "So what do you think of Act Three?"

His audience seemed unimpressed. *Bastards.*

Shaune's mood switched as he thought of Shanghai. His heart pulsed at full throttle as if Vara was peeling down her fishnets. "The respect, the prestige, and the fear will be unprecedented when the Utopian Society Alliance reveals itself next spring."

Shaune studied his audience a little more. He realized that some of the Society leaders' heads had a jack-o-lantern outline like Poppy's. Even Mummy's head seemed a little broader at the cheekbones than he remembered. He shook himself back into the meeting.

"After Act Three, I believe that I will have exceeded your expectations," he said. "The world's first gigakill will be achieved, setting us up for the takeover."

He cupped his hands around his head, feeling his temples. *They seem okay.*

Clemens responded with a contemplating grin. "Good idea. Like I said after the first SCED attack, there's too many people in the world. Thanks for your help in cleaning house."

Shaune beamed after hearing the US president flatter him. *Maybe the guy's not so bad*, he thought. *Just has bad taste in women.* Shaune bowed slightly.

"You're extremely welcome and when the bomb explodes, I'll be half way to Costa Rica to unwind."

Clemens walked up and shook his hand. "I look forward to your initiation."

"Me, too," Shaune said softly, squeezing his mouth into a tight, lipless grin. He glanced at his travel itinerary again and reminisced over the buffet of mind-altering drugs he'd ingested in his life. Nothing compared to the power high.

SUN 11/26/2130
USRG BASE QUARTERS
MORENO VALLEY, CA

The room was dark and warm but Daniel's eyes were wide open as always on bad nights. He heard the bedroom door swing open and slam off the doorstop. He immediately knew the sound. He curled up on his bed. A pair of men's boots started kicking toys across the floor. Backing up against the wall, terrified, he knew his ten-year-old body could not defend itself in such an unequal battle. The arm rose above him, enveloping his field of vision. Dad's fist was squeezed into tight ball, the knuckles a stark, angry white. And Daniel knew they would soon prove to be painfully solid.

The fist smashed Daniel's jaw into the back of his head. He spat away blood that was spilling from his mouth and nose. Lying on the mattress, he stared at the ceiling. His pajamas and face soon became damp and warm with blood.

The fist and forearm slid behind the curtains like a ghost and vaporized through the window. Daniel leaned on his side and hung his throbbing face over a trashcan. Bloody teeth fell from his mouth and clanked when they hit the can's metal bottom. He was startled by the sound of a baby crying.

Jeanette was standing over an incubator set up against a wall in his bedroom. Her hair flowed softly down her shoulders and over her lab coat. She looked at Daniel and then shook her head in disgust. He wiped his bloody face on the bedspread and padded across the carpet, stepping over his broken toys. Blood from his mouth and nose dripped onto his feet.

Raising her gloved hand, Jeanette gently rubbed the head of the flailing newborn. Daniel stood over the crib. Hannah stared back at him. She was wearing reindeer pajamas and a white stretch cap over her head. The ultraviolet light that kept her warm revealed her scrunched face. Wet loops of sweaty brown hair stuck to her head as she wailed. Her eyes were half open, their bluish brown irises and black pupils glaring at him.

Hannah stared at ten-year-old Daniel. Wrenching agony twisted her face, her organs and blood poisoned with pesticides. Tears mixed with the blood that already drenched his smooth, boyish face.

Suddenly her pupils turned white, making her look possessed. Jeanette sneered at him and stomped out of the bedroom. Hannah screamed louder and her mouth opened, filled with pointed teeth. Her anger burned toward Daniel through the incubator. She knew her pain was his fault. The pesticides that soaked the air around the lab he had worked at were tormenting her, killing her.

Daniel pulled off his pajama shirt and wiped blood from his face. How could he have known that the lab he worked at was soaked with deadly pesticides? Unable to look at Hannah anymore, his child-sized body collapsed on the floor. Blood spread over the carpet and he started sobbing.

* * *

Staring inside an empty trashcan with the March Base logo stamped on its front, Daniel trembled. Casey was belly-up and snoring on the carpet. At least his father hadn't killed him like in other nightmares. Smacking his dry lips together, he slowed his rapid breathing. But Hannah was right. He'd destroyed her. And Jeanette either knew or would eventually find out the truth.

Shaking his head from a sickly daze, Daniel shuffled into the attached bathroom. He brushed his index finger across a complete row of front teeth. He relieved himself and then rubbed cleaning gel on his hands.

Looking in the mirror, Daniel caught a glimpse of his sallow eyes. Then came his father's eyes, condemning him, growling about how he was a wimp that never fought back, or worse yet that word that started with a P. *No kidding. Ten-year-olds normally don't resist a two-meter tall, one-hundred kilogram black belt army general.*

He grabbed a bottle of antacid from the medicine cabinet and poured orange liquid down his throat. Gripping the bottle, he started out of the bathroom hoping for a morsel of peaceful sleep before going to SCED.

This can't be, he thought as small flashing lights caught his eye.

For a few seconds, Daniel stood and stared. His legs buckled under him. He grabbed the bathroom door to keep from falling down. There had to be at least twenty of them hovering over Daniel's bed, their faint hums forming a single howl.

Mateys filled his room, led by SG401, who was aiming its data upload beam at Daniel's Epad that was set on the nightstand.

Daniel bolted back into the bathroom and the door slid shut behind him. He leaned on the vanity to keep his balance. Everything would be okay. He could shout verbal commands to Pokey who would call base security. Speaking of Pokey, why wasn't he doing anything? Why was Casey still asleep?

Rubbing his hand over the base's emergency alarm, Daniel gasped for air. What were these flying robots doing here and worst of all, why were they following *him*?

He slid the door open enough to see that the Mateys were still there. SG401 swung around and aimed something that looked like a camera at him. Daniel froze as the light cut through the small crack in the door and glowed off his face and body.

"Observation of subject complete," SG401's voice chirped. "All necessary data uploaded."

Slamming the door shut manually, Daniel realized he was covered in goose bumps. Sweat beaded on his face and he began to heave. The DNA that gave him his high IQ and drive was releasing its dark side tossing him into the madness he so desperately feared. He'd cut back his counseling sessions to every two weeks. Maybe he still clung to old lies, that seeking outside help was shameful.

Sitting on the floor, he rested his head on his knees. He looked up when he heard knocking on the bedroom door and someone's voice.

"Daniel? You awake?"

Recognizing Matt's voice, Daniel shot out of the bathroom and the bedroom door slid open. "What's happening?" He shivered as he stared at his young coworker.

Matt backed away, seeming a little frightened. "Huh?"

Daniel spun around. Pictures hung on the walls. The HV was still bolted in the corner near the ceiling. The Mateys were gone. He sat on the bed, his heart aching for Hannah and hopeless about any prospect with Jeanette.

"I had this bad dream that I was a kid," Daniel said rubbing his eyes. "My dad was beating me. Somehow Hannah was there." He sniffled and wiped his nose. "She was in an incubator dying and she hated me for it. Jeannette Sparkman was there and she hated me too. I woke up and went to take a piss. When I came out, Mateys were floating in the room led by SG401."

"I'm sorry, man," Matt said. "You must've been sleepwalking the whole time. The Mateys and SG401 are on Earthstar bugging the shit out of everyone there."

"I almost pushed the emergency button."

"I'd hate to explain that one to General Jackson," Matt said as he motioned to Casey. "He didn't wake up so I think you dreamed it all."

Casey stretched and opened his eyes. He slowly rose to his feet and then sat down. "I didn't see or hear anything, Daniel. I woke up when I heard my favorite person's voice outside the bedroom door."

Daniel let out a light chuckle. "I hope I'm not losin' my head like, you know, General Griffin. Maybe Pokey didn't come out from hibernation because the Mateys weren't here." He looked at his Epad that had woken up and was showing all systems normal.

"Relax," Matt said. "You had a sucky dream. I hope you're hungry. I heated you an egg burrito from the freezer and made some coffee."

"Thanks." Daniel wiped his hair from his face. "What time is it?"

"03:00," Matt said. "We'll be meeting the others at 04:30. Just remember that this was all a nightmare."

"When I think about it," Daniel said, "I understand how Sanya could be tormented by bad dreams. Mine don't even come true and they're awful."

Folding his arms, Matt nodded. "Assuming she's telling the truth."

"I'm pretty sure she is. Let me take a quick shower."

"Okay, I'll meet you in the kitchen when you're done."

Casey jumped on Daniel's bed. He laid his head on the pillow and let out a loud startling belch. "Sorry, still recovering from the five tacos I had for dinner."

"Yeah," Daniel said. "I've smelled their vengeance since you ate them."

"Sorry about that, too."

Daniel walked in the bathroom and turned on the shower. Somewhere in the hissing spears of water spraying from the showerhead, he heard a faint hum and the electronic, inhuman voice of SG401.

SUN 11/26/2130
CALIFORNIA INTERSTATE 5 SOUTH
SAN CLEMENTE, CA

The bus headed south on the Interstate toward SCED. Daniel stretched across the third bench seat behind the driver. Closing his eyes, he was lulled to sleep by the tires' whoosh and the rhythmic chitchat coming from the back of the bus.

Daniel forced his eyes open. As exhausted as he was, he couldn't risk dozing off and having a repeat of his nightmare for everyone to see. Matt was behind him, leaning against the bus window in what seemed to be a contented nap. The general was sitting with his legs extended on his seat across from him, except he had to bend his knees so his feet wouldn't block the aisle.

Sanya sat in front of him next to a woman soldier. She stared out the window, her eyes vacant and rimmed with dark circles. Daniel understood her isolation. Her predictive powers had tossed her like a buoy into a psychic swamp, barring her from most of life's communal bonding. Just like his emotional wreckage had.

He started wondering if what he'd seen this morning in his bedroom was real. SG401 and the other Mateys *had* been there. Somehow, they'd left Earthstar to find him. But why? He was confused why Pokey hadn't done anything and Casey was never totally asleep. Looking at his forearm, he studied his Epad. He had to accept that the cartoon only seemed like a friend. The compact supercomputer was only a machine that detected more immediate threats. As much as the Dalmatian character seemed alive, he didn't have gut feelings.

"General?" Sanya said, breaking Daniel's mental fog. "Do I have to walk through SCED's remains? Can't I stay on the bus and look out the window?"

General Jackson turned to Sanya and pulled a large donut from his neoprene lunch box. "Unfortunately, yes and no."

"I *have* to see this firsthand?"

"Yes," the general answered then sunk his teeth into a pastry.

Daniel looked back out the window and shook his head. How could SG401 and the other safety guards really leave Earthstar to find him at March Base? Their adopted father, Kenneth Farrell, must be tracking them.

Stop, he thought. *What you saw had to be your imagination.*

He snapped out of his daze when he heard Sanya's voice quaver. "Can I view footage instead?"

"Neurotransmitters respond better with firsthand observation," the general said as he sipped on coffee. "Your brain will be taking in evidence you're not aware of. We'll also be collecting physical objects you'll be handling during the test."

"Isn't San Clemente a furnace?" she asked, as if hoping that would keep her from having to go.

Daniel noticed Sanya's voice sounded weak, even more so than during their first meeting in the interrogation room. He wrung his hands, worried over the impact that the testing could have on her.

The general shrugged, oblivious. "Lucky for us, it's not. A volcanic event of this level would be expected to release so much heat and ash into the atmosphere that we'd be dealing with mass deaths and evacuations. Instead, most of the effects seemed to quite literally disappear inside the earth."

"I don't understand."

"Neither do I," he said, motioning to Daniel. "That's why we hired the big guns."

"Is that supposed to be Matt and me?" Daniel said, feeling a bit defensive since he didn't ask to be a part of this and was somewhat forced to by Nielsen. "Big guns?"

The general narrowed his eyes at him. "Big guns at a big price. Even the animals are expensive."

Sanya sniffled and turned to Daniel. "What's SCED's environment like now?"

"The sun's gonna rise in a few minutes," Daniel said. "Most of the light will be blocked. The ground will probably be black and a bit squishy at times. More worrisome than SCED's physical state, though, is the nature of the attack. The destruction was surgically precise and challenges all of our knowledge on geology and natural law."

Sanya squeezed her eyes shut and faced forward. "I don't know if I can take the horror. My friends are there. Aaron's there."

Shoving more of the donut in his mouth, the general looked blandly ahead, reminding Daniel of the coldness he'd felt so much growing up. He remembered some of his dad's searing words: *Stop acting like a pussy, son. Be strong so you can survive.* He laughed aloud. And that was during a pep talk.

"Are you sure the risks of Sanya coming here have been assessed?" he asked General Jackson.

"I know this is hard for her," the general said, finishing off his donut. "But she'll be fine."

Sanya rubbed tissue over her eyes. "Daniel's right. I don't know if I can handle this."

The general shot Daniel a glare as he addressed Sanya. "We'd underutilize the testing if you didn't come here. If Aaron isn't a part of this, don't you want to find out who is?"

"Aaron worked for Emilio on Thanksgiving," Sanya said, her voice trailing off. Finishing off with a whisper, she added, "His wife was having a caesarean."

"Maybe we'll find out if Aaron Willis was the person you think he was," the general said. "The important thing is that we solve the case."

Daniel knew General Jackson was attempting to treat Sanya less like a prisoner, but exposing her to SCED could be traumatizing. If she had a complete breakdown, her thoughts could be reduced to gibberish like his were this morning.

The bus turned onto the off-ramp toward the towering barricades enclosing SCED and IRE. Black clouds slid across the sky. The area seemed devoid of any life except for the scores of guards in hazmat suits that looked like invading space aliens. SCED had become, in many ways, a different planet. Daniel watched blimps hover over the remains as they sprayed iced air over the coast to reduce the temperature.

General Jackson pulled a canvas bag from under his seat as the bus drove between two gates. "Put on your monkey suits. Even with the cooling blimps, some areas are hotter than hell."

As the bus came to a stop, two soldiers grabbed hazmat suits from the overhead cabinets and handed them to the passengers. Daniel took a suit and stepped into it. He pulled the top half over his upper body and arms, pulled on his boots, zipped up the suit, and snapped on the head covering. The ventilator and temperature controls started working automatically.

"Just seems like an endgame," he said to Matt from his headset.

Matt zipped up his suit and stretched his arms. "People have been saying that forever."

Through his head covering, Daniel could see how the earth's bowels had engulfed SCED and IRE. The sun was a brown, blurry smear subdued by the dense ash in the sky. A new coastline extended five hundred meters into the ocean. Narrow strips of red rock simmered but most of the lava was black and looked solid. In the distance, steam rose off the water as tides collided onto hot rock. The whole thing didn't make geological sense.

Daniel stood next to Matt as he stared at what was no less than annihilation. The death count was far less than the necrotizing strep tier of evil but was infinitely more sophisticated and in that way, much more frightening. How were they going to figure this one out? The bus doors opened and the passengers unloaded.

"So, buddy, no endgame?" Daniel said.

Matt scanned the coastline. "Okay, this doesn't look like the Earth I know. We'll figure things out," he smiled. "We're the big guns."

Daniel laughed. "I thought you were sleeping when he said that."

"No, just passively listening like the animals. Maybe sometimes they are awake."

"They'd appreciate that." Daniel visually washed over the area a second time. "This may not be an endgame, but it smells of a revenge or passion killing. Far more bizarre than the employee sabotage eco-attack JoMarie and I investigated."

General Jackson tapped Daniel on the shoulder. "Just wander around and explore. DHS and the US Air Force will be collecting rocks and other samples. If you can come up with any scientific explanation for this, let me know. I mean you should pick up something."

"I hope so," Daniel said.

Squinting at Daniel as if irritated the general folded her arms. "If you can't do that, at least help the soldiers with Sanya. Assess if her reactions seem appropriate. If she acts like she's not surprised or acts too surprised." He waved over DHS agents and soldiers, who followed him as he headed toward the shore.

Daniel started walking with Matt toward the tides and away from the investigation. He didn't feel like psychoanalyzing Sanya, particularly after his own mental voyage earlier. "Does the human race even belong in Earth's ecosystem? Maybe we don't belong here or don't deserve to be."

Matt looked at him through his head cover. "Then why are we here?"

"In my humble opinion, we stomped onto Planet Earth with a sense of entitlement and started screwing things up. If you want a more detailed answer, ask JoMarie."

"No thanks. I'll pass on the church version."

"Actually, there's not much difference between the two," Daniel said. "Her version has the potential for a happy ending."

Matt frowned. "They say that to manipulate people."

Daniel looked down at the volcanic rock. He really didn't know which version was true.

Suddenly, Sanya started screaming. He turned back to see her crawling on the ground. The two female soldiers lifted her back up. Daniel ran over to them and Matt followed.

"Can we help?" Daniel asked.

Sanya stumbled and leaned on one of the soldiers. "I can't believe it's real. Nothing's left!" She clenched her fist and stared at the melted rock. "Oh my God! My friends are lava! Aaron's lava!"

As she began weeping, Daniel bent down and touched her shoulder. "Today's walkthrough will help. Soon this will all be over. Your gift is evident."

"It's not a gift! It's a damn curse!"

A third solider ran to them and set a folding chair on the ground. Sanya sat down and sobbed, releasing her sorrow with what looked like painful thrusts of her head and chest.

"We'll leave you alone," Daniel said as he and Matt walked back toward the ocean. Waving at the soldiers, he felt awkward and guilty. He kneeled on the ground and pressed his fingers into a pile of warm, black rock. What scientific explanation could there be? He was well versed in geology to the extent that science had advanced, but this was far beyond anything he understood.

"I can't imagine what Sanya's going through right now," Daniel said to Matt. "So many of her friends are in this destruction."

"I have an idea!" Matt trotted to a mound of sticky, black sand and released the grains in the breeze that was spiraling down from the blimps. "Maybe I can build a bomb that stops people from building bombs."

Daniel grabbed his own handful of sand and threw the grains into the wind. "A serotonin bomb could be released in the atmosphere. Casey would probably find that unconstitutional, so we won't tell him."

"We should stop building any bombs for a while," Matt said. "There's plenty to go around. Flippin' burgers isn't so bad if you can get a good night's sleep."

"Sure isn't."

* * *

The bus pulled onto Interstate 215 North back toward the base. Sitting in his original seat, Daniel reviewed the images he'd taken with his Epad. There was nothing unique in the lava itself. None of his prior experiences had helped him come up with an epiphany or anything close. The mystery still lay in the force that manipulated it. The general and some of the others had nodded off. He understood why. The trip to SCED had been emotionally draining. As far as discovering anything new by trekking the shore, he drew a big, fat, white blank.

"I know why I avoid human attachments," Matt blurted.

Daniel stretched across his seat and propped his head against the bus window.

"Why?"

Matt leaned forward toward Daniel. "People are unstable. Why get attached to the unreliable? My mother died when I was eight. If you can't rely on having a mom, what else is there?"

"As a group, humans are often unreliable," Daniel said, "but your mom died. She didn't run away. I still get what you're saying. When I was twenty-seven, I thought my life was set. But the marriage lasted just three and a half years. When Cherril was pregnant with Hannah we lived in an upscale house that I'd selected so I could be close to work. You know how that story turned out."

"Why was there so much poison in the ground?" Matt asked.

Daniel's composure weakened and his words started splintering. "More people to feed."

"Nobody tested the area?"

"Fifty years ago," Daniel answered, "the world population was exploding. United States farmers were under huge pressure to feed the world. For the next forty years, they beat the shit out of the soil with anything they could to produce crops and stop the resistant pests."

"So the company you worked for bought the land after that."

"The investors and housing contractors bought land in 2112 and didn't receive proper disclosure." Daniel remembered July 2118, when the news broke on *Galax.net.* "The investors, my ex-employer, and I among others are listed as plaintiffs in an ongoing suit. I don't care about the money. I probably won't get anything and I don't care."

Looking out the window, Matt eyes filled with tears. "Like my mom being killed. My dad and I got a huge settlement after she died. But she's still gone. So the money meant nothing to me or him because for our purposes, it is nothing."

Feeling bad for Matt, Daniel realized he wasn't the only one who'd had profound sadness in his life. "Doesn't your dad work?"

"Yeah, but he doesn't have to," Matt said. "I used my settlement money for college, but I have a lot left over. We work because we don't know what else to do."

Daniel remembered how beautiful the Idaho plains had been, but the grassy knolls had been a grand illusion. Looking back, the one thing that had struck him after Hannah died was that he'd rarely seen an insect during the three years that he'd worked at the lab.

"The toxins were in the air, water, and ground in our housing tract," Daniel said. "While not so dangerous for adults, they were potentially deadly for fetuses and children."

Matt shook his head. "Are you sure the pesticides are what killed her?"

"Close enough." Daniel tightened his fists with resurging guilt. "Blood and organ tests verified prenatal exposure to pesticides known to cause birth defects. She was born with organ damage and leukemia. After four years of peaks and valleys, she died of pneumonia before the supposedly curable cancer was under control. Two other kids in our neighborhood were born with similar but less lethal conditions."

"That's a bad rap but not your fault."

"Cherril blamed me," Daniel said. "We'd moved to Idaho for my job. I picked out the cursed house. We could've lived in the city. I was still trying to impress my dad with a fancy home and big science career. I should've known better. I was never macho enough for him anyway."

"If your dad has a mental illness," Matt said, "you should try to let go. I realize he was an asshole when you were young, but a lot of time has passed."

"There's nothing logical about my state of mind," Daniel said. He thought about SCED's glossy black coast and realized Sanya was right. SCED was a graveyard. And he was afraid there was more to come.

"You didn't deal with your emotional shit before you got married," Matt said. "And you probably picked the wrong one. To some degree, you were also the wrong one."

Daniel felt a lump rising in his throat. "True. Cherril has come to terms with what happened. She remarried and lives in Seattle. She's got two kids. I'm glad she found her place. Now I need to find mine."

"With that doctor you met at Cedars?"

Waving his finger in front of his mouth, Daniel wasn't ready for his infatuation to be in the public domain. "I prefer that not be advertised."

Matt laughed. "You're joking, right?"

Daniel's face flushed from exhaustion. "Did I sound like I was trying to be funny?"

"Dude," Matt said, grimacing at him. He handed Daniel his Epad. "Hate to tell you but Casey has a posting on his social page about you in LA and at Cedars. He said you were staring at a doctor's derriere through her lab coat and you had a crush on her."

Staring at Matt's Epad screen, Daniel closed his eyes. "That dog's got to be shitting me! What chance can I have with Jeanette when crap like this is circulating on *Galax.net*?"

"This is my fault," Matt said with a guilty look on his face. "I told him because I was happy you seemed to like someone. I also told him to keep his mouth shut."

"Probably better this way." Daniel handed the Epad back to Matt. "Maybe I'm meant to be alone. When I saw the Mateys this morning, I wondered if my dad's insanity was closer to the surface than I realized."

"You were sleepwalking. You keep obsessing about being crazy. When you cross the line, I'll let you know. So will everyone else, especially that sadistic gray feline that's waiting for us back at base quarters."

"She sure would." Daniel checked his Epad for mail. "I haven't seen my parents in over a year. I know that's not cool, but I can't handle how they deal with things. Same old crazy shit over and over."

"You should still visit them," Matt said. "Compared to you I guess my life was okay. I sure wish I'd known my mom longer."

Daniel wondered where Hannah was right now. "We all have our aspirations." He watched Sanya stare out the window. The woman's swollen eyes were sad enough, but the void expression bothered him more. As awful as SCED had looked, Daniel knew nature would restore balance. He remembered what JoMarie said in Los Angeles about Earth's restoration ability: *That's what the system wants to do.* The word "wants" stopped his train of thought and a chill ran through him.

SUN 11/26/2130
USRG BASE QUARTERS
MORENO VALLEY, CA

Daniel jumped forward to avoid being clipped by the front door that started to slide shut a little too soon. He wondered if that was a subtle sign from General Jackson for the big guns to hurry up and start producing something. JoMarie sat on the couch talking to Casey and Cindera. Matt ran to Kosmo and Rushton and lay on the rug next to them. Rushton jumped on Matt and licked his face.

Daniel realized that the apartment was near capacity. All they needed was Robert and Sharon and then life would be like the good old days at Unity Station. JoMarie looked up and Daniel waved at her. "Hey, how's Nielsen?"

JoMarie wrapped her arms around Casey and Cindera. "He's pitching a fit because he wants you back on the mission."

"Ah, Nielsen started this whole thing. Why don't I feel bad?"

"I'm not crying for him, either," JoMarie said. "The mission's critical, but the situation here is disastrous. We have to figure out what's going on with these attacks." She picked up one of Sanya's files and began flipping through the papers and photographs. "What's your take on this?"

"I don't think Sanya Vasquez is a suspect anymore," Daniel said as he thought of her frail body at SCED sobbing in a chair. "Apparently her psychic abilities intake images of personal tragedies that are happening in other places. Her brain sniffs out personal trauma like Casey smells beef jerky under a bed."

JoMarie winced. "General Jackson did allude to that in an email. How unlucky."//

Daniel thought of Hannah. Some people didn't get a fair shake from the get go. Sanya was one of them, like his daughter. "We'll see how the military's AI program converts her thoughts into images. I hope the testing doesn't make her feel worse."

He noticed Casey was shaking his head at him with his arms folded. *I know,* Daniel thought as he turned away.

"Oh, I know," JoMarie said, reviewing her Epad. "It sounds like she's been through too much already. I'll be observing the reading with you, Matt, Casey, and Cindera. Maybe we can make some good come from all of this."

Rolling onto his stomach, Matt let Kosmo and Cindera jump on his back. Daniel was glad the whole animal crew was on Earth for a while.

"Whose idea was it to bring Rushton and Kosmo?"

"General Jackson," she answered. "He's so impressed with Casey and Cindera, he wanted to check out the whole troop to see if they can help. They're gonna unpack and get some rest. Robert's back at Unity Station, doing what he can."

"Well," Daniel said. "We need the animals' intellectual energy too. Is Sharon back on Unity to help Robert?"

JoMarie set the file on the table. "Not yet."

Knowing Sharon, he braced his hands on his hips. "Still at Cedars-Sinai." He raised his eyebrows and smiled. "With Jeanette?"

She pointed her finger at Daniel and nodded. Suddenly, he remembered what was on Casey's social page and his shoulders dropped.

SUN 11/26/2130
MARCH BASE INTERROGATION CENTER
MORENO VALLEY, CA

Rows of stadium seat padded benches faced a testing room with glass walls. Military brass and DHS agents filled the front rows. Daniel sat about five meters back. Casey sprawled between him and Matt while JoMarie sat on his other side. Cindera hopped on his lap and settled down.

Ignoring Casey's pout, Daniel gripped his computer tablet to input notes. He wasn't going to apologize for scolding the dog and insisting he delete the comments about Jeanette from his social page. Casey kept arguing that he didn't *say* anything. He just wrote a few things. Daniel knew that was "bull feathers."

General Jackson sat in the row in front of them. Daniel looked up at an HV hanging from the ceiling. A close up of Sanya was displayed. She lay back on a lounge facing the observers. Daniel studied her as several doctors checked her vital signs on a variety of machines. Electrodes were pressed on her chest under her tank top and a tranquilizer patch was pressed on her arm. Her saggy surgical pants revealed her thin frame. She seemed even more vulnerable than when she collapsed at SCED.

Daniel winced when the camera zeroed in under the rim of Sanya's hair cap. An implant was embedded in the nape of her neck. The back end of the implant exposed a small panel with flashing lights. As the camera zoomed out again, he noticed Sanya's fingers quivering like the whiskers of a nervous rabbit, as if sensing the presence but not the location of looming danger.

Looking at Casey, Daniel wondered if the dog had a point. Were they diving into scientific caves where a stalactite could dislodge from the ceiling and skewer those in its path? Were humans just another ingredient to increase knowledge for its own sake? Like the animals were for enhancements. Daniel stared at the floor to distract himself. That was how Casey knew. There had to be a risk the investigators were minimizing. He glanced back up at the HV.

A close up of the proctor, Dr. Ingles, displayed. The doctor turned away from several people in lab coats and opened a small refrigerator.

"Who are the others around her?" Daniel said, leaning toward General Jackson.

The general cranked his head sideways toward Daniel. "Neurologists. They're observing the procedure and will serve as assistants if needed for Dr. Ingles, the lead surgeon."

On the HV, Daniel watched Dr. Ingles pull a hypodermic needle from a case and slide the tip in Sanya's carotid artery. Aqua liquid seeped into her neck.

"I thought only the implant and nanos were needed for testing."

Pointing toward the HV, the general's voice fell to a whisper, "That stuff going in her neck is jellyfish juice to be absorbed by the brain tissue. That's how the nano computers can measure the brain activity so accurately. The stuff's harmless."

"I would've liked our lab to analyze the fluid's chemical makeup," Daniel said.

"You can later. This generic formula's been used forever." The general turned back to watch the testing.

Dr. Ingles released the last of the liquid into Sanya's neck and extracted the needle. He sat in a chair next to her.

Cindera tapped Daniel's chest. "Humans always say, 'this stuff is harmless.'"

Casey grumbled and nodded. "I call it people poppycock."

Trying not to listen to the animals because he feared they were right, Daniel fixed his eyes on Sanya, wondering if she had really recovered from the SCED trauma. Maybe they should have waited a day or two to test her. The info would still be in her subconscious. The lights in the ceiling faded until the observation room was dark. Dr. Ingles' voice was soft.

"Sanya, take a few deep breaths," Dr. Ingles said. "Close your eyes and think of pleasant memories—kids' birthday parties, walking through a park. Your unconscious mind will shift to the front lines and do the work."

The HV displayed a close up of the doctor unsealing the lid of a clear tube and then pinching tweezers around a small volcanic rock. He set the rock in Sanya's open palm. She closed her eyes and wrapped her fingers around the stones and the HV went white.

Reds, blues, and blacks swirled inside the HV. Daniel leaned forward.

A nighttime scene of the ocean emerged. A deep purple sky seemed ready to consume the water like a thirsty black hole in space. The surface was smooth and shiny as if lacquered. Accelerating wind pulled the water into the sky. Mountainous swells rose into waves that curved toward one another, touching at the top.

The waves rose higher, beyond the screen's view. A strip of sea floor became exposed between the walls of water. Dolphin fish and tiger sharks jumped from one wall to another. Following were oarfish, Pacific blackdragon and slender snipe eels. Daniel was impressed that the images were real species and not oddball concoctions from a mad hatter's mental salad. He still wondered if this would provide any useful evidence for the SCED investigation.

Casey tapped Daniel's shoulder and puckered his lips into a frown. "Bad."

"We'll see," Daniel replied. "You're probably wrong."

"I doubt it," Casey said.

Daniel entered descriptions of the images into the tablet, not because he had to but he needed a diversion from feeling guilty for being a part of this. He looked up and saw the exposed seafloor swell like a pregnant womb. The growing hill started moving under the sand toward the coastline. Plowing past the beach and through SCED's steel-barred fence, the hill ruptured. Daniel remembered watching the news and seeing snippets of the destruction picked up by the Skyguards. While this was far more detailed, he was still unsure.

Orange liquid blew in the sky over the buildings and flooded the ground. Sand crumbled under buildings. In the distance, cars screeched out of the parking structures and onto the freeway. Emergency vehicles pulled into parking lots near the buildings. The image faded to blue.

"Skyguards recorded the SCED implosion on *Galax.net*," Daniel whispered to JoMarie. "She might have picked this up from the news."

"What about the ocean life?" JoMarie said.

"She could've picked that up somewhere, too."

Daniel looked back to the HV. Dots blinked on the screen and formed into shadows. An image of Earth slowly formed. He realized that the land masses were different. He heard a few gasps coming from the other observers.

JoMarie pointed at the screen and whispered, "This is from the Triassic period, around two hundred million BCE. Look at the Pangaean supercontinent."

Squinting at the screen, Daniel wondered if he was seeing things right. He entered more information into the tablet. The image of Earth displayed had just one single landmass. Keeping Sanya and the HV in his peripheral vision, he leaned forward.

"Holy shit," Matt said. "Maybe she is psychic. This is in line with Charlie's story."

"Told you she wasn't making things up," Cindera said.

"I always doubted she was a terrorist," Daniel commented, "but I'm not sure these images are relevant."

The continent's tectonic plates seemed to enter a time warp and Daniel had to admit he was in awe of what he was seeing. Pangaea separated, forming Laurasia and Gondwana. He saw Casey shaking his head and making faces at Matt, who opened his mouth to say something.

"Both of you stop right now," Daniel said. "Watch the HV."

Matt and Casey leaned back and made one last face at each other. Daniel stiffened and studied the screen. *Some big guns we are.*

Pulling further from Laurasia, Gondwana separated into Africa and South America. Laurasia formed into North America and Eurasia.

"Did the Skyguards catch Gondwana splitting up, too?" JoMarie said to Daniel.

Daniel smiled. "They'd have to be prehistoric, alien Skyguards."

Cindera jabbed Daniel's forearm with her paw. "This isn't a joke. The thoughts going through Sanya could be hurting her brain. They seem too intense for a person to take in."

"Quit acting like this is my fault," Daniel said.

"I'm not," the cat snapped back. "I'm just warning you."

Daniel looked up to see several asteroids slamming into Earth. Fires and volcanic eruptions exploded and shook the surface. Dust enveloped the orb like a curtain drawing across a window.

A creature sprung at the audience. The three-dimensional image caused Daniel to flinch as if he were about to be body slammed. The thing expunging from Sanya's mind couldn't be what it appeared—a Tyrannosaurus rex.

The Tyrannosaurus flailed in the air as it was taken up by a tornado. A few seconds later, it toppled down a hill and slammed against a tree. A twister of spiraling snow and ice blew the tree on top of the wounded animal. Two pterodactyls flew in the distance.

"Could she like dinosaur movies?" Daniel said.

JoMarie raised her eyebrows. "Could be."

Casey snorted. "You two are misunderstanding what these images are saying. Everything is transitory. Humans are not the center of the universe, nor are they a permanent fixture."

"I never said we were," Daniel said.

Casey elbowed him. "You just act like it."

"Whatever." Daniel turned to the screen, which was now filled with blurry colors.

The image sharpened into an aerial view of a rain forest. The HV zoomed in on a burning Slojet wedged sideways between two trees. Snow was dusted over the greenery. *What a bizarre scene,* Daniel thought as more doubt about the testing weighed him down. Fire burst from the jet engines and turned into hot steam from the snow. Armed figures dressed in camouflage were running through the dense, snow-covered foliage away from the crash. A tornado bore down and pulled them off the ground.

"Some of the trees are fakes," JoMarie said. "I see the clean breaks in the trunks and branches. Something's being hidden."

The funnel tore more foliage out of the muddy, soft ground. Missile silos and tanks were ripped into the sky. The tornado reached a state of inertia and dropped its contents, including the people, like discarded trash.

Daniel tapped the general's shoulder. "Sanya's thinking stuff that reminds me of a series of B movies, edited and pasted into one flop. She could be spouting mental gibberish."

"This is coming from her unconscious mind," the general said as he turned to Daniel. "She's not thinking these thoughts, they're just there."

"Maybe she has gibberish in her unconscious mind," Daniel answered. "What can be done to make sense of this?"

"Asking me questions isn't what your team's getting paid the big bucks for."

Daniel looked back at the screen, sorry he'd bothered to say anything. He winced at the sight of frozen bodies sprawled over treetops and bushes. A building came to view. The roof was torn off and its walls had partially collapsed. As the image drew closer, he could see bookshelves tipped over in the remains of an office. A computer screen flashed *Miércoles, 06 Diciembre, 2130.*

He noticed the group of doctors gathered around Sanya and then the HV went blank. Dr. Ingles patted Sanya's arm and said, "Are you okay? You were shaking."

Sanya sat up and rubbed her forehead. "Really? I was asleep, probably from waking up so early. Don't remember a thing."

"We'll break for two hours," Dr. Ingles said. "I've done a scan and the nanobots have returned to the implant."

"Glad to know that," Sanya said. "Did you see anything that could help?"

"We're not sure what we saw." The doctor chuckled. "Go have lunch and sleep more if you need to."

Waving and smiling to the observers, Sanya walked through a door at the back of the testing room.

"JoMarie," Daniel said, "What did those scenes have to do with the terrorist attacks?"

"I don't know," she said still looking at the blank screen. "We'll have to sew them together and see what kind of quilt we get."

Cracking his knuckles, the general stared at floor.

"What's wrong?" Daniel said.

"She knew about that building in Costa Rica."

"The building we just saw that was partially collapsed?"

The general faced them, resting his arm on the back of the bench. "A few months ago, DHS received information that villagers were finding dead animals piled along the Pacuare River. Mercenaries were stalking the area and terrorizing anyone that treaded near. Those broken structures appear to be the aftermath of a similar intact building that Spyguard images captured a few months ago."

"You mean Skyguard?" Daniel said.

"No," the general answered. "Spyguards. Those are the classified eyes you don't see."

Daniel balked as he entered info in the tablet. *As if we're not watched enough already.* "You seem more shocked by the building than the dinosaurs."

"A T-rex and pterodactyl can be found in movies and textbooks. But I recognize some of those people thrown on the trees. Sanya Vasquez is either neck deep in international terrorists' circles or the inconclusive result on her predictive psychic capacity was, ugh, inconclusive."

SUN 11/26/2130
MARCH BASE INTERROGATION
RECOVERY ROOM
MORENO VALLEY, CA

Standing over the sink in the recovery room, Sanya finished her bottle of water. She massaged her temples with her fingers. The thick, padded chaise looked comfortable and she couldn't wait to land there. Her head was emitting a gentle throb; a figurative yellow light warning her to slow down or be hit with a migraine. But she had no control of this ride. The journey would end when the military decided that they'd traveled far enough into the abyss of her mind to get what they needed. She understood, but was still terrified.

She scratched the nape of her neck. The implant was itchy and downright annoying. Knowing it was there was half the problem. Hearing the door slide open, Sanya looked up. General Jackson was standing in the room holding a boxed lunch and drink.

Setting the food on the small table, he motioned for her to sit down. "You hungry? Gotta turkey and provolone cheese sandwich with chips and cookies."

Sanya nodded. "Sure am. I didn't eat much this morning after the SCED trip." Holding back a painful shudder, she had to push the SCED images away. There was too much going on to mourn anyone right now.

“Yeah, I understand,” the general said. “I’ve been through some tough interrogations and brain mappings myself. The good news is we already got some useful information from the testing.”

Pinching her brows with skepticism, Sanya took the wrapper off her sandwich. She took a bite then drank from the soda. “Dr. Ingles told me I solved the mystery on how the continents were formed.”

“Yes, thank you very much.” The general laughed. “I’m here to give you more good news. Because we’re pretty sure you’re not a terrorist, you’re being freed up a bit.”

Sanya’s food suddenly went down her throat before she was finished chewing. Trying not to choke in front of the general, she took a moment to compose herself. “What does that translate to?”

“We’re moving you from the jail cell to a studio apartment on the base. You’ll still be in our custody and electronically monitored but not so confined.”

Tears started welling in her eyes. *Dammit, don’t break down.* “Thank you,” she said.

Snatching a few of Sanya’s potato chips and tossing them in his mouth, the general stood as he crunched away. “We’ll allow you visitors three days a week for three hours duration. Call your daughters and parents after the testing. They can visit tomorrow.”

Sanya hadn’t seen any of her family ever since she’d been arrested. She had been allowed two brief phone calls. “I sure will.”

General Jackson headed toward the door and turned back to Sanya. “After you eat, I suggest you rest. You still have an hour and forty until we start up. Can I ask how long you slept last night?”

“About forty-five minutes.”

He looked up as if in deep thought. “That probably qualifies as insufficient. See you soon.”

After the door shut behind the general, Sanya chomped down her sandwich and chips, and finished her soda. She felt terrible that Marika and Jessie kept blaming themselves for purging the pain that they often felt forced to hold in. And how could she fault any of her coworkers or friends for calling the police? They were trying to stop the madness. She lay down on the lounge and closed her eyes. Sighing with relief as she felt the throb in her head calm a little, Sanya smiled at the thought of seeing the girls and her parents.

* * *

The rocks had faces. Swirls of wailing mouths and droopy, melted eyes stared at Sanya from SCED's rock-coated beaches. She stood over them wearing her beige suit—the same one she had on in May when she fell in the lobby. The faces started moving and speaking. They begged her to send messages to their families. She cupped her hands over her face as she heard Jasmine Eckert say, "Tell Krissy I love her."

The next voice was Caldwell McGinnis. "Tell my wife to move on. It's okay."

More voices joined in and the chatter become deafening, agonizing. Sanya had to escape. *Now!* She dashed over and around the rocks. She tripped and fell on her side, scraping her face. She wiped her bleeding cheek.

She forced herself up, her heart pounding as the voices kept pleading for her to come back. As she started running from the beach, she heard Dana Jones shout, "Please don't go! Tell Justin to take good care of the boys."

Her head pounding with dread and fear, Sanya pushed the sounds away and headed toward the SCED admin dome. She knew Aaron was in there. Storming inside the burning building, she headed up the stairs. As she climbed up each flight, her skin began blistering. Her throat burned as she tried to call out to him. Finally crawling onto the twentieth floor, she pulled herself up.

She staggered through Aaron's office door, which was slid halfway open. As she pushed her way through the flames that were burning her clothes and hair, she saw something in the corner. *Or is it two things?* Moving closer to the blurs, their forms became clear. She dropped to the floor and started shrieking.

Aaron was on fire, flailing his arms and legs. President Clemens was standing over him smiling, seemingly content to be engulfed in flames. Sanya felt dark energy swirling around the room like a hellish wind. She crawled toward Aaron and he extended his fingers. When she looked in his eyes, there was nothing but acceptance. Aaron knew he was going to die and wanted Sanya to hold his hand. Gently, she took his blackened hands and blew on them. His blue eyes were blistered and barely open. His lips were melted and disfigured.

Aaron lifted his arm and brushed his hand across Sanya's injured cheek. He closed his eyes and his head lowered to the floor. President Clemens laughed as he faded into smoke.

Sanya woke up curled on her side, her legs pressed against her chest like a fetus. Fighting the urge to scream, she yearned to stay on the lounge and not finish the testing. She clenched her jaw tight as her head throbbed mercilessly, punitively. The yellow traffic light in her mind had turned red as she slept and she was in no position to stop.

SUN 11/26/2130
MARCH BASE INTERROGATION CENTER
MORENO VALLEY, CA

Daniel sat back in the bench seat with the others. He made sure Matt was on the other side of JoMarie and Casey was on his far side. Dr. Ingles and the neurologists checked the monitors used to measure Sanya's vitals. The doctor reattached the electrodes to Sanya's chest and head.

"Okay, Sanya," Dr. Ingles said, "in a few seconds I'll be releasing the nanos. If you feel dizzy or have other side effects, let me know."

Daniel watched the HV. Sanya lay back and closed her eyes. Daniel followed the implant's status bar at the bottom of the screen. As the nanos released inside her brain, the bar quickly rose to one hundred percent distribution of the 1.5 million nanobots. Casey was pouting again. The dog folded his arms and then stuck his tongue out at Matt.

Daniel tapped Casey's shoulder and pointed to the screen. "It's not about you."

"He makes me so mad," Casey said.

"Ignore him." Daniel looked up as the lights went dim.

"And watch those bots going into Sanya's brain? I hate it here."

"I know," Daniel whispered as he saw General Jackson turn and give them a warning stare. "Just be an observer and take notes."

"I don't have to." Casey looked straight ahead. "There's nothing good to come of this."

Rubbing his finger on his tablet, Daniel brought up Hannah's picture and smiled. He was through arguing for now. He started inputting notes as Dr. Ingles recited facts about the LA strep attack. The HV in the room filled with color.

A Slojet glided over LA Valley. A man's face emerged in the plane's cabin and then faded. An older man was piloting the plane and a second man was sleeping in a back seat. The Cedars-Sinai emergency room displayed. Daniel turned away and took a few deep breaths as his hospital nausea revisited. A man and woman covered in sores were propped against a wall as they sat on the floor. The man was asleep, his head leaning on the woman's shoulder.

Dr. Ingles handed Sanya a small, burned figurine. "This is the George Washington statue we found at GlobeTek Finance," he announced to the audience.

A ball of light formed in the HV's center. Pixels spread from the ball and formed into a group of men and women gathered in an upscale meeting room. Daniel leaned forward and studied the images to see if anyone looked familiar. The faces were muted and generic, almost like police sketches that, while distinctive, could be any one of a thousand different people.

Daniel fixated on a man who appeared to be in his thirties standing behind a podium in front of the group. What seemed to be the same older man from the plane was behind the younger one in a chair against the wall. An HV hung from the ceiling and displayed an open suitcase. Daniel felt a brief déjà vu, but the image wasn't clear enough for him to figure out what was triggering his memory.

He turned to the sound of snoring. Casey and Cindera had fallen asleep. *Good*, he thought. *Don't want to hear complaining about things we can't change.*

"That's a suitcase bomb," Matt said motioning to a diagram displayed next to the case's contents. "Nuclear. Enough to take out a city."

General Jackson waved at the technician running the HV. "There's a printout of a travel itinerary on the podium. Try to zoom in on it."

The woman at the video controls nodded at the general and tapped commands into the computer. The images began to get larger.

"Those are airline confirmations," the general said. "See the destination? Shanghai. Who the hell's the man? Can we get a better view of him?"

Before the technician could respond, the image changed. A city that looked like Shanghai displayed on the screen. A blinding light flashed in the sky as a dreaded mushroom cloud rose over what Daniel recognized as Pakistan's capital, Islamabad. He and the other observers gasped at the HV in a single mortified breath. A closer view showed mountains of crushed concrete and glass. Charred bodies, cars, and busses were scattered across the streets en masse.

The general stood and waved at the technician. "Go back to the man behind the podium!" The screen turned white and then black.

Inside the testing room, Daniel could see Sanya's body shaking. She grabbed her tank top. A red light flashed in the testing area. Dr. Ingles and the other doctors stood over her, working the machines. The doctor lifted Sanya's shirt and pushed a heart defibrillator on her chest. Casey and Cindera woke up and ran to the testing room wall. They stood upright with their front legs pressed against the thick glass.

Audience members gathered around the animals, shouting questions through the testing room's glass walls. Daniel grabbed JoMarie's shoulder. Matt had closed his eyes and turned his head away. The lights were so blinding and the noise was so loud that Daniel couldn't hear or see a thing.

* * *

JoMarie leaned against the living room wall in their base living quarters.

"She's stable, but in a coma. General Jackson insisted that the computer and implant stay on with the nanos released."

Daniel felt sick. Of course, the animals were right. "How cruel can you get?"

"What did I tell you?" Casey said as he walked out of the bedroom wearing a backpack. "I knew those tests were dangerous!"

Cindera looked at Daniel with a tear in her eye.

"The fact that she has to keep the testing up is awful," JoMarie said with her eyes downcast. "But after she came up with those Costa Rica and Shanghai images, the general believes Sanya may be the only person who holds the key to solving the investigation."

"That's always the excuse you humans use," Casey said back. "The other animals and I are done here. We called Nielsen and he said we can leave today."

Daniel brushed his hand over Casey's back. "I want out of here, too."

"Be careful what you wish for." JoMarie frowned. "I also talked to Nielsen and General Jackson. You, Matt, and I are also returning to Unity tomorrow morning but not for the mission. DHS and the UN have scheduled an emergency meeting on the SCED attacks for December fourth at the base. We'll return here to present our findings and recommendations after analyzing Sanya's test results. Donovan and his IT crew are finishing the new AI program for us."

Daniel thought of Sanya at SCED and in the testing room. She was a guinea pig like all the rodents lined up in labs all over the world. "I care about solving the attacks but isn't there a better way?"

JoMarie turned on her Epad and displayed an email sent by Chistyakov. "I don't know. The faster we solve this, the sooner Sanya can be set free. So we'll have to work non-stop for a week to get this done," she said.

Wondering why he ever trusted the government or military, Daniel sat on the couch and rubbed his forehead. "Homeland Security and the UN have been working on some of their investigations, like the meteor storms, for decades and solved nothing. NASA blew me off when I contacted them about the blue light beam coming out of the ocean and we're given a week?"

JoMarie folded her arms and her face was tense. "That's right; seven days, twenty-four hours apiece."

MON 11/27/2130
MARCH BASE MILITARY HOSPITAL
MORENO VALLEY, CA

Just what Daniel didn't want to do—walk inside another damn hospital. But he had to for Sanya. The hospital floor's tiles were a glossy, mocking shade of white. He thought of how the hospital's brightness conflicted with the soiled science that incubated there. Matt walked next to him, carrying a glass vase filled with a bouquet of coral and yellow daisies. JoMarie followed slightly behind.

When they entered Sanya's room, the glare of a young woman locked on them. "Who the hell are you?"

Noticing the round, hazel eyes and high cheekbones, Daniel immediately saw the resemblance. "Are you Marika Vasquez?"

"Yes, now who the hell are you?"

JoMarie took the flowers from Matt and set them on a nightstand. Marika ruffled her hands through the daisies.

"We're Unity Station scientists assisting in the investigation," Daniel said.

"Oh, you're the people from the environmental mission. Can you understand why I'm upset about my mother being treated like a lab specimen?"

Daniel turned away from Marika's piercing gaze. "Yes and I voiced my concerns. Your mother's a heroine. She's tapped into something we haven't even begun to understand."

"If she dies," Marika countered, "what does heroism matter?" She rubbed Sanya's arm and her voice broke. "She had an aneurism that triggered a heart attack. Of course, the doctors claim the testing isn't at fault."

"Your mother has served her country above and beyond," Matt said. "We're so sorry."

"All I want is for my mother to leave this place healthy."

Daniel winced as he watched the jellyfish dye seep into Sanya's neck through an IV. "I hope the testing's over soon. We'll do everything we can to complete our part of the investigation so this can stop."

Marika blotted Sanya's chest and arms with a damp wipe. "The flowers are beautiful. I know she can smell them. A couple times today she's opened her eyes and nodded when I asked her questions."

"We'll go," Daniel said, walking toward the door with JoMarie and Matt. "Thanks for letting us drop these off." Marika nodded as she held Sanya's hand.

Walking down the hall toward the exit, Daniel stared back down at the hospital tiles. The floor wasn't deceiving after all. The science wasn't dirty, just cold like the colorless walkway. "I feel like a piece of shit," he said.

"Yeah," Matt added.

"Me, too." JoMarie looked at Daniel. "I'm not sure why. I just got here."

Daniel made sure he scuffed the floor with his shoes. "Could they be right about the mission?"

JoMarie looked at him. "Who are 'they'?"

Daniel thought of Gwyneth and Stephen. "The protesters."

"That depends on us," she said. "The mission will be what the USRG decides, no more no less."

"In that case," Daniel said, remembering his promise to Hannah, "let's go home to Unity and not settle for anything less than more."

PART V

RISE OF THE DOOMSDAY SUN

MON 11/27/2130
UNITY SPACE STATION
ALTITUDE 445 KM AT 28,150 KM/H

Daniel's brain was numb as he walked in the Thinkers Room. Donovan was reading his tablet, shot a glance at Daniel, and looked back down. It was already heading into evening and he'd be working through the night. He'd spent hours in his room working on files Donovan sent to him. He tried to cheer himself up by standing near the spruce tree in the far corner of the room. Clear lights twinkled throughout the tree's rubbery, aqua needles. Red, shiny ornaments hung off the branches. *Had to be JoMarie that did this.*

He thought of when he'd gotten back to Unity earlier. He'd headed to the observation room and dared to look in the scope again. The blue bolt of light was no longer a single beam. Now it stretched out like an arm with alien fingers, a frightening claw reaching out and pulling something toward Earth. The beam's base was still coming from the Pacific and had become ten times wider than the first time he'd measured it. *The thing is changing, expanding, perhaps overtaking.*

Looking back at the tree, Daniel noticed there were little presents shoved under the bottom branches. He breathed slow and tried to push away his worry. If only NASA had been as inviting as JoMarie. When he'd called the same woman as before to update her on what he'd just seen, she sounded irritated. She told him to call the Pentagon because it was probably a military issue.

He walked to his chair and nodded to himself. Maybe General Jackson would know something. He'd email the general the images from May and the ones he'd taken today.

Donovan pressed a button and a new computer rose from inside an upgraded conference table. "So, Danny, you have access to the world's most powerful AI software and the expertise of yours truly. What more could you want?"

"I'd like find to out what's causing the terrorist attacks, meteor storms, apocalyptic seismic events, and other shit that's going on."

"Boy, you're picky," Donovan said, turning on the computer.

"And as a bonus, I'd like to find out why the blue light coming from the ocean is expanding."

"It is?" Donovan said.

"Ten times the diameter as before."

"That's still pretty tiny. It's probably a weapon or spying tool that your military's responsible for."

"Never mind," said Daniel. "Let's just solve the world's problems in the next seven days."

Donovan arms stiffened into a kung fu posture. "If anything can help us with that, it's my HumanSpeak software."

"No horseplay," Daniel said still shaken by Casey and Cindera's warnings about Sanya. "Besides, I can't get past a brown belt. What databases are we using?"

Donovan grabbed a printout and flipped through the pages. "Here's a list. The main sources are from the UN and DHS terrorist databases, the US Geological Survey, and various technology libraries."

Taking the report and reading the list, Daniel believed the sources were plentiful but wondered if they'd help much. "What if these don't get us what we need?"

"The AI search engines will access a global lattice of alternatives," Donovan answered. Daniel imagined his dad watching the *Galax.net News* when the story broke that the USRG had found the cause of the storms and terrorist attacks. He wondered if his father would finally be able to utter one positive remark.

"Our research could change the course of history."

Seeming to sense Daniel's thoughts, Donovan squinted at him. "For yourself or others?"

"Hopefully both. I want to do more than conjure up methods of securing techno sludge," Daniel said. "But I try not to let this be my ego trip," he finished, angry at himself for still caring about his father's opinion of him.

Donovan began tapping on the keyboard. "Techno sludge is beneath your dignity?"

Yawning, Daniel was ready for bed. "My tenure at the EPA has served me well." He looked at the computer and remembered Public Hall; the bombing, the deaths. "We all search for some meaning in what we do. I want to change things so that other kids won't end up like my daughter, dead at four years old. It takes more than being status quo to do that."

Nodding, Donovan walked to the HV and grazed his finger over the screen to adjust the color and solidity of the images. "I was only half-kidding about implying some of your motives involve your ego. There are plenty of kids in China who need our help, too."

"The future generations deserve no less," Daniel said under his breath.

A few minutes later, JoMarie shuffled in the room. Sitting in her chair, she sipped on a cup of iced coffee. "You ready?"

Daniel pinched his brow. "I was born ready."

"Good. We'll be working sixteen-hour days, maybe more. Remember we only have six days left at...."

"Twenty-four hours apiece," Daniel finished.

"That's right," JoMarie said. "I talked to General Jackson. We can't discuss the bomb in our final presentation. He's using confidential sources to find out more about that. We can use the images for researching our hypothesis."

"He mustn't think Sanya's making things up anymore if he's using her readings."

"He knows she's not a criminal."

Daniel watched Donovan set up the equipment. "We'll play General Jackson's way, but I think I need a spacewalk to get some good ideas."

JoMarie set her coffee down. "You're too busy and so are Cal and the NASA group. Get working."

"Sorry," Daniel said. "Sanya's condition really bothers me."

“And me. I talked to the general and Dr. Ingles about the continued testing. They don’t seem concerned.”

“That’s bullshit. How could they believe the testing had nothing to do with this?”

“I know.” JoMarie stared at the floor. “There’s so much at stake yet putting her through the readings when she’s so weak is plain wrong.”

Daniel’s voice fell quiet as he pondered the options. “The sooner we get done, the sooner Sanya gets to be done. Sand’s pouring to the bottom of humanity’s fractured hourglass. As more grains fall, things could get ugly—very ugly.”

JoMarie walked to the tree and started straightening some of the ornaments. “We have Robert and the animals working on Phase II. Sharon’s pounding away at Cedars-Sinai. Working with the strep victims has been rewarding for her.”

“She’ll have to start moving with us on Phase II eventually,” said Daniel.

“Fear not, Danny,” Donovan said. “We’ll get this presentation done and Ms. Sharon can join us when she’s ready.”

Daniel looked up and saw Matt stomp into the Thinkers Room.

“What’s up?” Matt grumbled. “Was I tossed from the important AI project like Robert, Sharon, and the animals?”

“They weren’t tossed,” Daniel responded, exasperated at Matt’s childishness. “Sharon’s in LA saving lives and the others offered to work on Phase II in another conference room. They volunteered. Something you’re probably not familiar with. Try reading your mail and voice messages. You’re an hour late.”

“Oh.” Matt looked at Donovan. “What’s he doing here? I thought we were working the equipment.”

Donovan clapped his hands in front of Matt. “USRG Eco-terrorist Investigators featuring Matty Bertrand! Live on Channel Two, 18:00 Eastern Time. But before he puts on his outfit for HV, he must pick away the earwigs that were brought to the station in his dirty laundry!”

Daniel laughed and then tried to appear more solemn as he saw JoMarie turn from the tree and give Matt and Donovan an angry glare. Matt had set himself up with Cindera, General Jackson, and now Donovan. He seemed to be fishing for insults while wanting some type of acceptance at the same time.

"Go to hell, Don Poo," Matt said. "You're jealous because the UN didn't consider your job important enough to be a project specialist with Earthstar residence eligibility."

"Yes. I'm extremely jealous," Donovan said, laughing. "The Earthstar jackals make me sick. And don't call me Poo. Doug's little boy calls me that. From him it's cute. Not so much from you."

JoMarie sat in her chair and began tapping commands in the computer. Daniel could tell that she was starting to get pissed, so he'd figured he'd jump in. "Doug's kid, Brandon, was endearing on the shuttle ride in January. That is, after he stopped kicking my seat and crying."

Ignoring Daniel, Donovan froze in another kung fu pose. "My work is important enough to solve the terrorist investigations. I will also move us forward with Phase II. What would you do without my HumanSpeak, Matty?"

"I'd still be a genius."

JoMarie stood from her chair. "Did you two hear Daniel? Stop unless you want to be reported to Nielsen." She back sat down at the new computer.

The room fell quiet and Daniel breathed deep. *Hannah deserves better.*

Donovan peeked at JoMarie and whispered to Matt, "Please not your genius stories again."

Knocking his fist on the table, Daniel again fought to push away his dad's DNA. "We have children out there dying every day. Let's be a government agency that gives the public their money's worth. How much horsepower's in the computer, Don?"

"Lotsa," Donovan said. "You could run the world with this baby. The only things stopping you are firewalls and death row."

"No megalomania or lethal injections for me today," Daniel replied as President Clemens came to mind.

"Okay, no gold crown for Daniel," Donovan said. "I guess since we need AI programs, we should worry about the computer becoming too big for its micro-britches."

JoMarie turned her chair to Donovan. "What's to stop terrorists or governments from spying on us? What if we start closing in on someone and we're being watched?"

Donovan's smile expanded, covering the bottom half of his face. "Silly American, JoMarie. I work for the Chinese Ministry of State Security. I've been monitoring your DHS databases since I started working there during my sophomore year in high school. So eleven years!" He laughed and slid a small silver cylinder in a computer port.

"That's reassuring Lu," Matt said flatly. "What are you guys up to? Waiting in the wings to blow us up when you get the chance?"

Donovan saluted toward Matt. "No sir, Private Matty. We want to make sure you're not planning to do likewise to us. About your concerns JoMarie, I recognized the espionage capabilities of the superpowers and covert groups so I authored a routine that raises an impenetrable cyber wall that you Americans would be quite envious of."

"I'm glad you're on our side with this project," Daniel said, reminded again of how little privacy there was in the world. With the Epad, Skyguards, and now Spyguards, there wasn't much one could do without the risk of being gawked at in some way.

"That's right," Donovan answered. "Any attempt by a trespassing computer to poke its dirty little fingers into our masterpieces will find its knuckles cracked like peanut shells. We shall find the answers and divulge them only when ready."

Daniel stood next to Donovan, who was now reviewing HumanSpeak's source code on one of four table screens. "If we don't find a solution, the spying concern's moot."

"You entered the case data in narrative form?" JoMarie said as she looked at the screens with them.

"Yes, ma'am," Donovan said. "I entered them yesterday for the two SCED events. GlobeTek and the LA attacks are almost done but I know you wanted the SCEDs first. The IT department generated a narrative, flowchart, and raw data for each event. The information's organized into a data package. The package is structured so that the software can analyze the information in different ways."

"What databases are you using?" JoMarie said.

Donovan displayed the database list on the HV. "For general information, we're using applicable databases. For info specific to the investigations, we're including Sanya Vasquez's neuro readings recorded through this morning, as well as her arrest reports. We have

DHS investigation reports for each attack. HumanSpeak can analyze the SCED data packages separately or collectively."

He changed the display to the data package outlines. "We may get more than one answer or no answer."

"Sanya shouldn't be attached to that machine," JoMarie said. "I can only hope her misery isn't in vain." She scrolled through both SCED outlines. "We're starting by running a query on the SCED's together. I assume these have been reviewed?"

"Donovan emailed me both reports after lunch," Daniel said, his eyes getting heavy as he thought about the monotonous task he'd barely finished in time. "I reviewed them and made corrections. The assumptions and parameters are clean."

"No wonder you can't find a woman," Matt said. "You need to get a life."

"The mission isn't about focusing on our own lives but on others. And in case you've forgotten, I did have one."

"Yeah, but you need a new one now."

"Yes, but not right this minute," Daniel said. He thought of Hannah's urn at the condo in North Carolina. Jeanette passed through his thoughts. He cringed at Casey's now deleted derriere blurb on the social page and the embarrassment of having to call Sharon and explain what happened.

Matt looked around the room. "Where's Cindera when you need her? I want my seat warmed."

Donovan turned to Matt. "She's with the other animals and Robert avoiding you. All you do is harass her."

"I'm in the mood to annoy. Since Daniel and JoMarie are technically my superiors, I have to find a subordinate."

"Cindera outfoxes you every time," Daniel said. "Are you ever going to figure that out?"

Matt fidgeted with his Epad. "Maybe after we have a few drinks she can do a psych analysis on all of us."

"Matty," Donovan said, "I don't think you want her razor-sharp honesty even when you're drunk. Jake at least has diplomacy when he tells you what a mess you are."

"On that note," Daniel said, "I'm glad to be pushing middle age."

"Danny, for you I'll be nice. You did a fine job editing the redundancies and errors out of the data packages."

Donovan aimed a laser pointer at the text displayed on the HV. "The scientific assumptions regarding both SCED attacks are that all laws of physics must apply and all scientific theories may apply. Finally, all scientific hypotheses may also apply."

"Pretty broad," Daniel said feeling excited like a kid waiting to see what was inside a gift.

"We need leeway." Donovan laughed. "We're assuming a group of people carried out the attacks using unknown technology. Could it be space aliens?"

"Please." Daniel balked as dread replaced the gift. "That's a 'something more is going on' that I could live without."

JoMarie sighed and shook her head at Daniel as if worried that Donovan's comment would start a new conspiracy. "That goes for me, too," she said.

Straightening his lab coat, Donovan smiled. "What space aliens that can travel to different galaxies would want to stay near Earth longer than the time needed to get some pictures and fly off? I'd be gone in a jiffy."

JoMarie sat in front of the computer and read the SCED query aloud. "Generate one or more hypotheses that identify the perpetrators and describe the techniques that are responsible for events SCED-01 and or SCED-02."

Daniel's chin pressed on his chest as his head weighed down. He'd been awake over twenty-four hours. "Feed the computer and let her dance."

"She won't shortchange you," Donovan said. "This new computer and HumanSpeak are cleverer than any person."

"Clever?" Daniel said thinking of SG401. "I'm not sure I like that."

Donovan checked the computer diagnostics and executed the query. "That's our only hope."

MON 11/27/2130
FLC FAMILY TRUST RANCH
SOCORRO, NM

Shaune looked at the phone on his Epad as he stood in the gray, dim room. His dad would be calling and told him to be in the basement when he did. After talking to Clark, he was relieved that his buddy's newest arm was feeling like his own, albeit the skin wasn't a perfect match. At least the pigmentation treatment would work soon enough. Clark's financial settlement with the USA was generous and he was sunbathing on the Costa Rican beaches. He nodded. *And I will be joining him after Act Three is done.*

Lifting his sleeve, Shaune pressed his Epad against his forearm. He stared enviously at a picture of Clark had sent him while basking in the coastal sun.

He knew that despite some bumps in the road, Act Three would be a success. The People's Party was still polling lower than the Dems and Repubs and that was supposedly his fault too. Shaune had explained to his dad and Clemens what felt like a thousand times that polls would soon be irrelevant. As far as he was concerned, they already were. Peace on Earth was drawing near.

The Alliance members at Heathrow Airport were integrated into the staff. The bomb was approved to be loaded as a carry-on. Even though the case weighed twenty-five kilograms, hauling it onto a commercial airliner had to look easy to the other passengers.

Shaune's Epad rang. He saw his dad's face in the screen and answered. Forcing himself to make nice, he smiled at his dad's wide mug. "Hi, Dad, what's going on?"

"The bomb is done."

"I don't understand," Shaune said. "I was told it would be another couple days."

"I finished it—especially for you," Poppy said, his smile making his head look even wider. "Happy Holidays."

Wow! Shaune thought as he drew back from the Epad. It was the first time in years he'd ever felt his father's care or approval.

"Thanks so much. I didn't know you could build these."

His dad grinned at him. "How do you think I got to where I did?"

Shaune clenched his fists. "Where is it?"

"It's in the safe. The one inside the cabinet by the washer and dryer."

"I'll take a quick look and then put it back."

Poppy nodded. "The vitals are on the USA network. Call me if you have questions, but I prefer you don't." His eyes gleamed a little. "Don't screw this one up."

"I'll make you proud," Shaune said.

"That would be a first," his dad said as the phone clicked off.

Shaune pulled his sleeve down over his wrist. He was sick of his dad acting halfway human at first and then closing with his prick insults. "What an asshole," he said aloud then coughed out a snort. A voice coming from the stairs startled him.

"Yes, for all practical purposes, he is."

Shaune looked up and saw Bernard standing at the foot of the basements stairs. "I'm his kid."

"That probably makes it worse," Bernard said.

"What brings you down here?"

Walking to the cabinet, Bernard pulled out his Epad. "Your dad called and told me the bomb was in the basement."

"He thinks I'm too stupid to open it myself?"

"He didn't say that but my guess is probably so."

Shaune figured that his dad having a sliver of respect for him was too good to be true. He opened the cabinet where the laundry soap was stored. There was the safe. He reached his arm inside the cabinet.

The panel on the safe's door read his DNA and right thumbprint, and then clicked open. Pulling the case from the cabinet, Shaune winced as his shoulder yanked down toward the floor. Maybe more pushups were needed.

Bernard raised his eyebrows. "Pretty ordinary looking. I can't believe what it's capable of."

"Yeah," Shaune said as he set the case on the countertop. "It doesn't look like it could kill a million people."

Bernard pushed his forehead into a saggy frown. "So you really want to be a USA leader?"

"Well…why, yes." Shaune inserted his right thumb in the case's DNA reader. "Why else would I put myself through all this shit?"

"Exactly," Bernard said. "Once you become a leader this will only continue. You'll only be able to procreate from a select group. You may even be cut off from the Kat Shak."

Thinking of Vara, Shaune had lost most of his interest in the strip joint anyway but any serious thought of marriage and children hadn't occurred to him before. "I've gone too far, past a quarter million kills. And besides, Vara and my children would be so attractive and intelligent it would be a crime for them not to be born."

"I don't know. The USA is a pretty ruthless group in case you hadn't noticed."

"I will get my cake and eat it too," Shaune answered. "With all I'm doing for this group they should be kissing my ass, not whining all the time about the little hiccups in my plans."

Bernard stared down at the case. "Okay then. Open the hood and take a look at the engine."

Lifting the lid, Shaune knew the most plutonium that could be packed in a standard briefcase equated to a fifty-kiloton bomb. Good enough. He sat on a chair and set the open briefcase on his lap. "I have to make sure the girl I hired detonates this in the right place."

"That would help with your fatality benchmark," Bernard said as he paced back and forth with his face pinched tight.

Shaune patted the bomb's clear shell. "Yeah. She's gotta be in the heart of Shanghai's business center when everyone's heading to work. If she's in the middle of the desert, the exercise doesn't have much purpose. The city's population density is about twenty-five thousand per square kilometer."

"What's the estimated range of this beast again?" Bernard said.

"There are different levels. Three kilometers from the detonation point will kill either instantly or very soon after." Shaune calculated the estimates in his head. With his growing intelligence, these computations were becoming easy. "That's twenty-eight square kilometers. Multiply that by twenty-five thousand as your initial death count. Many more will follow over the months to come."

Bernard looked at him blankly. "More than seven-hundred thousand people. That's good I suppose, but it's not a million."

Feeling his face get hot as Bernard toyed with him, Shaune took a deep breath. *He's just an old, stupid man.*

"To help close the gap between that and the megakill, I estimate within a month another three to five hundred thousand or so will succumb to radiation poisoning. Then the war should start soon after, possibly resulting in the world's first gigakill."

The saggy skin around Bernard's eyes stretched to almost a tightened, youthful look as he said, "Unbelievable. One billion people."

"How many people are packed on this planet?" Shaune asked him.

Bernard raised his eyebrows up even higher. "I don't know."

"Nearly fourteen billion. I'm actually being green and promoting world peace. Yet most people don't see things that way."

Looking a little exasperated, Bernard shook his head. "No, they don't."

Shaune looked through the bomb's clear shell and studied the mechanism inside ready to obey on command. "USA leadership requires the ability to delegate tasks, so I'm delegating the gigakill to the unwitting militaries of China, Pakistan, and maybe more."

Bernard looked disturbed, as if these exercises were somehow offensive. Feeling suspicious, Shaune narrowed his eyes at his butler. "Remember, that warning I gave you before GlobeTek still applies."

"I'm not saying anything. I'd end up in a loony bin if I tried."

"Not to mention losing your kneecaps," Shaune said, and then shook his finger at his butler. "Not my idea, remember."

Bernard turned away and headed upstairs toward the main part of the house. "Thanks for the love."

Shaune set the case back in the safe and shut the door. He followed Bernard out of the basement and up to the first floor to the library. He sat at the computer and looked out the windows to Socorro. Taking the system out of hibernation and entering the USA network, he needed to verify the details about the bomb's detonation date and his flight schedule. Act Three was soon to make history. He could only imagine what the curtain call would be like.

TUES 11/28/2130
UNITY SPACE STATION
ALTITUDE 460 KM AT 28,800 KM/H

Daniel's heart pounded as he rushed to the Thinkers Room. The SCED mysteries could finally be solved. JoMarie walked up a few seconds later and nodded with a smile. The security panel scanned his thumbprint and read his DNA. Matt was probably still sleeping in his room and that was fine for now.

Daniel balked when the doors opened to Donovan snoring on the couch. He and JoMarie stared at Donovan and the query's results. The HV displayed 05:02 UTC.

Results of SCED Query - Logic Error:
Parameters and assumptions not applicable to events.

JoMarie read the display and in an unusual moment, dumped her etiquette. "Shit."

Donovan blinked several times and yawned. He sat up and rubbed his head. "Oh no! I performed a system check every hour from 22:30 to 04:30. The computer was executing the query and I dozed off."

"Re-execute," Daniel said, dreading the possibility that HumanSpeak may never generate anything that made sense since the attacks themselves didn't.

Donovan entered commands in the system and reran the query. Within a few seconds, text displayed on the screen:

> *This query has already been executed by HumanSpeak. Do you wish to rerun without modifying?*
>
> Donovan selected the "Yes" option on the computer's touch pad.
>
> *Results of SCED Query - Logic Error:*
> *Parameters and assumptions are not applicable to events.*

Daniel felt his spine compress toward the floor. He frowned at Donovan and pulled his Epad from his pants pocket. Pokey appeared on his Epad screen and pouted.

"This is not acceptable," Daniel said. "What do we do?"

"System diagnostics are okay," Donovan answered. "The program used the assigned databases. Based on the diagnostics report printed out, when the answer couldn't be found, HumanSpeak searched ten thousand more sources. Your assumptions are causing the problems."

"But Donovan," JoMarie countered, "our assumptions and parameters are very broad."

Daniel walked to the screen. "Instead of starting out with the SCED attacks, let's run a query on GlobeTek and Los Angeles. The science is known that caused those assaults. The program's response may give us clues about how to get answers for SCED."

"Okay," Donovan said. "While I'm sure similar tests have been run by DHS they didn't have software christened with my magic touch."

"Your magic touch needs to gather data and get some work done," Daniel said not wanting his impatience to bleed through his voice and create a distraction. "Make sure the information is formatted the same as the SCED data packages."

"Sure, Danny." Donovan sat in front of the computer and began completing the data packages for GlobeTek and Los Angeles attacks.

"Donovan," JoMarie said, "we'll name the first package GlobeTek Finance 2130 and the second one, LA Strep. I'll review the flowcharts and investigative reports. Daniel can review your narrative."

Daniel nodded, knowing their SCED presentation to the UN and the investigators at March Base would define their problem solving abilities. Any mistakes would be hard to offset.

"Donovan." JoMarie motioned to the computer. "Make sure we have the chemical structure for the SEV4 bacteria."

"Shall I send an email to our Dr. Sharon and request a reply to be provided now?"

"Please," she said. "I'll call her and let her know to expect an email."

"What's the estimated execution time for this query?" Daniel asked Donovan.

"Shouldn't be as long as the SCED/IRE queries," Donovan said. "We're dealing with a known method. Whether the perpetrators will be revealed is something else."

Daniel walked out of the Thinkers Room and headed toward the small gym. Uncertainty was not an option in this assignment because that equaled failure. He needed to distract himself and spacewalks were harder to schedule now that Cal and the NASA team were doing side jobs for Earthstar. Looking at his pants and button-up shirt, Daniel realized he had to change and not just his clothes. Feeling the burn in his stomach over Jeanette, the ache in his heart over Hannah and his reluctance to meet with Jake, he had to do something about the uncertainty within himself.

TUES 11/28/2130
MARCH BASE MILITARY HOSPITAL
MORENO VALLEY CA

Sanya gazed across the landscape. She was standing in the middle of a forest on a dirt road. *Where am I?*

Glimmering coniferous trees capped with snow stared down as if expecting her to do something. Blue iridescent birds soared overhead. Pinecones scattered along the roadside reflected light. Shimmering warm fog drifted toward what looked like the sun at the distant end of the road. Looking down, she saw that awful hospital gown draped over her. Her slippers were dry despite the air being damp with mist. Grabbing the material of her gown, Sanya checked the ties in the back to make sure she wasn't exposing herself.

As Sanya's vision expanded, she realized she was in a ravine. Snow-covered mountains towered behind each side of the forest. A waterfall cascaded from one of the mountain tops and into a creek that turned parallel to the road. Fish jumped out of the water and dived back in. Ducks stared at her quizzically as they waddled along the water's edge.

A very old man, perhaps in his nineties, walked past her, followed by two old women and a little girl. A glowing figure held what looked like two premature babies in its arms. Following them was a group of animals—cats, dogs, lions, and deer trotting together as a group as if their association was nothing out of the ordinary. A swarm of illuminated orange bees floated over a bed of flowers. More people walked past her.

Sanya fixated on them, wondering if she would recognize anyone. She didn't. They were dressed in varying types of clothes and pajamas. A few wore hospital gowns. Others were naked, the details of their anatomy muted by the fog. They didn't seem to know or care about her or each other, as if they were seeking their own destiny. Yet they all seemed to be going the same direction.

Backing up a little, Sanya was still. A human-looking form was coming toward her. *A male?* Based on the broader shoulders and larger arms—yes. He waved, and then trotted down the path toward her. A sting of fear shot through her and then she relaxed. Hearing a voice coming from the form, she struggled to figure out if the person was somebody she knew. Maybe he could at least tell her where she was and why she was here. Or perhaps he'd tell her to lay off the migraine drugs for a while. She'd allowed the nurse to put a few drops on her tongue this morning. The next thing she knew, she was here. As the man got closer, Sanya listened carefully to make out his words.

"Don't worry, there's no…."

"Can you please speak a little louder?" Sanya said hoping not to make him mad.

The man's magnified sigh was startling, his voice clear and firm.

"What I said," the man responded, "was don't worry. There's no whoopee cushions hiding in chairs on this side of the light!"

Sanya started laughing and crying at the same time. Her chest filled with warmth as she felt Aaron's arms wrap around her. She hugged him and buried her head in his iridescent shoulder.

Wiping a tear from her face, Sanya pressed harder against him. "Are you okay? I want to know you're okay!"

Pulling away a little, Aaron stared at her, his eyes bluer than ever and casting a mild glow. With his trademark smile, he said. "Now I am." He paused. "Are you ready to come with me?"

Unable to move, images of Marika and Jessie flowed in Sanya's thoughts. Her daughters still needed their mother. Her mom and dad were calling her back. She looked down the road.

"You don't have to join me right now," Aaron said as he held her hands. A cloud of glittering mist blew past them. "I can wait. You'll be back eventually."

Sanya grabbed Aaron and kissed him on the cheek. "I'll wait for you, too. I promise."

Aaron smiled and gave her a tight hug.

"You should watch your daughters grow up if you can. Your parents will need you in their declining years and if you want to marry someone, I understand." He hesitated. "But don't feel you have to." He let her go and started to back away. "I didn't have a choice, but Sanya, for now you get to choose."

Crying, Sanya nodded. She wasn't ready to be here. And because she could go back, she would.

As his figure began to drift away, Aaron's voice grew soft. "See you soon, my dear. Until then, I'll save a chair for you."

TUES 11/28/2130
UNITY SPACE STATION
ALTITUDE 460 KM AT 28,800 KM/H

Daniel stood in front of the Thinkers Room doors. He felt like he was living the same day over and over rehearsing a play he was unable to get right. He looked at his Epad, 21:00 already. Donovan had executed the query and the results were ready to review. He groaned, thinking of the possibilities. Back on stage, read the lines. Take two, take three—take a hike.

He and JoMarie spent most of the afternoon reviewing and editing Donovan and the IT group's work. JoMarie had gone to her room to call Ed and sleep awhile. Daniel had a feeling she'd probably sleep all night, and he wasn't going to wake her up unless they found something worthwhile.

Matt came up behind him and released a loud obnoxious yawn. Daniel felt his Mexican dinner began to settle and stared at the doors. He rubbed his tired eyes then turned to the familiar panting of breath.

Casey galloped to him and bucked in the air. "Ready for work!"

Matt scowled. "What are you doing here? This is classified stuff for real scientists."

Daniel rubbed Casey's back. "There's nothing him wrong with him joining us. Robert said it was okay."

"Yeah." Casey swatted Matt's arm. "Mind your own business."

"Me?" Matt pushed Casey's arm back. "You've got the biggest mouth in Unity Station. I told you something in confidence then you ratted out Daniel on your social page."

"I was told not to say anything and I didn't. Besides, that was a public service. Someone's got to get Daniel a girl."

"You really helped too," Matt said. "You're a bigger gossip than most women."

"What would you know about women? Hah!" Casey gave himself a high five on Daniel's pants.

"Okay." Daniel thought of Jeanette and felt an empty ache in his chest. "Let's not go there. He's not the only one."

"The difference is…." Casey paused and grinned. "You can get women but you're shy and kinda picky. Matt's not picky or shy and he still can't get them."

Matt nudged Casey with his hip. "Canine, don't meddle in things you don't understand."

Casey stood on his hind legs. "I was teasing. You can get girls too. Just stop being a sourpuss."

Daniel pressed his thumb on the Thinkers Room reader. "Get your priority's straight buddies. The source of the GlobeTek Finance and the LA attacks may be inside this room."

"I hope so." Matt yawned again.

The doors slid open. The HV flashed a mocking message that levitated in front of them.

Hail to the Chief.

"Donovan!" Daniel was startled at the anger in his voice. *Push away Dad's DNA*. He stuffed his hands tight in his pockets. "Your department's charging the project specialist budget a fortune. Are you sure Humanspeak is capable of the complex analysis required for this?"

Waving his hand at the screen, Donovan leaned back in his chair. "What do you mean? You got an answer."

Daniel paced in front of the words. "I agree Clemens is an asshole and probably a megalomaniac. While I've always suspected he could be involved, the truth is I don't know what he'd be hoping to achieve." Looking around he whispered, "You sure this room's surveillance free?"

"Yes," Casey interrupted. "Nielsen had me and Rushton sniff for hidden cameras and the like. All we found were stray donut chunks and peanuts, which we ate. He doesn't trust governments or authority either, especially deities. And I think the computer's right about Clemens."

Daniel didn't bristle at the idea of the People's Party and Clemens being involved in heinous acts but couldn't figure out the why. There was no benefit he could think of. So he'd have to think harder. He had to be missing something.

"Hopefully, just the data package needs some tweaking," he said. Grabbing a bottle of water from the refrigerator, he walked to his chair. "Forget these unsolved cases. All we're getting is smoke and mirrors. Let's test something we know the answer to. If the computer proposes a hypothesis that agrees to the case's real outcome, we have assurance that Humanspeak is operating correctly. Then we can consider revising our assumptions or parameters in the data packages."

"Good idea," Donovan said. "Maybe you'll get a gold crown after all."

Casey clapped his front paws together. "Let's see if Humanspeak can solve a murder mystery!"

Nodding, Daniel hoped a breakthrough would be forthcoming. "Not a bad idea."

Donovan sat in front of the computer and accessed *Galax.net*. "Okay, Casey. I'll download the facts of a case and exclude the resolve. You got one in mind?"

Dropping in his chair, Matt switched on the heating element. "Don't ask him. He doesn't read stuff like that."

Casey aimed his paw at Matt. "Despite the skepticism of the ignorant, I do have an idea—*The Minneapolis Murder of Sarah Jacobson.*"

"I remember that case from a couple years ago," Daniel said bringing up the book on his Epad. He read the back cover. "The story had twists and turns. Everyone thought the husband killed the wife but the brother was convicted. He got the death penalty even without the body found, at least in its entirety."

“Are you sure the husband didn’t kill the wife?” Matt said. “Normally that’s who does.”

“He got the insurance money,” Daniel said.

Matt grabbed a box of donuts off the kitchen counter and set them on the table. “Oh.”

Casey brought up a true crimes book on his tablet. “Mr. Poo, you need to make sure the computer can only access information from your data package. No uncontrolled *Galax.net* searches. Otherwise, the program’s solution won’t be the result of AI analysis. It will just find the information on a news site.”

“I’ll limit the computer’s searching ability,” Donovan said. “Casey, you have the soul of a programming architect. Are you part Chinese? I’ll contact the Minneapolis PD to gain access to their database.”

“What if they say no?” Matt said.

Baring his teeth, Donovan grinned. “Silly American, Matt. What do you think?”

* * *

Daniel stood by Casey in front of the screen. He scrolled the HV to the query’s end for the conclusion. “Casey you want to do the honors and read the query’s results?”

Grinning, Casey read aloud. “Hypothesis: Sarah Jacobson faked her death and is living in the French Polynesian Islands. Her arrest is imminent.”

Pressing his tongue against his clenched teeth, Daniel fought the urge to shout. “Donovan, I know you’re working hard but this is unacceptable.”

Matt spun his chair in a circle. “The faked death theory was investigated. Police found the woman’s severed arm and leg in a freezer hidden in the brother’s shed. They believe he kept the parts as a memento to punish their parents. He was supposedly the black sheep.”

“Sounds like it,” Daniel said as he grabbed a jelly donut from the box on the table. “Let’s get everything straight. Sarah Jacobson’s brother, Franc Bowers, was convicted and sent to death row for killing his sister. He was heir to half of her $20 million life insurance policy."

"Her husband was the other beneficiary," Casey replied.

Daniel shook his head concerned this was going the wrong direction, just like the Public Hall meeting back in January. "Remember, he was eliminated as a suspect and received all insurance proceeds."

"I'll review the program code," Donovan said. "The computer's either thinking too much or she's come down with a virus. I won't charge this to your department."

"Thanks," Daniel said starting to feel tired. He was glad JoMarie was getting her sleep. "We need your help moving forward."

Donovan sat in front of the computer's table screen and reviewed the program code. "For the murder query, I prohibited Humanspeak from searching *Galax.net* or other means. Her only authorized source was the data package." He frowned. "I don't know why she accessed unauthorized sites."

"Good job, Dog and Poo." Matt folded his arms. "Hey that should be the name of your team, Dog Poo."

"Be quiet!" Casey said. "Do you have a better answer? We're at least trying."

"I haven't wasted the computer's time on wrong ones."

"The program accessed databases on its own?" Daniel winced, more uncertain than ever.

"That she did," Donovan said as he glared at Matt. "Compared to other AI software, HumanSpeak is exceptional at following orders. The data package provided enough information to solve the case. Maybe it had a bug that led it to a criminal conspiracies website."

Matt pointed to the computer. "While computers sometimes malfunction, that one's getting too big for its micro-britches like that dog is."

"Her britches," Donovan said with a serious look on his face.

Daniel stared at the computer and his shoulders dropped. "I don't care if the computer and the software is a he, she or it. We'll sit here all night until this is fixed. You have to understand Donovan, time's running out and we're haven't accomplished a single thing."

TUES 11/28/2130
THE BIOLOGY LAB
MOHAVE DESERT CA

Gwyneth stood up from the worn recliner. She stretched her arms toward the ceiling and studied the old manufactured home. *Some laboratory*. She heard Stephen rustling around in his room. "I'm ready, Stephen. You need to get in here."

Stephen ran past her and in the kitchen as he ate a soy hotdog. "Oh, the burden of skinsuits! They have to be constantly nourished and washed. And this mustard's giving me heartburn!"

"This is my duty, your duty," Gwyneth said feeling slighted. This assignment was one that most apprentices would beg for and Stephen was plain whiny today.

She waved to him. "Hurry up."

Stephen ran in the living room and stood next to her. "Ready?"

Gwyneth nodded and stared into the air. White light emanated from her eyes. A tunnel opened and filled the room. It blossomed into a yellow glow with a white center and then exposed the trans-atomic realm. She watched people inside move about and talk.

"Daniel is really smart," Stephen said, watching the Unity project specialists do their research. "He has depth and a dry sense of humor. That's what I like about him. He and the others look like they're making progress."

"And they must continue," Gwyneth said.

“They sure don’t want to deal with the alternative.”

Turning to Stephen, she folded her arms into one. “That they don’t.”

Gwyneth motioned to Daniel talking to Donovan Lu. “Daniel has a high motivation through his daughter’s death to improve humanity’s state. The real progress will be made later when he goes against his peers and insists on an unconventional solution to a problem.”

“And that helps us,” Stephen smiled. “I can’t wait.”

“Yes,” Gwyneth said. “The sooner they get their mission done, the sooner ours will be finished.”

“And how!” Stephen said. “I’m sick of this place. Back and forth, back and forth for sixty million years. Ugh!”

Watching Donovan working with the computer, Gwyneth let out a sigh. “That’s nothing. Try billions.”

“Didn’t you kind of bring that on yourself?” Stephen said, and then covered his mouth. “Sorry.”

“You’re right,” Gwyneth mused as she closed the tunnel. “There’s something about this place that keeps bringing me back.”

WED 11/29/2130
UNITY SPACE STATION
ALTITUDE 487 KM AT 27,750 KM/H

JoMarie stood over Daniel tapping his shoulder. "You can go to your room. I'll let you know if anything exciting happens."

Pressing his Epad against his arm, Daniel stretched in his Thinkers Room chair. Tuesday had slipped to Wednesday 00:45. "I'll stay in case you need me."

"Okay," JoMarie said, "but I'll take over for a while."

"Fine with me," he answered. Barely able to stay awake, Daniel realized that General Jackson had replied to his email. He touched the icon and read the response.

> *Hi Daniel,*
> *Interesting images. I checked out the coordinates using the scope at the base and saw the same thing you did. That bolt of light does seem to be transforming when compared to the earlier images you sent me. But it is still very narrow in diameter. It doesn't appear to be an immediate threat. Try contacting NASA again and tell them I sent you. Bug the shit out of them until you get to someone with clout. I bet at least one of those assholes knows what it is. You just haven't talked to the right person. I'll call them if they ignore you again. Hope*

your research on SCED is going well. Contact me if you have further questions. A. Jackson.

Pokey shook his head. "Geez, he wasn't much help."

Daniel saved the email in a folder. "Well at least he cares."

"That's good he does," Pokey replied, "but we need to hurry with the cases. Your deadline's getting closer."

Daniel knew all too well that the investigation's hourglass was dumping time faster than they were making progress. He wasn't going to sleep. Opening the Phase II files sent by Robert and the animals, he tried to read but the weight of midnight pulled his head closer to the table.

Matt was watching a game show on HV and popping donut holes into his mouth. Casey gnawed on a giant piece of jerky that looked like a pizza slice. JoMarie sat with Donovan and was scanning through what seemed like endless screens of program code.

Grabbing the HV's remote, Daniel changed the channel. Matt shot him a scowl and then returned to eating his donut holes. After jumping past hundreds of ho-hum comedies, classic movies, and music channels, he settled for the *Galax.net News*.

He felt even more tired as he watched the supermodel-turned-newscaster twist her brown hair in repetitive small circles. She spoke in a monotone voice about the health risks of molds, pet dander, and air ferns. Some of the things that passed for news amazed him. His eyes started to close as he slumped in his chair.

Another, more intelligent-sounding, female voice interrupted. Daniel blinked and straightened up in his seat.

"We have a special news report," the woman said. "Homeland Security officers have arrested a Minnesota woman believed murdered in 2127. Sarah Jacobson is believed to have faked her own death for life insurance money."

"Yesirreee!" Casey shouted and swiped his paw in the air. "I knew it all along!"

JoMarie and Donovan turned to the HV. Daniel leaned forward as the woman managed a bright, cheery tone.

"Her brother," the woman continued, "who was convicted of the murder and was sitting on death row, has been granted clemency."

Daniel's mouth fell open. He tried to muster a cough but any audible response was wedged deep in his throat.

Donovan ran to Casey and did a quick two-step. "Time for me and my fellow Chinaman to have a snack!"

As Casey and Donovan headed in the kitchen to raid the refrigerator, Daniel turned back to the HV. The supermodel had returned and was finishing up the story.

"French authorities have surrounded a mansion in the French Polynesian Islands where an American woman, Sarah R. Jacobson, and her husband Gerald Z. Jacobson are living." Her perky voice irritated Daniel, but he was entranced. "An investigation by DHS and Metropolitan Life Insurance discovered that the woman had faked her own death by having a doctor in Mexico amputate her left arm and leg and replace them with two transplanted donor limbs."

A news clip displayed French police storming the manor and running up an expansive marble staircase. A few seconds later, Daniel stared at the handcuffed woman wearing a sweatshirt and jeans as she limped down the stairs toward the front door.

The newswoman returned to the HV and continued her spiel. "Ms. Jacobson and her husband planted the limbs in her brother's freezer. During and after her brother's trial, various agencies continued to investigate. The couple had been living off the insurance money and royalties from Mr. Jacobson's book."

Brushing his lab coat like a preening peacock, Donovan smiled. "I think certain people owe me an apology!"

"Lu," Daniel said, "your AI program kicks ass."

Matt waved at Donovan. "Sorry, man."

Donovan bowed. "Apologies accepted. My moment of glory, however, is short-lived. We must now return to our original testing. My suggestion is to execute the SCED queries with no parameters. Let the computer do her dance on a big stage."

"Sounds good," JoMarie said. "Based on current physical law and technology, we have no idea how the SCED attacks were implemented anyhow. Remove the assumptions."

Daniel kept watching the HV. As the Jacobson's were being driven away by the authorities, HumanSpeak's "Hail to the Chief" response to the GlobeTek and LA attacks stuck in his thoughts. The smart aleck blip suddenly became much scarier.

"What do we have for parameters?" Donovan said as he ate a candy bar and walked back to the computer.

Pushing his eyebrow into his Sherlock Holmes motif, Casey chomped on another slab of jerky. "How about 'All things are possible.'"

Daniel walked to Donovan, his gaze fixated on the HV. "You believe that command will reject?"

"If it does," JoMarie said, standing next to him, "we'll have to change it. We're running out of options. Clearly this is something outside of our science."

"We'll have to see," Donovan said as he deleted the assumptions for the SCED attacks. "Maybe Casey has a point." He input 'All things are possible.'

Feeling a sense of urgency, Daniel walked to Donovan and JoMarie. "Can you add that there may be a blue light beam involved? Those bolts, or whatever they are, have been verified as coming from the Pacific Ocean between Asia and Central America."

"Oh that," Donovan said. "Okay, as long as it's not a required characteristic."

"Doesn't have to be," Daniel said. "I think the light spearing from the ocean could be a covert weapon used to execute these attacks. General Jackson is wondering what's going with this as well."

JoMarie motioned to Donovan. "Do what he says."

Shrugging, Donovan tapped information into the data package about a blue beam stretching from Earth as having a possible correlation to the attacks. "The coordinates of your beam are listed as being at a latitude 18.56 and longitude of minus 122.52. That's sixteen hundred kilometers in the Pacific Ocean from the west coast of Mexico."

"That's what the telescope reported," Daniel said. "Did you put that the beam extends past the solar system?"

"I will but I hope this doesn't confuse the AI program."

"Stop arguing with Daniel or we'll never get anything done," Matt said to Donovan.

"We'll remove the possibility if the program rejects it," Donovan said as he narrowed his eyes at Matt.

Daniel rubbed the back of his neck as he felt his muscles tighten. They were probably all tired and a bit testy from working so much. "I can't sleep. I'll stay here and wake up everyone if anything happens." He looked at the computer again and wasn't sure if he wanted to know or not.

"Then I will go to your quarters and sleep in your honor," Casey said.

Smiling, Daniel patted the dog's back. "You've helped a lot. Take the rest of the day off if you like."

Casey sat up and brushed his right paw over his left paw. "I shall visit *Galax.net's* shopping network. I need to purchase some attire for casual events."

THURS 11/30/2130
UNITY SPACE STATION
ALTITUDE 487 KM AT 27,750 KM/H

"Wake up, Daniel," Pokey said. "The time is 07:09 UTC and the query's coming up with something. Hooray!"

Donovan was staring at the HV, scrutinizing program codes.

Daniel yawned and sat up. "You've been here all night, Don?"

"I don't leave anyone alone with Gina," Donovan said. "Not that I don't trust you, I'm protecting mission assets."

Rolling his eyes, Daniel figured he'd play along since Donovan might be on the verge of actually producing something.

"I'd never touch Gina or her likeness without asking you first. That's just the kind of guy I am. My Epad woke me and said the query was almost done processing."

"We're at ninety-five percent completion. JoMarie and Matt are on their way here. I let you sleep because you've become so moody."

Daniel was motionless as the words started flashing on the HV.

System executing - hypothesis generation in process: Estimated completion of analysis: 95.6 percent.

He heard the familiar whoosh of the Thinkers Room doors sliding open. JoMarie and Matt ran in.

"I'll be damned," Matt said. "No rejection."

Donovan folded his arms and smirked. "Told you."

JoMarie stood next to Daniel and watched the HV. Suddenly worried, he tightened his fists. "Could the computer generate something totally stupid or impossible?"

"Absolutely not," Donovan said. "The machine, being non-human, is purely logical. She has no bias that will interfere with sound analysis."

JoMarie braced her hands on her hips. "But yesterday you said the program disobeyed your commands."

"Only for our own good. She solved the Jacobson case."

Donovan started shaking his hips in a victory dance. He read the diagnostics report on one of the table screens and smiled at JoMarie. "The hypothesis is printing, boss. We're not getting a report, we're getting an encyclopedia!"

"Congratulations," she said. "You paved the road. Now let's see where it takes us."

Chills ran up Daniel's chest and down his arms. He tried to shake himself out of the nagging suspicions that seemed to follow him wherever he went. Staring at the papers as they were being bound by the printer, he opened the lid and grabbed the report. He read the cover.

Unity Scientific Research Group:
Project Specialists' Hypothesis
Origin of San Clemente Electrical Distribution Events I and II

Daniel reviewed the database search list. "HumanSpeak used almost forty thousand databases and searched over fifty thousand." He balked. "One of the sources is listed as unknown."

"We can check that later," Donovan said. "Sometimes that happens but I knew she'd come through."

Donovan motioned to the diagnostics report on the table screen. "The query results show that all assumptions within defined parameters were met, whatever that means because we had none."

JoMarie displayed the introduction page on the HV. "Check this out."

HumanSpeak's analysis and conclusion regarding events SCED-01 and SCED-02 is named: The Cosmic Instinct Theory—referred to hereafter as the CI Theory.

The attacks on San Clemente Electrical Distribution were not terrorist acts but a response from the cosmic ecosystem. For the Homosapiens, Doomsday's sun has risen.

Humanity's destructive nature has activated a celestial warrior's sword from Earth's core identified in the optional parameters as the "blue light beam." The ascent of this planetary dagger that utilized intergalactic sources, was required to temporarily suppress the invasion of ultramatter into Earth's ecosystem.

Feeling faint, Daniel stared at the report. In some way he knew they'd hit pay dirt, but he didn't know what to do with it. He leaned back and stared at the text. "No wonder NASA was clueless. I thought they were being lazy asses."

"Maybe they were," JoMarie said, "but they couldn't have figured this out anyway."

Matt turned to Donovan. "I think Gina made this shit up. What's it saying? What the hell is ultramatter?"

"I don't know," Donovan said. "You guys provided the source data for the packages and defined the parameters."

"Practically speaking, there weren't any," Daniel said, "except the blue beam of light as a possibility and we got something from that."

"Plus," Donovan added, "Gina and I couldn't even think of words that abstract, much less put them together. While our Chinese vocabulary is excellent, our English is only very good."

Staring at the words, Daniel's heart pounded. "According to this report, the SCED attacks were not acts of terrorism but a natural defense against something called an ultramatter invasion that was caused by humanity's destructiveness. So the blue light appears to be a natural force, not human or alien."

He looked at JoMarie. "What have we found?"

"I'm not sure yet," JoMarie said as she advanced to the next page of the report.

The Cosmic Instinct has existed since Earth's formation. Earth is a womb that incubates the souls of its species whose destinies lie beyond the rim of the third planet. The Earth will rise to protect its offspring, annihilating that which stands in its way.

Tuesday, 6 November 2096 CE to current date: *Stage I—Earth's life system is seriously weakened due to destructive events. Ultramatter is able to enter the atmosphere in minute quantities.*

Stage I CI Defense: *Meteor storms occur at selected locations and dates as warning system for future destructive events.*

Thursday, 18 May 2130 CE to current date: *Stage II—Ultramatter expands in Earth's atmosphere as the weakening ecosystem becomes unable to resist invasion. Doomsday's sun has risen over the planet.*

Stage II CI Defense: *Seismic events SCED-01 and SCED-02 are early Stage II defenses used to annihilate sources of human destruction.*

Date is pending: *Stage III—Ultramatter assimilates into tangible forms and consumes the ecosystem.*

Stage III CI Defense: *Prior to completion of Stage III, defenses will retaliate against the Homosapiens' threatening acts until ecosystems are restored to equilibrium.*

Daniel noticed that Matt had slipped into the kitchen, just as he'd withdrawn from the frontlines at Cedars. *At that age*, Daniel thought, *I wouldn't have been able to cope, either.* "This is bizarre."

"But it makes sense," JoMarie said, putting her hand on her chest and staring at the stars outside the window as if seeking advice. "We're entering some type of apocalypse."

"I already tried that explanation on you at Times Square," Daniel said. "I got ignored."

"I didn't want to overreact," JoMarie answered, "but I never dismissed your concerns. Ultramatter, whatever that is, began entering our atmosphere on Election Day 2096. Stage II started the date of the first SCED attack. So Stage I has been here thirty-four years."

"Come to think of it," Daniel said, trying to grasp the totality of what they'd read. "Meteors hit DC the day before that election. I was eight and my mom was watching the results. Rocks started raining down over the Capitol. A terrorist attack hit Spain a few days later. *Galax.net* spewed out stories for a day or two, and then nobody thought much of it."

"I'm surprised rocks haven't rained down on that place more often," Donovan said.

"Maybe my daughter would be alive if they had."

"I know." Donovan's face grew pale. "My grandparents died prematurely from exposure to toxins during China's economic boom near the same time. Maybe citizens in my country will get justice as well."

Daniel looked at Hannah's picture on his Epad. "I hope so."

"So we have a meteorite storm," JoMarie said. "Within a week, a terrorist attack or some other destruction happens. We discussed this with Robert when we were in LA, but didn't have enough of the story. I think the missing pieces are now emerging."

Daniel brought up the 2096 election results on his Epad. "That's what I've been saying and everyone thought I was crazy. That was the year the People's Party had more members in Congress than the Dems and Repubs. So much for the third party everyone wanted."

"I remember learning that in high school," Donovan said. "The Chinese government was happy that the US socialists had more members than the other two parties."

"That's what they called themselves," Daniel said. "They're not socialists but tyrants. Your government's probably not so happy now."

"No—but we can still break into most of your computers."

JoMarie flipped through the report. "The People's Party didn't get a president until 2108, but they had a simple majority in the house and sixty-two in the senate."

"Yeah," Daniel said. "And what happened the day before?"

"There were meteorite storms in DC and Tokyo. After that, we had the election and a terrorist attack hit Japan." JoMarie looked at Daniel and started to laugh. "We can't present that to the UN leaders. They'll think we're nuts."

Daniel turned away from the screen. “We could be, but that doesn’t mean we’re wrong. We can bring up the ultramatter invasion…when we figure out what it is.”

“At the very least,” JoMarie said her eyes intense, “we have to figure out how to stop this so-called invasion. We’ll have to work around the People’s Party element in secret. We don’t even know what they’ve supposedly done.”

“I can only imagine,” Daniel said.

“Daniel.” Donovan motioned to the HV. “Read this part. Does this sound like language a computer would use with my English?”

Daniel read the block of text Donovan had displayed on the screen.

As part of the Engineer’s oversight system, the Cosmic Instinct monitors destructive behavior in the universe and its effect on evolution’s destiny. Threatening Homosapien acts are setting the stage for an ultramatter invasion. The Cosmic Instinct will manipulate Earth’s natural forces to engage in major destruction to stop ultramatter’s total destruction.

“The Engineer?” Daniel said. “I feel like a lab rat in some grand experiment.”

Donovan uneasily laughed. “Maybe we are.”

Matt returned from the kitchen holding a donut. “Maybe this is all crap. Couldn’t HumanSpeak have generated the wrong information? After all, this is just a hypothesis.”

“More like a prophecy,” JoMarie said. “Do I dare say, of our Creator?”

Chewing on his pastry, Matt shook his head. “Not quite yet. Donovan said himself that his English wasn’t that great. Maybe this program misunderstood the data packages.”

“Even coming from you Matty,” Donovan commented, “I hope Humanspeak’s wrong.”

“And it’s so abstract.” Daniel stared at the screen. “I’m not sure it’s practical. The more we learn about these events, the more deliberateness seems to be revealed. Why am I not happy about being right?”

“Because the possibilities are terrifying,” JoMarie said. “We have to research the analysis the report used and figure out what to do.”

She switched the computer into audio mode and the text was read aloud using the voice of Donovan's ex-girlfriend, Gina.

> *"Abstract of Formulas that Support the CI Theory: System was unable to generate formulae in their entirety. HumanSpeak's estimate of calculations required: 1.6 billion formulae, 5.6 trillion variables."*

JoMarie paused the computer and studied the formulas. "Matt, Donovan, look at these. Do they look familiar to you?"

"I recognize the symbol of infinity and the Greek letters," Matt said from his chair as he stared at the screen. "There's the standard deviation. The Theory of Relativity is embedded in the large formula on page four hundred and sixty-two. I have never seen most of the symbols and formulas. Donovan?"

"I know less than you, Matty," Donovan answered. "My expertise lies in translating human instructions so computers understand them."

Daniel reactivated the computer's voice and was startled when it sounded like it was clearing its throat. He looked at Donovan who was grinning at him. He almost dreaded learning more information because he was unsure that the tools existed to do anything. "Hey guys, listen to this," he said as he started the audio.

> *"SCED-01 and SCED-02 are the Cosmic Instinct's responses to forbidden metamorphosis that threatens to destroy the barrier between the Organic and Ultramatter Dimensions."*

Daniel studied the words, more confused than ever. "The terms evolution's destiny and the Ultramatter and Organic Dimensions don't exist in science. We have until Monday to explain them and the blue light bolt. Could we be sailing toward shit creek?"

JoMarie paced in front of the screen. "Shit creek, as you put it, is not an option. Let's use common sense. Ultramatter is alien and lethal; very bad, not wanted here. There's an implication that if we stop humanity's bad behavior and heal the ecosystem, ultramatter will not enter our atmosphere or at least take it over. The blue beam has something to do with that. It seems like some type of communication system is drawing meteors to Earth when certain things are going to happen."

"Why didn't the ridiculous text propose solutions?" Matt said to Donovan.

"The solution could be," Daniel said, "for us to find the solutions ourselves. The problem is solvable, but something apparently had to step in."

"Does that mean we don't have to figure out those formulas?" Matt said.

"Hopefully not." JoMarie stared blankly at the screen. "Daniel's probably right. Solving the big problem with the big formulas requires using street smarts as much as science. We all know what forbidden metamorphosis means—bad changes."

Daniel grabbed an iced coffee from the refrigerator, again wishing there was something a little stronger than caffeine stirred with the cream. "These cryptic texts are saying in practical terms that Phase II must advance. The ecosystem is weakening in ways that are allowing a deadly force to enter the atmosphere and take over. Destructive behavior, including those in the People's Party must be stopped."

"And we can't say that when we present our findings to the UN and DHS," JoMarie said.

She skipped to the printout's next page. "We have to know what the destructive acts are and stop them without publicly pointing fingers."

Daniel felt another chill run through him. He stared at the hypotheses' name for the force: *Cosmic Instinct.* He took a big gulp of his drink. "Instinct requires a type of survival mechanism and because of the deliberateness of its actions, intelligence."

He stared at the screen and his chill shifted to nausea. *Intelligence.*

"JoMarie," Daniel said, his hands trembling, "there's one more page in the file. It's titled 'The Final Analysis.'" His voice trailed to a whisper and his shoulders dropped. "Can't wait to read it."

JoMarie scrolled to the last page of the file. Daniel read the words and then stared at the floor. Donovan and Matt recoiled, as if moving further away would somehow send the truth to a distant land for someone else to deal with. Of all things, Casey had figured out the scenario that proved HumanSpeak's logic to be reliable. Chistyakov would be proud and for sure, Elvis would be. Daniel felt his stomach rumble and he began to hyperventilate. He could tell he was going to get sick.

Looking at JoMarie, he hoped for the inspiration she always managed to give him in his darkest moments—after Hannah's death, at Times Square, then at Cedars-Sinai. She put her hand on his arm and stared at him. Her eyes were wide with fear.

"Daniel, you were right the whole time. There *was* something more going on."

THURS 11/30/2130
FLC FAMILY TRUST RANCH
SOCORRO, NM

Mummy was in the dining room standing over Bernard who was nervously zipping and buttoning her blouses and dresses onto flat mannequin torsos stacked on the table. The butler hung the clothed torsos inside suitcases that stood upright. He looked worn out for just turning seventy-four. Of course, he had been working for the family for fifty years. Shaune felt some sympathy for the guy.

Bernard's crepe paper hands twitched as he moved. "Madame Tricia, is there anything else?"

Mummy's statuesque frame towered over the butler. "Roll my ankle socks into balls and gently insert them inside my sports shoes."

Shaune heaved out a loud moan. *I have so much to do*. He had to take the jet to the family castle in Warwick. Then he had to make sure the USA affiliates would be at Heathrow Airport and Turkish Airlines when he arrived. He'd already booked the flight and wished could've flown from the United States straight to China. But boarding the bomb in the United States was too risky because many leaders in the TSA were not USA members yet.

Spiking a ball of yarn on the floor, Shaune watched it unravel after a few dull bounces. The remaining ball hit the leg of a stool. He upped the heat on his beige recliner and leaned against the fantasy fingers in the back cushion to massage his shoulders.

"Dammit, Mummy! This fuckin' yarn keeps tangling up. How in the hell am I supposed to learn this before I leave for Shanghai?"

"I don't know, Shaune," she said. "You're thirty-seven years old. Figure something out on your own for a change!" His mum stormed past him and up the spiral staircase that led to the master's quarters. "See if one of the maids can help."

Shaune frowned. Nobody paid any attention to him anymore. "What's more important than Act Three?"

She shouted from the balcony. "Checking on your lazy father to see if he's finished packing for Earthstar."

"But Mummy, you and Poppy weren't selected for residency."

"We have selected ourselves. That is sufficient. And I know that Gigakill will affect England. If nothing else, we'd end up with unwanted refugees."

"I suppose so," Shaune said as his gaze darted through the house's passageways, searching for any moving body with half a brain. If only Vara was here. She'd help him organize his yarn, get the project done, and would have sex with him afterward.

One of Mummy's executive assistants bustled past. The old Welsh hag would help…with the yarn anyway. On the other he'd take a huge pass.

"Hey Annilyn! Can you show me how to manipulate this damn needle? I'm starting to go nuts!"

Annilyn turned and stomped toward him. "What's with this raging army of yarn balls around you?"

Shaune puckered his chin. "I'm making a blanket for Mummy."

"How touching," she said. "Bullshit in its pure chemical form."

"I'm expressing a sensitive side that's usually hidden."

Annilyn folded her arms. "I stand corrected. *That* was bullshit in its pure chemical form. Give me the hook."

She rolled the crochet hook between her fingers. "This is too small unless you're making doilies. Do you have anything else?"

Shaune popped open a large plastic box stuffed with craft tools in disarray. "I had Bernard purchase different sizes at the cyber store. The right one has to be here somewhere."

Annilyn pulled a hook from the box. "This is the size G, normally used by beginners. Take this in your hand and make a slip knot."

Watching Annilyn as she twisted the needle to make a row of loops and knots, Shaune tossed a yarn ball against the wall. "This is so goddamn stupid."

"You should minimize the vulgarities," Annilyn said as she weaved a second row of loops. "They patronize your highly evolved intellect. Following my lead will be easy."

"It has nothing to do with easy," Shaune said. "I engage in tasks much more complicated than this. All sorts of things you could never conceive of. I just have a problem doing stupid things!"

She stopped weaving and stared at Shaune. "Why on earth am I helping you learn something you have such contempt for?"

"Okay, I'm not making a blanket for Mummy. I'm on a top secret mission."

"Crocheting an afghan?"

"No, Annilyn," Shaune groaned. "It's so much more than that. One day, when I'm a world leader, I'll visit you at your Shady Valley codger home and clue you in."

She laughed. "World leader of what? *Afghan*-istan?"

Shaune ignored her foolish humor and thought of the bomb in the safe. A mushroom cloud rose in his thoughts. The brilliant splendor shone against the turquoise Asian skies. The subsequent war would be quick and dirty. Once the takeover stepped in to rescue humanity from itself, the world would be forever better.

"Help me with the godforsaken stitches, please!" he said.

Turning on the HV, Shaune watched *Galax.net's* twenty-four hour international news channel. He lay back as Annilyn started crocheting his afghan. Bored with the endless coverage of his strep attack, he opted for the local news. A scene displayed of the art district. He turned up the volume.

Suddenly, Shaune couldn't breathe. He gasped and Annilyn dropped the patch of stitches on the end table by the chair. Bernard ran from the dining room and knelt on the floor next to him.

Shaune grabbed Bernard's arm as they listened to the HV.

"A renowned artist from Socorro, New Mexico, was kidnapped from her apartment. Vara Jasmine Bradley was last seen on camera footage as she left her studio last night. She is believed to have been kidnapped by three men who threw her in the trunk of a black BMW with no license plate."

Agony and fear boiled in Shaune as his body shook. He stared at the HV, hypnotized with rage as the news continued.

"Based on an interview with a DHS source," the newscaster said, "she could be the victim of a South American group that kidnaps attractive American women for the sex trade and to be wives of wealthy, polygamous men."

Trying to restrain himself from smashing the HV to bits, Shaune clenched his jaw tight and painfully. Vara's mother and father were on the screen, begging and crying for the return of their daughter. He'd find out who did this. Vara's kidnapping was no accident. Somebody was on to him and he would find who. Then he would give new meaning to the word terror.

Shaune closed his eyes and imagined his mushroom cloud planted and blossoming like a beautiful, potent flower. Any bullshit doubts that Bernard tried to pound in his head over the gigakill had evaporated. Once the first flower was released more would rise to the sky and form the biggest flaming garden the world had ever seen. Then Shanghai and much more, would be just like his beautiful and loyal Vara—gone.

THURS 11/30/2130
UNITY SPACE STATION
ALTITUDE 487 KM AT 27,750 KM/H

Daniel slipped on a pair of sweat pants and a t-shirt. His bones and brain ached, overwhelmed by realities too heavy to bear. He turned off the artificial gravity in his room and felt himself lift off the floor. Casey floated off the bed and started pawing his way toward him.

While thankful he'd prodded Cal into letting him go on a quick space hike earlier, Daniel was embarrassed that he'd also vented his grief and anger about Hannah's death. Stress was drowning him like the whirlpools in his nightmares. The good old days were so much better when he was ignorant and could only imagine what was causing the meteor storms, the SCED attacks, and the blue light beam.

He watched Casey dart down and whip his paw underneath the dresser. The dog pulled out a half-eaten jerky stick. "I was wondering where this went," he said as he started chomping on the dried, brown meat.

Taking a deep swallow, Daniel stared at the jerky. "That old stuff isn't going to give you stomach problems, is it? I need to sleep tonight."

Casey glided closer to Daniel and seemed to be scrutinizing him. "I do have digestive mishaps sometimes, but I have a good feeling about tonight. By the way, you look pale, even more so than normal."

Daniel's mood darkened. "That's a big understatement."

"Before you share," Casey said, "I need to tell you something about Clemens. I should have told you before, but I get scared when I think of him."

"Can't be worse than what I found out today."

"It's about that 'Hail to the Chief' message on the computer."

"I can't wait to hear what's next."

"You might," Casey said matter-of-factly. "He's been enhanced. Which also means he's nuts."

"He was already that way," Daniel said rubbing his temples. "But now he's a super genius and nuts. Fantastic."

Frowning, Casey nodded. "Sorry."

Daniel lowered his head. He knew this could be the beginning of new horrors to deal with and probably part of the reason the Cosmic Instinct was intervening. The destructive possibilities of mad super-geniuses were virtually endless.

"How do you know?"

"After the UN meeting back in May, Cindera and I were on the cabana. Clemens stomped out and was rude as always. Then he stole Cindera's lounge." Casey released a Cheshire cat grin. "Then President Butthole started itching his socks and face. A rubbery coating fell off his head and he had bruises around his eyes."

Daniel wiped his forehead with the back of his hand. "While that's not complete proof…." He stopped and looked at Casey who had far more understanding of enhancement labs than he did. "Never mind, I think your hunch is strong evidence."

"I've seen other humans operated on in the lab I was in," Casey continued. "They start acting bonkers around six months to a year after the surgery. After that, they're plain blahooey. Maybe it brings out the craziness already within them."

"With a cherry on top," Daniel said. "The People's Party must have a bigger scheme planned as I've suspected. That's why the SCED disasters happened. IRE storage facilities are a big cash cow for key People's Party members and they're planted in many of the US and global nuclear power plants."

Casey floated past Daniel toward the dresser. "I'm not sure I understand. Please elaborate."

"At times," Daniel answered, "I thought Clemens could have been involved in some conspiracy with other party members. Other times I thought I was the crazy one." A thought suddenly hit Daniel.

Why would Clemens attack the United States? Because he was also attacking other places and had to make the assaults look random. *Could the People's Party really be behind the US terror attacks?* Like Donovan's program said, 'Hail to the Chief.' *Shit!*

He looked at Casey. "I think the People's Party may be using the false flags strategy."

Casey twirled around. "Where you attack yourself?"

"To stay in power," Daniel said feeling a surge of victory. That made sense. He sighed.

"But why would he attack other countries when he's moving to Earthstar?" Casey said.

"Terrorists have always used false flags. It's the lowest form of war," Daniel answered. "They attack elementary schools and churches in their own cities and then blame people they don't like. The People's Party hasn't done much to make life easier for the public so they stay in power through fear."

Releasing a disgusted snort, Casey shook his head. "Many of you humans, especially your leaders, are quite despicable. Present company is excluded for the time being."

Daniel turned on the small HV in his room. "You're not the only one with that opinion. Let me show you HumanSpeak's conclusion regarding the SCED attacks." His stomach began to tighten again. He'd always suspected there was something under the radar but hoped he was wrong. Clemens' enhancement was more evidence and there had to be others.

Daniel now knew more than ever that his chaotic upbringing and his dad's crazy DNA had given him an ability to detect threats that were imperceptible to most people. That was why he understood Sanya's isolation and pain. That's how he knew the meteor storms were targeting things. As he loaded the CI Theory report from his Epad to his HV, his hands shook. Sweat stuck against his face in zero gravity.

Will Hannah ever get the justice she deserves?

Thinking of JoMarie's sparkling spruce tree and the stars that seemed to be watching him during his spacewalks, Daniel saw a flicker of hope. Hannah and the other children who had already perished would force humanity to change its ways. The project specialists would have to find out the bigger reason for the People's Party's evil acts. That was his promise, humanity's promise.

He thought about the CI Theory, a final solution that was more frightening and less stoppable than Hitler's original. And unfortunately for humanity, perhaps justifiable. The meteor storms and destruction of SCED and IRE were caused by the Cosmic Instinct to save a collapsing ecosystem that was allowing a substance called ultramatter to break into the atmosphere.

Daniel remembered the grassy knolls of Idaho where Hannah was exposed and the scorching African nations that were suffering beyond compare with plagues and water rationing. This downward spiral was being halted by something not yet fully understood. Forced into a role of self-defense, the ecosystem responded after abandonment by a population that was mentally absent through choice or oppression. And through that absence, evil grew bigger wings, allowed to soar over the Earth and its inhabitants without reproach.

Daniel and the other USRG scientists would help save the planet's ecosystem and that destiny whatever it was. He'd fight to the death for children like his innocent Hannah. He thought of Larisa and the other kids on Earthstar, as well as those in the hot continents.

The words he dreaded started to form on the HV. They tore into his brain like the blue beam clawing out of the Pacific Ocean, ready to tear the pretty, little head off anything that stood in its way.

The closing paragraph of HumanSpeak's analysis displayed and Daniel felt his stomach seizing again. He headed toward his tiny bathroom for some meds. Casey shot him a worried glance. Daniel looked at the golden retriever. He motioned to the HV. "Read this and be glad you were born a dog."

> *The Cosmic Instinct is in Earth but not of Earth. To achieve evolution's destiny, the CI Theory predicts that the Cosmic Instinct will impose its most compelling manifestations on Earth's most threatening enemy and needy child: the Homosapien.*

6055209R00245

Made in the USA
San Bernardino, CA
01 December 2013